INTERSECTING BELIEFS

A Novel of Mystery, Romance, and Reflection

Linda Edmister

ISBN 979-8-9863138-4-9 (Paperback)
ISBN 979-9-9863138-5-6 (Digital)

This is a work of fiction. Any resemblance to persons living or dead is purely coincidental. The Lansdowne Correctional Facility, Tinkers Well and Harrington County, Kansas, and Spurlock, Virginia are entirely fictitious.

where fiction meets fun and faith
www.misteredbooks.com

Books in the *Intersections* Series

Intersecting Lives
Intersecting Dreams
Intersecting Beliefs
Intersecting Destinies

Author's Note:

The third installment of "Intersections" seeks to explore the fascinating connection between Jesus and Jewish history and feasts and the sad reality of antisemitism. I trust no offense will be taken at the sparing use of very mild, colorful language in keeping with the equally colorful characters. The scripture passages, which begin each chapter, are intended to be read as poetic pointers rather than taken contextually. All other passages relate to the storyline.

For Major Larry Taylor,
who taught me to face adversity
with grace and humor.
Soar with the angels, dear brother.

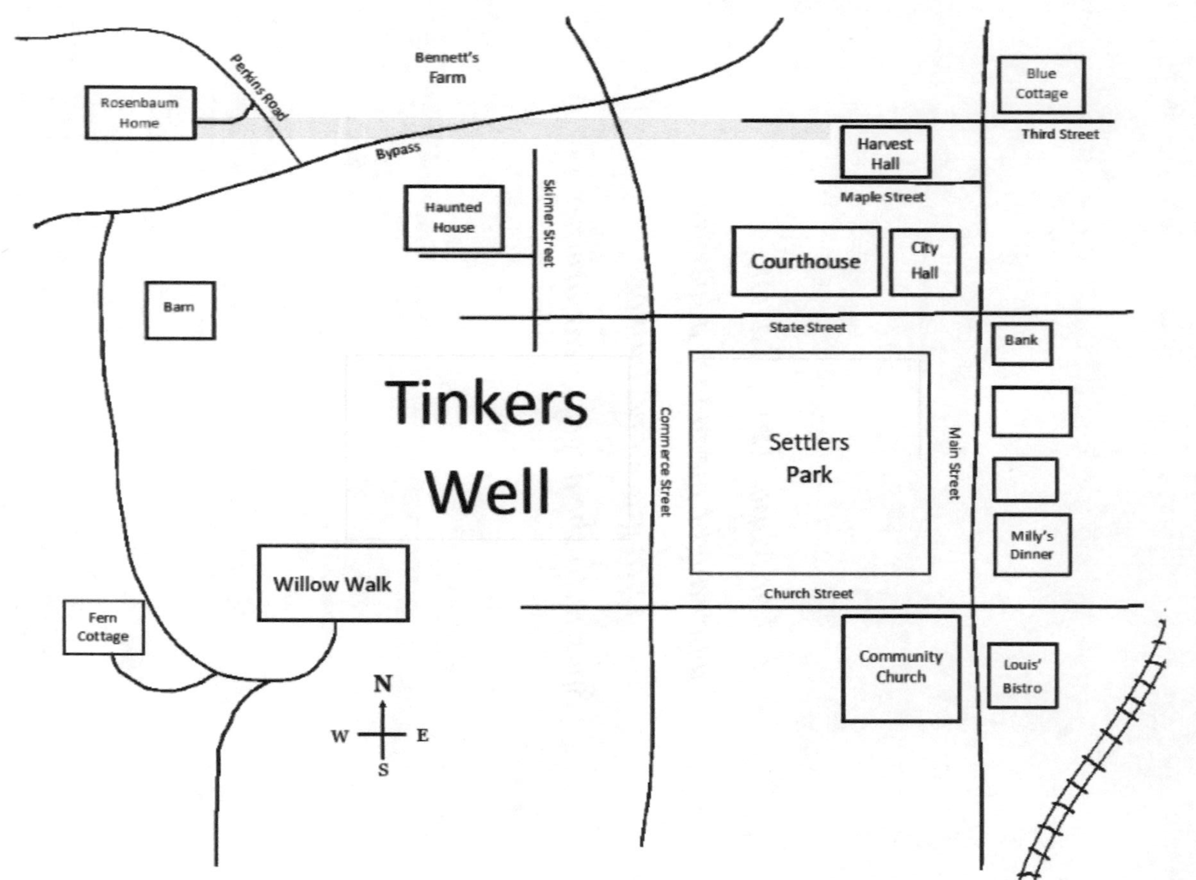

Perkins Road
Bennett's Farm
Blue Cottage
Rosenbaum Home
Bypass
Harvest Hall
Third Street
Haunted House
Skinner Street
Maple Street
Courthouse
City Hall
Barn
State Street
Bank
Tinkers Well
Commerce Street
Settlers Park
Main Street
Milly's Dinner
Willow Walk
Church Street
Fern Cottage
Community Church
Louis' Bistro
N
W
E
S

PROLOGUE

"Therefore, repent and turn to God, so that your sins may be erased, so that times of refreshing may come from the Lord's presence; and he may send the Messiah appointed in advance for you, that is, Yeshua.

Acts 3:19-20 (CJB)

The last remnants of daylight slowly retreated with the setting sun, allowing the garden, with its lingering shadows and fading birdsong, to settle into dusk and silence. Before twilight ebbed completely into darkness, a short, but dignified woman in her seventies turned from observance of nightfall to stand at one end of a mahogany dining table draped in lace. Her husband, at the other end of the table, dropped a few coins into a *tzedakah,* or metal box, as a reminder to do what is right by helping others. He smiled at his wife of 53 years and offered her the traditional Sabbath greeting.

"Shabbat shalom, my dear."

"Shabbat shalom, Isaac."

Striking a match, she held the feeble light to the wick of a single candle where it caught and flared into a soft glow that was multiplied by a second candle standing, like its neighbor, in a brightly polished silver candlestick. The woman, whose neatly plaited gray hair was covered with an intricately embroidered shawl, waved her arms in a circular motion toward her face three times before placing her hands over her eyes. Her lips parted, and the silence was broken by a rising chant-like melody in a kind of modal scale that would defy analysis by modern music theorists. The words were half sung, half wailed as the centuries-old blessing rose to infuse the moment with reverence, just as the candles graced it with light.

Baruch atah, Adonai Eloheinu, Melech ha'olam Asher kid'shanu b'mitzvotav V'tzivanu l'hadlik ner shel Shabbat.[1]

There were no children present to receive a blessing. They had grown and left their parents alone decades before, so Isaac offered the *kiddush* blessing for the wine and the *challah*, a loaf of braided bread gleaming from an egg wash brushed on prior to baking earlier that day. The woman lifted the decorative linen covering and cut the loaf using a knife that had also been covered during the blessing. Offering her husband a piece of the bread, she sighed in an eerie echo of the chant.

"So, Isaac. We are alone again to celebrate Shabbat." It was not a complaint, rather a fatalistic observation born of years of resignation.

"As you say, Deborah. But thanks be to Adonai, we still have each other." His gentle optimism shamed her.

"You are right – as always." She allowed a twisted smile to appear. "I don't know why you have put up with my kvetching all these years, but I am so glad you have."

"Without you, who would I talk to?" His philosophic reply was tempered with a wink.

"You save your winks for your grandchildren, bless them, and have some more matzo ball soup. You are too thin." She ladled more of the hearty soup into his bowl before he could stop her.

"Too *thin*? I haven't seen my belt buckle in years! What you need is more people to cook for," he grumbled in protest. "I can only eat for one."

"Yes, but no one from our synagogue wants to drive out here to join us for dinner. They feel they must stay overnight, saying it would be an

---

[1] Blessed are you, Adonai our god, Sovereign of all, who hallows us with mitzvot, commanding us to kindle the light of Shabbat.

imposition, even though I have told them they would be most welcome. And they know the rabbi has told us it is permissible to drive into the city to attend Shabbat services." After a moment of reflection, she added, with that fatalistic sigh, "I suppose we thought our children would visit more often."

"Perhaps we should have stayed in Kansas City, but we both agreed, when I retired, that we would enjoy having a little Eden in the country to call our own. Besides, has it not been the lot of our people to be outcasts?"

Deborah idly tore at her bread. "Yes." There was a hint of bitterness in her voice. "Because we have prayed and prayed for Messiah to come, and yet he tarries, even though Isaiah proclaimed that he would '*comfort all who mourn, yes provide for those in Tziyon who mourn, giving them garlands instead of ashes, the oil of gladness instead of mourning, a cloak of praise instead of a heavy spirit.*'[2] Perhaps it is just as our Reform friends say after all; he is only an idea, a state of existence."

"Perhaps. Or maybe he is as real as you and I, just as the prophets foretold. And even if he tarries, we have still been blessed, no?" Isaac went to his wife and knelt by her chair. Taking her hand, he looked into her troubled face and sought to bring her comfort. "Our children and grandchildren and soon, *great*-grandchildren, are healthy and happy; we have a beautiful home to share in our old age; and we *will* find friends here in Tinkers Well. I am sure of it. And if you insist on questioning Adonai's timing, remember that after two thousand years of wandering, exile, and occupation, Israel is again a nation. Is not that a miracle?"

With tears in her eyes, the woman touched her husband's lined face. "No, Isaac. *You* are the miracle."

The tender moment was broken when a frown gathered on Isaac's face, and he suddenly reverted to a matter-of-fact tone.

---

[2] Isaiah 61:2, *Complete Jewish Bible*

"I'm glad you think so, but you may change your mind when you have to help me get up from here."

It took the combined strength and laughter of both to restore Isaac to his feet. He hobbled to his place at the table and tackled his brimming bowl of soup. The peace of Shabbat reigned once more.

Chapter 1

While the young women were dancing, each man caught one of them. They took them away and married them. Then they went back to the land God had given them. They rebuilt their cities and lived there.

Judges 21:23b (ICB)

A warm breeze rustled the leaves of overhanging palms, creating a kaleidoscope of shadows on the sandy lawn. At its gentle urging, a few stray hairs escaped the colorful headband tied around Rose Ludlow's auburn curls as she sat up. Reaching out to lay her hand on the recumbent figure in a neighboring lounge chair, she said, "Tim..."

"Mmm?" he responded, not moving a muscle.

"Honey, it's almost time to get dressed for the banquet. Let's take another quick swim. It will probably be our last chance before we leave tomorrow morning."

"No," came the mono-syllabic reply.

"No, you don't want to swim?" persisted his patient wife.

Tim Ludlow finally turned his head in her direction. Without opening his eyes, he covered her hand with his and said in a slow drawl, "No, I don't want to leave here tomorrow. I want to stay and float along on a lazy river, surrounded by white sand beaches and exotic birds, where the most difficult decision we have to make each day is which swimsuit to wear. And by the way," he said, opening one eye to look at his wife, "I'm a *big* fan of every one of yours." With eyes closed again, he continued in a faraway voice. "I want to spend every day in the sun snorkeling over a coral reef, or parasailing in the bay, or zip-lining through a tropical rain forest until we're old and gray and tired of each other's company. In other words: I'd like to stay forever."

A predictable giggle followed as Rose pulled him unwillingly to a sitting position. "Come on, you handsome slug, I'll race you to the beach," she said and took off running through the opening in a hedge of pink hibiscus. The vivid, living wall provided both a lush color palate and much-desired privacy between the cottages of their secluded Belize resort. Tim waited till she was almost to the water before hopping up to race after her. Catching her neatly in his arms, he tossed her into the breaking waves. She wiped the salt water from her eyes and pulled him in after her, and the two forgot about everything but one another. The banquet could wait.

The Ludlows shivered and pulled their light-weight jackets tighter as a cold blast of Missouri wind blew through a gap in the jet bridge.

"Brrr!" Tim said with feeling. "I think we're almost in Kansas again, Dorothy."

Rose reached up to touch her husband's bronzed cheek. "I believe I can actually see your tan fading."

"No, that's just the way my face looks when my teeth are chattering uncontrollably." He put his arm around his wife to pull her close as they shuffled toward the gate.

She arched an eyebrow and inquired softly, "Surely, you're not feeling romantic *now*?"

"Don't be ridiculous. I need you to block the draft."

Derek Warner and Amy Walker were waiting for them in the baggage claim area while Amy's fiancé, Abe, circled the airport to keep the SUV warm. They didn't want the newlyweds to catch a chill after their tropical honeymoon. With everyone soon loaded in the blissfully warm vehicle, the five friends headed to the place they called home – Tinkers Well, Kansas.

"Before heading to the airport, we ran by the house to turn up the heat there for you, too. There are freeze warnings in the forecast for the next three nights. Welcome home!" Amy said gaily and moved her left hand behind Abe's headrest. Something caught the light from passing cars and twinkled as she wiggled her fingers.

Rose gasped and switched on the dome light in the back seat. "Amy, is that your…"

"Engagement ring? *Yes!* Isn't it perfect?" Abe grinned silently in the driver's seat.

"It's gorgeous! We haven't even been gone a whole week. When did *this* happen?"

"Some of us do not benefit from the largesse of long-lost grandmothers, so *my* fiancée had the privilege of choosing her *own* ring," Abe declared proudly.

His fiancée punched him lovingly on the arm. "I had an in-service day on Wednesday, so we drove to Kansas City and came home with – this," she said simply. "I love it."

"I can certainly see why." Addressing herself to the driver, Rose added with spirit, "I'll have you know, Abraham Yousef, that I love mine, too. And I couldn't have found anything I'd like half as much as the ring Tim gave me."

"Way to stick up for your man, sweetheart," Tim said with a cocky smile.

"Don't you people ever think about anything but love and engagement rings and honeymoons?" Derek asked, folding his arms in disgust.

After short consideration four voices replied in unison, "No."

"But we'll be very happy for you when it's your turn, Derek," Rose said sweetly. "You're just waiting for a very special lady who deserves a wonderful man like you, right?"

"*Finally*, someone who understands the essence of Derek Warner. Rose, you can be my best man. These two losers aren't good enough."

He endured the rest of the drive to Tinkers Well subjected to wild speculation on the improbable accomplishments and sterling virtues of the future Mrs. Warner.

A harassed young man nearing 40 paced aimlessly around an expensively decorated living room and wondered how he had ever gotten to this place. Matt Murdock looked across the room at his wife, and a familiar pang of longing wrenched his gut, as it often did when he considered the woman he had married. Matt had never had any delusions about his attraction for a woman like Brittany. He was not physically impressive, though he had a pleasant, if rather non-descript face. Nor was he particularly charming. His personality was amiable and his temperament placid.

Matt and his wife had met at an investment seminar where he was a presenter. His immediate, inexplicable yearning for her would ordinarily have been quenched by his own self-doubt and rational attitude toward life. But *she* had miraculously chased after *him*, and with her advances, reason flew out the window. He could only attribute her interest in him to the mystique of being pursued by an older man. The attraction of a moderately successful financial planner had to be limited for a bubbly college sophomore who exuded the sex appeal he believed her to be yet unaware of.

At 29, Matt found her fascinating and unbelievably desirable. Every scruple and restraint regarding the proper courtship of a woman had been swept away in his quest for the unattainable prize – a prize that seemed to be offered to him, impossibly, by a bewitching innocent who responded to his tepid advances with burgeoning sensuality and wild abandon. He was no match for her youthful exuberance and passion. It was the news of an unplanned pregnancy, two months after they began dating, that catapulted the unlikely pair to the altar.

After eight years together, Matt still remembered every detail of his dream bride on their wedding day: her rich, deep red hair flecked with green and bronze as it cascaded over her pure white shoulders, framing a face as lovely and willful as its mistress. Naturally dark brows and lashes added drama to the wells of her sparkling green eyes. Her shapely figure had not yet fully succumbed to the ravages of maternity, having, instead, taken on an entirely flattering rounded fullness which only added to her allure.

Theirs had been a successful union in the sense that he worked tirelessly to build his client base and their net worth, and she fulfilled his every fantasy when her desire for ever-increasing wealth and status was incrementally satisfied. If motherhood seemed to have little impact on her habits or interests, Matt reasoned that everyone expresses their love in different ways.

Little Mattie and Drew were always turned out in the most fashionable children's clothes, and behaved admirably, if a little rambunctiously, when around their father. He adored his "little men." At times, he thought Brittany treated them like dolls. She played with them and pampered them, then relinquished them to others more suited to dealing with the whims of two little boys when they showed signs of being inconveniently human. He believed her affection for her children, however, to be real and abiding. She was rather like women of the aristocracy who warmly welcomed the company of their offspring for a few hours a day after they had been duly prepared for presentation by a nanny.

Matt further reasoned that the circumstance of having invited his aunt, Irene Fields, to live with them just after Mattie was born, might well have caused the new mother to feel inadequate in the presence of so capable and managing an older woman. But the gesture was sincerely offered, rooted both in a desire to lessen his wife's load of responsibility, and to provide a home for a dearly loved aunt. Mindful of his part in forcing his wife to find alternate interests to fill the time away from her babies, he was always quick to acknowledge her commitment to ensuring their home was inviting and stylish. Matt also appreciated her selfless dedication to meeting the social obligations he abhorred solely to further her husband's connections and career.

Beautiful Brittany. Beloved Brittany. Devoted Brittany.

How could I have exposed her to such scandal and embarrassment? Matt had just spoken the unspeakable and watched her naturally vibrant, expressive features go utterly blank. He didn't know what he had expected – anger, despair, compassion – anything but this absolute absence of emotion. But then, how does an otherwise vital, passionate woman react to the news that her husband might shortly be going to prison?

He had fought like a madman over the past month to make sense of the discrepancies in his clients' accounts. The errors had come to light through a changeover audit performed by the new accountant of one of those clients. Matt subsequently reviewed all his other accounts and found similar discrepancies. He had postponed meetings to try to figure out what had happened, but the few who kept a close eye on their shares and funds had started openly questioning his reluctance to meet with them. One of the more diligent investors had finally called in the State Securities Regulator when failed attempts to contact their financial advisor raised more red flags than they were willing to ignore.

"I can't figure it out. I've tried and I've tried, but none of it makes any sense." In frustration, Matt ran his fingers through his best feature – thick, light brown hair turning prematurely gray through worry and fear. "And I can tell by your response that you don't believe the only possibility either, but what else can it be? One of the other agents must be manipulating data, but I don't see how they could have gotten my passwords, and I just can't believe it of any of them. They are all stand-up guys."

Brittany remained silent, but an alert wariness crept into her eyes.

"The only other explanation is that Frank had something to do with it. After all, he founded the firm 40 years ago. I really know very little about him; he's always been so standoffish. Maybe there's some motivation in his life leading him to desperation. I mean, who really knows what's going on with him?" Matt focused on the elaborately twisted sculpture on the coffee table. He dared not look at his wife. Her silence unnerved him.

Finally, she spoke.

"You think it could be Frank? Hmm, that's interesting."

Matt looked up to find an arrested expression on her face. It passed so quickly he wondered if he had imagined it.

"Oh, come on, baby, don't look so grim," she said. The quicksilver change in her manner had its inevitable effect. Matt's despair was tempered with hope. Maybe things weren't as dire as he had imagined. Brittany stood in front of her husband and tilted his head, drawing his eyes with the light in her own. "It'll be all right," she said in a playful, childish voice. "You'll see, baby. Now let's go to bed. Things will look all better in the morning."

She slid her hand down to his tie and gently pulled him to his feet. Matt followed her just as he always had. He was powerless to resist her. She had gone from bruised angel to provocative paramour, and his need to possess her blotted out every other consideration. As he focused on the mesmerizing sway of her hips, he slowly reordered the agonizing thoughts that had tortured his brain over the past few weeks. Perhaps, things *would* look better in the morning…

CHAPTER 2

They celebrated and enjoyed good food. They were glad and full of joy.
Esther 8:17a (NIrV)

Rose watched critically while her husband of four weeks made his way around the veranda of their massive, newly restored Victorian home. Fading afternoon light added an additional challenge to the already tortuous process. He could only move an extension ladder along the rail in short, three-foot increments in order to reach the overhanging roofline. As an expert carpenter, Tim Ludlow did nothing in a shoddy manner, even if it was simply hanging Christmas decorations, though he was beginning to think his bride's ambitious decorating scheme was anything *but* simple. Methodically mounting screw hooks under the roof's edge to avoid the gutters, he made his way around to the front steps, securing long, even lengths of plug-in Christmas string lights to the screws as he went. Or so he thought.

"Tim," Rose pointed out patiently for about the fifth time, "that section is sagging a bit."

And just as patiently, her husband responded, after pulling up a little slack, "Better?"

"Perfect. I can't wait to see what she'll look like with all the lights turned on," Rose answered with mounting excitement. She invariably referred to the house with a feminine pronoun, for to Rose's mind, the Victorian period piece represented a grand old lady.

While Tim mounted the larger lights, Rose wrapped the swags of greenery adorning the porch railings. There were so many strands of twinkle lights, Tim feared the house might be mistaken for a landing beacon by passing planes. But he left all the decorating details to her. He merely offered himself as the technician who had to work them all out from a practical standpoint. He certainly possessed the necessary skill set and strength to do so. The tall, sturdy building contractor, whose powerful muscles were more a testament to his profession than any workout regimen, had intentionally affixed lights to the two second-story balconies and attic turret while Rose was out earlier on a strategically timed materials run. He knew she'd have suffered agonies of worry over watching him balance precariously to hang lights on the higher rooflines.

"Okay, now move the ladder over to the parlor window so we can hang the wreaths and bows." Tim grinned at Rose's use of the royal "we." She had instinctively embraced the role of project manager in the many jobs they had undertaken together during the process of renovating their home.

Rose had immediately fallen in love with the old house on her arrival in Tinkers Well, more than five months earlier. It took several weeks, however, before she realized she was also in love with Tim Ludlow. While they were sorting out their relationship, they at least agreed on a shared vision for bringing the neglected 150-year-old Victorian gem back to life. Rose had christened the stately home *"Willow Walk"* in a fanciful moment. Much to their delight and amazement, Tim's grandmother, Aletha Mason, had given them the unexpected gift of the deed of ownership to the old house at their engagement party in August.

Since then, the couple had worked tirelessly to restore the three-story building to its former glory. Working around the other demands of his renovation business, Tim put his considerable skills in architectural carpentry to the test. And when it got down to the wire, he brought in his whole crew to finish the main living spaces before his wedding in October, when the house welcomed the wedding party and extended family for the rehearsal dinner. It was the first of many events to be held in the spacious home. When Aletha presented the young couple with the key to Willow Walk, she quickly overcame their objections to the outrageously generous gift. *"She needs to be a home again,"* she told them, *"to hear the sound of children's voices and the laughter of many guests. She needs to be loved and to shelter love."*

The couple had enjoyed a blissful six days in Belize for their honeymoon before returning to the less than balmy breezes of early November in Kansas. Brisk weather, fallen leaves, and the lure of football as viewed on what Rose considered a ridiculously large LED flat screen TV inspired them to invite a crowd for their first Thanksgiving together. Having already planned to spend Christmas with Rose's family in her hometown of Winchester, Kentucky, the occasion afforded the newlyweds the opportunity to share at least one of the year's major holidays with their Tinkers Well family.

The weeks prior to Thanksgiving Day found the newlyweds settling into the haphazard process of learning to live in each other's space with grace and laughter – and a few ruffled feathers. Despite keeping his work areas clean and organized, Tim failed to treat his living spaces the same way. He had a tendency to leave articles of clothing – jackets, boots, and clothes – wherever he discarded them. Rose patiently picked up after him while gently pointing out the hall tree in the foyer and the shoe rack for muddy boots in the laundry room. Rose invariably drove their vehicles until they were on empty then neglected to mention it. And whenever she borrowed a tool from Tim's workshop in the garage – needed to complete her current decorating project – she always returned it to some other spot. Using a permanent marker, Tim drew outlines around each tool hanging on the pegboard, or laying on the bench, to indicate their assigned places. He also had small dashboard signs made.

You are my wife
Add fuel to my life

Not only did the reminder make her more attentive to the gas gauge; it invariably made her smile.

Fortunately, the two agreed on some of the more critical aspects of co-habitation. Dirty dishes belong in the sink, not scattered all over the house. Vehicles are to be parked in the garage, not left in the driveway – especially in wintertime. Whoever empties a trash can is expected to replace the liner. And lastly, the toothpaste tube should *always* be squeezed from the end rather than the middle. Occasionally, husband or wife intentionally violated a house rule in the hope of starting a friendly squabble. They thought it good practice for future quarrels of substance, believing that rehearsing the kissing and making up part could not be overdone, though evenings spent holding one another in the mellow light of a flickering fire usually cast any trifling infraction into obscurity.

Other couples were also learning the ropes of a changing relationship. Ahmad "Abraham" Yousef and Amy Walker had announced their engagement the day before the Ludlows' wedding. A difficult separation and emotional reunion left them more convinced than ever that they were meant for each other. They set their own wedding date for the last Saturday in March. It worked out to be the weekend between standardized testing week, which Amy could miss for last minute wedding prep without any setback for her classes of music students, and spring break. Abe would have preferred something a little more immediate, such as New Year's Day, but after their rescheduled visit to her parent's home two weeks after the Ludlow wedding, he was obliged to agree to a longer engagement.

Amy's dad, though impressed by Abe's intelligence, enterprise, and obvious love for his daughter, was not as eager to forgive and forget as his wife. Wayne Walker never appeared to take much notice of the emotional upheavals experienced by his children, leaving his wife to wade through those murky waters. But he had been acutely aware of Amy's distress when her supposed sweetheart had up and left her at the end of September without any solid explanation. Though Wayne said little about it, Amy's tears and troubled spirit had cut him to the quick. Young Mr. Yousef, though obviously once again in Amy's good graces, would have to prove himself a little more before Wayne was convinced that he was good enough for his daughter.

The rest of the extended Walker family, however, weren't willing to wait to see if Abe could successfully run the gauntlet of Wayne's contriving, so it was a houseful of siblings, aunts and uncles and grandparents who greeted the couple on their arrival. Abe experienced much the same kind of mass meet and greet that Tim had endured when meeting Rose's extended family in Kentucky during an engagement reception there. It was Abe, however, who felt more comfortable amid the big, noisy group, having grown up in a large family himself. But after the recent painful quarrel over his rejection of Islam in favor of Christianity, and his consequent evangelism efforts, he had been cut off from his own people a second time. Through the precious gift of Amy, God had blessed him doubly with another family.

Since the Walker clan wasn't likely to get everyone together again anytime soon, Joyce Walker suggested they call that weekend "Fakesgiving." Her lack of enthusiasm over the prospect of preparing a second feast for a crowd, just weeks later, left the engaged couple free to celebrate the Thanksgiving holiday as they wished.

Believing that love was wasted on the young, the male member of a third couple worked diligently to make a dream come true for the love of his life. God had brought about a miraculous work of spiritual redemption in the heart of Miles Hawthorne – Tim's formerly estranged biological father and only child of Aletha and her first husband, James Hawthorne. God had also awakened in Miles a knowledge of true, unselfish love, opening his heart to long buried feelings. After 30 years of separation, Miles was as sure of his love for Tim's mother, Marilyn Ludlow, as he was of his next breath, for he could sooner stop breathing than stop loving her. And the element of their relationship that most amazed him was his ability to love her without knowing how she really felt about him.

Miles and Marilyn continued to enjoy outings together, or meeting at church, and what had become their ritual of co-hosting her Sunday potluck brunch. Their conversations were easy and illuminating. He learned more about the rich depth of her character with every word spoken. Marilyn knew only that she was happy in his company and deeply thankful for the relationship that he and Tim had forged. She believed her affection to be purely platonic now and was grateful to Miles for not pressing her for anything more. She would have been less than human, though, had she not noticed that he had aged well, having somehow grown more handsome than she remembered. A feathering of gray at his temples complimented the lines of living etched in a face set with a square jaw — the face mirrored so clearly in the chiseled features of his son. The still attractive middle-aged couple were old and, once again, dear friends who had come through the trials of life with their relationship stronger for having been tested. Marilyn would not allow herself to consider a different interpretation. She convinced herself that she was perfectly content as things were.

All these familiar players, and several others, once again took the stage when Thanksgiving Day dawned cold and bright on the fourth Thursday of November during that glorious autumn when love found a home in Tinkers Well.

All the leaves of the dining room table were needed to accommodate the guest list. Garlands of silk-colored leaves hung from the central chandelier, while its crystal pendant drops covered the wood-paneled walls with dancing reflected light. A long, narrow centerpiece with tapered candles graced the table draped in multiple tablecloths to cover its length.

Abe and Derek were worried that the decorative pumpkins and gourds on the sideboard wouldn't allow enough room for the food that filled the whole house with tantalizing scents. Cloves, thyme, sage, and roast turkey vied for honors. The big kitchen, lined with white shaker cabinets and anchored by a large gas stove in fire engine red, provided ample space for the four ladies prepping food. Aletha settled herself at the farm table to supervise and comment on recipe variations as needed.

Another veteran and construction crew member, Jada Young, along with her brother Jamal, had accepted the invitation to join her boss for the holiday. Though Rose and Amy invited her to join them in the kitchen with the other ladies, she declined in favor of hanging out with the crowd attempting to watch multiple pre-game shows simultaneously in the conservatory. Tim had moved the big flat-screen TV into the music room because the space could accommodate more individual seating. It was also strategically located next to the kitchen and any potential leftovers that might be available later. If Jada seemed more comfortable in the company of men, she had plenty to choose from that day.

Other than the only absent team member, José Nuñez, who was celebrating Thanksgiving with his aunt and uncle, the rest of the *Three Brothers Construction, Inc.* crew were present. Jason Buchwald and JT Gaines both joined the Ludlow clan, preferring to save their money for Christmas trips to visit their respective family homes in Savannah. The two traded smack over long-time rivals Georgia and Georgia Tech like the best of enemies while Derek and Abe provided unnecessary – and unsolicited – additional commentary on every player, statistic, and coach in college football. Observing the strange, centuries-old ritual of male bonding with amusement, Miles surprised himself by discovering a latent interest in the finer points of battle on the gridiron. As host, Tim made sure everyone was comfortable and relaxed. He also had the unenviable task of announcing that the time had arrived for the football lifeline to be temporarily severed in deference to the feast awaiting them in the dining room.

Every inch of the laden table was filled with enough food options to tempt even the most finicky appetite. All the traditional elements were present from turkey and stuffing to mashed potatoes and gravy and cranberry sauce. Other tantalizing offerings included sweet potatoes Jamaican style, cheese grits (courtesy of JT) and a fruit platter big enough to cover an entire place setting. The sideboard groaned from the weight of pies, cakes, cookies, homemade caramel corn and fresh fruit cobbler. Rose had thoughtfully worked out a seating arrangement for the mixed crowd and, using her newly honed calligraphy skills, she had created autumnal themed place cards accordingly. The collective crowd may not have alternated boy-girl, and the total came to the dreaded 13, but no one seemed to notice or care. Finally sorted out and seated, those present followed a signal from their host to join hands in preparation for the Thanksgiving prayer. Tim cleared his throat and began.

"Father God, you are awesome and worthy of praise. We come before you today to give thanks for your abundant blessings that, if mentioned individually, would result in cold food. So, I simply say thank you for the gift of your Son and your merciful grace, for family and friends old and new, for honest work and purpose, and for the biggest feast this old house has seen in decades. Please bless it for our nourishment that we might serve you with strength and joy to the glory of your name. And all God's people said…"

A hearty, "Amen!" followed, and the feasting began.

Six hours and two football games later, Mr. and Mrs. Ludlow bid the last of their guests goodnight and fell, exhausted but supremely happy, onto a deeply cushioned loveseat in the parlor. They were free to savor the peace and quiet of the moment without the worry of facing a mountain of dishes in the kitchen thanks to Derek's mother, Angelica Warner, who had made short work of after dinner clean-up. She may have been a strict task master, but everyone knew her orders were spoken from a heart of kindness, with the words uttered in a voice flavored by the warmth of the Caribbean. It was only after the dining room and kitchen had been cleaned, and leftovers packaged up for all to share, that Angelica realized she might have overstepped as a guest in another woman's home. She pulled Rose aside to say as much.

"Rose, I am sorry for bein' so bossy. This is your home now, and I just took over your beautiful kitchen like I owned it. Please forgive me, child."

Rose hugged the older woman. "Angelica, you have the biggest servant heart of anyone I've ever known. And you've taught me more in the past six months about selfless ministry to others than I might otherwise have learned in a lifetime." She added with a twinkle, "I've been taking notes."

Angelica smiled in relief and kissed Rose's cheek. "That may be a lot o' nonsense, but it's kind o' you to say so." Nodding significantly at Tim lounging in a chair among the football crowd, she offered the new bride some sage advice. "And don't let that man o' yours get in the habit of thinkin' he doesn't need to do his part."

Rose laughed. "I promise I won't. Though, in his defense, I must say that Tim's been wonderful about helping me with anything I've asked of him."

Angelica smiled knowingly. "My husband Isaiah was as fine a man as you could meet anywhere, but even he needed a little remindin' every now and again. Now you go on and join the young people. Marilyn and I need to discuss some ideas for the party we're plannin' before you two and Abraham and Amy disappear for Christmas."

There was no mellow firelight in the two-bedroom duplex that Amy Walker called home, but she and her fiancé were perfectly content to sit side by side on a worn, sagging couch while they followed the dancing patterns of flickering light reflected on the opposite wall. The fascinating spectacle was formed by an eclectic collection of scented candles and tapers of differing heights secured in various secondhand candle holders. Covering the top of a beat-up, hand-me-down entertainment center, the odd assortment of lights provided the only illumination in the small living room. Three long legs rested on a wide ottoman, while Abe's prosthetic knee bent to balance the artificial lower section of his leg on the floor. Slipping her left arm under the sinewy one stretched out to allow Abe's hand to rest on her knee, Amy intertwined her slender fingers with his, moving her fourth finger to capture the random light in the prism of her diamond engagement ring.

Both tall and slim, they made a striking couple. Abe's black hair and goatee framed angular facial features and accented his olive skin. Those characteristics were perfectly complimented by Amy's softer brown hair and a face dominated by large, expressive eyes and a generous mouth.

Raising her head from its resting place on his shoulder, Amy said, "Babe, I don't want you to think that because I am so happy right now, I've forgotten what you must be missing. I wish I could somehow help you bear that more easily, but I don't know how."

Abe turned his head to look into her troubled eyes. "But Amy, you help me bear it every single day." He rubbed her cheek with his finger. "You are my rock. Every time I look at you, I am reminded that any hurt can heal and any wrong be forgiven with grace and love. And honestly, I have more hope now of reaching at least some of my family than I did before my trip to Virginia, especially my mother. I think our conversations helped her to recall long-buried memories of the Jesus she knew as a child before her adoption by my Muslim grandparents. It still blows me away that she never told me about her early life in a Christian family. But I believe that was probably due more to respect for my father's wishes than any hesitancy on her part."

"What about your siblings? You haven't said much about them except that you can still whoop Husam at basketball. But then, so can I." Her sally drew only the hint of a smile from her fiancé. "Did you get a sense that any of them might be open to hearing the gospel?"

Abe considered the question before answering. He and Amy had spoken little of the relationships within his family since his return. It was partly because he was still processing their parting and partly because he didn't want to burden her with heavy thoughts when they had so much to rejoice in. But he understood the need to be open with her, and he loved her all the more for caring. After all, whether they were estranged or not, the Yousefs would soon be her family too.

"I believe Samia would at least listen to my testimony. She is also closest to Ommy, and if the two would be willing to hear me out, they might even discuss the ideas together. She also stays in touch with her former nursing instructor, Noor; you know, my friend that came to faith in Christ as I shared my story with her."

"You mean the woman I thought you'd fallen for while you were away?" Amy couldn't help teasing him.

"Amy Walker, you know perfectly well that I had no interest in her at all – at least not romantically. You are, and always will be, the only woman for me."

Amy rested her head on Abe's shoulder again. "Feel free to remind me of that as often you like." He laughed and kissed the top of her head, then grew serious once more.

"I'm afraid that Fahkir and Radeyah's husband, Asad, are both wholly on board with my father's vision to spread the influence and scope of Islam across America."

Contemplation of that plan, as laid out by his father during the recent Virginia homecoming, always cast a paralyzing fear over Abe's heart. It also fortified his determination to answer the call to attend seminary. Amy had greeted the news of his scholastic goals with complete support, though she might not have fully understood the driving force that his father's unholy crusade had inspired in Abe. He would not, however, allow those sober reflections to cloud a day of thanksgiving.

"Radeyah is so influenced by her husband, she will be hard to reach. I do believe, though, that Husam might hear me, if he hasn't decided to turn against religion altogether."

"What do you mean? I thought he was a lot of fun to hang out with when he came to visit you last summer. He was certainly friendly to me, and I could tell that he truly admires you."

"Oh, he's a great kid, and he thought the world of you, which shows he has excellent taste. But what you may not realize is that, as the youngest child, he has been far more indulged than his siblings. He alone was allowed to leave home to attend college in a different state. The rest of us lived at home and continued to attend our local mosque with our parents while receiving our education at the university nearby. But as I watched him, when he was around the rest of the family, I began to wonder about the depth of Husam's devotion. He participated in the prayers and traditions of Islam, but I had a sense that he was just going through the motions. If anything, I think it more likely that he will turn to atheism. If he does not discover that Christianity is all about relationship, not religion, he may lump it in with all that he is probably being taught by his peers and professors to disregard as irrelevant."

Abe was silent for several moments, lost in his thoughts. Shaking himself out of his passing melancholy, he spoke on a more hopeful note. "But I will not give up on any of them."

"Then neither will I," Amy responded with a supportive smile. If all she could do in the present was to lift his spirits, then she would do it with all the fervor of a champion cheerleading squad. His revelations encouraged her to pursue her efforts to reach out to people she had never met simply because of their importance to Abe.

"Now, enough of these heavy thoughts. What else shall we discuss, my love?"

It was the opening Amy had been waiting for. "Well, we've been so busy getting engaged and spending time with my family, and you getting caught up with everything at Three Brothers that we've never actually talked about where we'll be getting married or what we want our wedding to look like. I know that four months seems like a long time from now…"

"About a hundred years," her fiancé supplied, unhelpfully.

"I think you'll find that four months will pass faster than you think," she said, smiling at his nonsense.

Abe turned his head to look at her with more than a hint of skepticism. "I am fairly certain we will *never* agree on that point." She merely dropped a swift kiss on his full lips and disentangled herself to look for a pen and paper. Returning presently with two mugs of hot cider in hand and a notebook tucked under her elbow, she settled herself at a strategic distance, knowing they would accomplish more without the distraction of one another's immediate presence.

"Hey, what are you doing all the way over there?" Abe frowned at Amy who sat in an armchair four feet away. "This is Thanksgiving Day – Night and I'm more thankful than I can say that God brought us together. But I would be even *more* thankful if you sat here," he suggested, patting the vacated space next to him, and flashing his eyebrows like a cartoon villain. Amy laughed and shook her head, opting to stay put. She reached to turn on the lamp next to her.

"Nice try, Mr. Yousef. *I'm* thankful we're getting married, but that won't happen if we don't get to work."

Abe frowned and commented, "You know, sometimes you can be such a schoolteacher."

"Thank you," was her only reply as she began making a list of all the details to be discussed.

A month had elapsed since their stormy, emotional reconciliation at the Ludlow rehearsal dinner, and Amy was ready to move from the hazy glow of the newly engaged to solid plans for a wedding and the start of their life together. Abe wanted the same things, though he was far more interested in the latter part of the equation. Despite his preference for more snuggling on the couch, he sat up straight and turned his attention to his fiancée. "I am ready to do your bidding, my darling," he said formally in his well-bred, slightly accented voice.

Caught off guard by his change in attitude, Amy's face adopted a familiar smitten look, and she said tenderly, "Oh, Abe, I do love you," which nearly brought him off the couch, so she quickly got back to the business at hand. "Okay, first things first. Should we get married in my original home of Council Grove, where a lot of my family live, or here in Tinkers Well, which is and will be our home, or maybe have a destination wedding?" The last suggestion wasn't offered with much enthusiasm.

"Amy, I would marry you at the South Pole or in the middle of a desert or on a mountain top; in jeans or in a tux; with 200 guests in attendance or just us, the pastor and a few witnesses. I know that's not very helpful, but I want whatever makes you happy, as long as you promise that I get to take you home with me after it's all over."

She took a deep breath and said with decision, "Then, if it's all the same to you, I think I'd like to get married here with all our friends and our church family. My family can drive over for the weekend – I'm sure we can find enough people to put them up – and we can go to *our* home afterward, instead of a cold, impersonal hotel." Amy had her own reasons for wanting to get married in Tinkers Well.

"Tinkers Well, it is. What next?"

"I suppose we can always get married in the church. Rose and Tim's wedding was certainly beautiful there. But I was thinking it might be fun to do something… different. Something uniquely 'us.'"

Abe pondered the possibilities for a few minutes then snapped his fingers and exclaimed, "I have it!" Amy waited expectantly. "We can be married in your classroom with all your students lining the hallway, playing the wedding march!" Amy threw a pillow at him. "If you continue to abuse me like that, my darling, I won't be responsible for any retaliatory actions."

"Abe, be serious!"

"I am *always* serious," he said, with his eyes crossed.

"Abraham!" she said severely, trying hard not to laugh. "Would you prefer an afternoon wedding with light appetizers afterwards, like Rose and Tim's, or an early evening ceremony followed by a full meal?"

"A full meal, definitely. A *very* full meal. With cake. Lots of cake." Abe's appetite was legendary. "And before you ask, plan whatever you want for music and flowers. That's your thing. But I will humbly offer my services as taste tester for all the edible elements."

"Fair enough, but since you're the computer genius, do you think you could design the wedding invitations?"

"Do you know, I believe I *am* a genius," Abe said reflectively, rubbing his chin as if pondering a deep philosophical construct. "Therefore, I can surely produce invitations that are not altogether contemptable." Amy threw another pillow at him. "I warned you, my girl…" he said, and started to rise from the couch.

"Now Abe…" Amy couldn't help laughing as he approached her with ominous intent. "We need to brainstorm a little more about possible venues." He took her notebook and pen and tossed them onto the floor before pulling her to her feet. She put up little resistance when he wrapped his arms tightly around her waist.

"You can talk to Rose about it," Abe mumbled while placing a judicious kiss under Amy's right ear. "She's got a million ideas about everything." He planted a kiss on the end of her nose before moving to the corner of her mouth.

"Good thinking," Amy sighed and turned her head slightly to assist his errant lips in finding their ultimate target. The pen and notebook still lay on the floor when she sent him home a few minutes later, the only concession to wedding planning being a shared conviction that it needed to happen soon.

Rose took Angelica's advice to heart, allowing Tim only one day after Thanksgiving to relax and absorb several more hours of football. Inspired with a vision, she enlisted his aid in digging through the endless boxes of ancient decorations she had unearthed when cleaning out the third-floor storage area prior to its conversion to a grand master suite. Tim had moved the boxes down three flights of stairs to the cellar until they were needed.

During the house's renovation, he had taken great care with the foundation, knowing the rest of the process would only last as long as that which supported the whole. After encapsulating the floor and walls of the cellar with tough, heavy plastic sheeting, he had installed an airflow system and a dehumidifier to keep the air fresh and the environment suitable for storage. It didn't take him long to realize how much storage his imaginative bride would require. Tim was thankful for the foresight that had inspired him to add shelves along the entire length of a perimeter wall. He easily located the Christmas boxes, but after dragging them all back to the main level, he mentally chided himself for not tossing several of them into the skiff dumpster on their initial trip downstairs.

Indeed, many of the items had aged beyond saving, but there was one huge box full of nothing but delicate glass ornaments. Another contained miles of strung beads and baubles and a set of intricately detailed hanging figures depicting all the characters of Tchaikovsky's *Nutcracker Ballet*. Rose was enchanted by everything she discovered in the musty boxes, mentally making notes on where to place each figurine and candlestick while trying to decide on what place of honor to designate for the hand-carved nativity scene.

She told Tim that they would need at *least* three Christmas trees to hold all the decorations they had found. In his ignorance as a new husband, he made the almost unforgivable suggestion that they didn't necessarily need to use *every* item in *every* box just because it was there – especially since they weren't even going to be at home for Christmas. Rose quickly set him straight. Her contrite but willing groom spent the rest of the weekend squiring his wife all over town in search of the requisite trees (they ended up with four) and both fresh and silk greenery. He then manfully scoured stores in two counties for enough extension cords and Christmas lights to blind all their visitors and effectively keep the electric co-op solvent for decades to come.

After hanging the final wreathes on the side transoms of the front bay window, Tim went to put the ladder away in the garage while Rose made sure that every light chain, electric candle, and miniature streetlamp in the house was switched on before joining him at the front gate. As agreed, they both turned around to look back at the house at the same time. Rose danced in delight. "Oh, Tim, she is so *beautiful*."

He just stood there with a wide grin on his face. "Wow!" said it all.

It was a sight to gladden anyone's heart. The intricate levels of roofline were clearly outlined in ordered white lines, while the numerous balcony railings, wrapped in greenery and twinkle lights, provided a more blurry, muted radiance. The main Christmas tree stood triumphantly in the bay window enclosure, with a second fully decked out tree displayed on the second-floor balcony at the front of the house. Tim had even managed to attach a glowing solar-powered star atop the weather vane standing at the pinnacle of the turret roof.

After taking it all in, Rose glanced up anxiously at Tim's face. "You don't think I overdid it with the lights do you? Please say no."

He pulled her into his arms and said softly, "I wouldn't change a thing."

"You goof, you're not even looking at her," Rose protested, laughing.

Tim's eyes gleamed. "Oh, yes I am," he said, and kissed his bride long and lovingly. Finding no fault with his response, Rose snuggled closer in his embrace.

After a while, she said, "Tim?"

"Mmm?"

"Do you ever… have you ever felt so… so happy that you were a little… afraid?" She spoke hesitantly, a slight frown between her eyes. Hearing the disquiet in her voice, Tim pulled away a little to search her face.

"Afraid?" he asked gently. "What are you afraid of, sweetheart?"

"It's hard to explain." Rose paused for a moment, then continued as if not quite sure of how to express her feelings. "Ever since our wedding, I've been filled with a kind of… glow, deep inside me. I feel it when you're sitting at the breakfast bar drinking your morning coffee while I prepare your lunch, secretly hoping you'll be home to share it with me. I feel it again when I see you walk through the door at the end of the day. I feel it when we're worshiping together in church and when we're sitting quietly in the evenings looking into the fire, not saying anything. I feel it when I lay in bed at night waiting for you to finish your shower, and when I see your lazy smile next to me in the morning with your hair all rumpled from sleep." She laughed, then added, "I even feel it when I'm washing your dirty laundry." Tim smiled, fairly certain that the novelty of that task would fade quickly.

"Sometimes I have to pinch myself to make sure I'm not dreaming – that I'm really your lucky wife and you're my adoring husband." She hesitated again, searching for the right words to go on. "I know I will always love you, but I also realize that this prolonged feeling of euphoria can't last, and I wonder what life will be like when the newness of being together has worn off. It – the prospect – frightens me."

Rose stopped and was silent for so long, Tim felt compelled to comment. "Well, I'm not sure – "

"I don't ever want to take you for granted, my love," she blurted out over his words, touching his face with her hand.

Tim covered it with his own, lifted it to lightly kiss her palm, then drew both her hands to lay against his heart. "I don't ever want to take you for granted either," he said tenderly. "And yes, I feel that same sense of wonder and deep happiness now." He grinned and pointed out, "Why do you think I agreed to buy out an entire tree lot and two electrical stores," drawing an inevitable giggle. "But even when that passes – and it will – there will still be more great moments of joy to come than we can possibly imagine. And there will also probably be seasons of trouble or sadness, but God gave us each other to share the joy and to cling to one another in grief. And he promised to be with us through all of it. He also gave us a host of people to surround us with love and encouragement," he said, adding ruefully, "and advice – whether we want it or not. So, for now we just glory in the moment, and six days or six months or six years from now, no matter what life brings us, we will *choose* to be happy even when we don't necessarily *feel* like it. Agreed?"

"Agreed," Rose replied, taking Tim's hand as they walked toward the house. "Have I mentioned lately that I am *so* glad I married you and that I love you to the moon and back?"

He considered for a moment before answering. "Well, not in so many words, and I was planning to mention that inexcusable oversight, but can I do it inside? I'm freezing!" Tim started running toward the porch pulling his wife behind him. Her light-hearted spirit restored, Rose left the lilting peel of her laughter floating like effervescent bubbles on the cold night air.

CHAPTER 3

They were to be days of feasting, rejoicing, and of sending gifts to one another and the poor.

Esther 9: 22b (HCSB)

"I don't know why you're in such a goldarn hurry to see this farm. And for that matter, how did you even know it was for sale?" The forthright question was as close as Ezekiel Gerzsewski ever got to showing he was out of sorts.

Zeke serviced Harrington County as a realtor, an auctioneer, and an agriculture agent when he wasn't farming his own acreage, and he preferred to do all things in his good time. He liked to get to know his clients over lunch at the diner or fishing on a Friday afternoon. His walk was slow, his talk was slow, and according to his wife, his thought processes weren't much faster. Were it not for his obvious Polish heritage, he might have been mistaken for a displaced southerner. Given a choice, he would always opt for sitting on the porch swing sipping iced tea over mending a fence rail in the hot sun. If Zeke hoped that his comments would unsettle his passenger, he was destined for disappointment.

The well-dressed gentleman riding next to him showed no signs of umbrage whatsoever. His square jaw and classic features were schooled to impassivity, though the piercing blue eyes took in anything visible through the streaming car windows – which wasn't much. The forecast for light rain showers had been a miscalculation of epic proportions. The error manifested itself in torrential downpours and extremely limited visibility, causing the ditches on either side of the road to swell into competing rivers. Turning his attention to the driver, he simply offered, "Let's just say I have a friend at city hall," by way of explanation.

Zeke snorted. "That'll be Lucy Bennett. How that woman gets to know everything a week before everybody else does beats me. She should have gone to work for the CIA." His passenger merely smiled, thinking they had finally hit on a subject about which they were of one mind. After a few moments of intense silence, when Zeke had to focus entirely on the road after an unpleasant episode of hydroplaning, he said, still annoyed, "Mr. Hawthorne, I can't figure out what you expect to see today. Why, it's raining so hard out there, it's not fit for ducks! Couldn't this have waited a few days?" Zeke never understood why anyone wanted to rush through life when it was so much more pleasant to stroll. But then, he had never met anyone quite like Timothy Miles Hawthorne.

When Miles set a goal, or made a plan, or designed a well-thought-out development scheme, he kept his hand to the plow and his eyes on the horizon. In past years, he had been known to work for weeks on end without taking a break and without flagging. That had been the ruthless Miles Hawthorne who had made a name for himself in New York City. Since relocating to Kansas City and establishing his reputation locally, he had continued the same focused working practices that had garnered him so much success. But they had been tempered to more reasonable levels as Miles learned to reorder his priorities. He discovered that he rather enjoyed his time off. Zeke Gerzsewski would have been amazed to learn that Miles rarely worked weekends now, preferring to spend time in Tinkers Well with the estranged family who had welcomed him back into their lives. But the project that inspired him to insist on hurtling through the rain and sleet was a rare mission that brought those two worlds together.

"In answer to your question, Ezekiel – "

"Make that Zeke, if you don't mind. Anytime someone calls me Ezekiel, I feel like one of those Old Testament prophets breathing fire and fury. Doesn't quite fit my personality. I'm more of the 'take it easy' type, if you know what I mean."

Miles knew exactly what he meant. Unfortunately for Zeke, Miles was in no mood to take it easy. He had been on the lookout for some months for a certain type of property in just the right location for his purposes. He had enlisted the aid of Lucy Bennet several weeks earlier when cornered by her at a church social event. It seemed they shared parallel goals. She, unlike most women, failed to fall for his innate charm, but she was astute enough to recognize his intelligence and professional skill, and she intended to make use of both.

Lucy was, in theory, secretary to the mayor and city council. She had also, somehow, assumed self-appointed membership to any board or committee she felt would benefit from her native shrewdness and historical perspective. Recipients of her generosity included the Regional Planning Commission, the Zoning Commission, and the Industrial Development Board, to name a few. As someone who had been born and raised in Harrington County, she knew everyone that was anyone, and a whole lot more besides, and had stayed abreast of every issue involving the city since she was old enough to read the local newspaper.

After her children had grown and flown the nest, Lucy wasn't quite ready to settle down to waiting on invitations for babysitting gigs as an itinerant grandmother. Though she had originally volunteered her services to the city council, her unrelenting energy and drive quickly made her indispensable, and she was hired on a permanent part-time basis. Her husband, Tom, happily supported her in her work. When he saw Lucy drive away to her appointed rounds, Tom knew he had several hours of blessed peace in which to enjoy taking care of his farm in the truly estimable manner he had employed for over 30 years without his wife's well-meaning, but not particularly helpful, interference. She was a force to be reckoned with, though those who knew her best acknowledged that her finest quality was a tender heart that melted like butter for anyone in need.

Lucy Bennet had not aged as gracefully as many of her peers, having no desire or interest in fighting the effects of time. Her graying hair and serviceable attire – at least two decades behind the mode – made her appear older than her 50-odd years, but her youthful energy and a forthright manner swayed the scales more favorably. She certainly got Miles' attention when she wanted it. Catching him on his way to the kitchen, Lucy wasted no time. She asked him bluntly on that occasion whether he had any suggestions for expanding the influence and scope of Tinkers Well.

"The mayor and his pals, though I'm sure are all fine men and women in their way, have no eye to the future. They're more interested in the daily special at Milly's Diner than looking past the nose on their collective faces. And I have a notion that you're just the man who might be able to make something happen around here where they can't." Lucy stared fixedly at Miles, demanding an answer.

"I like a person who comes right to the point," he said just as bluntly, though whether she noticed the twinkle lurking in his eyes was anyone's guess. "I do happen to have a few ideas, but for now, I must insist that you keep this conversation in utmost confidence."

Where charm had failed, the suggestion of intrigue did the trick. Lucy dutifully kept her ear to the ground, and, three weeks later, contacted Miles. Her information sent him to the office of one Zeke Gerzsewski on a day that should have been called, county wide, on account of bad weather.

"I do apologize for inconveniencing you on such a day, but it has been my experience that ideal opportunities are made, not presented by the erratic whims of chance." The inconvenience also affected Zeke's car, which started showing signs of water leakage around the worn seal surrounding the passenger window. Miles moved his legs slightly to the left and continued his focused surveillance of the scenery.

"This property hasn't even been officially listed yet, so what's the big hurry?" Zeke growled, frowning.

"I'm sure you appreciate, as few others would, the rare combination of the property's proximity to town and its access to city water and sewer. Furthermore, the sizeable acreage is surrounded on three sides by roads, making it easily accessible both for development and traffic from multiple directions." Zeke had never given those qualifications any thought at all. In Lucy Bennet's estimation, his lack of vision lumped him in with most of City Hall. "All I ask is that you drive me around the entire perimeter so that I can get a feel for the land and its relative position to other communities." Keeping one eye on the mostly obscured landscape and the other on a detailed map he had pulled up on his phone, Miles felt a building sense of excitement.

Zeke might have grumbled a little longer, but they suddenly drove straight out of a particularly heavy deluge into nothing more than a thin mist lightened by a breakthrough sunbeam. His attitude lightened accordingly. By the time they circumnavigated the property and stopped to drive around the farmhouse and outbuildings, the rain had stopped altogether. A rainbow appeared in the sky as they drove back to Zeke's office. Whether it was the colorful reminder of God's covenant with Noah, or belief that he might be able to close the office a little early that afternoon – probably the latter – Zeke wasted no time. He processed Miles Hawthorn's offer as quickly and accurately as possible, knowing a sizeable commission awaited him in the end. What Zeke failed to realize was that Miles could just as easily have purchased the property directly from the Cooper family. But after an almost calamitous misunderstanding over a land deal in Kansas City that had nearly brought him to blows with his son just before the latter's wedding, Miles chose the more transparent approach so that no hint of impropriety would cast doubt on his motives.

God had redeemed more than Miles' soul on a fateful day in July; he had redeemed his heart as well. And that heart now swelled as Miles checked off the second step in a quest that drove him like no other pursuit before. Having completed all the formalities, Miles shook Zeke's hand and drove toward the bypass and the driveway to Willow Walk. He needed to talk to the one person whose advice he had spurned for so many years and whose gentle words of encouragement now helped keep him grounded. Turning onto a lesser driveway before reaching the big house, Miles parked in front of Fern Cottage and walked quickly to the door. He knocked decisively before letting himself in and waited with barely contained impatience for his mother to answer his summons.

Wassail simmered on the stove, sending tantalizing waves of cinnamon, clove, and citrus scents wafting through the house. The ladies of the Ludlow/Hawthorne family had just completed an exhaustive tour of Willow Walk so that Rose could describe all the decorations as Aletha touched each one and remembered. Her sightless eyes beheld nothing, but the eyes of her mind still saw every detail. Her companion dog Scout, a golden retriever who rarely left her side, looked on attentively.

"Oh!" she cried in delight as Rose guided her hands to the Nutcracker ornaments hanging front and center on the nine-foot tree in the parlor. "I thought these must have been lost." She touched first the princely nutcracker, then the sugar plum fairy and the reed flutes, until she had held and reacquainted herself with each piece. "My parents gave me this collection when I was eleven. It was the first of many years they took me to see the *Nutcracker* ballet when I was a girl. I was so enchanted by the costumes and the music that I must have danced around the house for weeks afterward humming the *Waltz of the Flowers.*"

Gratified that she had brought pleasure to someone who had known so much tragedy in her life, Rose was inspired to pull up a recording on her phone. Grabbing Aletha's hands, Rose helped her sway in time to the lilting melody. Tim quickly relocated the coffee table to allow for more freedom of movement.

Miles, watching from the hallway, marveled as he witnessed one of the magical impromptu moments of Christmas. The familiar decorations had roused memories in him also, but his memories were clouded with guilt and remorse. His youthful rebellion and hardness of heart had cost him as much, if not more, than his mother. A young Marilyn, insecure yet devoted to her husband, had tried to bring that note of gaiety and wonder into their home during the holidays. But Miles had already begun slipping into a lifestyle more focused on ambition and personal gain than selfless giving or the sharing of sentimentality. As he followed his mother's hesitant, yet determined steps, the guilt was lifted by the liberating knowledge of the grace and forgiveness he still sometimes struggled to acknowledge and accept. Without really thinking, he walked over to his ex-wife and literally swept her off her feet as he began waltzing with her to the brilliant strains of Tchaikovsky. Marilyn was at first a little self-conscious, but the music and Miles' approving smile helped her to relax in his embrace while they danced around the room like the seasoned partners they were.

Tim, not content to be left out of the fun, tapped Rose on the shoulder and cut in just before the ending flourish. He twirled his grandmother around the parlor floor until the final cadence when she collapsed against him. Her fine porcelain features were flushed with exertion and happiness, and she laughed like a carefree schoolgirl.

"Oh, my goodness," she said, trying to catch her breath, "I haven't felt so young in years!"

Marilyn, too, laughed when Miles bowed gallantly. But as he raised his head, he looked at her in a way that made her heart beat even faster than the accelerated rate caused by the dance. Suddenly breathless, she instinctively looked away to break eye contact, unsure of what the intent look meant and unwilling to consider the possible answers. Instead, she ushered the ladies into the kitchen to finish after dinner clean-up, while Miles, glancing significantly at Rose, asked Tim to step into the library to discuss "the collaborative project" they were working on.

While Rose emptied the drying rack of pots and pans and whisked them away to their appointed storage spots in the spacious cabinets, Marilyn placed a cinnamon stick in five Christmas mugs and filled them with the fragrant wassail. She and Rose had spotted the brightly colored mugs at a thrift store near Leavenworth, and Rose couldn't leave the store without all twelve, and a matching red pitcher, despite their evident chips and imperfections. She later discovered that they were originally from a well-known pottery called *Wächtersbach,* near Frankfurt, Germany. The mugs instantly became family heirlooms. And being the romantic she was, Rose treasured them all the more for the little dings that signified they had been loved by some other family before hers.

While the other ladies completed their tasks, Aletha entertained them with accounts of Christmases past.

"We had very little money those first few years of marriage. James flatly refused to accept any financial help from my family, you see. But we saved enough to make a trip to upstate New York to see all the beautiful fall colors during that first autumn after our wedding. That was before Timothy was born, of course."

Miles had grown up as Timothy Hawthorne, and so he would always be to his mother and his former wife. The continued use of his first name by the two women who had loved him all those years ago filled his heart with hope tinged with humility, because it also reminded him of their radical pardon and renewed support.

"I remember we stayed in a quaint little town, hardly more than a village really, that hosted a yearly fall festival. Artisans from all over New England came there to sell their artwork. The town's population just about tripled over that weekend, so we were lucky to rent a room in a boarding house right on the town square." As an aside to Rose, she explained, "I suppose it's what you might call a B & B nowadays."

Rose and Marilyn sat with Aletha at the farm table, both anxious to learn more of Miles' past. Despite having been married to Miles, these were stories Marilyn had never heard; she understood why and could only be thankful that Aletha shared them now.

"Now where was I? Oh yes. That's how we met the woodcarver," Aletha said, and beamed happily at her audience who felt they had missed out on a few chapters of her tale.

"I'm sorry, but are you saying you met a woodcarver at the boarding house?" Rose asked.

"Well, of course not. Why would he need a room when he had his own little camper parked in an alley off the main street? Wasn't that clever of him? He set up a display of his wares under the camper's canopy instead of trying to vie for attention amid all the booths set up around the square."

Rose and Marilyn recognized Aletha's singular narrative style with a wink and a nod.

"He carved the most exquisite figurines, and his specialty was nativity sets. That set that you pointed out in the parlor was made by him. It does look lovely displayed collectively. What you couldn't know, however, is that we asked him to make a few modifications and commissioned an additional piece from him, though I suppose it has been misplaced by now."

"No, it hasn't," Rose said, intrigued by Aletha's story. "I *did* find another figure of Mary, but she was shaped in such a way that she didn't fit into the display, and quite frankly, I couldn't figure out what to do with her. Wait right here. I think I left the box in the corner cupboard in the dining room."

As she moved toward the doorway to the neighboring room, Aletha called after her, "Bring the donkey back with you, too."

A few minutes later Rose placed the carved figures on the table, then watched in fascination as Aletha gave a little twist to the donkey's blanket and lifted it to reveal a tiny peg on the animal's back. Rose placed the other figure in the old woman's searching hand, and with a snap, Mary was riding sidesaddle on the donkey – a very pregnant Mary.

"That's brilliant!" Rose cried in delight. "Now, why did I not notice Mary's swollen belly?"

"Because you weren't looking for it, I suppose. There's one other detail you might have missed. There is a little groove in Joseph's right hand that you can slip the donkey's reins into – for when they are making the journey, you understand." Aletha smiled, remembering the practice of recreating the Christmas story from five decades earlier. "We always made a practice of leaving only the animals in the nativity scene during the weeks leading up to Christmas, while Mary and Joseph and the donkey advanced by small stages down the hall on their 'journey' to Bethlehem. Oh, if you could have seen Timothy's joy in finding the baby Jesus in his manger every Christmas morning, with the shepherds in attendance. It almost eclipsed his excitement at the plethora of gifts crowding the base of the Christmas tree."

Sadly, over the years, joy had deteriorated into indifference and distain as Miles reached young adulthood. A heartbroken mother had boxed up most of those cherished memories with the ornaments that recalled them, consigning them to a forgotten past. Now the memories, the sounds of music and laughter, and the sights – as only Aletha was able to see them – came to life again.

Rose, on her way to rearrange the nativity scene and announce that it was time for the gift exchange, caught up with the two men as they entered the hall. Miles looked up and down the long expanse and frowned.

"Everything looks just beautiful, Rose, but I can't help thinking something is missing – here." He gestured vaguely at a spot midway along the wide corridor.

Her eyes twinkled with her newly discovered knowledge. "Don't move. I'll be right back."

Miles looked at his son for enlightenment, but Tim just grinned and shook his head. "She surprises me about every five minutes, so I'm as clueless as you are."

Returning with the expectant Mary, Joseph, and the donkey, Rose directed Tim to clear off a display shelf.

Frowning, he asked, "Let me get this straight. You want me to *take down* Christmas decorations – *before* Christmas?"

"Ti-im!"

"Okay, okay." Presently, Victorian streetlamps and carolers were replaced with Joseph leading the donkey carrying its precious load.

"Oh, good Lord! I'd completely forgotten about these." Miles touched the pieces, inspired by the freshness and meaning of another long-forgotten tradition.

It was the long-standing tradition of gift giving, however, that created memories for everyone, for the exchange signaled a new beginning all around. The hope and promise that entered the world with the birth of the Christ child seemed to spread its gentle power over all those present. Mother and son were reunited; Miles and Marilyn sat in comfortable anticipation as old friends; father and son added another leg in their journey of bonding; and bride and groom waited anxiously to see if the love and thought that went into their gifts would be greeted with pleasure by the other.

In recognition of her role as family matriarch, Aletha opened her presents first. It was unlikely that the presentation of the crown jewels would have eclipsed the gift dearest to her heart. An unbelievably soft monogramed bathrobe from Miles brought happy tears to her eyes. But such was her state of mind that she would have been thrilled had he gifted her a pair of serviceable wool socks! Miles unwrapped blue jeans, work shirts and steel-toed boots, all the while keeping an eye on his grinning son and wondering what future projects were planned that required such serviceable splendor. Miles' gift of tickets for the Kansas City Symphony both astonished and delighted Marilyn. Her deceased husband, Peter, had shown little interest in the classics, and had tolerated good-naturedly, rather than enjoyed, the few concerts they had attended together. She had almost forgotten how much she enjoyed the thrill of great musical works performed by professional musicians. Yet, Miles had remembered.

"Timothy, I don't know what to say except 'Thank you.'" She stood impetuously and hugged him without thinking. He savored her nearness but pulled away first to spare her any awkwardness.

"They're box seats so you can invite three people. I thought you might take Tim and Rose and mother, or Angelica and the Lindeman's. I believe Mark mentioned that he was a jazz fan, and they're playing Gershwin in the spring."

"But surely you'll come, too." Marilyn couldn't disguise the wistful note in her voice.

"I will be there any time you ask." He held her hands and her gaze as if they were the only two people in the room. Rose was enthralled by the exchange. Her husband judged it time to move on.

"Okay, enough about music. What do I get?" he said in the manner of a much younger Tim.

Rose was momentarily eclipsed in Tim's esteem when he opened an envelope from Miles containing a hodgepodge of tickets to various professional sporting events, but she happily seconded plans for father and son to spend more time together. If she was disappointed at Tim's lackluster response to her first gift – a new suit for Abe's wedding – she appreciated the effort he made to act pleased.

Tim's forced smile inspired Miles to comment affably, "Turnabout's fair play, my boy. Now you can get used to *my* 'work clothes.'" The forced smile turned to a lopsided grin. Tim humbly thanked his wife for taking care of him and moved on to a second offering from Rose. His reaction this time was more satisfying.

"Honey, where did you *find* these?" Tim asked in wonder. From an old wooden toolbox, he pulled out the creative gems used by craftsmen of a bygone era. Holding each treasure reverently, he tested the wooden level, gingerly checked the blade on the planer, spun the hand drill to watch the wheel teeth move smoothly, and traced the barely discernable markings of the carpenter's square.

"I know you can't actually use them, but you're such a talented carpenter that I thought you might appreciate some classic hand tools. Maybe you could display them in the library, or… or maybe in your Three Brother's office in town…" Her voice trailed off as he replaced each tool in the old toolbox without speaking.

Finally, turning to Rose, while ignoring the rest of the room's occupants, Tim gathered her in his arms, kissed her tenderly, and whispered, "Sweetheart, this is the most thoughtful gift I've ever received." Her cup of happiness was full to overflowing, though it lost a few drops when she opened her first present from Tim.

"I know you're going to love this. And it's really the reason I suggested we exchange our presents here instead of taking them to Kentucky with us. Go ahead. You're going to love it," he repeated with assurance.

New husbands rarely know their brides as well as they think they do.

Rose took the box held out to her. It had a little weight to it, and she couldn't help allowing her imagination its full scope. She envisioned an elegant ceramic sculpture or perhaps a delicate porcelain figurine. This time, her imagination failed her completely. Quickly removing the lid and sorting through the tissue paper, she stopped and stared blankly at the contents.

Misinterpreting her muteness, Tim lifted the object from the box and placed it in Rose's hands. "Isn't she a beauty?" he remarked with pride.

Rose looked at him in confusion. "It's a gun."

"Well, actually, it's a Springfield Armory™ 9mm pistol. It's just the right size for you. And look, it comes with two 10-round magazines."

Rose continued to stare in bewilderment. "But… it's a *gun*."

Miles lips began to twitch.

"Yes…" Tim finally, reluctantly, registered her lack of enthusiasm.

"I've never fired a gun." Rose's blank stare turned to a worried frown.

Mistaking her reaction to his gift to be grounded in her inexperience with firearms, Tim assured Rose that he could teach her how to use it in no time. "I'll get some hay bales and set up some practice targets so you can build your confidence."

"But I… I mean – who am I supposed to shoot?" she asked in dismay.

Miles clapped his hand over his mouth to silence the shout that threatened to escape his lips. His shoulders shook with ill-concealed laughter. Marilyn purposely kept her head down to hide a wide smile. It was Aletha, having missed all the visible signals inherent in the dialogue, who said placidly, "Now I call that a very sensible question." Miles hurriedly left the room, no longer able to control the mirth that consumed him.

Totally ignoring his less than helpful family, the harassed groom said to his bride, "You're not *supposed* to shoot anybody."

"Then I don't understand…"

"Honey, I want to know that you can protect yourself when I'm not around. I'm gone for at least two weeks every summer and a weekend every month with my Army Reserve duties, and we live out here isolated from any neighbors except Aletha…"

"But Aletha lives out here alone," Rose pointed out.

"An excellent observation, dear. Why doesn't someone give me a gun?" asked the blind woman, setting Miles off again. His laughter rang from the dining room while Scout, laying by the fire, tucked his tail and whined a little.

Rose squared her shoulders and said with resolution, "If you think I need one, then I'll learn to use it." She would have agreed to mastering the workings of a bazooka, if only to wipe the look of hurt and frustration from Tim's face.

He quickly removed his gross misfire and replaced it with a small gift bag. "It isn't much, but I thought you might like it." His confidence in shreds after missing the mark so widely with his first offering, he held out little hope that the second would be any more successful.

Determined to make much of whatever she found, Rose pulled out a jeweler's box and opened it tentatively, then cried out with pleasure at its contents. A brushed silver heart with two colored stones affixed to one side dangled on a silver chain. "Oh, Tim, it's *beautiful!*"

Encouraged by her response, he explained, "These are our birthstones, and you see this little ring at the base of the heart? That's where we'll attach smaller hearts with each addition to our family, and each will have its own birthstone."

Tears filled Rose's eyes. "Tim, I've never received anything more beautiful or meaningful. I love it and I love you."

All thoughts of previous disappointment were relegated to the distant past. The evening ended on a triumphant note when Marilyn emerged victorious from a board game she had given Tim.

"I smell a rat," Tim said, looking suspiciously at his mother. "Did you practice this game before you wrapped it?"

"I had to make sure all the pieces were there," she replied airily. Miles found her artless response captivating, and his unguarded expression said as much.

Bidding farewell to their guests from the kitchen porch, Tim stood with his arms wrapped around his wife for warmth. "I'll be darned if I can figure out what's going on between my parents, but it's certainly not going to be dull around here anytime soon."

Marilyn was a little surprised to find Aletha absent when Miles picked her up a week later to attend the Christmas Eve service at Community Church.

"I know. It was Mother who suggested the eleven o'clock service rather than attending the earlier evening service. But she said she could feel a cold coming on, so I left her listening to Dicken's *Christmas Carol* from the collection of old radio show recordings Tim and Rose gave her."

"I guess it's just you and me, then."

"Just you and me," Miles echoed softly.

Community Church glowed with warm candlelight from candelabras by the altar and candles in the windows. The flickering light set the banks of poinsettias ablaze with rich tones of red and pink. A minimal use of music provided maximum effect as the pianist and flutist played a prelude medley of gentle Christmas carols: *Still, Still, Still; Infant Holy, Infant Lowly;* and *Away in a Manger.*

Miles and Marilyn slipped into a pew midway up the aisle just behind Tom and Lucy Bennett.

"I'm a bit surprised to find so many families with children at this later service," Miles observed after the formality of pleasantries.

"Ha! They're the smart ones. You keep a seven-year-old up till midnight and you won't have to get up before nine o'clock Christmas morning!" Nothing got past Lucy Bennett.

Despite having turned his back on the faith of his youth, Miles had attended a few Christmas Eve services over the years. It had been more a cultural gesture than a religious one, and the churches in question had offered the pinnacle in musical excellence. With deep appreciation, he had listened to a world-renowned boys' choir perform arias and choruses from Handel's *Messiah* at the National Cathedral in Washington. He had marveled at the sheer power of the pipe organ at London's Westminster Abbey when the low pedal stops were engaged, shaking the very foundation of the ancient church.

At the time, he had believed that such magnificence represented the height of what worship should be. Standing next to Marilyn, however, and singing carols with the clarity of the words made paramount, he was reminded again that the essence of worship is actively participating in the music and the spoken word rather than passively listening to a performance, no matter how grand or glorious. As they sang the final verse of one of his favorite carols of childhood, set to a tender melody by Gustav Holst, the simple message spoke to him more effectively than a clarion call.

> *What can I give him, poor as I am?*
> *If I were a shepherd, I would bring a lamb*
> *If I were a wise man, I would do my part*
> *Yet what can I give him; give my heart*[3]

It was the carol sung at the end of the service, however, when everyone held their individual candles aloft and the house lights had all been dimmed, that took Miles back to the awe and simplicity of Christmas as a child. Congregants, gathered to celebrate the birth of a Savior, made their way outside singing the timeless words of *Silent Night.* Miles and Marilyn walked into the cold night air, and snow began to fall. The timing of the unexpected

---

[3] Christina G. Rossetti, "In the Bleak Midwinter" (1872) Public Domain.

flurries might otherwise have felt like a cliché but for the tribute of the collective raised voices. The silent snow added its own unspoken homage.

Christmas hugs and well wishes were exchanged before families and friends drove off to dream of the joyous morning to come. While others drifted away, a middle-aged couple stood fast, not wanting the moment to end, though they could hardly ignore one of the deacons locking the church doors. Marilyn laughed softly and took Miles' hand.

"You have made this a truly special Christmas, Timothy. Thank you… for… for being here."

"Thank you for welcoming me home. Merry Christmas, my dear." He kissed her gently on the cheek. A sudden, frosty breeze extinguished their flames, and they turned to walk slowly to the car.

CHAPTER 4

January heralded a new year with a frigid wind that blew an endless parade of snow flurries into mounting drifts. Chilly gusts covered any obstacle in their paths with white powder, while the mercury struggled to reach 30 degrees by mid-afternoon. Only the hardiest and hungriest of wild things ventured from their dens and thickets in search of food hidden under the frozen blanket of snow. The barely perceptible lengthening of days following the winter solstice became obscured by leaden skies that continued to insist on an early twilight, driving the inhabitants of Tinkers Well into the warmth and security of their homes. In future years the harsh forces of winter would become merely seasonal trials to be endured, but for the present, they provided the newlyweds with an extended honeymoon of sorts — a time to dream before the fire without the likelihood of anyone dropping by or any social demands to disrupt their leisurely routine.

The Ludlows spent hours wandering through the rooms of Willow Walk arguing good-naturedly over decorating schemes and room uses. Rose favored flowers and wallpaper; Tim wanted cleanly painted walls accented with plaid. She was destined to win, of course, but they struck a mostly mutual agreement on style ideas to be implemented as time and finances permitted.

Rose had achieved just such a meeting of tastes for their own attic suite. It was neither overtly feminine nor distinctly masculine. Their king-size bed was draped in a neutral damask striped duvet and accented by rows of pillows in varying shapes and patterns – too many pillows to Tim's way of thinking, though he wisely accepted the futility of a battle hardly worth fighting. An oversized plush area rug in a muted abstract motif gave their feet a warm place to land in the morning before hitting the shining hardwood floor on the way to the bathroom. Rose had her reading nook in the turret space, and Tim got his ventless gas fireplace on the wall opposite the bed – the wall that backed up to the mechanical room housing the heating and cooling systems for the entire house. Unlike its cousins on the ground floor, this fireplace surround was composed of layers of irregular stone topped by a rustic wooden mantelpiece. While it was the antithesis of the other intricately carved surrounds adorned with marble tops, it suited the room perfectly. Rose admired it as much as Tim did.

They also agreed, essentially, on space allocations on the second floor which boasted five bedrooms, amply proportioned. Both husband and wife were committed to hosting as many guests as they could hold for special events such as the Walker-Yousef wedding or visits from the Kentucky contingent of the family. But Rose also wanted a project room for sewing and following her new passion of repurposing or refinishing thrift store finds. She pointed out that Tim had essentially turned her lovely music conservatory into a football man cave for every male relation and friend in town *and* had a workshop on one end of the old carriage house. For the sake of sport, he made a show of disputing her claims, enjoying her spirited comebacks, and invariably grinning in defeat. Rose, in turn, agreed that the parlor was the more practical setting for the piano and graciously accepted Tim's offer of rounding up a group of able-bodied men to move the instrument to its new home. The conservatory was renamed the family room and tranquility settled over the Ludlow domain.

On dark evenings, when taking a break from reading an engrossing tale in the big wingback chair before the library fire, Rose adopted the habit of watching over her husband's shoulder while he sat at the desk working on post-holiday project schedules and plans. She began asking about the projects and discovered that she found the process interesting and Tim's ideas intriguing. Rose had been so focused on their own home for the past few months that she had almost forgotten about his other construction obligations. Her questions initially showed her lack of knowledge about anything but the superficial elements of Victorian restoration. But as Tim patiently explained the work to be done and the architectural considerations involved, her interest was captured.

Rose began offering hesitant suggestions on practical issues, such as space usage and layout options. As her knowledge grew, so grew the validity of her comments, until Tim made it a practice to run new remodeling projects by her without waiting for her to ask. It meant the world to him that Rose genuinely cared about his profession. And he had to admit that her observations – coming from a woman's perspective – were often quite helpful. So in tune were they as a team that he began to assume he had discussed *all* his upcoming jobs with her. One glaring oversight rippled the waters of their placid, halcyon existence, exposing the inevitable reality of human error. Honeymoons don't last forever.

The hours of prior planning enabled Tim to send the newer members of the crew out on their respective assignments with little additional oversight. Momentarily free of immediate supervisory responsibility, Tim met with the original members of *Three Brothers Construction, Inc.* at Milly's Diner on a gloomy, frigid day that showed no signs of warming. Having invested so much time and attention to its renovation the past summer, the diner had become their home away from home. They each sat clutching a mug of hot coffee to ward off the lingering January chill that seemed to permeate everywhere, despite a gas fire burning merrily in the corner stove. Abe alone dared let go of the mug to finish off a piece of apple pie; after all, he hadn't eaten anything for over an hour! Before getting down to business, they shared tales of their respective holiday adventures on the road. Derek had spent a quiet Christmas with his mom in Tinkers Well, but Tim and Abe had enjoyed more chaotic Christmases with the families of their respective sweethearts.

Gertrude Gunn, Rose's outrageously outspoken grandmother – known as Granny Gert to her family and Gertie to her friends – had been instrumental in bringing Rose into Tim's orbit. He, therefore, held her in high esteem despite her propensity to say exactly what she was thinking at the most embarrassing moment possible, then taking perverse pleasure in the ensuing confusion.

The young couple had barely gotten settled into Rose's childhood home in Kentucky for Christmas before Beth Thompson's only sister, Patty Gunn, had been compelled by their forceful mother to drive her from their shared home in Versailles to Winchester. Granny Gert was determined to greet her granddaughter at the earliest opportunity and to hear all the latest news from Tinkers Well. Having spent several months there earlier in the year with her old college friend, Aletha Mason, Gertie had become a staple in Aletha's social circle at church. She had also been a hit among the seniors crowd that gathered for Bingo every Thursday evening. Granny Gert was greeted with genuine affection by the Ludlows, and with guarded optimism by her daughter Beth and the rest of the Thompson family.

Both of Rose's sisters and their husbands were also present to welcome the newlyweds. The oldest of the three sisters, Violet, had presented her parents with their first grandchild only two weeks earlier, so it was almost a competition between the women to be granted cuddling rights with little Ian. Giving deference to Rose, who had not yet held her nephew, the others watched indulgently as she cooed softly to the precious life in her arms.

Tim, who was engaged in the more manly pursuit of swapping predictions for bowl game victories with the other men present, happened to glance over at his wife and captured a glimpse into their future. The sight of Rose rocking the baby warmed his heart, even as he relegated the foreshadowing of that image in their own home to a nebulous "someday." During pre-marital counseling, they had both agreed on the desire for a large family, but Tim was in no hurry, selfishly savoring his wife's complete attention and the total lack of restraint they enjoyed as they learned to live life together. He imagined parenthood some two or three years distant. Rose's maternal instincts kicked in the moment she held baby Ian in her arms.

Granny Gert, never loathe to pry into anyone's affairs, demanded in a voice calculated to be heard for two city blocks, "Rosie, you were born to be a mother. When do you and that handsome husband of yours plan to present me with another great-grandchild?" Totally ignoring Rose's fiery blush and Tim's sudden interest in his feet, she added, "Why, you've been married two whole months already; seems like you could have figured everything out by now. And I'm not getting any younger!"

Tim smiled ruefully as he recounted the episode to his buddies. Derck gave a shout of laughter, mentally picturing the event as if he had witnessed it firsthand. It was his belief that a little embarrassment was good for the soul, unless, of course, it was experienced by him. Abe, on the other hand, responded with empathy.

"I would laugh, but I so get where you're coming from – unfortunately. I think Granny Gert and Amy's Great Aunt Ruth – I now think of her as the 'Ruthinator' – must be distantly related. But honestly, I find her even more dangerous than Granny Gert. She's small and dainty and looks as guileless as a cherub, but hiding behind that angelic facade is a wicked tongue and an impeccable sense of timing for optimum effect. She has this sweet smile that reminded me of Aletha, and she kept calling me 'dear boy.' That deadly combination caught me completely off guard.

"You'll probably think me paranoid, but I swear they all conspired to have her sitting right next to me for dinner the first night we were there. No sooner had I taken a big bite of sweet potatoes than she asked me how high up my leg had been amputated. I couldn't very well talk to her with my mouth full, so I gestured to indicate where my leg ended and the prosthesis began. She patted the spot gently and smiled at me. Then that sweet old lady tapped her water glass with her spoon until she had *everyone's* attention and announced to the entire room that I hadn't lost anything *really* important." Abe shook his head as Tim and Derek burst out laughing.

"That is awesome!" Derek said. "I would have paid good money to see that."

"I'll be sure and invite her to *your* wedding," Abe replied with heavy sarcasm.

"Like I've been telling you, Derek Warner plans to escape the bans of matrimony for a while yet. This whole extended family thing sounds a little like navigating a mine field."

"Not getting married, huh? Should we get that in writing?" Tim looked at Abe who replied in an off-hand way.

"I wouldn't worry too much. I fear he lacks the charm and good looks to attract any sensible woman."

Derek retaliated by wadding up napkins and throwing them across the table at his friend.

"Hey, hey, *hey*, you two. Back in your corners," Tim said, shaking his head. Derek made much of appearing offended, though neither of the other two paid any attention to him. "Speaking of weddings, I'd like to run an idea by you both. It was a suggestion made to me by Miles and I'd like your feedback."

They spent the next hour discussing a comprehensive overhaul of the large barn located on Tim's property. He had drawn on his father's years of experience in property development by asking for practical ideas in putting the old structure to use. The one Miles endorsed the strongest was the one Tim had the hardest time wrapping his brain around. Despite his doubts, he had drawn some preliminary sketches and made a list of materials and machinery required, including some sub-contracted work.

After reviewing everything, Derek commented with some concern, "Phew! This is a big project. We've never really taken on anything of this scale before."

"I know, but from a structural standpoint, it's actually less complicated than the work we did on my house or even the Bennet's place."

"Yeah, but if you decide to make it useable year-round, you're talking about a massive heating and cooling unit," Derek countered. "Is that even cost effective?"

While the other two traded ideas about industrial duct work, blowers, and fans, Abe sat quietly pursuing his own line of thought. As if finally working something out, he said, "What if I do some research into leasing the specialized equipment you would need. It's possible we could get a price break if we started work now before the busiest part of the building season."

"You want us to work in that old barn *now*, when even *polar* bears are hibernating?" Derek was not a big fan of temperatures below 50 degrees, despite having grown up in Chicago. He attributed his antipathy toward the cold to his Jamaican heritage. Abe preferred to call him a wuss.

"I'll wuss you," Derek muttered. Tim rolled his eyes as napkins were once again hurled across the table by the two twelve-year-olds he called business partners.

"I have an idea on how to keep it warm enough to work in while we're sealing it and installing insulation," Tim shouted over the chaos until he finally succeeded in recapturing the attention of the combatants. "At least we could try it out and go from there."

"I vote we give it a try," Abe said. "Do you think we can make it functional in say… less than three months?"

Tim looked at Abe, a speculative gleam in his eye. "Are you suggesting some guinea pigs?"

Derek grumbled, "Pigs are about the *only* things that would be interested in that frozen cave."

Abe had higher hopes. When he picked up his fiancée after school on Friday, he broached the idea to her. Amy's exuberant response nearly caused him to swerve off the road. She was instantly on board and offered her services to help in any way she could. Her plans were falling into place.

Midway through January the snows finally stopped. The temps rose sufficiently – aided by the return of a weak, if insistent, sun – to turn the white wonderland outside Rose's windows into a sodden, patchy landscape spotted with stubborn, dirty snowdrifts. She attributed the depressing atmosphere to Tim's unusual verbal reticence and preoccupation. *Three Brothers Construction, Inc.* was again fully staffed and making headway on all the projects he had organized during the holiday lull. When asked if he had any new plans to show her, he merely replied that everything was in the execution stage, so there was nothing of interest to share. Rose sensed that Tim was worried about something and felt that he had withdrawn from her in some intangible way. Determined not to be troubled by the subtle change in her husband, or to push for a confidence he obviously didn't feel inclined to share, she set out to woo him back to good humor.

While Tim was meeting with Derek and Abe, Rose was focused on trying every possible ploy to brighten that particularly bleak day and recapture her husband's fancy. She added a tablecloth and candles to the kitchen table and prepared one of Tim's favorite meals for dinner: a succulent standing rib roast, garlic and green onion potatoes, and peas with bacon. She even offered hot homemade biscuits dripping with butter and honey.

Rose greeted Tim at the back door with her most beguiling smile, wearing an outfit she knew to be one that he particularly admired. A very flattering white ruffled blouse, topping a tweed pencil skirt, never failed to catch Tim's eye, and her shapely legs, made even shapelier by ankle boots, inevitably drew a whistle. But after depositing his muddy boots in the laundry room, he returned her welcoming kiss almost mechanically, and the rest of the obvious extra effort made on his behalf went largely unnoticed. Now *she* was getting worried.

Rose had barely finished the washing up – accomplished uncharacteristically alone – when she was summoned by her cell phone. *Finally,* Rose thought, *someone I can talk to.* But the eager bride-to-be on the other end of the call did most of the talking and left the seasoned wife of less than three months even more puzzled and concerned. Rose left her phone and went in search of her husband.

She found him in the library with his nose practically glued to the computer screen. She would ordinarily have stopped on the threshold to admire the artistic setting. The golden glow of the fire cast moving fingers of light onto the multitude of mismatched volumes shelved on the bookcases lining the better part of two and a half walls. Their colorful spines and irregular heights produced an abstract note in the otherwise solid backdrop that surrounded a stately walnut writing desk with curved legs. Its bulk, coupled with the modern incongruence of a desktop computer, declared it to be functional without detracting at all from its timeless elegance. The ornate scrolled outline of the side and front panels, however, might have been the utilitarian frame of a cardboard box for all Tim noticed. The arresting tableau also left Rose unmoved. She was a woman on a mission.

Rose moved to look over his shoulder, as she often did. But she stood with her hands on her hips and a look on her face that would have warned Tim of treacherous waters ahead if he had had eyes for anything but the information he studied on the screen.

"Tim, why didn't you *tell* me?"

"Hmm?" he answered, keeping his gaze focused on the various dimensions of large industrial fans.

"Why didn't you tell me about the barn?" Rose asked again, hoping the clarification might get his attention. Hope died quickly. "I had to find out about it from *Amy*," she added for effect.

"That's nice…" Tim's voice trailed off as he clicked on a close-up of technical specifications.

She tried again. "Why didn't you tell me about turning the barn into a wedding venue?" Determined not to be ignored again, she leaned over so that her face blocked the screen from his vision, demanding he shift his focus. She at least succeeded in getting him to look at her, even if he was still distracted.

Attempting to hide his annoyance, Tim said shortly, "I'm sorry, sweetheart. Did you ask me something? I'm working on some detailed logistics research." He glanced back at the screen, hoping she would let him finish what he was working on.

"Timothy James Ludlow!" That did it.

"Okay, okay, I'm listening." Tim pushed his chair back and folded his arms, no longer making any effort to hide his evident impatience.

Rose pushed the keyboard aside and sat on the edge of the desk to block his view of the screen, her expression a composite of hurt, resentment, and concern. "Now that I have your attention, let me try this again. Why didn't you tell me about the barn project?"

Tim's frown turned to overt exasperation at her question. "Rose, I told you about that months ago. I distinctly remember – "

He stopped abruptly, and quickly whipped through a mental inventory of all their recent conversations concerning every project proposal on the books for Three Brothers. Tim couldn't remember ever leaving her out of that process. When he dredged up the memory of his first discussion of the barn renovation with Miles, his heart sank.

Tim slapped his forehead as awareness of his gross oversight finally registered. He stared into the fire and began mumbling disjointed sentence fragments. "I told Miles not to… I wanted to run it by Derek and Abe… just jumped to the conclusion that you… *especially* since it's Abe and Amy…"

Eventually catching up to the present, Tim looked at his wife. "I never told you."

"You never told me," Rose repeated, though confirmation was hardly necessary.

"I *do* remember asking Miles not to say anything to you about turning the barn into a wedding venue when he first suggested the idea back in September – "

"*September!*" Rose leaned forward, now even more upset. "You've been planning this since *September*, and you didn't think I needed to know?"

"Honey, it's not like that. I didn't intentionally mean to leave you out of the decision – "

"You just forgot to mention to your wife that you were considering the creation of a whole new business venture literally in our backyard."

"Well, yes – apparently." Judging by Rose's reaction, that was the wrong answer. "I mean – no?" Her exasperated expression indicated that she wasn't crazy about that response either.

"What I'm trying to say is, yes, I honestly thought I *had* discussed it with you, and no, I *never* left you out of the equation for a minute. In fact, I've known from the start that if we decided to do this, you would probably be more involved, from a business standpoint, that is, than I would. I just wanted to know that it was feasible financially before getting your feedback." Tim paused to gauge her reaction. Though he had excluded her on such an important undertaking, whether justified or not, he felt a little resentful that his efforts at explanation still met with such evident disappointment and indignation.

"Tim, I felt like a complete fool when Amy called to tell me about getting married in our barn, and I had *no* idea what she was talking about. Fortunately, she was so excited that she did most of the talking, so she probably didn't notice how clueless I sounded. I was so embarrassed." There were tears in her eyes now. "You are under no obligation to tell me anything about your work, but you have, and it has meant *so* much to me that you value my input. It made me feel like I was really part of a team. But for almost a week now, when I've asked you about *anything*, you've brushed me off with a few superficial comments, even though I could tell that you were really worried about something."

Tim stood there, rendered speechless by her accusations because he knew them to be true.

Rose took a deep breath to steady her voice. She felt she was finally getting through to him. "You have every right to keep your own counsel, but evidently you've been willing to discuss this venture with Miles and Derek and Abe, even letting Amy in on it, but you can't talk to me – your wife." Her final words were a cry from a wounded heart.

You have really stepped on your poncho this time, Ludlow! Tim thought, followed quickly by, *How can I fix this?* Running his fingers through his hair in frustration, he took another stab at explaining.

"I don't know if I forgot to tell you about the barn *because* we've shared so many work-related projects lately that I just assumed we had discussed it, or because I was trying to spare you the worry over financing and taking such a big gamble without any real guarantee of it being a success."

"But Tim," Rose replied, voicing her own frustration, "I'm not some fragile flower that can't handle pressure. I'm your wife, and I can sense when you're troubled even if you don't tell me what's going on. And quite frankly, worrying alone without knowing why is much worse than facing – whatever – together. And this barn renovation isn't just another project, it's *our* project. Besides, if it involves a gamble, shouldn't I have a voice in that decision?"

"Of course, you should, and if I did unconsciously leave you out of the loop, it certainly wasn't intentional. And I promise you that I fully intended to bring you in when I had all the facts and figures lined up. In fact, that's what I've been working on this entire week," he said, gesturing at the computer behind her. "I am truly sorry I didn't discuss this with you sooner, but you must know that I would *never* set out to hurt you or to overlook your contribution to *any* decision that concerns our family and our home. And no one knows better than me what a strong and courageous woman you are. Unfortunately, I can't help wanting to shelter you from worry and trouble, regardless of how capable you are to handle it." He could see her anger begin to fade as she considered his words.

"As an excuse, it's pretty feeble, Ludlow," Rose said, allowing the use of his last name – always reserved for mock censure – to give him a glimmer of hope. "But I'm not ready to let you off the hook so easily." Tim dared to permit the shadow of a smile to break the stiff contours of his face as he watched her hop off the desk and walk slowly toward him. Taking his hand, she led him back to the desk and indicated that he sit in the big desk chair. After grabbing the footstool by the fireplace, Rose knelt on it so that she could see the computer screen clearly. "Okay," she said, "tell me *everything.*"

Tim spared her nothing. They pored over plans, materials, timelines, and finances. He explained that his pre-occupation that week had largely been attributable to having met on Monday with the investors Miles had lined up. Though guardedly interested, they wanted to see a mock-up of the property the following week, including sketches for the addition of special features, such as the kitchen, restrooms, and balconies. Those added requirements had only added to Tim's stress level. Rose listened with rapt attention, jotting down her own ideas on a notepad as he showed her the plans and addressed his chief concerns. When she added her own suggestions to the discussion, Tim was humbled again by her insight into improvements on the layout and space allocations. He should have had more faith in his Rose. He wouldn't soon make that mistake again.

"Well, what do you think?" he asked anxiously at the conclusion of his presentation.

"Before I answer, what is it about this project, out of all the others you've done, that has you so worried?"

"It's the speculative nature of it. Whenever I contract to do work for someone, I provide them a comprehensive estimate that I know will be paid at the completion of work. I know I can count on that financial outcome. But this – this is a shot in dark. It may well succeed, but it could just as easily fail if we're not able to market it properly." Tim looked away from Rose to stare again at the spreadsheet on the screen. A sea of red numbers stared back at him. "And then there's the idea of starting out in the hole and being beholden to investors – it's just not… me. I want to control every situation, and this forces me to let go of control. And the more I investigate the potential pitfalls and uncertainty of this kind of undertaking – well, to be completely honest, it scares the snot out of me!" He sought solace and wisdom in her understanding smile.

"I know this is hard for you, my love, but I'm going to be completely honest, too." Her smile widened, and she said on a sigh, "I think it's an answer to prayer." Her response left him stunned. Whatever he had expected, it wasn't that. "I've been aware for some time now that as much as I love you, and living here, and fixing up our home, I need to have some kind of occupation that takes me outside of myself." Tim looked puzzled and a little hurt, prompting her to hurry on. "I am happier now than I ever thought possible, but I'm not sure it's good for me to pour all my energy and creativity into what is essentially just – us. And because it *is* just us now, I've gotten a pretty good handle on our daily routine, and well, it simply doesn't take up all my time. Even with visits to Aletha and getting involved with a ladies Bible study at church and small group activities, I have ample time now to throw myself into something… big."

Rose waited for Tim's response. All he said was, "I'm listening…"

"This is the perfect season to take on a venture like this. I can build relationships with wedding planners in Kansas City, visit every bridal store in a 50-mile radius with boxes of brochures, and create a Facepage or website for the business. I'm sure Abe would help me with that, especially since he and Amy will be our first customers."

As Tim remembered an earlier conversation, he smiled. *Guinea pigs!.*

Encouraged by his evidently lightened mood, Rose added, "And if we can get this up and running now, I can still manage the scheduling and hire of local help for the events, even after we start a family. By then, whenever that may be," she said a little wistfully, "it will be a well-oiled machine." Tim's wary consideration of her vision finally turned to resigned acceptance. Rose twinkled engagingly at him, "You were right when you thought I might jump all over this idea, and *maybe* I understand why you didn't say anything sooner."

"I will probably never live that down, but since we seem to be in agreement over 'The Ludlow Wedding Chapel' – "

"Oh, I don't think so." Rose quickly corrected him. "*Willow Walk Weddings.*"

Tim grinned. "I defer to the expert. As I was saying, since we're in this together, I think you should come to the meeting next week. It's important that we present a united front, and your enthusiasm alone will probably carry the day."

Rose paled a little at his suggestion. "You want me to make a business presentation – "

"Honey, if you show up with even a tenth of the excitement you showed me tonight, they'll be begging to be a part of this project. I know you sold me on it."

"Yes, but – admit it – you *wanted* to be convinced." She stood at last to let the circulation work through her cramped knees. "Ow! I think my legs have gone to sleep," she said as she limped around the room.

Tim took advantage of her preoccupation to flip back to the website he had been studying.

"You know, those big fans are manufactured in Lexington." Rose had returned to the desk and was doing deep knee bends while gripping the desktop for balance. Tim quickly scrolled down to the bottom of the webpage.

"I'll be darned. How on earth did you know that?" He couldn't imagine why she knew anything about Industrial fans.

"Oh, the dad of one of my college roommates is a senior member of the company and Jen works there now in their sales department," she replied as she bent double to stretch the backs of her stiff legs. "Why?"

Tim smiled in wonder at the woman who continued to surprise him, even when she had to brow beat him into listening to what she had to say. "Are you telling me that you know someone who works for Big Action Fans?"

"Of course." Rose swung her arms from side to side and pulled on her elbows to loosen her shoulders. "Would you like me to talk to my people about making us a deal?" she asked with a cocky air as she leaned over his chair.

Without warning, Tim grabbed her and deposited her neatly in his lap. Leaning his forehead against hers, he spoke softly. "I love you, Rose Ludlow. Are we okay again?" He was now assured of her answer, but when she pulled away, and her face grew serious once more, a twinge of doubt pierced his confidence.

"I don't mean to be overly critical, my love, and I know you've been distracted lately, but there *is* something else you've neglected, despite my best efforts to help you remedy your oversight." She crossed her arms and stared fixedly at him, her lips clamped tightly together.

Tim frowned for a few minutes, trying unsuccessfully to figure out in what other way he had failed his wife. Just as he was about to give up in defeat, clueless bewilderment changed to almost comical dismay and unbelief.

"No. No, *that* can't be right." Rose raised her eyebrows slightly and lowered her chin as if daring him to refute her claim.

Tim slapped his forehead again – a gesture that was quickly becoming a habit – and groaned. "I am such an *idiot*." With commendable remorse, he addressed his wife. "If anyone had told me on my honeymoon that in less than three months, I would be taken to task for being an inattentive husband, I would have laughed in his face." He cupped the rounded softness of her jaw and gently rubbed her cheek. "If *ever* I allow myself to get so sidetracked again, I not only give you permission, I *beg* you to hit me over the head with a large, blunt object, if that's what it takes to make me treat you like the treasure you are." He kissed her firmly and asked again, "*Now* are we okay?"

Rose hopped off his lap and strutted to the doorway like a runway model. Turning, she struck a "come hither" pose. "That depends," she replied in a sultry voice, with pouty lips that would have done Marilyn Monroe proud. Tim certainly approved of the performance.

"Depends on what?" Tim was halfway to the door.

"It depends, big man, on how quickly you can finish what you're working on." Rose shrieked when he lunged for her – unsuccessfully. "Catch me if you can," she taunted as she ran into the kitchen and up the back stairs.

Tim shut down the computer and turned off the gas logs in the fireplace in record time, then raced after his wife, determined to make up for his lamentable lapse.

CHAPTER 5

But if the thief is not found, the owner of the house must appear before the judges, and they must determine whether the owner of the house has laid hands on the other person's property.

Exodus 22:8 (NIV)

Tick, tick, tick, tick.

The second hand moved relentlessly around the face of an ugly utilitarian clock, striking an oddly harsh note in the otherwise elegant appointments of a courtroom marked by marble and rich wood wainscoting.

Tick, tick, tick, tick.

The sound echoed in the almost silent chamber occupied by a smattering of people awaiting the judge's verdict. The trial had been short and succinct. Matt Murdock had paid his lawyer a large retainer that seemed directly disproportionate to the defense provided. He held out little hope of an acquittal, though the evidence against him was largely circumstantial. Sadly, the damning point regarding account passwords and the bogus bank account in his name, about which he knew nothing, could not be discounted. Judge Johnson, moreover, was of the old school that believed someone must pay for crimes against the community, and Matt had enough documentation stacked against him, circumstantial or not, to qualify as appointed scapegoat.

Tick, tick, tick, tick.

During the trial, the interminable sound had gone unnoticed, drowned out by questions, arguments, statements by investigators, and denial of knowledge by his longtime co-workers and boss. The memory of their betrayal rang in Matt's ears. But the questioning had stopped, and the determined heartbeat of time had again asserted its dominance over his consciousness. He began to feel the weight of its unyielding import, a harbinger of the marking of time that must surely be his future.

Tick, tick, tick, tick.

Matt dragged his eyes from the hypnotic movement of that incessant hand to look around the scarcely populated room. Frank Hibbard had remained to wait for the verdict. *Is his presence motivated by a desire to provide moral support,* Matt wondered, *or to assuage a guilty conscience?* He certainly had a vested interest, from a purely professional standpoint, in how the trial's outcome would affect the reputation of Hibbard and Associates. Matt decided that Frank's support, or conversely, callous self-interest, hardly mattered anymore. He had located the only face that really mattered.

Brittany sat against the back wall, an exotic flower in a dull garden of suits and uniforms. She had been a brick throughout the whole process. Matt swallowed a lump in his throat as he gazed at her loveliness, only slightly subdued by the wide-brimmed hat and colored glasses that shielded her face and her privacy. She smiled bravely at him and blew him a kiss. He tried to return her smile, but his lips wavered, and he turned away abruptly to hide his shaky emotional state.

Tick, tick, tick, tick.

To block out all other thought, Matt allowed his attention to be drawn once more by the hypnotic effects of a piece of machinery surely possessed by Satan himself. The offending noise didn't even bear the alternating novelty of a tick, *tock*, tick, *tock* to break up its infernal monotony. But the demoralizing power of the clock, Brittany's blessed presence, and every other consideration were suspended when the judge entered the room and assumed the bench. Matt stood on shaking legs to hear words that numbed his heart and mind.

"Matthew Murdock, you have been found guilty of embezzling funds through undisclosed manipulation of client financial accounts, falsifying statements, and funneling funds to a non-registered charity established by yourself. You are hereby sentenced to eight years in a state penal facility."

The last thing Matt remembered was the crash of the gavel adding an exclamation point to the pronouncement of his doom.

February might rightly claim the title "Gloomiest Month of the Year." Its skies seemed to be perpetually overcast – overcast with rain or overcast with a snow and sleet mix. The freshness of soft white powder covering dead grass and trees with a touch of purity was the only hope for alleviation of nature's winter misery. No such change in the weather occurred to brighten the first glimpse of Tinkers Well by the four passengers of a sleek foreign coupe turning off the bypass on its way into town. The two who showed the greatest interest in their surroundings were the little boys in the back seat who sought distraction from the ache of losing their father and the only life they had ever known.

"Look, Mattie, sthere's sthe school." Young Drew Murdock's missing front teeth failed to dampen his eagerness.

"Uh-huh." The thought of trying to fit into a new classroom with a million kids who would have a bazillion and one questions about where he came from and why he had moved to Tinkers Well was the last thing eight-year-old Matthew Murdock wanted to consider. He turned his attention instead to the town square coming rapidly into view.

"Do you see over there, Drew? It looks like a real gazebo. And I think I see – yeah, there are some swings and climbing ladders on the other end of the park."

"Now, you boys know the first thing we must do is get the house set up before we think about anything frivolous. You know how I hate a messy house."

"Yes, Mama," Mattie answered, a little deflated.

"But I'm hungry. Couldn't we get sthomeping to eat firsth?" Before his mother could answer, Drew pointed excitedly at a welcoming sign. "Look! Sthat says 'Milly's Dinner.'"

"That's 'diner,' dummy."

Drew ignored his older brother. "Could we eat sthere, huh?" Each word grew louder with the longing inherent in contemplating a long overdue lunch.

"Please, Andrew, you know how Mama dislikes loud voices. But we won't have any food in the house yet, so I suppose we could try it out. Though it hardly appears worthy of a review in *Fine Dining* magazine," she mumbled under her breath.

As the driver pulled into a vacated spot just in front of the establishment in question, the fourth traveler beamed at the inviting exterior. "I think it looks quite charming."

Aunt Reenie perpetually looked for the charming in everything. With her spare figure rounded by an oversized coat, and her head crowned by tightly wound gray hair, she bore a remarkable resemblance to the iconic "Aunt Bea." She might have been stepping onto a sound stage when she crawled, with some difficulty, out of the low-slung vehicle. Now in her late 70s, Aunt Reenie found the task increasingly challenging. But she accomplished it as quickly as age and passing rheumatism allowed, then turned to usher the boys out of the back seat and into the restaurant.

They had been in her charge since birth. Her nephew Matthew, who had also grown up under her tutelage, had asked her to move in with the young family at a time when she literally had nowhere else to go. As the oldest of eight motherless siblings, it had fallen to her lot to raise one generation of Fields children after another until a final act of service left her homeless. When her aging father, handed into her care by the rest of the family, finally passed on to his eternal reward at the ripe old age of 94, Irene was sure she had outlived her usefulness and her meager savings. But Matthew and Brittany's need had been her salvation. The young mother had happily relinquished the reins of childrearing and housekeeping into Aunt Reenie's experienced hands, finding fulfillment in effortlessly assuming the role of trophy wife.

As usual, Milly's Diner was bustling on that Saturday, despite the weather. Tables around the corner gas fireplace were in high demand, and Milly's staff struggled to keep up with the requests for coffee and hot chocolate. It was the perfect moment to make an entrance. When the party of four paraded to the only empty table in the place, the subdued tones of 1960s bubble gum rock became suddenly louder as conversation all around temporarily stalled. Brittany was never put out by undo attention; she thought it her due. So, when all eyes in the diner turned to look with native curiosity at the strangers in their midst, she attributed their interest to the luxurious folds of her mink coat and the underlying cashmere suit displayed beneath. One table took particular note of her novel sophistication in such a rural setting.

"Do you know who that is, Marilyn?" Rose Ludlow asked her mother-in-law. The two, plus Amy Walker, had met for lunch on that bleak Saturday to bolster Aletha Mason's flagging spirits. Despite not being able to see the gloom outside, the elderly lady, nonetheless, felt its creeping cold and acknowledged its prohibition against enjoying the pleasure of sitting on her porch swing and feeling the warmth of the sun.

"I have no idea, and I've lived here a couple of years, but she just oozes 'wealthy and stylish,' doesn't she?" Marilyn's back was to the newcomers, who had taken the second booth behind theirs. Rose and Amy, however, had a clear view from their side of the table.

"Can you describe them to me? Perhaps I've met them," Aletha suggested, her curiosity aroused.

"For one, think of your favorite 60's TV sitcom and imagine Aunt Bea, only thinner," Marilyn answered, peering into a strategically held compact mirror.

"How clever of you. I can picture her perfectly, though I'd hardly call Aunt Bea stylish."

"No, no, I'm sorry, that's the – companion? grandmother? I'm not sure. But it's the young woman, who can't be much older than Rose or Amy, who has everyone staring. Girls, how would you describe her?"

"Tim would probably say 'hubba, hubba,'" Rose commented critically, "but not in a cheap kind of way. Very Fifth Avenue, if you know what I mean. She has gorgeous red hair – deep, not brassy – perfect facial features, and a figure that surely owes two of its outstanding attributes to plastic surgery. I mean, *honestly…*"

"Rose, you are so bad!" Amy chimed in with a laugh. "But, I must admit, pretty spot on. She's sitting next to a little boy with brown hair. I'd guess he's about eight or nine, and the one next to the older woman is a redhead like his mother, complete with adorable freckles. He's probably a few years younger. The thing that's odd about the boys is the way they're dressed. It looks like they just escaped from a prep school."

Aletha nodded her head knowingly. "That will be the Murdock family recently relocated from Kansas City and living in the little blue cottage on Third Street."

Staring in disbelief at the blind woman, Rose said in a voice tinged with awe, "How do you *do* that, Aletha? I've always wondered if you weren't a little clairvoyant. What's your secret? Come on, confess."

"Oh, there's no secret," Aletha replied with a twinkle. "Just two words. Lucy Bennett." That explained everything to her tablemates – well, almost everything. Aletha obligingly filled in the missing pieces. "Lucy heard the news from Carmen Ramirez, who works for the electric co-op, who found out when Zeke Gerzsewski called to get the power turned on after leasing the cottage to Mrs. Murdock."

"Wow! What town needs an internet search engine when they have a Lucy Bennett?" As always, Amy was impressed by the speed and accuracy of the local grapevine.

"You know, I have an empty desk in my classroom since the Bakers moved to St. Joe after Christmas," Marilyn said. "I wonder if I'll be meeting the oldest boy soon. And possibly the mother?"

Speculation was suspended as a busy waitress arrived with two loaded salads topped with grilled chicken, a steaming bowl of chicken and rice soup for Aletha, and a BLT with onion rings for Amy. Rose looked longingly at her friend's plate.

"How can you eat like that and still maintain the figure of a supermodel?" she sighed. "I'm jealous."

Dipping an onion ring in a pile of ketchup, Amy replied with a grin, "I know I can't keep this up forever, but I'm sure going to enjoy it while I can!"

As they savored their meals, the four ladies passed the time trying to guess the background and possible reasons the three fish out of water and "Aunt Bea" had relocated to Tinkers Well.

"Do you suppose we ought to introduce ourselves and welcome them?" asked Rose, her conscience stinging a little from her earlier catty comment.

"Oh, I don't think so," advised Aletha. "After all, we probably *shouldn't* know who they are yet. Why don't we just leave them what little privacy they have left in Tinkers Well. I'm sure we'll cross paths soon enough."

It was Aletha, oddly enough, who first made the acquaintance of one of the newcomers.

Matt Murdock stared at the only speck of natural light visible from his cell. It was hardly uplifting. Rain lashed at the high window over a backdrop accented by variants of gray. He had been the guest of Lansdowne Correctional Facility for just over a month, and though he was housed in the East Unit – considered minimum security – he felt as bound and isolated as any inmate in Alcatraz. After the initial shock of sentencing and the subsequent indignity of relinquishing anything that spoke of his individuality in exchange for a nondescript orange jumpsuit, he had come to terms with his situation. His only comfort lay in the memory of his last precious minutes with Brittany before being led away in handcuffs. She had promised tearfully to take care of the boys and to do everything in her power to prove his innocence. When he closed his eyes, he could still feel the power of that final kiss.

But his eyes were open now. Matt had only spoken to Brittany once since his incarceration in mid-January when she visited the prison to tell him about the sale of their home. She had honored his wish to never bring the boys there to see him. They had been told simply that Daddy had to go away for work – maybe for several years. He never wanted them to see him in such a place. In light of the trial outcome, it was fortunate that he and his wife had discussed the path she must follow in the event he was found guilty of a crime of which he was innocent. In addition to an eight-year prison term, Matt had been assessed a hefty fine that had wiped out their considerable savings. With no money left in the bank and only the $100,000 Brittany had netted from the house sale, she and the boys and Aunt Reenie would have a meager $25,000 annually to live on until he was eligible for parole in four years.

They had agreed that it would be best to keep a low profile, so remaining in Kansas City was out of the question. But living within a reasonable radius of Lansdowne, located twenty miles north of the city, would make frequent visits a greater possibility. Their search led them to the town of Tinkers Well. The cost of living would be considerably lower, and Matt had suggested the boys might benefit from living in a rural area. Brittany had barely controlled a shiver of revulsion at the thought, but it would only be for a time, and even life in a backwater town might be endurable given its proximity to Kansas City from the west.

Driving up to the tiny blue, shingled cottage on that raw February day, Brittany's determination to see the plan through nearly came to naught. But Aunt Reenie's habitual comment, "Now isn't this charming," coupled with the boys' satisfaction in being situated within easy walking distance of the town square, had propelled her through the front door. Once inside, she was pleasantly surprised to find that the house had been well-maintained, and that it did indeed have its own sort of charm.

The door opened directly into the living-dining-kitchen space where the focal point was a large stone fireplace. When Brittany discovered that it required actual wood to work, she lost interest. She was also disappointed by the absence of a dishwasher, though since she rarely washed dishes, she dismissed the oversight as trifling. When further exploration disclosed that the little home had only one full bathroom, she nearly declared that critical shortfall a deal breaker. Fortunately, for the peace of all concerned, Brittany found that a tiny half bath had been added in a corner of the generously proportioned upstairs loft, which she instantly claimed for her own. Besides its openness and private amenities, it was clearly the only space large enough to accommodate the king-size bed she had insisted on bringing with her.

Furniture arrived minutes after their own arrival, and Brittany was caught up in the novelty of setting up house. Her focus being primarily on her own comfort, she left Aunt Reenie to make up the boys' bunkbeds in a room that was half the size of their previous individual rooms before unpacking and organizing the kitchen. While the others were busy unloading boxes and storing their contents, Brittany volunteered to find the local grocery store and procure supplies. Aunt Reenie was hardly surprised when the doting mother of two returned with nothing more than frozen dinners and microwave popcorn. But she resolved to stock the cabinets and refrigerator first thing Monday morning, despite knowing she would be required to walk to the market since she was unable to drive her niece's car.

Feeling that she had made sufficient sacrifices on behalf of her family, Brittany had flatly refused to trade in her expensive, low-profile sports coupe – complete with a manual transmission – for a more practical vehicle. Believing that everything they needed was within easy walking distance (except, perhaps, for an elderly woman who might find it difficult to navigate slippery sidewalks in the snow and rain), Brittany congratulated herself on having made the right decision. She nobly offered to drive the boys to school, given that it was on the edge of the town proper and over a mile away. The paltry gesture was wholly in keeping with Brittany's character.

Aunt Reenie began wondering about family dynamics soon after joining the Murdock household. She loved her nephew dearly, having been very present during his childhood years. And being a spinster, she had always looked on her nieces and nephews as her children. Little Mattie quickly became the apple of her eye and the grandchild she would never otherwise have had. When Drew joined them two years later, she was as content as any woman had a right to be. The only ripple in her tranquil existence came as uneasy misgivings began to take hold regarding the relationship between her nephew and his bride.

It was patently obvious that Matt adored his wife. And why not? She was a paragon of beauty and charm, and she knew just how to cajole and tease her husband into acquiescing to whatever plans she concocted. The fact that these began to involve her attendance at events not requiring her husband's escort, caused Aunt Reenie to speculate as to Brittany's activities.

When a casual comment at dinner one evening regarding her busy schedule brought a wary look to Brittany's eyes, Reenie grew more certain that her suspicions held merit. Matt appeared blind to anything untoward, but afterward, his aunt noticed a subtle change in Brittany's daily patterns. She was at home more and insisted Matt accompany her to evening events where, as she put it, "You can meet important people that could potentially be very lucrative clients."

Whether it was her intended aim, or simply a fortuitous outcome, Matt obliged his wife for a while, but quickly grew bored with what he considered insipid evenings among shallow people. He infinitely preferred spending time with Mattie and Drew, who grew more endearing and lovable with each passing day. So, he gratefully left social networking to Brittany, content to welcome her home and listen to her lively accounts of dull evenings she endured on his behalf. His manifest gratitude was warmly reciprocated, and he was pleasantly surprised to see his list of affluent clients growing just as she had predicted.

When Mattie began preschool, Brittany argued that a prestigious institution, which was both expensive and located on the opposite side of the city, was the only place for him. She believed in giving her children every advantage and argued that it was a waste of fuel to make the round trip twice a day, so she drove him to school and waited the three hours until it was time to bring him home. That process changed only slightly when Drew followed his brother to the academy. He attended full day Preschool to accommodate Mattie's schedule, allowing Brittany to maintain the practice of one round trip a day.

Matt was stirred by her motherly devotion and was doubly pleased when she began coming by the office at least once a week to help him in any way she could. He was touched by her interest in his work and slowly began shifting routine paperwork into her surprisingly capable hands. Brittany's presence freed a shared, overworked administrative assistant to focus on supporting the rest of the office. In Matt's estimation, their marriage had never been stronger. Aunt Reenie still had reservations.

As Matt's success grew, so did their lifestyle. Brittany insisted the Murdocks leave their comfortable three-bedroom home in a family friendly neighborhood. They took up residence, instead, in a grand five bedroom, four bath home in a highly prized subdivision. It had the advantage of being closer to the boys' school, allowing Brittany more flexibility in her schedule. She continued to faithfully assist Matt in his work – until everything came crashing in.

If Brittany was ever going to display her true colors as a mercenary wife and indifferent mother, the time had come. Her steadfastness in standing by her husband's side only intensified his adoration of her, and instilled in him a deep sense of humility. It flatly astounded Aunt Reenie. She had to give Brittany her due. Even though the most important person in Brittany's world would always be Brittany, she had conducted herself through all the mortifying trials of that dark season with admirable strength and fortitude.

One aspect of her character had remained constant throughout their marriage, however. Despite Matt having been brought up in a Christian home where everyone attended church regularly, Brittany had quickly convinced him, after their wedding, that Sundays were more productive if spent as family time, especially after Mattie was born.

"It's so hard to keep a baby quiet during the service, and as he gets older, it will be hard on him to have to sit still through all that talking."

Matt had given in to her arguments, as he invariably did, despite having gone to church almost every Sunday since birth. Because of a need for spiritual nourishment and renewal, and because she was rarely invited to join the rest of family on their Sunday outings, Reenie went alone to a neighborhood church near the house. She longed to take the boys with her but contented herself with reading stories to them about colorful Bible characters and introducing them to the person of Jesus.

Perhaps the one positive outcome of the sordid life chapter that turned their world upside down was the opportunity – or necessity, depending on one's viewpoint – for the Murdocks to begin again. Too exhausted from unpacking and decorating her lofty personal space to designer levels the day before, Brittany put up little argument over Reenie's suggestion that they all attend church that first Sunday. Reenie understood, rightly, that Brittany meant the old woman was welcome to take the boys with her to church. The emotionally shattered mother would stay home and try to recoup her strength by soaking in a surprisingly comfortable claw foot tub left in the cottage after a decades-old renovation.

The day was cold, but the clouds had cleared out overnight, allowing a wintry sun to greet the intrepid threesome as they bravely trekked into town and found Church Street.

"Look, Aunt Reenie. Sthere's lots of kids going into sthat church," Drew pointed out hopefully.

"Let's see. Can you read the sign from here, Mattie?"

"It says Community Church."

"I like the sound of that. Shall we try it?"

After duly escorting each boy to his respective Sunday school classroom, Aunt Reenie shyly entered the room designated for seniors. Conversation was in full swing, so she took a seat on a sidewall where she could study the others present. She liked what she saw. She guessed the simply but neatly dressed crowd to be mostly in their seventies or eighties. As was usually the case with that age group, women outnumbered men. It was a nattily attired gentleman in coat and tie, however, who first approached her and introduced himself.

"Good morning, ma'am. I'm Bob Taylor, but folks around here mostly just call me Bobby. If I'm not being too nosy, what brings you to our little town?" Having gathered the pertinent information, Mr. Taylor turned to report his findings. "Hey, everybody. This here is Miss Irene Fields. She's the one that just moved into the blue cottage on Third Street. Well, her and her niece and nephews."

"That's niece-in-law and great-nephews," Reenie pointed out. Best to start off with clarity, she always believed.

A confusing crowd of well-wishers greeted her with more names than she could possibly hope to remember, though one stood out – a petite woman with a gentle voice and the deepest china blue eyes Reenie had ever seen. It quickly became apparent that the eyes were equally sightless, which explained the presence of an unusually well-behaved dog at the woman's side.

"I'm Aletha Mason, and I do hope you'll join us for worship today, too. Pastor Lindeman is teaching through the letters of Peter. I believe today's lesson is the warning of corruption of doctrine and false teachers in the larger Christian church. Next, we'll be studying First and Second Thessalonians. It quite reassures me to study Bible prophecy, and to know that God has a plan for the future of the world, especially as I observe it growing more heathenish and confused around me. It helps all the senseless nonsense make sense. I'm sure you understand."[4]

With Mattie and Drew in tow, Reenie found places for them in the pew directly behind Aletha's. Once comfortably settled, they were introduced to worship, Community Church style. It was all a novel experience for the boys, who scanned the pews during the prelude time to locate new friends from their Sunday school classes, now sitting with their parents. Drew was fascinated by the flute and violin accompanying the piano. Despite being located in a small, Midwestern town, the congregation was made up of an interesting mix of people, which rather surprised and pleased Reenie. It was what she fancied heaven would look like.

---

[4] Olive Tree Ministries, *"The Last Hour,"* Dr. Ed Hindson, December 23, 2022 (Maple Grove, MN, 2022) https://olivetreeviews.org/radio-archives/page/3/

She saw a number of Hispanic families, at least two Black families, two adorable Asian children, who she later learned were adopted from China, and a very tall, striking young man who, she guessed, must surely be of Middle Eastern origin. The music was rich and meaningful without being overpowering, and the sermon was soundly Biblical and factual — not the wishy-washy social and "culturally correct" fluff heralded in most churches today. When the three newcomers were invited to share in a potluck brunch at the home of Aletha's daughter-in-law, Reenie nearly wept with gratitude for God's provision of fellowship and welcome in their new community.

Matt hadn't attended church in years — not since he'd married Brittany. He had initially felt guilty about giving up what had been such an important part of his life. But having gotten into the habit of convincing himself that whatever Brittany suggested must be what was best for the family, he had agreed with her perspective that one didn't necessarily need to attend church to be a Christian. He had cringed a little at the "churches are all full of hypocrites" argument but had sublimated his conscience to her desires.

Now there was no Brittany to walk with through a park on a Sunday afternoon, after sleeping in and consuming a late breakfast. There were no little boys to tug at his hands, demanding he push them on the swings or wrestle with them in the grass. There was only Matthew Murdock, convicted felon.

On his fourth Sunday at LCF, his emptiness and loneliness had finally driven him to seek out the prison chapel. As he entered a surprisingly large worship space, Matt experienced an odd sense of freedom. It was as if, since losing everything he held dear, he felt like a true individual, a person of worth. Singing old hymns brought back memories — safe memories — of a carefree childhood unencumbered by the weight of being a husband and father who had failed his family. For a few blessed moments, he was granted the privilege of being a child again, the child of a Father who never makes mistakes or fails his children. While a sermon about unmerited grace and forgiveness was not new to Matt, he heard the message with new ears as if he had never fully understood it before.

As is sometimes the case with "good" people, Matt had always wrestled with the idea of being a sinner in need of a savior. He had made a profession of faith as a young boy because he wanted to please his parents and Sunday School teacher. He believed it was expected of him, though he hadn't fully understood the significance of the words of the prayer he repeated. As the middle sibling in a family of three children, he grew up being the fair-haired child, the peacemaker. To spare his parents any more angst over less than stellar grades – something his brother and sister created in spades – Matt worked hard and followed a course of study in college that led to a stable, self-sufficient career, if not a particularly impressive one.

His church attendance as a single adult was more habitual than spiritual, continued out of a deep-seated desire to live honorably, to do the right thing. It wasn't until he encountered the unstoppable force that was Brittany that Matt experienced any real remorse. His actions during their dating season caused a fleeting sense of guilt, but when in her all-consuming company, he often felt as if he had no real control over his actions at all. A gentle, but inherently weak nature never had any hope of asserting itself during their marriage, so Matt unconsciously settled into the familiar, comfortable role of peacekeeper.

Then all the past and future had been swept away with the strike of a gavel. There was only now, and in the now Matt began a personal awakening. The comforts of family and career were gone, along with his identity in both. He found himself, for perhaps the first time in his life, coming to grips with who Matthew Murdock really was. He was a man wrongly accused – but hardly without fault – forced to pay the penalty for a crime he did not commit.

Something clicked in his brain. There was no dramatic falling of scales from his eyes, as happened to the apostle Paul after his encounter with Jesus on the road to Damascus. Nor did he undergo a sudden sense of rebirth. It was more a shift in thinking, a change in focus. He saw Jesus in a fresh light – someone who really *could* understand what he was feeling. Jesus, too, had been a man wrongly accused, a man who had suffered a terrible punishment in a perfect state of innocence for the sake of those he had created and loved. He was a Savior worthy of worship. The closing song triggered another moment of clarity. It was a song Matt had sung many times as a younger man, but at this place in time, surrounded by as strange and foreign an environment as anything experienced by Daniel and his friends in Babylon, it made total sense. He sang the second verse like he was singing the lyrics for the first time in a familiar language.

We are the broken, you are the healer, Jesus Redeemer, Mighty to save
You are the love song we'll sing forever, bowing before You, blessing Your name

Holy, holy, Lord God Almighty, worthy is the Lamb who was slain
Highest praises, honor and glory be unto your name, be unto your name[5]

The words of the chorus surrounded him, pierced him, and took him out of himself, allowing the knowledge of unconditional love to slowly penetrate the recesses of his heart and mind so long shut off from its healing touch. Though there were no tears or outward signs of emotion, Matt knew he had turned a corner and had begun a journey of discovery. Part of him feared what he would find, but he faced that fear with newfound courage, strong in the certainty that he would never be truly alone again.

---

[5] Lyrics derived from *Be Unto Your Name* by Lynn Deshazo and Gary Sadler. ©1998, Integrity's Hosanna! Music (ASCAP) (adm. at Integrated Rights.com). All rights reserved. Used by permission.

CHAPTER 6

No part of the process was easy. Ever since Tim and Rose made the decision to take on refurbishment of the large barn on their property in earnest, it had been one long, uphill battle. Tim confirmed that a well fed the pump in the old barn, but multiple years of hard freezes had turned the supply line into a sieve. A new water line with ample insulation, and a greatly modernized, mechanical pump, solved the water problem. The pump fit snugly in the barn's basement, which had functioned for decades as lifesaving shelter for livestock during hard winters. With the basement's newly designated role as storage and mechanical space, its dirt floor required better covering, but pouring cement proved difficult when temperatures rarely rose above 45 degrees. Tim hit on the idea of running hyper-insulated duct work from portable heating units through the windows of the lower level. The finished product provided a solid surface and ample capacity for tables and chairs that would ultimately be hoisted to the main floor by way of an open service lift. To ensure the entire structure met ADA standards, the lift continued all the way to the catwalk connecting the balcony and the musician's loft.

With Rose's blessing, Tim decided to play-up the barn theme by covering the inside walls of the "great hall" with barn board rather than sheetrock, but it was in short supply. An unexpected and unlikely source, however, saved a huge hit to the budget and allowed progress to continue. Rose contributed where her limited skills allowed, though when she brought a hot meal for the crew on an especially cold day, she decided it was time to find some other way of contributing to the future of *Willow Walk Weddings*. The horrified bride walked in to find her husband dangling from a crossbeam 15 feet above his fallen extension ladder. When she heard him yelling at Derek to move the elevated work platform over because his fingers were getting numb, she quickly realized that there were elements of Tim's job she preferred to remain ignorant of.

Focusing instead on what she could control, Rose pledged to offer the ultimate down-home experience for future patrons. With a clear vision in mind, she enlisted the aid of Amy Walker, and the two spent each Saturday in February hitting every thrift store and flea market within sixty miles of Tinkers Well. So intent were they on their single-minded purpose, that they begged the proprietors to call either of them when likely items were donated or consigned. In four weeks' time, the two savvy shoppers had purchased 15 completely different table settings of varying pieces, two old church pews, and an assortment of antique mirrors and pictures to hang in the restrooms and hallways. Checking every conceivable block they could anticipate, the girls added multiple wooden buckets to hold random flowers or antique tchotchkes, and a disparate collection of vases to be used as needed. But the real prize they both set their hearts on required approval from the master carpenter who thought they were both nuts when he heard the suggestion.

"You want to use a bunch of old, worn-out windows that don't even match, instead of the energy efficient, well-sealed, double-paned, prairie design windows we already agreed on?" Rose found Tim, on a rainy afternoon, in the kitchen of the barn hanging drywall. When it came to building, everything that went into a project (products, designs, proposed usage) had to make sense to Tim. He planned sensibly, and he executed each plan with almost flawless accuracy, but when confronted with the avant-garde, he felt a little like he was wading in quicksand.

"It's not a bunch, it's just three… well, maybe four. And when you describe them like that, it sounds terrible." Rose was momentarily rattled, but she refused to have her dreams squelched.

"You mean I'm speaking like a rational man who is renovating a *barn* for weddings I'm still doubtful of?"

"But don't you see? That's exactly why they're perfect!" Arguments with Rose were at all times entertaining and frustrating. Tim loved the way she poured herself into everything she did, especially things they did together, but their ultimate endgame concepts didn't always coincide. "The most attractive quality about a place like this is its total lack of style," she continued at her persuasive best. "It gives us the opportunity to meet preconceived expectations with out-of-the-box novelty. We can set tables with actual Wedgwood™ china, some with old dishes originally purchased with grocery store stamp books, and others with obscure, but unique patterns. Nothing matches, but it somehow comes together in carefully ordered disorder. And the windows will add a flavor of the past." His look of skepticism deepened.

"Besides, you're already using a lot of repurposed materials," Rose pointed out with what Tim considered annoying accuracy. "You got most of the barn board you covered the main interior walls and insulation with from Miles, right?" Tim opened his mouth to answer, but she swept on. "I'm not sure where he got it, but he recognized how useful and fitting it would be."

Before Rose could add another brick to the structural wall of her argument, Tim pointed out, "Yes, but I put *barn* board… inside a *barn*. That's hardly thinking outside-the-box."

"Well, maybe." She hated to concede even that small point, but she stuck to her guns. "Don't say no yet. The stores – "

"Stores? You mean the windows aren't all in the same place?"

"No, but all three stores – "

"Three?"

Rose ignored the interruption. "All three stores will be open on Sunday until six. I thought maybe you and I, and Amy and Abe…," she said, and paused to nod at the two standing in the doorway, waiting to see who would win the day. Both put their money on Rose. "I thought that maybe we could all go check them out after brunch on Sunday. We'll have room for everybody in your truck plus space for the windows. That is, if we buy any." Rose finished on a coaxing note and a captivating smile that rarely failed to work their magic.

"Aargh!!!" Tim grabbed his wife's shoulders and stared sternly into her upturned face. "Do you know how unscrupulous it is to bat those gorgeous eyes at me and turn on your atomic-powered charm when you know I am utterly defenseless against either one? But to use them in tandem – that's just down right…"

"Unscrupulous?" If anything, Rose's assumed air of innocence became more pronounced. Abe, rightly anticipating the end of the discussion, grabbed Amy's hand and the two set off to discuss wedding details. Tim, left with no other recourse to vent his feelings, pulled his wife roughly into his arms. A thorough kiss left both combatants satisfied. Rose released Tim to continue the drywall process she had interrupted and immediately made several phone calls to ensure her plan could be carried out on the weekend.

The adage that "clothes make the man" might hold true for the vast majority of the male population, but in the case of Miles Hawthorne, it might reasonably be argued that the man makes the clothes. His reaction to the Christmas gift of practical, if less than fashionable, rough work attire had been one of genuine gratitude. They represented to him that he was fully accepted and welcomed by the family he had spurned so many years before. Now, stepping out of a truck whose door panel placards announced *L & L Homes*, he began to fully appreciate the truly practical side of the clothing. By February, Miles had taken possession of the property sold to him by Zeke Gerzsewski. The prevailing weather patterns of sleet and rain hardly contributed to the land's appeal. But appealing or not, progress on the proposed development was essential for completion of his master plan.

"Ideally, the main building needs to be closer to the town end of the development with streets for housing construction spread out around it. As agreed in our initial consultation, each property must be at least three quarters an acre, and the individual houses will range from roughly 1,800 to 2,300 square feet. I don't want enormous homes that no one from the area can afford. I'm also mindful of drawing young families from the city who are willing to swap convenience for affordability."

"I agree. I think this'll make a nice little subdivision, and I promise to do everything I can to make it fit in stylistically with the houses in town. You saw the plan options for wide front porches and garages in the rear, connected by a breezeway? And we can do a mix of siding, brick, and stone. That'll take the facades back a few years."

Jim Lindell had a reputation for incorporating aesthetics and individuality into his homes, which cost a little more up front, but the value of timeless quality is difficult to incorporate as an after-purchase add-on. Miles had chosen this specific builder after considering, and subsequently discarding, all the producers of cookie cutter houses, whose lack of imagination was usually reflected in a lack of attention to detail during the construction process. If he had learned anything from his son, it was to recognize the mark of someone who took pride in his work.

"You're going to waste some buildable acreage if you insist on broader streets," Lindell observed, "but it's your dollar, and I suppose Kansas *is* supposed to be known for its wide-open plains."

The two men were walking the property on a day when mud and muck slowed progress to a slippery crawl, but they made their way to the farmhouse where Lindell stopped. He frowned and shook his head.

"I can follow your vision until we get to this old place. Why, it must have been built around the turn of the last century. What do you plan to do with it? Surely, you don't expect me to…"

"No, no, no. I apologize for not making myself clear. This project will be left to my son. He has already inspected it and given me several options for renovation. Tim has an extraordinary talent for architectural restoration and has assured me that this weary old house has several novel characteristics worth preserving."

Lindell looked dubiously at the weathered structure, but as long as it was off his plate, he was quite willing to leave it on someone else's.

"I don't know who you subcontract with for landscaping, but I'd prefer that they plant indigenous trees and native grasses in the open common areas as if the neighborhood simply emerged from the existing fields."

"I've got to say, working with someone who knows exactly what he wants and is willing to commit to those decisions makes my job a lot easier."

Miles smiled, but responded a little ruefully, "Pardon me if I sound a bit rude, but little consideration was given as to any ease with which my plan might be carried out by you. Though I must say, it also pleases me to work with a company capable of catching the ball of my vision and running with it, so to speak. No, this is a project that goes well beyond the limited scope of my specialized experience, and it must be done right. It must pay tribute to the town of Tinkers Well and its history, to the Creator who birthed the town around a life-giving well in the middle of a sunbaked prairie, and to someone who deserves all that is honorable and pure. I don't expect you to understand all or any of that, but I do expect you to uphold those ideals."

Jim Lindell had agreed to build the relatively limited development in the small satellite community mostly because of Miles Hawthorne's reputation for professionalism and focus. He had expected to meet someone with an edge and an eye for cutting costs and inflating profits. The professionalism, knowledge, and focus had been apparent from their first meeting, but with each subsequent encounter, Lindell found himself recalculating his initial assessment of the legendary Hawthorne. The man knew his business, but he was as pleasant and genial in conversation as he was clear-sighted and to the point. This latest revelation as to the unexpected depth of Miles' character inspired Lindell. He was, himself, a respectable, God-fearing man, but he rarely dealt with others who held such high standards. He found those qualities refreshing and motivating.

Extending his hand, he said, "I'll do my best, and that's a promise."

Miles returned the other man's grip firmly and nodded toward the farmhouse. "I was going to suggest stepping inside to sketch in some roads and building layouts on the prints of property perimeters I brought with me, but it's probably as cold in there as it is out here. Might I suggest we remove to Milly's Diner in town for a late breakfast?"

Since Jim Lindell's breakfast had consisted of one stale granola bar, he needed no urging. An hour later the two were well away on development planning, barely aware of the constant coffee refills.

A swath of orange, personalized only by beards, or tattoos, sat as one at the conclusion of an opening song sung with gusto, if a little off-key. Chaplain Reardon invited those present to turn in their Bibles to a passage in 2 Corinthians, chapter two. Sitting in a semi-circle before him, many of the men struggled to find the page indicated. One prisoner located it quickly, then turned with assurance to help his neighbors navigate the book's unique layout.

Nearly a month had passed since Matt Murdock had sought comfort and reassurance in the only sanctuary left to him. It had been an experience at once familiar and completely alien, but he had clung to the songs and spoken word like a lifeline, knowing it to be his link to the past and his only hope for the future. Weekly Bible study augmented services, and he never missed either. He dug into Paul's letter to the church at Corinth with hunger and humility, finding solace for the lack of letters he received from his family.

He had no delusions about Brittany's efforts at letter writing, but he was sadly disappointed in Aunt Reenie. It was she who had taught him as a child the importance of that increasingly antiquated form of communication. He knew her to be a disciplined letter writer during her residence with him and Brittany, and yet nothing came – no pictures of the boys or by the boys, nothing with which to decorate the dreary walls of his cell. Matt consoled himself that it was surely due simply to the exigencies of getting settled in a new home and community. Letters would come. Encouragement would come. Until then he sought both in the eternal pages before him. With their help and leading he built for himself, stone by stone, a foundation of faith – faith in his God and faith in himself. Each dawn was a fresh victory, and with each victory came the desire for more. While still an alien in a foreign land, Matt grew thankful for the cycle of morning and evening, for he saw that it was good.

Flying fingers tapped away at a laptop keyboard. Amy's thoughts almost outstripped the ability of her fingers to keep up. She only paused to formulate her next careful sentence, then away flew the useful appendages. The author finished the note and reviewed it with satisfaction, only to look up and see her fiancé coming through her front door. So engrossed was she in her task that she failed to hear his brief knock. Glancing quickly at the screen to ensure she'd covered all the crucial details, she pressed "send" and launched the message into cyberspace.

"Quick, take the cups so I don't drop the pizza," Abe said, wrestling to close the door without sacrificing dinner.

"Why did you get drinks? You know I have plenty here," she said, grabbing the freezing cups balancing precariously atop the pizza box.

"Yes, but you don't have milkshakes so thick you have to eat them with a spoon."

Amy's eyes brightened. "Yum! Did you remember…"

Abe grimaced. "Peanut butter and bacon? Yes, though it took every drop of my devotion to you to place the order. How you drink that mess is beyond me."

"Don't knock it 'til you've tried it." She couldn't help laughing at his look of disgust.

Abe carved out some usable space on the little table in the corner of the kitchen. The adjacent designated dining area had been repurposed for office space and boasted a desk scattered with papers, an electric piano, and a music stand rising bravely from a pile of instruments crowded around it.

"I *have* tried it, remember? Which is why I stick with chocolate. It is, and always will be, a classic."

"Just like you, babe." Amy's hands, now free after depositing the frosty shakes on the table, found their way around Abe's neck where their icy touch got his attention, as did her kiss on the point of his chin. They might have kept his attention, but a loud rumble emanating from the nether regions of his abdomen caused the two to move apart, unable to ignore the interruption.

While devouring his three-quarter portion of the pizza, Abe looked around the small home, already full to overflowing with Amy's scattered belongings, and frowned. He eventually left off eating altogether to absentmindedly calculate the limited space and tried, unsuccessfully, to imagine how he would ever fit into the jumbled clutter. Amy was a little surprised at his suspended consumption of dinner, and the frown frankly left her puzzled.

Abe paused in his musings regarding the small space to ask in an unusually somber tone, "Are you *sure* you want to marry me?"

The unexpected question blindsided Amy. She nearly choked on her milkshake while random, horrifying thoughts flashed through her brain. *No, no, no, this can't be happening! We are engaged now and a month away from our wedding. He promised he would never disappoint me or cause me to wonder about the strength of our relationship ever again. He's kidding. That's it – he's kidding. But he looks so serious…*

Those thoughts and more jostled for prominence in a brain rendered numb by worry and disbelief, leaving Amy incapable of a rational response. A few seconds later her tumultuous emotions rose from the depths of doubt when she realized with relief that no answer was expected. Abe continued to look around the room, not at her, and spoke in absent observation.

"I know I don't have a lot of stuff, but I do have my own TV, laptop, and books, and I'll probably get tons more of those when I start seminary. And then there are my clothes. I've seen your closets, and I don't know how all my things are going to…"

Abe stopped when he heard a shaky laugh. He glanced at Amy and was horrified to find her wiping her eyes and trying to staunch more unbidden tears.

"My darling Amy, what's the matter? You look like your dog just died and you're trying to keep a stiff upper lip."

Though her spirits had rebounded from despair, she, nonetheless, failed at a lighthearted response and irrationally began tearing up again. With a quivering lip, she attempted to respond casually. "I'm just being silly. Ignore me. I'll be fine."

"I will *not* ignore you," Abe said, and reached his hand across the table to take hers. "Tell me." His touch and gentle urging had the opposite effect he had hoped for. Despite her best efforts to gain control over the erratic feelings brought about by her misunderstanding of his idle comments, Amy found it difficult to recover on a dime after riding the surging wave of her misplaced fears. It didn't help any that she felt ashamed for doubting him.

"Oh, Abe, I thought it was just like before… out of the blue… just when I thought everything was wonderful, and I was sure of a future together. I mean, one minute you're eating p-pizza and teasing me about my m-milkshake, and the next minute you're… you're asking if I really want to m-marry you… I was so… scared."

Abe came around the table in a flash and pulled Amy into his arms. Gently stroking her soft brown hair, he murmured reassurances into her ear. "I am so, so sorry, my darling girl. It never occurred to me that my foolishly frivolous words would be misinterpreted. I only began to wonder where you will put me after we are married."

A watery chuckle encouraged him. He pulled away to wipe the tears from her cheeks and look intently into her eyes.

"I may be a fool and hopelessly unworthy of you, but I promised you when I returned from Virginia, as I promise you now: I will *never* leave you again. Do you hear me? Never."

Amy was only able to nod her head, but a wobbly smile shone once more. Abe held her tenderly for a few more minutes until he could hear her breathing grow steadier, then released her to turn his attention once more to his neglected pizza and his suspended cogitations. Back on top of the world, Amy attacked her milkshake with relish, and offered a tentative solution to their dilemma.

"The obvious answer is a bigger place, I suppose." Abe lifted his eyebrows and nodded his head in agreement. His mouth was full. "We could probably find another rental somewhere in town. That new family, the Murdocks, certainly lucked out."

"You mean the 'hubba hubba' lady," Abe mumbled out of the corner of his mouth.

"You just stay away from her, mister," Amy said severely. "Her aunt seems very nice, and the two little boys are both cuties, but *Mrs.* Murdock looks like a man-eater if ever there was one, and I won't have her eating mine!"

Abe grinned, enchanted by the sudden appearance of Amy's tigress claws.

"How would you feel about a little stroll after *you* finish eating?" she asked, slurping the last of her milkshake.

"Are you kidding? It's freezing out there." No sooner had the words left his mouth than his conscience reminded him of the pain he had unintentionally caused his beloved just moments before. "I'm sorry – again. Of course, we can take a walk if you want to."

"No, you're right. It is pretty nippy outside. What do you say to a nice, warm drive instead? There's something I'd like to show you. Well, technically, it's something you saw many times when we were first dating. Remember how we used to walk together almost every evening? But I want you to look at it now with refocused eyes."

A few minutes later they were driving down State Street in Abe's SUV when Amy told him to turn left and pull over in front of a long length of wrought iron fencing. Skinner Street had been named for a former state representative and mayor, and owner of the grandest house in the town proper.

"The *haunted* house? *This* is what you wanted me to see? People warn their kids to stay away from this place. Neighbors claim they've seen strange lights at night through the slits in the wood window coverings. You told me yourself that your students are scared to walk by it after dark."

"Are you finished yet?" Apparently not.

"This isn't a house. It's a mausoleum fit only for the dead – *not* the living." Abe spoke with finality and a pronounced grimace.

"Maybe it's just been misunderstood."

"*Misunderstood?* This place doesn't need a psychologist. It needs an exorcist!"

Amy's only answer was a quick exit of the vehicle so she could peer through the rungs of the sturdy fencing. Whether women in general have an affinity for old, deserted houses, or because she had walked, run, or driven by the house many times since moving to Tinkers Well, Amy had for some time thought of the classic colonial revival structure as *her* house. But until she could picture a future with a family of her own, her dreams had just been passing fancies. She had never said anything about her thoughts to Abe on their earlier excursions simply because she knew them to be nothing more than silly, wasted whims. She had discovered early on that the property was tied up in a decades' long legal suit – that is, until five days earlier.

Amy, representing the town's music teachers, had gone to city hall to apply for a permit to use the gazebo in the park for a spring combined school music concert. After ensuring that every box and line had been completed satisfactorily, the ever-helpful Lucy Bennett handed Amy more than a permit; she gave her the 411 on the Skinner home.

"Can you believe it? After all these years, the whole lot of the clutch-fisted generation that inherited the place after the death of their father, the late Honorable Moses Skinner, is gone or mentally incapacitated. So, all their stingy parsimony netted them absolutely nothing. None of *their* descendants have any desire to live here – just want to make a quick sale and split the money." She caught a speculative gleam in Amy's eye and rambled on.

"It's a pity there's no one who needs a big house like that. Why it'd be perfect for a growing family with that great big lot and all those trees. Plenty of rooms, too. I went there once for somebody's birthday party when I was a kid. I remember thinking it looked like the kind of house some high muckety-muck government official should live in. Turns out it was. It'll take some elbow grease to put it in order – just the sort of thing that would be right down your fiancé's alley, with the help of Tim and the other boys, of course." Lucy hadn't lived with a farmer for over 30 years without learning a thing or two about planting seeds.

Now Amy was ready to share her thoughts with Abe, and the discussion about their impending crisis of square footage seemed the perfect opening to launch her campaign. An early dinner had bought them enough time to view the abandoned building, with its boarded-up windows and creeping ivy, in the fading glow of quickly retreating sunshine. The subdued lighting underscored the emptiness of the house as if its very essence had departed with the last residents 30 years before.

Long neglected hedges created so much shadow that the once artistic cobblestone walkway to the front door had become nothing more than a host for patchy moss. Mottled, mixed brown brick did little to dispel the gloom. The only remaining hint of the home's former dignity and stature was found in dual chimney stacks standing as tall and straight as the day they were built, one on either end of the two-story home. Blank windows, boarded over to prevent damage by kids with a destructive penchant for pitching practice, and the "Private Property, Keep Out" signs, caused Amy's spirits to flag a bit.

Not easily beaten, Amy gathered her courage and poured out her ideas to Abe, who had reluctantly left the warmth of the car to join her at the gate. He listened politely, but without much enthusiasm. Amy, like Rose Ludlow, admired the traditional elements of architectural style, while Abe was more inclined to favor sleek, clean lines and a minimum of frills. All he could see were hours and hours of renovation work in the evening after he'd done hours and hours of renovation work during the day. That kind of schedule might suit Tim, but Abe needed time to refresh his mind and his stomach. Amy, of course, reminded him that most of his work was done in the office. And because she had it on good authority that the family meant to auction the property "as is," her source assured her it would go for a song.

"With what we could potentially save on the initial purchase price, we could hire Three Brothers to do the heavy work. I mean, think about it. Look, there's that big, enclosed sunporch off to the side where I could set up a real teaching studio with its own outside entrance. And I'm guessing those roof dormers are not just there for show, because there are windows on the ends of the attic too. Can you imagine how much room there must be up there? It probably housed servants at one time, but we could use some of it for storage and still have room left for a big movie room." *And maybe someday, it could be refurbished for some other use.* Amy had in mind a playroom for little Yousefs, but that discussion could wait.

"And I've been doing some research online to try to figure out what the interior might look like. These houses usually had formal living and dining rooms on the front of the building with an eat-in kitchen and a den at the back. Just think how nice it would be for you to have your own study. And look way in the back of the yard, which, you'll notice, is *huge* and has all those fabulous mature trees. I know it's hard to make out much in this light, but it looks like a sizeable garage with what might be an office, or workshop, or maybe a small guesthouse on one end."

Abe felt like he was drowning in a sea of house specs and wondered why Amy hadn't pursued a career in real estate instead of teaching. She would certainly have succeeded at both. He couldn't help but smile as she painted layer upon layer of a possibility she had clearly been contemplating for some time. He allowed her to wind down before reluctantly painting a different picture.

"Amy, I can see why you think this would be a great place for us, but have you forgotten that I'm starting seminary in the fall? That will last three years – "

"Yes, I get that, and I know it's probably a terrible time to buy a house, with our income shrinking and the expenses for school, and everything…"

"No, you misunderstand me. It will take me three years to get through seminary, but I'll be looking for pastoral opportunities after that, and there is little likelihood that I'll find any in the immediate area. I know we talked about that." Abe could see Amy visibly second guessing herself, but he judged it kinder to help her face the truth now rather than later, after she had set her heart on something unattainable.

Abe had succeeded in curbing her excitement, but she wasn't giving up yet. Measuring her words carefully, Amy bravely fought against Abe's verbal deluge of cold water. "Everything you say is true, and yes, we have talked about relocating someday. But I think we both agree that we will need to move *somewhere* here in Tinkers Well, and soon. Can we at least consider this possibility? Depending on how much work needs to be done, we could live here for three years and still come out ahead when we sell it later."

Abe stood there in silence – an immovable object that would only bend to an irresistible force. Amy applied it. "*Please?*"

"Ugh!! How do you *do* that?" Abe threw his hands up in defeat. "You're as bad as Rose. Do you girls get together and compare notes on how to wind your weak, spineless men around your little fingers?" Amy kissed him soundly and pulled his hands around her waist before resting her head on his shoulder.

"Don't be silly, babe. It's a superpower attached to our second X chromosome. You didn't stand a chance."

The proposed window excursion went off without a hitch. Perhaps it would be more accurate to say without *much* of a hitch. Despite Rose's excitement over her "finds," Tim couldn't get past the frailty of the frames, and the fact that they weren't quite as square as they needed to be.

"But can't you just cut the hole in the wall a little lopsided? That would certainly add an interesting touch," Rose suggested hopefully. It never crossed her mind that the process might also add a nervous tic and an ulcer to her sorely tried husband. Abe and Amy left the Ludlows to hash it out and went in search of anything that might serve as a second desk for him.

Tim sought in vain for a compromise that would satisfy both Rose's artistic soul and his more pragmatic approach to the barn restoration, all the while silently praying for the wisdom of Solomon. Knowing his wife would be disappointed if they returned to Tinkers Well empty handed, he decided to do some searching of his own. Five minutes into his quest, he gave a shout that caused everyone in the store to look in his direction. Spying an old newspaper through the warped glass of an even older window than the one Rose had pointed out, he hit upon the answer to incorporation of his wife's sketchy treasures while adding something of real value she wasn't expecting. Tim headed off Rose before she could reach the real gem he had found hidden on the top of an armoire in a cluttered corner. And because he could be just as determined as she was, the two entered into a short, but satisfactory, round of negotiations.

"You can pick out three windows all together, so one at each stop or – "

"Four windows," Rose countered. Tim pursed his lips and considered her demands.

"Four windows at two stops and that's my final offer," he said as if he had been driven into the last ditch. Rose only hesitated a split second before allowing her saucy smile to appear.

"Deal." Tim gravely shook her outstretched hand, then told her she and Amy had to wait in the truck while he completed the sale.

"But they're our windows. We found them. Why can't Amy and I claim them?"

"Because, Ms. Bossy, there's something I found that I don't want you to see until I have everything in place and installed properly."

Rose narrowed her eyes suspiciously, but reluctantly agreed to his wishes. Both girls watched Abe carry a tarp into the store but couldn't discern any details of the items wrapped tightly inside it on its return to the truck. They repeated the process in the next town before heading home.

A week later, Tim led a blind-folded Rose into the barn at dusk when little natural light remained to penetrate the cavernous space. He turned her around several times to confuse her sense of direction and instructed her to wait while he flipped a few switches. Returning presently, Tim removed the blindfold. Her reaction was all he had hoped for and more. She was so surprised by the unconventional but brilliant use of the old windows that she was uncharacteristically bereft of speech.

Tim had mounted a thin metal bar about eight feet high on the walls separating the kitchen and restroom areas from the main hall. Dangling from chains affixed to the bar hung two windows on each side roughly two inches away from the walls. Rose gasped at the unexpected presentation accented by chains of tiny LED lights surrounding each window frame. The subdued spotlighting gave life to the captivating array of photos set at odd angles on each piece of glass. But these were no random photos. Rose gazed in wonder at pictures of herself and Tim from infancy through their wedding day, each representing a step on the journey to their life together. Her eyes misted with sentimental tears as she slowly walked along the gallery of memories. When she considered the hours he must have spent gathering and mounting the photos, and the care he took to incorporate her impractical ideas into something they could both be proud of, she turned and ran into his waiting arms.

"Oh, Tim," she said, her voice muffled by his substantial shoulder, "why are you so good to me?"

"Because," he replied, his lips brushing her hair, "I love you to the moon and back. I heard a hopeless romantic say that once." Her ever-ready giggle followed. He held her at arms' length to look into her eyes. "And lest you think me more of a superman than I really am, I should tell you that Amy and Abe put together all the pictures. I gave them the scrapbooks you brought with you from Kentucky, and they got a bunch of pictures from my mom. And all the wedding pics came from the photographer's website." Anticipating her next comment, he added, "And before you suggest it, Abe has already uploaded photos of the display to the *willowwalkweddings.com* website.

"Thoughtful, handsome, *and* resourceful. You're quite a catch." Looking lovingly at her husband, she continued on an apologetic note. "I don't tell you that often enough, do I?"

"Well, a fellow can always use a little reminding now and then…"

Rose spent several leisurely minutes reminding him. Tim was so enamored by her methods of persuasion that he almost forgot his final surprise.

He gently placed his finger over her parted lips. "Hold that thought 'til we get back to the house. There's something else I want to show you."

A second gasp escaped Rose when Tim flipped a switch, and muted rays of light in rich jewel tones added their radiance to the growing darkness. He had mounted an intricately designed, three-foot-square stained-glass window between the high wall in the ladies restroom and the main hall. It was a treasure surrounded by rough barn wood, an artistic element among the simple and common. Rich gold and yellow petals against a blue mosaic sky, framed by imaginatively variegated green leaves, drew all eyes to the queen of Kansas horticulture – the sunflower.

"How do you do it? How do you add excellence to perfection?" Rose turned from contemplation of Tim's inspired design ideas to contemplate her husband.

"Just remember this someday when I mess up big time. And speaking of reminding, we need to get back to the house." He made his way along the row of windows, switching off the LED lights as he went. Rose followed him down the hall where he reached in to switch off the light in the ladies' room, and she stood back as he slid the huge barn door closed and locked it.

"We just got here, and now you're in a hurry to get back to the house." They were walking quickly toward *Willow Walk.*

"I'm sorry, sweetheart. It's my *terrible* memory."

"Your *what?*" Rose couldn't help laughing at the exaggerated crestfallen tone in his voice.

"I've already forgotten why you think I'm so awesome, and I need you to tell me again. Or maybe *show* and tell…?"

"Timothy James Ludlow, you are incorrigible!" Rose said severely.

"It's one of the reasons you're crazy about me. Go ahead, admit it." He was right, of course, but she refused to pander anymore to his male ego – not until they reached the house, at any rate.

CHAPTER 7

Tim knocked soundly on a door bearing emblems of the many hats worn by Zeke Gerzsewski in serving the residents of Harrington County. He and Derek attempted to look through the window to determine whether the office was occupied, but sheets of housing specs for numerous properties, many sold months earlier, were taped to the windowpanes, making it impossible to tell. Receiving no answer to Tim's hail, and finding the door unlocked, they let themselves in and looked around the cluttered space. Multiple signs leaned against the outer wall announcing, "For Sale," "Coming Soon," and "Absolute Auction," along with agricultural field markers for several varieties of wheat, corn, sorghum, and soybeans.

"Mr. Gerzsewski, are you here?"

A muffled, "Just coming," sounded from behind a wall, and presently Zeke's backside presented itself to be followed by the rest of its owner fussing over a fishing reel with a tangled line. His bald head was hidden by a floppy hat adorned with numerous fishing flies, and the pockets of an extremely well-worn vest bulged with bobbers, weights, pliers, and other tools of the dedicated angler. "These darn things get hung up so easily." Zeke fiddled with the line a few more minutes, eventually freeing it, and addressed his guests. "She's a beaut," he commented, carefully winding the line onto a shiny reel, "but almost as much trouble as a woman. Now what can I do for you young fellows?" he asked, leaning his rod and reel in the corner where it slid sideways in fascinating slow motion to be lost among the signs.

Mesmerized by the slow decent, Derek jerked his head back when the rod hit the floor. Tim wasn't so easily distracted.

"I'm Tim Ludlow. I called you earlier in the week about getting a key?" Zeke squinted his eyes, trying to remember. Nothing registered.

"For the Skinner house?" The detail, furnished by Derek, brought an arrested expression to Zeke's face, but the lifted eyebrows demanded more clarification.

"The Skinner property you're auctioning off in five days?" Tim exaggerated the words as if communicating with someone of a different species. Light dawned. Zeke snapped his fingers.

"That's right. You told me you have a friend who might be interested in the place?" He shook his head. "To be honest with you, I don't know why anybody would want that old house. Why, it scares *me*, and I've been over it several times."

Tim's ears perked up at Zeke's innocent comments. Any inside information might prove useful. "Can you tell us anything about the history or the condition of the house? I understand it's been unoccupied for 30 years, and I just wondered what kind of improvements, if any, have been done to the place, or even minimal maintenance, for that matter."

Now Zeke Gerzsewski prided himself on being a man in the know, and he enjoyed displaying his knowledge to all comers. His chest swelled importantly, and he reached for his fallen rod hidden behind the signs. "Oh, I could tell you a thing or two, but I always feel that sharing information is best done in a congenial setting – somewhere you can relax and spend your time. How do you boys feel about a little fishing?" he asked hopefully.

Tim, as impatient as his father Miles, frowned and started to say, "No thanks," but Derek headed him off.

"Why, we surely do enjoy fishing, but we have a few other things to get to this afternoon." He sensed Zeke's withdrawal and added quickly, "But there's always time for a piece of pie and a cup of coffee, right?" thus successfully recapturing Zeke's attention. "I hear Milly's been serving a mixed berry pie all week. What do you say we mosey over there and claim a piece before it's gone?" Derek clinched the deal when he suggested, with his irrepressible smile, "A man's gotta eat, right?"

"That's what I keep telling my wife, but she still complains when I pop into Milly's for a bite."

"Oh, Tim understands all about that. He's been married a whole four months now." Tim understood nothing of the sort. Rose was completely supportive, loving, and if anything, urged him to allow himself more time to relax and take it easy.

Zeke turned to the affronted groom and winked. "Got you on a short leash, has she? Here, hold this," he told Derek and handed him the fishing tackle. Digging into his cluttered desk for the house key, he missed the tight-lipped glare directed at Derek.

"Here we go," Zeke said, emerging triumphantly with key in hand. "You can have this," he said, handing Tim the key, "and I'll take that." Derek surrendered the rod and reel only to watch Zeke lean it in the corner where it again disappeared after another painstakingly slow slide down the wall.

Zeke ushered the younger men outside and suggested they all pile into his cramped sedan for the drive. Tim managed to avoid a carpool to the diner, but when he and Derek stepped out onto Main Street an hour and a half later, he had to admit that asking a few adroit questions, and letting Zeke monopolize the conversation, had been time well spent. It was only after he and Derek had scoured the house in question from top to bottom, however, that he fully appreciated the value of that insider information.

"I've never seen anything like it in my life, and if I hadn't seen it with my own eyes, I wouldn't have believed it. But everything in this report," Tim said, handing Abe an envelope, "is the gospel truth. Derek is my witness."

They were sitting around the Ludlows' kitchen table. The walls in the house were ten feet tall, but Rose had somehow transformed the large room into a cozy gathering place for their closest friends and family. While she and Amy had ostensibly been making the thrift store rounds in search of dishware and windows for the wedding barn, Rose had collected a few more colorful artistic elements for her own home.

There were now two more ceramic roosters strutting across the top of the shaker cabinets in addition to the one given to her by her mother-in-law at Christmas. Random sprays of greenery broke up the large expanse of white cabinets and muted the LED lighting that ran along the top. A huge oval serving platter in a sort of blue willow pattern, large enough to accommodate a 25-pound turkey, was mounted on the wall between the mud room and the window by the table. Several lesser platters in varying shapes trailed down the wall under it. Rose and Tim weren't the only ones who found the room warm and inviting, and though those gathered there were fully aware of its charm, all eyes and ears focused on Tim, who had the floor. Rose listened attentively from the stove where she whisked together the ingredients for a creamy garlic sauce.

Neither Abe nor Amy was sure of how to take Tim's words. "So, is it good news or... bad?" Abe asked cautiously. Amy held her breath. Her intent stare practically bore a hole through Tim.

He chose to answer Abe's question with a question. "When you were kids, did you ever go into one of those houses at an amusement park where everything *looks* right, but you feel like you're walking sideways as you go through it, and everything is somehow cock-eyed?"

It must be really bad. In her abject disappointment, Amy fought back threatening tears. As much as Abe was relieved that Tim's report would finally put a stop to her insistence that they consider buying the Skinner property, he couldn't help sharing her letdown a little.

"You know how much we appreciate you and Derek spending your Saturday like this on our behalf – "

"You know that's right!" Derek said.

Abe paid no attention to him. "But perhaps it would be helpful to be a little more forthcoming…"

"That's what I've been trying to say. Yank off that band-aid, brother." When Abe glared at him, Derek judged it time to clamp his hand over his mouth and study his table setting.

Rose deftly placed browned chicken tenderloins in the thickening sauce and added angel hair pasta to a boiling pot. After setting the sauce to simmer, she joined the others. All eyes were on Tim. "Okay, here's the bottom line. Are you sure you're ready for this?"

Amy gulped, and Abe nodded his head solemnly.

"Everything from the dark, dungeon-like foundation and boarded over windows, to the wiring, woodwork, cabinetry and heating systems," he said, listing each building element like an executioner announcing those to be hung or decapitated, "are not what they seem. It's a house full of optical illusions that appear to date back some 10 to 15 years. Like I said, I've never seen anything like it."

"What does that even mean?" Abe demanded. Amy was too confused to say anything. Derek grinned broadly. Keeping a straight face had nearly killed him.

"But how does that fit into what Lucy Bennett told Amy about the Skinner siblings," Rose asked, trying to make sense of Tim's words. "Does it have something to do with why they wouldn't agree to sell the house after their father died?"

"You're on the right track, sweetheart, but it's thanks to Derek that we got the answers to a lot of questions we didn't even know we needed to ask of Zeke Gerzsewski, the auctioneer. Derek plied him with non-stop pie and coffee, and the guy talked his head off. I know I was impressed."

"A simple thank-you will suffice." Derek looked at Abe expectantly and was rewarded with a big hand shoved in his face.

"But what could he *possibly* have told you that would make you say something so crazy? I warn you Tim, if you don't give us a straight answer soon, I'll turn Amy loose. She'll come across this table and *shake* the truth out of you!" Amy was wound so tight at that point, she looked to be in danger of jumping the gun.

Tim held up his hand, laughing. "Okay, okay. I promise, I'm not intentionally torturing you or trying to confuse you. I merely thought that having more background info would make our findings easier to understand. So here goes. You were right, Rose, about the six children of Moses Skinner disagreeing over the house, but it's more complicated than that. Apparently, the siblings had never really been close because each one was jealous of the others, believing their father to have favored a different brother or sister over themselves. Whether that's true or not, we'll probably never know. Anyway, I guess Skinner decided he would force them to reconcile and cooperate if they wanted any inheritance.

"As Zeke tells the story, Moses tied up his entire fortune in the estate, meaning that his heirs had to agree to one of them living there and buying out the shares in the house belonging to the others, after which their father's fortune was to be divided among them. *Or* they all had to agree to sell the house, then split that income and the remaining fortune. And because none of them trusted the others, thinking all but the one owning the property would somehow be cheated, they refused to agree on that option. Likewise, they refused the second option, each one thinking they would outlive the others and claim everything. But if they failed to agree on either option, which is ultimately what happened, they inherited nothing. The money would be left in trust for necessary repairs to the property until an agreement could be reached. And here's a critical point. *Any* of the siblings could request funds to make repairs to the house without the others being notified, but neither could they tell their own children. No one was privy to the estate's value except the executor – hold onto that.

"The stipulations of the will were to remain in effect until the last sibling, necessarily being of sound mind and having outlived the others by a minimum of six months, inherited everything. If *none* of the six met those requirements, the estate, including what was left of the fortune, was to be divided by their descendants. That's why it's finally being sold. None of the original six made the grade. Like Lucy Bennett told Amy, four died within months of each other and the other two live in memory care facilities."

"Wow! That's incredible." Abe shook his head in disbelief. "So, because they couldn't agree on sharing everything, they ended up with nothing. It sounds like a parable."

"Crazy, isn't it?" Derek deemed it time for a little attention aimed in his direction. "Like he said, the best Tim and I could figure is that one or more of old Moses Skinner's kids were banking on the possibility of being the last man – or woman – standing. They made improvements to the house, then *hid* them, so the upgrades were unrecognizable to the others."

Amy had been silent for so long the others were almost surprised when she finally spoke. "You know I want to jump up and down and start screaming now, right?" Her hands shook slightly. "Because I sense that there's awesome news buried somewhere in this story, but you'll have to explain a little more. For instance, why hide repairs?"

"Because they didn't want the others to know they had been dipping into the estate till and because an old house in a seemingly advanced state of decay would lower the value of the property for probate." As an afterthought, Derek added with feeling, "Makes me glad I don't have any brothers or sisters."

"Zeke did tell us that they came together over a few points. There was no room for squabbling over the need for roof repair, reinforcement of the chimneys before they collapsed, and covering the windows to protect against damage," Tim explained further. "I didn't arrive at the 10 to 15-year-start date solely because of the work done. That's, coincidentally, how long Zeke thinks there has been power to the place, and that's probably because the next project, from a practical perspective, was lining the crawl space with heavy black plastic sheeting. Nowadays, white sheeting is used, but without a powerful utility light, the black stuff is almost invisible. It kind of looks like tar paper. There are also some added wooden support beams mounted on cinderblock bases which are nearly indistinguishable from the original foundation."

"And who do you think crawled around in that spider-infested dungeon to discover all those details?" Derek shivered at the thought. "That's right, yours truly."

"Spiders? You are such a wuss. Whatever happened to 'Rangers lead the way'?"

"Dude, when I was going through Army Ranger School, I was so mentally and physically whipped, I could have slept with a *tarantula* on my face. But now I'm a man of more civilized habits, thank you very much." Believing himself to have scored a point, Derek went on. "That's how I found the dehumidifier behind one of the cinder block posts. It clicked on just as I was crawling around the corner – scared the crap out of me!"

"But when we went inside," said Tim, "and tried the light switch by the door, without success, we looked up to find that the light fixture had been removed. That seemed odd, so we split up. Derek took the den and living room, and I went through the kitchen and dining room. *All* the light fixtures had been removed. Who does that? We already knew there was power to the house, so why remove the lights? The back door opens into the hall that runs straight through the house to the front door, so very little natural light makes it into the adjacent rooms. All we had were our flashlights and headlamps.

"At first the kitchen cabinets looked like the simple style of a hundred years ago, and the old, rusted hardware was either hanging crookedly from drawer fronts and cabinet doors or missing altogether. I don't know what made me look closer, but I did. The handles were hanging loosely because there was only one mounting hole, and when I pulled on one to look inside, I got a real surprise. Each cabinet had clean, smooth surfaces, and brand-new, stainless steel *hidden* hinges. The old hinges were still attached to the door fronts, but they were only taped in place. I looked at the cabinet doors more closely and discovered they're actually pale gray, not white, and appear to have a new ultraviolet finish. Pretty high-speed stuff. That's when I started looking at everything differently. Nothing was as it seemed."

"Like the cock-eyed houses when we were kids!" Amy could barely sit still.

"Exactly!" Derek replied with a grin. Turning to her tablemate, he asked pointedly, "Now what would you say is the easiest way to cover up something you don't want anyone else to see?"

"I don't know," Abe said, shrugging his shoulders. "Hide it somehow?"

"Really? That's the best you've got? Have you forgotten all those night patrols in Afghanistan?" It said much for the emotional healing of both men that they could discuss, objectively, such events as the one that had touched each of them with shattering effect.

"Night. Darkness," Abe replied thoughtfully.

"Bingo. One of the next big projects must have been the windows. You know how they're boarded up?"

"We assumed it was because of broken windowpanes."

"That's what Tim and I thought too. There are even broken shards of old glass on the floors. But the weird thing is that the windows are also boarded over on the *inside*. Now *that* doesn't make sense. So, Tim – "

"My curiosity got the better of me. I was wearing my tool belt – you never know when you'll need something. I grabbed my hammer and pried one of the covers off. I've never seen anything like it."

"Please stop saying that!" Abe's nerves, like Amy's, were vibrating like the plucked strings of a finely tuned instrument. "We're still mostly in the dark since the first time you said it!"

Tim grinned his apology. "It was a custom window in pristine condition. And not just your run-of-the-mill replacement window of ten years ago – probably about the time they were added. It's top of the line, both functionally and architecturally, and you can bet the rest of them are identical. By then, we began to feel like we were on a treasure hunt, and oh baby, did we find some treasure!"

Rose had completely forgotten about dinner. The sound of water boiling over on the stove recalled her to her hostess duties. After popping some breadsticks in the oven, she finished off the salad, moving mechanically through the shredding and chopping while she focused on the discussion beyond. Tim was clearly enjoying himself.

"When I studied the rest of the interior, something about the wood molding – and there's a lot of it – kept tickling my brain. It appeared to be in pretty good shape – well, more precisely, great shape. That struck me as odd in a house that has been uninhabited for thirty years with no climate control for much of that time. Then I looked closer. It's been recently refinished – all of it. By recently, I mean in the last five years or so. The change might not have registered if we hadn't done the exact same thing at our place seven months ago. The varnishes we use today leave a different sheen, and the stain is a darker brown than would have been available in the period the house was built – almost espresso. But again, in the dim light it's hard to tell. The wood floors, also refinished, are a little lighter."

"Dude, your eyes are glowing. How do you do that?" Derek asked, peering at Abe.

"Tell me about some other fantastic discovery and they'll get even brighter."

"You're on. This I've got to see." Derek shared his own remarkable find with the group while keeping an eye on Abe's face. "So, while Tim was recovering the window, I spotted rectangular blocks on the ceilings. When I climbed up to take a look (Tim also brought a ladder) I found ductwork grates that had been covered over. The odd thing is that there were also radiators under the windows. Remember, I'm doing all this by flashlight and head lamp. On my earlier caving expedition, I found an old coal furnace in a deeper dug out space under the house. That would explain the radiators, but why the grates? There should have been one or the other. I found the answer in the attic. There's a good-sized room separating the two ends of the space – *but it has no door*.

"I'm not kidding," Derek asserted in the face of everyone's obvious skepticism. "A secret room. How cool is that! Without thinking, I leaned my shoulder on an outside corner while I was scoping it out. When I stood upright, that section of the wall hit me in the butt when it swung out on a hinge. There was a spring-loaded latch on the inside, but more importantly, there was a *dual zone HVAC system* – probably one for the first floor and one for the second floor and attic. But neither Tim nor I had seen a thermostat anywhere. *Someone had completely hidden a modern heating and cooling system!* That made me wonder how we could have missed the exterior A/C units. So, while Tim was snooping around inside, I looked outside again. I made another circuit of the house and discovered the reason we missed the A/C units the first time. They were completely covered over by boxes painted in a dark green camouflage pattern, making them virtually undetectable behind the untamed bushes around them. These people must have been *nuts!*"

"Or very cunning," Abe observed, his eyes narrowed. "The interior work must have been done at night. That would account for people seeing lights through cracks in the window covers."

"Oh, they were definitely cunning, all right. One of them, probably the one who added the HVAC system, replaced all the old plumbing, but covered the work up by leaving a mess. Tim figured that out."

Rose had completed dinner preparations and set the serving dishes on the table, an act which, ordinarily, would have signaled that Abe turn his attention exclusively to his food. The breadbasket at his elbow went unnoticed.

"What kind of mess?" he asked, watching Tim rather than the steaming bowl of chicken scampi sitting directly in front of him.

"What I noticed were large sections of the lath and plaster interior walls where the covering had been torn off, leaving old paper insulation hanging out all over the place. Everything I'd seen so far was a misdirect, so I started digging into the walls. That's when I found new plumbing lines, which prompted me to look under the sinks – no more lead pipes or leaky supply lines. They've been replaced by PEX lines and PVC, cleverly masked with scrappy-looking, old tube insulation."

"But why update the pipes and not the insulation and then leave the walls a mess?" Even Abe knew that didn't make any sense.

"Now you're thinking like a contractor."

Tim grinned appreciatively. "Because nobody looks twice at torn-up walls. Who wants to mess with that? And the odd thing was that there were also exposed *exterior* wall sections – "

"Where there shouldn't have been any plumbing. Are you telling us…"

"That if you don't buy this house, *I will.* I could flip it with little effort and make some serious bank." Abe allowed himself a speculative smile. And though Amy was far from understanding the implications of Tim's find, she was pretty sure the jumping up and down and screaming would start soon.

"Wait, I don't get it. Or I should say, I don't get the last part about the walls, but I have a feeling I'm going to like it," she said optimistically.

"After all the other hidden treasures I had unearthed, I wasn't about to take anything at face value. I had initially just chalked up the walls to something needing repair or replacement, but taking everything else into account, I started poking around those, too. At first glance, they seem to be covered by aged wallpaper, but it's only stapled on, and the walls in a few of the bedrooms and one bath are covered in fabric that peels off easily. But the best part is what's *underneath* it all. Except for the torn sections, which were surely left unrepaired to throw others off the scent, the interior of the whole crazy house is covered in sturdy, modern drywall."

Amy had survived her share of disappointments in the past year. She couldn't bear the thought that the promise of her dream house – having turned overnight into her miracle house – might be added to the list. But it all sounded just too good to be true. She hardly dared look at Abe to gauge his response. His frown did not encourage her until she realized that it was more a frown of concentration than one of disapproval.

"You can't run 21st-century heating and cooling units off old wiring." Abe looked up to find Tim nodding his head as if encouraging the other to complete his thought. "Which means that…"

"I found new wiring *and* R-23 insulation when I dug into one of the end walls in the living room. And all the power receptacles have been replaced with vintage designed modern ones. That, and the new drywall throughout the house, tells me that the whole thing has been rewired. I'm telling you, this old house is not only in impossibly good shape; it's a once-in-a-lifetime find."

Amy and Abe turned to one another. With a smile lurking at the corners of his mouth, he nodded slightly. That was all the encouragement she needed. The jumping up and down and screaming had begun.

Abe was so quiet on the drive home Amy began to worry. *How could he possibly not be excited over their impossible luck? Surely, he must recognize this as a blessing from God.*

"Babe, you haven't said a word since we left Rose and Tim's place. Are you just feeling overwhelmed? I know I am – in a good way."

Abe didn't answer right away. Finally, shaking his head, he said with reserve, "It's not right."

"What's not right?"

"Amy, we can't, knowing what we know, go to that auction on Wednesday and bid significantly less than we know the house to be worth. It's not right," he repeated.

"But you heard Tim say he would buy it if we didn't. His inside knowledge obviously didn't stop him from recognizing an incredible deal."

Abe responded a little tersely, "I am not responsible for Tim's conscience, but I am responsible for mine."

Amy fought her growing resentment without success. "I see what you're doing. You *never* wanted that house, and now you're just making up excuses. Why couldn't you have been honest with me in the first place instead of letting me get my hopes up?"

Against his will, he allowed himself to be stung by her infectious anger. "Okay, you're right. I *didn't* want that house because I saw it as a bottomless pit. But you either can't or *won't* understand that it would be wrong to purchase it now under false pretenses."

"We haven't done anything wrong. Don't think you can come all holier-than-thou over me, Abraham Yousef!"

"I am only saying that there are sins of *co*-mission and sins of *o*-mission, and buying the place without at least sharing our knowledge with the auctioneer would fall into the latter category."

"Ugh!" was her only reply. The rest of the drive passed in a heavy silence, broken only by the slamming of the passenger door when Amy left the vehicle without a word.

"I just felt that I had an obligation to share with you what I know about this property before the auction tomorrow."

By the time Abe had located Zeke Gerzsewski and convinced him to meet at the Skinner house, the sun, partially hidden by gathering clouds, was dropping quickly on a frigid Tuesday afternoon that threatened rain or worse.

"I don't mean to be rude, young man, but I think it's safe to say I know this property better than anybody, and the things you've told me just don't add up."

"Look, I know it sounds impossible. I can still hardly believe it myself, but I thought it only right that you see for yourself, so that the auction will be conducted in a way that is both fair to the buyers and the sellers."

Zeke was clearly skeptical, but he was a respectful, good-natured man, and though he was anxious to head home to warmth and his waiting dinner, he agreed to indulge Abe "for a short spell." He had come armed with a flashlight, but little enthusiasm. Abe first suggested he investigate the crawlspace. Looking through the opening was as far as he got.

"I'm not getting on my hands and knees to go crawling around under the house. My wife would have my hide if I got these new pants dirty. And going by what I see here, it looks like a dark, dank, dungeon – just like any cellar of this building period."

"Yes, but it doesn't smell dank, does it? That's because of the dehumidifier."

Zeke sniffed and shrugged his shoulders, then strained to hear an automated motor.

"I don't hear anything, young fellow."

"Well, maybe it has cycled off. I can assure you it's there."

"Maybe so," Zeke said doubtfully, "but it's starting to drizzle so would you mind if we moved inside?" He had already closed the cellar door. That day, his head was capped neither by a fishing hat nor any other covering to ward off the cold seeping into his bones. Once inside the backdoor, Abe pointed out the missing light fixtures. "Doesn't surprise me at all. Knowing that family, I'm shocked they left anything but the bare studs."

In the kitchen, Abe went to a set of cabinet doors and pulled, but they wouldn't budge. He couldn't have known that that specific section of cabinetry was destined to contain a double oven and was covered by old doors tacked in place to hide the opening. Zeke shook his head and mumbled, "Young fool."

"I don't know what could be wrong with those but look at this. Do you see how the vinyl floor is merely stapled in a few places to the toe kick board? If you lift up on a corner you should be able to see the slate floor under – "

"Now hold on there, Mr. Yousef. You can't go around taking things apart. I have strict instructions from the family that the house is to be sold 'as is.'" Noting Abe's frustration, Zeke generously offered, "Why don't you show me something else, say in the dining room." They moved into the adjacent room where Abe quickly moved to a window and drew a hammer out of his pocket.

"Let me pull this wood off and you'll see for yourself that there are beautiful, upgraded windows underneath."

"I told you, you can't go taking things apart! You just leave that alone. Why, anyone can see glass from the broken panes all over the floor."

"But what about the covered ceiling vents?"

"Vents?" Zeke snorted. "That's just a ceiling patch. They're all over the place. Look at those walls. They didn't even bother to patch those."

"Yes, but if you dig into the old insulation, you'll find new wiring and plumbing."

"Sure, I will." Zeke rolled his eyes and shook his head. "Are there any other great discoveries you'd like to share with me? It's getting a bit late." His patience was wearing thin.

Knowing his words might make an impact if he could just show Zeke the secret attic room and its contents, Abe pulled and cajoled the other man up the stairs. Reaching the top floor out of breath, Zeke stared resentfully at Abe who pushed multiple times on the corner of the hidden room without success. Derek had not been specific about *which* corner held the latch, and Abe chose the wrong one. Zeke had seen, or rather not seen, enough. Without a word, he started down the stairs. Reaching the back door, he held it politely while Abe begged him to check just a few more things.

"Oh, I don't think there's anything else I care to see. I don't know why you pulled this crazy stunt, and I can't for the life of me figure out how you thought you'd benefit by trying to pull the wool over my eyes. All I can say is, I hope you're better at home renovation than you are at telling tall tales."

"But Mr. Gerzsewski, if you would only look at the A/C units on the side of the house. I'll hold the bushes back as best I can so that you can get close enough to see them." The drizzle had turned to snow mixed with freezing rain.

"I have no intention of climbing through wet, prickly bushes so you can have a good laugh. Good evening to you, sir."

The warmth of Angelica's kitchen notwithstanding, Abe sat shrouded in a blue funk that refused penetration. He had tried to do the right thing, and it had gone decidedly wrong. He hadn't spoken a word to Amy since

Saturday night, despite calling her several times to hear only her voicemail message. She had chosen to sit with the other musicians at church and was absent from Sunday potluck brunch. The tantalizing aroma of jerk chicken over seasoned rice might as well have been smoldering ashes for all the pleasure it afforded Abe. The Warners looked at each other, wondering how to help him. Finally, Derek made a command decision.

"Enough, already. Will you just try calling the girl again? She can't ignore you forever, and you can't keep avoiding each other. Not only does it make everyone around you miserable, it's a stupid way to prepare for marriage. I mean, if you can't get past arguing over a little thing like buying a house, how are you going to manage the really tough stuff, like who gets control of the remote?"

A twisted smile appeared on Abe's face just as his phone began to ring. It was Amy. He excused himself and hurried to his room. Putting the call on speaker, he sat down on his bed and burst into pent up speech.

"Amy, my darling. I have been such a fool. I didn't mean to hurt you – I never mean to hurt you – but I stupidly keep doing it. I went off the deep end without welcoming a discussion or respecting your feedback. Can you forgive me – again?"

"There is nothing to forgive. It's all my fault. I behaved like a spoiled child who didn't get her way. You were right, and I was wrong. I don't know how I let myself get so wrapped up in that silly house. I mean, I would be happy living with you in a grass hut, or a cave, or my little place. Can *you* forgive *me?*"

Abe couldn't help laughing. "Well, if I have a choice, I think I would prefer the duplex over a hut or a cave." He was instantly serious again. "Of course, I forgive you. But I must tell you – "

"No, let me finish. One of the things I admire most about you is your integrity, and I foolishly questioned that. I am *so* sorry." She added on a forlorn note. "I don't deserve you."

"If by 'don't deserve you' you mean that you are as capable of error as I am, then I'd say we were *meant* for one another. But you need to know – "

With a laugh, she cut in once more. "I love you, Abraham Ahmad Yousef. And I think you're right about being meant for each other, so I'm afraid you're stuck with me."

Savoring the tenderness in her voice, he made a final effort to communicate his vital piece of information. "I met with the auctioneer today, but he didn't believe me."

"And now that we've gotten past this ridiculous fight, I just want to get – wait. *What?*"

"I met with Mr. Gerzsewski and tried to point out several of the things Tim and Derek told us about, but it all went wrong. Or maybe I should say it all went right. The auction is going forward as planned tomorrow, and I intend to be there with bid in hand."

Angelica and Derek could hear Amy's scream of elation all the way in the kitchen.

The Skinner estate was sold at auction for $109,000 and, after tacking on the auctioneer's fee, Abe and Amy walked away with a bill of sale for just over $125,000. The closing date was set for the week of the wedding, and even though both would have preferred moving in immediately, they recognized the impossibility of embarking on such a task with all the other activities planned prior to the celebration. After all they had been through, it didn't really matter. Move-in could wait until after the honeymoon. They had a home.

CHAPTER 8

Don't lust for her beauty. Don't let her coy glances seduce you.
Proverbs 6:25 (NLT)

The Murdock family had fallen into a satisfactory and surprisingly restful routine, as far as Aunt Reenie and Mattie and Drew were concerned. Brittany alone seemed to grow increasingly irritable and on edge with the realization that their residence in Tinkers Well was permanent, at least temporarily. While the others became more involved with activities in the local community, Brittany grew more aloof.

When not languishing around the cottage, she spent most of her days driving off to who knew where in search of her own unique brand of entertainment. Aunt Reenie could only speculate on what attractions drew her niece so frequently to the city. As far as she knew, they had severed any social ties there, other than those with distant relatives in whom Brittany had little interest. But she rarely failed to make it back in time to pick up her sons at school, and in those few instances, she had been so touchingly contrite that Reenie had withheld judgment.

Living simply, as limited finances constrained them to do, brought into sharp contrast the different worlds inhabited by the two women. Reenie lived to serve and to make a home for whatever relation she was currently living with. She found comfort in providing a place of constancy and shelter for two little boys who understood little of what had happened to the father they adored, or why it was necessary for him to leave them. She encouraged each one to bring home every scrap of artwork they created at school and found cheap, secondhand frames in which to display them. Periodically, she included one of their childish drawings with her letters to their father.

The primitive, colorful designs added a splash of color to walls that were otherwise devoid of personal touches, except for a large oil portrait of Brittany commissioned by Matt on the occasion of their wedding. The idea had been planted by the bride without any conscious awareness by her groom. He had thought it a gift for him to treasure. Brittany had encouraged him in his mistaken belief. When the fatherless family moved to their present home, she had sold any other paintings, wall hangings, or sculptures from their previous lavish home décor in order to pad their limited coffers. Mattie and Drew hardly missed that aspect of their former life. They rather preferred runny finger paint art and paper plate flowers with droopy, glued on leaves. And with the help of Aunt Reenie, they folded enough Origami animals to constitute the zoo currently residing on the broad mantle over the fireplace.

Compassionate teachers helped them make the transition to a new school, even going so far as to provide them with what they called "play clothes" in place of the khakis and button-down shirts the boys wore on their first day of class. Children can be merciless when teasing peers that look different than the local norm. Brittany had been a bit put out by such interference until she understood that she was not expected to bear any expense for the clothes. The downgraded wardrobe was drawn, unbeknownst to her, from donations to the school for students in need. She kept her comments of censure for her sons, who seemed unaccountably proud of their jeans and flannel shirts worn over colorful tees.

Though the boys continued to struggle with the loss of their father, they felt more at home in the small town than they ever had in the larger city and happily accompanied Aunt Reenie to Sunday school and church each week.

Their eyes and hearts were open to the novel experience of singing about a Heavenly Father, someone who created them and loved them, even though they had never seen him. As children do, they quickly picked up on the tunes of the hymns and worship songs, and eagerly participated in the responsive scripture reading. Some of the words were beyond Drew's vocabulary, but Mattie helped him where he could. And as much as they enjoyed taking part in the Sunday potluck brunch held at the home of Mattie's teacher, Mrs. Ludlow, they appreciated the impromptu football games instigated by the young men in attendance – weather permitting – even more. The men invited all the kids to participate – including girls (which Mattie and Drew thought quite unnecessary), and coached them on catching the ball, throwing the ball, and avoiding touch "tackling."

Brittany began to dread the arrival of the three churchgoers on the return from their rounds. She listened with barely concealed boredom to weekly recitations of new Bible verses, the recounting of everything they had eaten for lunch, and boastful accounts of their rival glories on the backyard football field. The boys couldn't conceive of anyone not wanting to hear descriptions of their new friends and role models. They made much of "Big" Tim and "Funny" Derek, and Drew took a deep interest in Abe, whose metal leg he had yet to sort out in his mind. Brittany listened until she could bear no more. She gently but firmly reminded them that it is not polite to talk about people with whom others in the conversation are unacquainted.

Reenie watched her reaction closely. She had been watching her nephew's wife for some weeks, trying to figure out what was driving the young woman to such ill temper. Brittany had never been quite so overtly critical when they lived in Kansas City, or while Matt was still in the picture. Reenie might have suspected her of pining for her husband except that her professed devotion to him had always seemed a little too artificial, too overdone, as if she was merely playing the part of the dutiful wife. And the role of doting mother was obviously wearing thin, especially since the boys had begun to assert their own personalities after discovering that jeans, sweatshirts, and sneakers were preferable to their previous "preppie" look. They also begged to have a pet of their own, like their classmates, who boasted of puppies, kittens, a pig, and even a descented skunk. Their mother quickly squashed that idea on the grounds of limited funds.

"We can barely afford to feed ourselves. You wouldn't want to get a pet and then not be able to take care of it, would you?" Brittany crooned at her persuasive best.

"No, Mama," answered a dejected Mattie.

"No, Mama," echoed little Drew.

"Good. Now that we have that settled, why don't you run along and play, or finish your homework, or whatever it is you do."

Aunt Reenie felt her fingertips digging into the palms of her hands as she watched the selfish young mother thoughtlessly wound her children yet again. Maintaining a generous spirit with an effort, Reenie told herself that Brittany never intentionally hurt anyone – she was simply blind to anyone else's cares but her own. In short, Brittany's ill humor and petty complaints arose from nothing more than being exiled from her self-appointed place as the center of the universe.

The Murdock family might have officially removed themselves from Kansas City society, but Reenie, without knowing it to be so, eventually decided that Brittany's frequent trips to the city could only be explained by a desire to mingle with her former society friends. The fact that she could no longer invite those friends to a stylish, professionally decorated home must have galled her. And as the weeks wore on, those trips became less frequent, causing Reenie to further speculate that those "friends" had begun to lose interest in Brittany or – what was just as likely – Brittany had lost interest in them.

As an only child born late in life to a kind, but simple couple who wanted nothing more than to indulge their lovely daughter's every whim,

Brittany discovered early on that, with a little coquettish urging, she could manipulate her doting parents to bend to her will. It became a game to see how far she could push them. Acquisition of a pony, dance lessons, a convertible on her sixteenth birthday, and the promise of her own furnished apartment when she went to college were tests of her power over them. Their agreement to a "little" plastic surgery for the vibrant young woman, who had convinced them that the procedure would boost her self-confidence, taught Brittany to expect to receive any and everything she demanded. Her parents were hardly affluent, but they were both committed to making their "princess" happy.

The more they spoiled her, the more she charmed them with her natural beauty and lively personality until she finally persuaded them that she would only be *truly* happy if she attended a college 300 miles from her home. They only agreed to the proposition after she broke into impassioned tears and professed how much she would miss them, adding that she was determined to make them proud through her academic pursuits. Brittany knew them far better than they knew their daughter. The distance had been carefully calculated to ensure that timid, parental home bodies would remain at a healthy distance. She reassured them with the fact that their darling could make the drive to or from their home in a day, thus negating the necessity for her to stop overnight on the road.

The promised apartment greeted her on her arrival, arranged over the internet by Brittany herself, who only demanded her parents' credit card to finalize the rental agreement. She quickly rushed several sororities but ultimately chose the one claiming honors as the most prestigious and well-connected. Then she embraced a new game – one with infinite possibilities. When she had wielded her bewitching appeal on the male members of her high school class, her success had been almost too easy. And her parents' ever-present oversight had limited her avenues of experimentation. Brittany, the college co-ed, spread her manifest charms indiscriminately. Athletes, scholars, frat boys, and young professors and teaching assistants were all grist for her mill. The more unlikely the conquest, the greater her desire for victory. Her more strait-laced sorority sisters frowned on her exploits. But those with a morally free and open attitude envied her the ability to bring any man under her power, then toss him aside when her attention was captured by a more promising quarry.

Though possessing a well-developed intuitive knowledge of male human nature, Brittany was certainly no scholar. She used her romantic liaisons to ensure passing grades in all her classes. The academic success she had promised her parents may have been merely a pretense, but their largesse and lenience in supporting her lifestyle might have dried up if her grades had gone down. The only true goal she had set herself was to marry well. Sprung from plebeian origins, Brittany had no intention of remaining in that class. She liked comfort, clothes, and pretty things, and she was smart enough to know that such treasure would only come her way if she found a man who had the one thing she lacked – money.

Unfortunately for her schemes, the connections she had hoped to make through her highbrow sorority had come to naught as jealous or overly judgmental sorority sisters had blocked Brittany's efforts to mix with the upper crust. Not one to be easily thwarted, she sought other avenues to the wealth she craved. It wasn't until she agreed to attend a boring investment seminar with another ambitious friend that her luck changed. The other girl, not so self-assured as Brittany, dared her friend to try her hand at one of the financial advisers giving presentations, arguing that anyone who manages other people's money must have a lot of his own. Enter Matthew Murdock.

A passably good-looking, soft-spoken young man ten years her senior, Matt would ordinarily have failed to catch Brittany's eye. But the outrageous dare had put the bit squarely between her perfectly even white teeth, and she switched on all their glittering power when introducing herself, asking with a pretty pout if he could help her with her "silly finances." She knew precisely how to gauge a man's interest, and Matt's had been pathetically obvious. So began a campaign that rivaled Sherman's march to the sea.

It was hardly an immediate *fait accompli*, however, for with every thrust forward by Brittany, Matt countered with intriguingly prudish objections despite his blatant desire. All the men in Brittany's other romantic encounters had understood the rules of engagement and had tacitly agreed to abide by them. Matt not only misunderstood Brittany's rules, he mistakenly reasoned that she didn't know what inner conflict her innocent actions produced in a man so in love. He was caught in a battle with his own honorable instincts all the while wanting to turn a blind eye to them. Matt's gentlemanly rejection of her more brazen advances was cat nip to a woman who had always had her own way, inspiring her to bring out the big guns and fire barrage after barrage of assaults on his senses and his shrinking conscience. Inevitably, he surrendered, as she knew he must, but her success presented two unforeseen and unique situations.

Brittany had enjoyed the battle far more than those so easily won previously, and she found herself actually caring for Matt, in as much as she was capable of caring about anyone besides herself. The second presented a problem she had carefully avoided in previous relationships. But her involvement with Matt had forced her to change her strategy, leaving an unexpected chink in her armor. While her eyes had been so focused on the prize, she had lost sight of her usually strict practice of employing precautions against collateral damage. While the resulting unplanned pregnancy had shocked her almost as much as it had Matt, she took it in stride and informed Matt that she would take care of it. His horrified reaction to her implied suggestion surprised her, though she was forced to admit that it was totally in keeping with his character.

"Brittany, my beautiful, wonderful Brittany, you can't possibly tell me that you would *ever* consider that option."

Brittany thought that a foolish statement, since that was precisely what she was considering, as had several of her friends who had followed through with such a decision at a clinic conveniently located near the campus.

"Oh, my sweet, innocent girl, this was never the way I planned to start a family, but it seems we already have. Forget that unthinkable choice. I know you want this child as much as I do, because it was conceived in love – our love."

Passion had driven him to his knees.

"If you'll have me, I promise to be the best husband and father in the world."

Matt's blind devotion, coupled with the sudden image of a wedding – a lavish wedding where all eyes would be on her – saved the day and little Mattie. Brittany had no sooner reluctantly surrendered the novelty of being a blushing bride than her attention was claimed by the need to augment her wardrobe to accommodate the life growing inside her.

Matt could barely keep up with the string of packages arriving almost daily, or his rapidly growing credit card bill. But as the game changed, Brittany adapted. She grew quite adept at pacifying her husband's qualms even as she was adding to his financial burden. Aunt Reenie's arrival had been a godsend, rescuing Brittany from the tedium of caring for an infant after the newness and adulation of producing one had worn off. But after two babies – and she made certain there were only two – her interest in playing house quickly began to wane. Her tepid affection for her husband and children remained, but her soul craved more – more attention, more stature, more excitement.

It had not taken Brittany long, after their whirlwind wedding, to figure out that Matt's financial standing was not quite what she had understood it to be. But she wanted what she wanted, and he had done everything in his power to meet her demands. When she finally emerged from the cloud of home life and took stock of her emotional needs and the family's monetary ones, as measured by her standards, she hit on an idea whereupon she could contribute to both. Slowly, one charitable board appointment or garden club membership at a time, Brittany made contacts and began to climb the elusive social ladder. The wives of affluent men might not have appreciated everything she had to offer, but their husbands did, insisting that she and that fellow – what's his name – be invited to whatever get-together they were hosting.

"Why, it wouldn't be a party without Brittany," was the statement heard in many a household, whether welcome or not.

As her popularity grew, so grew Matt's client base, and subsequently, their income. Brittany celebrated the achievement of one life goal after another: an expensive foreign sports car, a bigger home, invitations to the most exclusive events. Her plans were neatly falling into place when they were suddenly derailed without warning.

Sitting in the living room of a tiny cottage in the small and insignificant town of Tinkers Well, Brittany had to take several calming breaths to ease her strained nerves. She contemplated with disdain the primitive artwork adorning the walls, while the irritating sounds of high, childish voices at play rang in her ears. *Is it really worth it?* she wondered. *Can I see this through?*

"Granny Gert! Aunt Patty!" Rose jumped up and down, waving her arms to catch the eyes of two travelers stepping off the escalator on the airport's baggage claim level.

"Rosie!" Granny Gert shouted. With single-minded determination, the old woman, built along the lines of a miniature wrecking ball, plowed a path through slower moving passengers to embrace her granddaughter, then stood back to look her over with a critical eye.

"I suppose that young giant is still treating you right?" Rose radiated her happiness. "And I suppose you're still set on spending the rest of your life in Kansas, miles away from your old granny."

"If you mean, do I plan to spend the rest of my life with the kindest, handsomest, truest man I've ever known, then yes." Rose laughed when her grandmother rolled her eyes. "And yes, that means living in Kansas, which you know full well. And you *also* know that you're welcome to visit any time. Though I noticed you were quick to accept Aletha's invitation to stay with *her*, which tells me that the two of you will probably be plotting mischief before you've even settled in at *Fern Cottage*. It's a good thing you brought Aunt Patty with you."

A fair facsimile of her mother in both mien and physical make-up, Patty Gunn offered her niece a gruff but kindly greeting. In an aside, Patty warned Rose that her mother had insisted on bringing enough suitcases to clothe half of Harrington County, despite their limited one week stay.

"Oh, I know how she packs. Remember, I drove with her from Kentucky to Kansas – twice."

"You girls quit jabbering. I want to make sure no one accidentally grabs my luggage." After decades of dragging around the same two suitcases she'd had since she married Grandpa Ernie 60 years earlier, Gertrude Gunn's grandchildren, spearheaded by Rose, had presented her with brand spanking new, hard-sided luggage for Christmas, complete with wheels and adjustable handles. She was extremely proud of them and had checked and double-checked the labels on each one before driving to the airport with Patty. Now she watched the odd assortment of duffle bags, suitcases, and boxes circling around the carousel with an intent gaze, until she spied hers making their way towards her. She could hardly miss them – nor could anyone else. They were her favorite fire engine red.

She cried out in a voice loud enough to be heard on the flight line, "There's the first one, Rosie. Grab it! Quick, girl!" Rose retrieved it and the second, following close behind, while Patty claimed her own modest bag. Tim drove up just as the three ladies walked outside, and quickly loaded the bags into the bed of his truck. Loading Gert and Patty was a little more challenging. The young couple alternated between lifting and shoving their passengers into the back seat.

"I'd forgotten how high this monster truck of yours was, Sonny. You need to keep a little step stool in here for those of us who don't have legs that are ten feet long!" Tim made a mental note and the journey to Tinkers Well continued without incident.

"Is that you, Trudy?" Aletha had hurried outside when she heard Tim's truck pull up in front of Fern Cottage. She stood on the porch with Scout at her side to greet each visitor.

"Of course, it's me, Letha. Who else were you expecting?" The old friends slipped into the use of college nicknames, and the comfort of a long held and cherished friendship, as if donning well-worn gloves. Aletha excused herself from Gert's effusive greeting to welcome Patty, who had stood back to watch the reunion with an indulgent smile.

Leaving the threesome to sort themselves out, Tim commented with a grin, "I don't know how your Aunt Patty will get a word in edgewise."

"Oh, she doesn't mind. I think she's just pleased to see her mother so happy. So am I. I can't help thinking that Granny Gert has been a little… well… off her game over the past few months. She hardly teased me at all when I last called her. She even referred to you as Tim instead of 'Sonny.' Aletha has at least had the distraction of weekly visits from Miles, but since Christmas, those seem to have shifted to more time spent with *your* mom than *his* mom. I think this visit will do both our grandmothers good."

"I agree. And surely, they can't get into too much trouble in just one week," Tim prophesied optimistically.

Rose speculated in silence. *Or could they?*

"I know how busy you are right now, honey, but would you at least consider it. Those little boys are struggling. I've seen it before in kids of divorced parents, and though I can't give you any specifics, the situation they're in now is almost worse. And I know they'll feel comfortable around you, because of the time you spend with them on Sunday afternoons." Without giving her son a chance to protest, Marilyn hurried on. "And you mentioned asking Derek to fix up a flophouse while he's living in it… What? …Oh, sorry. You want him to *flip* a house after Abe's wedding, and Abe will be busy learning to be a husband. That leaves you as the only other childless adult male the boys know. The program doesn't start until after Easter, so you won't have any conflicts, especially since Rose attends the women's Bible study on Thursday nights. It's not like you'd be missing anything."

Except a few precious hours of blessed peace when I can vegetate in front of the TV in solitude, thought Tim on the other end of the phone conversation.

Marilyn mistook his silence for agreement. "Tim, you know how much this will mean to them. Thank you, thank you, thank you, honey. Your dad would have been so proud of you. Remember how important the Pinewood Derby was to you both when you were a Cub Scout? You and Peter used to spend hours designing your car, then building it, and finally watching it fly down the track. I don't think you ever won, but it didn't seem to matter. I expect it will be the same for Mattie and Drew.

"…No, I don't think I'm the one that should approach them about it. The idea would be much more effective coming from you. And you'll need to get permission from their mother. I've only spoken to her once, but I should think she'd be thrilled to have them taken off her hands for a few hours. Oh, goodness, I probably shouldn't have said that. I was unfairly critical. Let's just say she's not like any other mother I've ever met… No, Tim, you can't wait until after the wedding to talk to them. The other kids at school are already challenging each other for the trophy, and I can see how the talk affects Mattie, at least. I think if they knew they had something to look forward to, it might lift their spirits a little.

"So maybe you could drop by their house on the way home from work if you're in town in the next few days?...I know the barn takes priority right now, but I could have sworn I heard you mention to Derek last Sunday that you had to give the final stamp of approval on the bathroom remodel JT and Jason were finishing this week, so maybe then?...I know, I know. I am unprincipled, annoyingly persistent, and should be ashamed of myself for being so nosy and pushy ...I love you too. Give Rose a hug for me. 'Bye."

The glossy pages of a fashion magazine flipped past Brittany's listless gaze without making any impression. She threw the periodical back onto a coffee table littered with tiny trucks, children's books, and an odd assortment of rocks that seemed to enthrall Drew for no apparent reason. Strolling to the front window, she looked for a diversion, any diversion. Mattie sat at the kitchen table finishing his homework under Aunt Reenie's supervision, while Drew practiced reading out loud using the new phonics techniques he had learned that day.

Oh God, life is boring, Brittany thought. She was just about to turn away from the window when she saw a large, white pickup truck pull up next to her sports car. She waited long enough to spy two men getting out of the truck, then stepped back to run her fingers through her hair, and waited for the bell to ring. Her languid attitude left her abruptly as she opened the front door. If she'd been looking for a diversion, she was in luck; she had found not one, but two.

A ruggedly handsome man with blonde hair and shoulders that nearly filled the doorway smiled a shy "Hello," and entered the house as Brittany waved her arm in welcome. The gesture also included what, to her mind, was a shorter, deliciously chocolate version of the first, who flashed his own brilliant smile.

"Mrs. Murdock, my name is – " The introduction was cut short as two little human missiles launched themselves at the visitors.

"Derek!" Drew hit his new friend with such force that Derek had to grab the doorframe for support.

"Whoa, little man. You almost knocked old Derek over. How's it going?"

Mattie followed suit with "Tim!" but stopped short of wrapping his arms around Tim's long legs, awkwardly offering his hand instead. Tim shook it, then grabbed the little boy's shoulder and shook it roughly, which brought out Mattie's broadest grin. A fierce competition for airtime then ensued.

"Derek, you wanna hear a good joke?"

"Hit me with your best shot," Derek said, squatting to address Drew eye to eye.

"What do you call a lazthy baby kangaroo?"

Derek gave his best impersonation of someone thinking hard. "Umm – a sloey joey?"

Drew responded with glee. "No, thilly, a *pouch* potato!"

"Why do you keep trying those dumb jokes?" Mattie said with the disdain of an older brother, trying, unsuccessfully, to sound more mature. "They don't want to hear those. I'll bet they came by to play football, right Tim?" The pitifully hopeful suggestion hit Tim squarely between the chambers of his heart.

"Now boys …" Brittany began, miffed that she had been thrust out of the limelight.

Quickly forgetting his brother's earlier critical performance review, Drew jumped on the idea with both feet. "I'll bet you're right, Mattie," he said with a partially toothless grin.

Brittany tried again. "I'm sure these nice gentlemen didn't come to – "

"We don't have a very big yard but – "

"But the park ith juth down the street," Drew finished Mattie's thought eagerly.

Far from appreciating his younger brother's assistance, Mattie turned in resentment to the usurper who had stolen the idea that would secure him a place of prominence before his two idols. "Hey, I was gonna say that."

"Boys, really, you must remember your manners…" Brittany had clearly lost control of the situation.

Tim, recognizing the signs of anarchy building at an alarming rate, placed a finger in each corner of his mouth and split the air with a piercing whistle that shocked everyone into momentary silence. He placed his hands on two little heads, forcing them to look at him and said, not unkindly, "Pipe down, you knuckleheads," a form of address that found instant favor with the would-be assailants. They both grinned sheepishly and shoved each other lovingly.

"Sorry, Drew."

"Me too, Mattie – but I thtill don't see –"

"Uh, we're not starting that again. Now you need to apologize to the ladies present. Gentlemen should never start fights in front of ladies." Shamefaced regrets having been duly directed at their Aunt Reenie, who was quite impressed by the way the situation had been handled, and at their mother, who was still dazed by Tim's masterly conduct, Mattie and Drew got back to the matter at hand.

"Why *are* you here?" Mattie demanded.

"And where ith Abe?" Drew added.

"You'll have to excuse Abe, little man. He's getting married this weekend, so he's a little busy right now," Derek explained.

"Getting married?" Drew was not impressed. "To a *girl?*"

"Well, yes. You see, God made us men so that we'd *want* to marry girls."

Drew pondered the explanation for a few seconds and finally announced, as if working out a perplexing problem, "I gueth Daddy married a girl." Glancing at his shapely hostess, Derek nearly burst out laughing.

In an effort to keep the visit on a more sure footing, Tim spoke quickly. "I'm sorry I let these two goofballs get a little out of hand, ma'am. My name is Tim Ludlow, and this is my friend and business partner, Derek Warner. We're here to ask your permission to invite your boys to participate in the Pinewood Derby workshop at our church beginning the week after Easter. They're already Cub Scouts, so they're eligible to compete. The weekly Thursday workshops help fathers and kids prep their cars. And, well, since your husband is away on business, and my wife and I don't have any children yet, I hoped you might let me borrow Mattie and Drew for a few hours each week."

Football was forgotten. The boys stared in awe at Tim, then at their mother, and held their breath. She didn't even look at them. Her eyes were on Tim. She had never met a man with such authority before. Matt was a loving father, but he coaxed rather than commanded obedience from his children. Here was a man who spoke kindly and diffidently one moment, then, almost effortlessly, demanded adherence to his words without question. She liked it. She liked it very much.

"I've always said it's healthy for boys to let off a little steam now and then," she said in such a way that Tim was a little in doubt as to what boys she was referring to. Derek, watching like a fly on the wall, bit his lip again. He was pretty sure he knew. Mattie and Drew stood with their mouths hanging open. They had *never* heard their mother utter such words in their short lifetimes.

"I'm sure we can work something out. Why don't you and your friend," here she paused to wink at Derek, "have a seat and we can chat." There was no escape. Brittany wrapped a hand around the pronounced biceps in each man's arm and led them to the couch where she positioned herself between them. She seemed incapable of saying anything to either of her guests without leaning close to them while keeping a hand on each man's leg. With an effort, they managed to escape 10 minutes later.

"Phew!" Finally headed to Derek's house, Tim spoke his mind. "That woman scares me to death!"

Derek let out his bottled-up laughter. "Dude, I wish you could have seen your face. You looked like you were being hypnotized by a she-wolf ready to pounce on her prey."

"I think I was." Unable to withstand Derek's infectious laughter, he added on a chuckle, "I'm not going anywhere *near* that woman again unless Rose is with me."

"Coward."

"You better believe it!" Tim agreed readily. Brittany would have been shocked by his comments. She found Tim a fascinating replica of Matt, only bigger, stronger, more handsome, and infinitely more masculine. The immediate future suddenly looked brighter.

CHAPTER 9

"Don't be afraid of them. Remember the great and awesome Lord, and
fight on behalf of your brothers, your sons, your daughters, your
wives, and your families!"

Nehemiah 4:14b (NET)

"We are sorry. The number you dialed is disconnected or is not in service."

Matt Murdock tried the phone number three times with the same unsatisfactory result. Other inmates were waiting to make calls, so he reluctantly hung up and made his way back to his cell. It was the middle of March and two months since he had seen his wife during her sole visit to LCF. The absence of any written communication during the intervening period had disappointed him more than it had alarmed him. But the total lack of contact with his family began to worry him — a lot.

Images of the worst kind flashed through his mind: Brittany injured in a car accident — he had warned her numerous times that she drove too fast; one of the boys sick or missing — what did they really know about the community of Tinkers Well; Aunt Reenie near death — after all, she was seventy-eight. *No*, Matt told himself. *You're overreacting. There must be a simple, reasonable explanation.* He sat on his bunk, staring at the opposite wall as if seeking answers from the rows of unyielding cement blocks. His eyes kept coming back to a three-by-five-inch index card mounted among many others. The prison chaplain had provided the cards for members of

140

his weekly Bible study, encouraging them to capture what he called "inspiration verses" that could speak reassurance or comfort or confidence at a glance.

Only the wise know what things really mean.
Wisdom makes them smile and makes their frowns disappear.
Ecclesiastes 8:1 (GNT)

Though he didn't feel much like smiling, Matt closed his eyes to seek the source of all wisdom. He opened his mind to an answer, to reason. He sat there breathing deliberately – in and out, in and out – when an infinitesimal flicker of light darted across his brain. It passed so quickly as to be almost imperceptible, but he had been learning to examine himself, to be open to truth as he faced his weaknesses and failings with humility and candor. He was totally unprepared, however, to do the same as regarded his beloved wife. So horrified was he at the implications of the impossible, unwelcome thought that he shut it out, tried to slam a heavy iron door against its intrusion into his consciousness. But it was too late. The arrow of doubt had penetrated his thought processes, and he almost cried out in revulsion.

It's not possible! His agonized brain shouted. *Brittany would never intentionally cut me off. She loves me, loves our family.*

"That's it!"

His own protestations had provided the answer. Weak with relief, Matt muttered aloud in an undertone as if to add credence to the assurances that had finally broken through his tortured mind. "She changed the number on her phone to protect her and the boys and Aunt Reenie from annoying condolence calls." They had never really had any close friends as a couple, but old acquaintances and work associates might think they were being supportive by calling her. "Brittany would hate that," Matt continued to mutter. He had to admit, though reluctantly, "And she's so busy taking care of our family that she just forgot to tell me. Oh God, what a mess!"

Even if he'd had access to Facepage, which he didn't, he knew she rarely bothered to check the page he had set up for her. Matt was prepared to acquit his wife of any willful action in their present communication conundrum, but for the first time in their marriage, he felt a twinge of annoyance toward her. He shook off the strange sensation and set his mind to solving the problem at hand. He was not about to lose touch with his family. If he had to fight for them from a prison cell, then so be it.

"Maybe I could bring in a third party somehow…"

Joy should be pure and unalloyed, not tinged with pain or regret or sadness, though it so often is. Mothers endure intense pain and indignity to welcome a precious new life into the world. Parents must resign themselves to no longer being the most important people in their children's lives when a son or daughter-in-law joins the family amid jubilant celebration. A successful career with highly coveted promotions often demands sad farewells when the job moves a family across the country or across the world.

Abe experienced just such a dichotomy of emotions. His wedding was less than a week away, and he looked forward to the event with barely contained impatience. But he also carried a constant ache for what he would miss on that day. The big barn would be filled with Amy's family, Community Church friends and co-workers, but no Yousefs would be present to witness and celebrate this milestone in Abe's life. He had always imaged that one of his brothers, Fahkir or Husam, would be standing by his side as he spoke his marriage vows, and that his parents would be sitting in the front row, anxious to welcome their new daughter into the family. But he had regrettably accepted the truth – that image would never be realized.

His father had utterly cut him off at their last parting, and subsequent emails between himself and his mother had been somewhat stilted, almost insistent on enforced commonplace. He had accepted her absence at the festivities; he would have feared his father's retribution had she dared to disobey his mandate of separation. But he longed for the deeper understanding they had shared immediately following his departure. It was almost as if she had retreated behind a shell of affectionate pleasantries. Perhaps she wrote in a more reticent vein in case his father somehow intercepted their correspondence. Whatever the reason, Abe was doubly thankful for his adopted brothers, Tim and Derek and committed to embracing the occasion of his wedding without any hint of regret. He loved Amy with every fiber of his being and with every conscious thought, and the beginning of their life together *must* be a day of rejoicing, with or without any other Yousefs present.

"Chaplain Reardon, I need your help." All the other regulars of the midweek Bible study had left, and Matt was helping the prison chaplain load folding chairs onto a rolling rack. A guard looked on from the doorway.

Jeff Reardon had been a prison chaplain for over ten years. It was a uniquely challenging calling, but he had embraced it, and he had learned the ropes with his share of missteps. Religious figures and social workers are easy targets for prisoners who attempt to use the innate kindness and sympathy of such people to their advantage. After falling prey to such manipulation a few times, Chaplain Reardon's discernment skills had been sharpened to a keen level of perception. He welcomed all newcomers with warmth tempered by a healthy dose of skepticism. Upon meeting Matt Murdock, however, he had taken to the younger man immediately. Matt's ingenuous attitude and naturally respectful behavior spoke more of an honest seeker than a dissimilating schemer.

"You understand that I cannot promise you anything, and that I must clear your request through the warden, but I'll see what I can do. I think you are wise in contacting the school as a starting point. They won't be able to answer you directly – probably won't even answer me, for that matter – but they can forward your concerns to your wife. It will be up to her to act or not." Matt's frown deepened at the other's final words. Instinctively, the chaplain reached out to squeeze Matt's shoulder. Physical touch was something he rarely allowed between himself and prisoners.

"Put your trust in the only one capable of carrying your burden, son, and let go of worry. Your family is in his hands, and nothing you, nor I, nor your wife can do will ever change that. Have a little faith."

For the first time in weeks, Matt felt his load of cares growing gradually lighter.

Wedding week was well underway with plans coming together. Dresses had been picked up and music rehearsed, and accommodations stood ready for visitors. A final grading of the new gravel parking lot at the barn, marked off by railroad ties, received Tim's stamp of approval. And an industrial size gas stove and dishwasher, salvaged from a repurposed restaurant two counties away, were delivered and installed three days before the big day.

The inaugural booking for *Willow Walk Weddings* was more than a grand opening. It was a special event for the Tinkers Well community and *Three Brothers Construction, Inc.*, and marked the beginning of a new life for two of the most likeable people in town. Abe and Amy had wrestled for hours over how to limit numbers; they wanted to invite everyone from the mailman to bank tellers to the entire staff at *Milly's Diner*. They managed to cap the invitation list at 100, which was reasonably conservative considering part of that number represented several places for individual guests the two had allotted one another after mutually refusing to disclose who the guests were.

The air was charged with excitement when Abe knocked on Amy's front door. He wasn't sure why she had been so insistent on his attire for the evening, but he had duly donned the leather jacket and soft pullover sweater she had given him. His jeans were freshly pressed (representing one of Angelica's last acts of maternal care) and his black cowboy boots shone. Amy's parents had gone to great lengths to find low cut boots that would accommodate his prosthesis. Their efforts on his behalf at Christmas signaled not only their acceptance, but their sincere affection for their prospective son-in-law.

While he waited for Amy to answer the door, which was curiously locked, Abe wondered if her parents had arrived early, and the evening was meant to be some kind of pre-rehearsal wedding dinner. Just then, the door swung wide, and Amy stood there looking as lovely as he had ever seen her. She wore a loosely fitted blue dress with sleeves to her elbows and a rounded neckline that highlighted her well-defined collarbone. Her hair was shining, her face was beaming, and she was clearly filled with so much excitement and anticipation that she looked ready to jump out of her skin. Abe was a little mystified when she held him at arms' length instead of willingly accepting – and returning – his kiss of welcome, as was her custom. His eyes followed her arm pointing toward the living room where three figures jumped up from the couch and turned to yell, "Surprise!"

Abe stood rooted to the spot, unable to believe his eyes. Words failed him; his only feeble attempts at speech amounted to nothing more than suspended questions.

"What-?" was his first try, succeeded by "How-?" and followed up by the brilliant "You-?"

Thoughts failed him. Abe looked from Amy, who jumped up and down, clapping her hands like the bonus winner of a TV game show, to the three unexpected guests who waited impatiently for a signal from him. He managed only, "Uh-" before he was almost knocked over when first his mother, then his sister Samia, and finally his brother Husam alternately kissed him, hugged him, and slapped him on the back.

"Ahmad, my son, you look so thin," Mrs. Yousef cried, then looked at Amy. "You need to put some meat on his bones. I can give you recipes for all his favorite dishes."

"Ommy, I get plenty to eat —" Abe began protesting out of habit.

"Ommy, why are you so worried about food? Doesn't he look well? Ahmad, I told you the new haircut and goatee suited you. Amy agrees with me." Amy grinned and nodded on cue.

"Give the man some space. Good grief, you women will smother him before he has a chance to see my new basketball moves." Husam danced around his brother and jumped up to feign a shot. "I'll show you who's got game now, bro." He smirked like a million other cocky college students, sporting a school hoodie bearing the image of a navy commodore, with the motto "Anchor down" under it.

It was impossible. His family was here, in Tinkers Well — for his wedding! Abe would have pinched himself, but his limbs were still temporarily paralyzed. Surprise was replaced by supreme happiness until the magnitude of the situation pierced the bubble of his joyful delirium. It *was* impossible — if his father knew of their actions. They must have plotted around him, hidden the excursion from him. How would he react if — no, *when* — he found out? A cold wave of concern, almost of fear, washed over him. If his father could disown him, kick him out of the family, and forbid the others to speak of him, what would he do in reprisal for daring to actually associate with the outcast, and for the occasion of a Christian wedding at that?

"I would never have believed I could get you to shut up for so long." As the younger brother, Husam claimed credit for Abe's prolonged silence. "Amy, I don't know what you see in this tall bag of bones, but he doesn't deserve you." The two exchanged a high five and all eyes rested on Abe who continued to stand helplessly silent.

It was clear to Abe that what, at first, had appeared as the glorious impossible, was the result of a collaborative effort between his fiancée and the more foolhardy members of his family. That it had quickly degraded in his stupefied mind to one fraught only with peril, resulted in his initial delight being equally downgraded to fear – fear and irrational resentment. The saner, reasoning half of his brain recognized that Amy had only acted out of love and a sincere desire to lessen the unspoken pain that Abe bore over separation from his family. Regrettably, that rational voice was drowned out by one shouting, *How could she have put them in such danger? God only knows what the consequences of their ill-conceived folly may yet be!*

As Abe fought to keep his voice steady, he looked at Amy and said in measured tones, "May I have a few words in private with you, my darling?"

Amy knew her success to be complete. Abe's wish for privacy could only be explained by a desire to thank her in a more tangible way, one that might prove embarrassing for the others present. Iffaa Yousef knew better. She had not been his mother for 30 years without recognizing the signs of controlled anger and chided herself for not anticipating this reaction. Not willing to allow Abe's foolish notions to ruin the evening or to hurt the young woman she had grown to love through the witness of Amy's demonstrated character, Iffaa broke quickly into the conversation to intercept her son's misguided thoughts.

"That's all well and good, my children. You two will have the rest of your lives to moon over one another, but I claim a mother's privilege to speak with my son first. Come, Ahmad. There is much I would say to you before you embark on the path of matrimony. Will you forgive me, Amy?"

Amy found it so touching that Mrs. Yousef wanted to give Abe some pre-wedding advice, she gladly relinquished her claim on his time and affection. "I'll just finish getting dinner ready. Samia and Husam can help me."

"Cooking is woman's work," Husam responded with mock scorn. "I think I would rather relax and check my phone." But the overconfident young man had met his match in Abe's bride-to-be.

"Do you want to eat, buster?" Amy demanded, brandishing a wooden spoon. Husam grinned in defeat and accepted the knife held out to him. "That bread needs to be buttered and sprinkled with garlic powder before it goes in the oven."

Samia put her arm around Amy and sighed. "You're my *favorite* sister-in-law."

Ordinarily, both Abe and his mother would have enjoyed Amy's masterful handling of the youngest Yousef, but one was too focused on coercing the other into unwelcome dialogue for either to notice. Abe's mother pushed him through the bedroom door and shut it.

She held up her hand to stop Abe before he could speak. "Don't you say a word, Ahmad, until I've said my piece." She motioned toward the bed. "Please sit down. You have me at a supreme disadvantage when you are standing." Abe obeyed silently.

His mother began to walk nervously around the room, which wasn't easy considering it was now crammed with boxes of Abe's belongings. She, like Samia, wore a long, full skirt and a long-sleeved shirt, but both had dispensed with the hijab for the evening, enabling her son to take note of the gray hair he remembered from the trip to his parents' home six months earlier. It was now liberally streaked with white, causing him to wonder at the strain she might have been living under.

"Do you have any idea what that young woman has gone through on your behalf? She had to track down Samia's email address from Husam. She helped Samia set up a new email account – one unknown to your father – and set up a schedule of regular messaging. Either Samia or I have been writing to Amy almost every day for the past three months, and we called her on the burner phone she provided us to use when we were away from the house so that we could speak with one another. It was mailed to Samia's student mailbox. Amy's actions sprang purely from a loving heart. She wanted to introduce herself and get to know us, because she understood how important we are to you.

"But let me make this clear. Although Amy expressed a desire for us to be here for your wedding, she voiced the same concern over angering your father that you, no doubt, are laboring under. It was Samia and I who ultimately made the decision to make the trip. Amy was thrilled with the news, though she still worried about us. I assured her then, as I am assuring you now, that I can handle anything your father chooses to accuse me of. We have been married for over 30 years, and believe me when I tell you that there is much I have forgiven him — things that were far more hurtful to me than his merely being forced to accept the natural desire of a mother to be with her son on his wedding day." She stopped for a moment to still her rising emotion.

"Ommy, are you telling me that Aby *knows* you are here, and he is okay with it?" Abe could hardly credit such a preposterous idea with truth.

"It was a happy coincidence, or as Amy put it — God's timing — that your wedding occurs on the same weekend as the end of both Samia's and Husam's spring breaks. I explained to your father — truthfully — that she and I wanted to drive to Tennessee to visit her brother over the holiday. Husam was ready to continue the journey when we got there."

Abe's continued grimace goaded her to add, "And if you wish to chastise me for not sharing the *whole* truth with your father, feel free to do so, but understand that I have every intention of telling him when we get home. If he wants to rant and rave and act like a child, then so be it. I was not about to let him ruin this opportunity for me and your brother and sister." Abe still looked worried. She sat down next to him and took his hand, speaking gently.

"Ahmad, marriages are complicated, and your father's and mine is no exception. I respect him and care for him as any woman would who has shared a home and a bed and children with a man for so long. But you cannot judge my actions or his based on your understanding of them from your position as our son. I never set out to defy him, but if I must, in order to fight for my children's happiness, I will."

Abe put his arms around his mother and leaned his cheek against her head. "Ommy, please forgive me. I have *no* right to question your motives, and even less to scold you for your choices." He kissed her forehead and looked at her with a rueful smile. "I am truly, *truly* happy that all of you are here, and I promise to be on my best behavior from now until – well, until I forget what you told me, which won't be anytime soon." Iffaa Yousef touched her son's lean cheek.

"Do you know who you reminded me of when you scowled at Amy and told her you 'wanted to speak to her privately' like the emir of the palace?"

"I did not scowl."

"You scowled. Just like your father." Abe was shocked and more than a little displeased at the comparison. But he was an honest man, and he immediately cringed as he remembered his dictatorial attitude about the house purchase and his unwillingness to listen to Amy's input. "Oh yes," she said, nodding. "You sometimes assume that same autocratic air. And where do you think you got your rebellious, independent streak? You two are more alike than you may care to admit. Think about that."

With a few judiciously placed comments, she had succeeded in getting through to him more effectively than four weeks of pre-marital counseling. Iffaa stood and bent to kiss her thoroughly chastened son. "Now I will send Amy in to you, and I trust that your words to her will be full of love and gratitude and humility. She is a gift beyond price, Ahmad. Never forget that."

Amy entered the room a few minutes later with an impish grin on her face, but when she found her groom staring out the window with a frown between his eyes, the grin faded. Abe glanced at her and held out his hand. When she placed hers tentatively in his, he pulled her into the circle of his embrace and stroked her hair, saying nothing. She could feel the thudding of his pulse where her ear lay against his neck. Finally, he spoke with careful deliberation.

"Before I put my foot in my mouth or say anything stupid that can be misunderstood or unintentionally hurtful, I want you to hear this." Abe looked into her eyes, her glorious eyes, and said purposefully, "I love you, Amy Walker, more than I have ever loved anyone or anything this side of heaven. And I have every intention of marrying you on Saturday whether I'm good enough for you or not. I don't now, nor will I ever, deserve you, but I hope you will continue to overlook my failings and love me anyway."

"Oh, Abe, of *course* I love you. But why do you look so… so solemn? I thought you'd be more… well, more excited and happy about your mom and Samia and Husam coming to the wedding." She added doubtfully, "Did I do something wrong in reaching out to them?"

"No, my darling. You did everything just right, and you've given me a wedding present far beyond the scope of my feeble imagination." Abe smiled tenderly and pulled her close once more. "Have I not thanked you properly?" Without waiting for an answer, he proceeded to leave her in no doubt of his gratitude. Stepping away with some reluctance, Abe muttered, "Three more days. Just three more days."

Amy laughed the laugh of an ebullient spirit released from all care and worry. She grabbed Abe's hand and pulled him toward the door. "Shall we go take Husam down a few more notches? He's decided he's God's gift from heaven to the culinary world after prepping a loaf of garlic bread."

"Amy," Abe said, looking as if a peculiar notion had just occurred to him. He stopped short of the door. "When you suggested getting married somewhere other than the church, did it have anything to do with my family members being here?"

"Well, to be honest," she said, smiling ruefully, "I didn't really have much hope of any of them coming. I hadn't even tried to contact your mom or sister before Thanksgiving, but on the slim chance that anyone from your family *could* make it, I thought they might be a little more comfortable in a neutral setting rather than in a Christian church. I didn't say anything because I wanted to surprise you if it all worked out." As Abe stood there shaking his head, she asked with a little of her earlier misgiving, "Are you mad at me?"

"*Mad at you?* Are you kidding? I still can't believe you pulled this off!" He held the door gallantly for her, and they rejoined the family.

Abe hugged everyone again, this time without restraint. He might have withheld his unreserved affection had he known the visiting threesome would spend the next two hours dredging up innumerable embarrassing anecdotes of his youth and childhood. The stories kept Amy in stitches and instilled in the butt of every agonizing detail a calculated desire for revenge.

When the party broke up for the evening, Abe learned that his mother and sister were to stay with Amy until the wedding when they would join Husam at the Warner home. Angelica insisted that since she was losing one Yousef, she should have the honor of hosting the others. Iffaa was especially touched by the invitation. She felt she owed much to the woman who had offered such kindness to Abe in her stead. Iffaa and Samia retired to the bedroom to allow Abe and Amy some privacy while Husam took advantage of his brother's absence to claim the driver's seat in Abe's SUV.

The groom-to-be held his chosen bride's hands in a firm clasp against his chest.

"I won't see you again until the rehearsal on Friday," he said wistfully.

"I know. Rose told me all about your stag party – well, at least what she knows, which isn't much. She told me even less about my hen party, but I'm so glad your mom and Samia are here to share that with me."

"If I know Tim and Derek – and now Husam – they'll drag me out into the wilderness and expect me to sleep there."

Amy pulled her hands away to cradle his face. "My big, tough man," she teased him tenderly. "I'm afraid you probably won't get much of a reprieve from my brothers either. I *can* tell you that you won't be at Willow Walk. The ladies are taking over the whole house for the evening."

Abe's empty hands found their way around her waist. "Don't let Granny Gert or your Aunt Ruth say anything too outrageous. I shudder to think how Ommy and Samia would react."

"I'm pretty sure they can handle whatever shocking stories those two old dears can dish out. Remember, your sister is a nurse. I shouldn't think she would be much surprised by anything. She is, after all, a grown woman. I really like her. I think we'll be good friends."

Abe pulled Amy close and murmured in her ear, "It's obvious that they all love you. How could they not? I know I do." A brief kiss, and he was gone.

Amy leaned against the door after Abe left, still a little bemused by all that had passed that evening. She hugged the warm glow of those golden hours to herself and went about settling her new family members for the night.

Chapter 10

The month is the one when everything turned around for them from sadness to joy, and from sad, loud crying to a holiday.

Esther 9:22b (CEB)

A groundswell of excitement swept through those well-wishers who knew Abraham Yousef and his story best: rejection by his family, a tenuous reconciliation, and final separation. Now, miraculously, part of that family had arrived in Tinkers Well for his wedding. Certain plans had been set into motion the minute Amy received confirmation that Iffaa, Samia, and Husam would be in attendance. She may have successfully kept Abe in the dark, but other key players were notified in anticipation of the need to rework the wedding week schedule to include the newcomers. Chief among those was Angelica Warner.

Rightly anticipating Iffaa's desire to meet the woman who had acted as surrogate mother in her place following Abe's hospitalization, Angelica wisely asked Amy to bring Iffaa to visit her the morning after her arrival. Despite her son's evident excellent health and present happiness, Iffaa, nonetheless, carried much guilt for her complicity in his family's initial disavowal. She approached the Warner home with some trepidation. It dissipated quickly as Angelica's smile of greeting dawned.

Amy and Samia stayed only long enough for initial introductions before they were shooed out the door to finish some last-minute wedding shopping. Angelica invited her guest into the kitchen. Nothing breaks down barriers faster than a shared cup of tea at a kitchen table. Iffaa graciously accepted the gesture of hospitality and resolved to pay tribute to all Angelica had done for Ahmad in her place. She began a rehearsed word of gratitude and apology, which was all she had to offer for the love and care extended to Abe by the Warners. But Angelica stopped her when the other woman's voice began to tremble.

"Now enough o' that. It's really *I* who owe you a debt o' gratitude." Tears stopped abruptly to be replaced by surprise. "You see, Abraham — " Angelica stopped, suddenly aware that the adopted name might be offensive.

"Abraham is fine," Iffaa assured her. "He is a new man in so many ways. Perhaps his new name suits him better, but he will always be Ahmad to me."

Patting Iffaa's hand resting on the table, Angelica continued. "Abraham came to us at a time when *my* son was wrestlin' with his own wounds and scars. Abe helped Derek to find his faith again, in the Lord Almighty and in himself. They became brothers, and with Tim puttin' everyone to work and helpin' all o' them to find direction, those three grew to be as close as David and Jonathan in the Bible." Noting Iffaa's arrested expression, she added, "Here I go, makin' a reference to somethin' that must be strange to you."

"Is that the David who was a shepherd boy and fought a great giant?"

Now it was Angelica's turn to look surprised. Abe had only shared his mother's early history with Amy. "I didn't know that story was told in Islam."

"No, but I remember hearing it from the time I was a little girl." So at ease was Iffaa in Angelica's snug kitchen, that she shared the story of her Christian parents' sudden death and how she came to be raised by a Muslim family. The discussion was open and honest, and afforded Iffaa a curious sense of freedom. Eventually turning their attention to planning for the rehearsal dinner, with a menu that incorporated both their native origins and cuisines, their differences dissolved into nothing, and they became friends. By the time they had created a splash in the local grocery store by purchasing as exotic an assortment of ingredients as Tinkers Well had to offer, and then spending the afternoon prepping food for the feast, they were sisters.

Much to his relief, Abe's grave predictions about his bachelor party were so far off the mark, he would happily have repeated the program the following day if not for his wedding rehearsal and dinner, and the fear that Amy would disown him if he was absent for either.

The evening began with a rough, cold ride in the back of Tim's pick-up truck surrounded by ominous piles of camping gear – Abe's worst nightmare.

"I am *so* paying you back for this when you get married, provided you can ever find a woman foolish enough to take you on," Abe grumbled when Husam blind-folded his brother and helped him into the truck.

"And I am *so* going to remind you, you said that." The reply gave Abe pause to speculate on what was coming next.

A mid-trip transfer to a van, when he was thrust unceremoniously onto the end of a bench seat, only left him more confused. Though he was surrounded by voices, no one spoke to him or responded to his demands for information. It was if he had been sequestered in a reverse soundproof booth – he could hear everything in the van, but those around him seemed incapable of detecting his presence.

Rough roads were left behind, and eventually stop and go movement indicated city traffic. Abe's hopes rose. Exiting the van in a parking lot, he sensed crowds around him. When he was finally allowed to remove the annoying blindfold, Abe obeyed and was immediately struck dumb. Derek slapped him on the back of the head, and then there was no stopping the ensuing monologue.

"I can't believe it! We're in Mercy Park," Abe breathed in awe, slowly looking around. "I can't believe it! We're in the *Landing,* and, and – no it can't be." Turning to Husam, he grabbed his brother's arm, shaking it relentlessly, and commenting in amazement, "Do you *see that?*" he demanded, pointing at the scoreboard. "Washington United is the visiting team. *Washington United!* That's *our* team." Abe had only ever attended one soccer game, and that was when he took his two brothers to see their favorite footballers on a visit home to northern Virginia after joining the army.

"I can't believe it!" he said for the umpteenth time and quickly donned the Washington United jersey handed to him by Husam. Everyone grinned at his pleasure – everyone except Derek, who looked on with his hands on his hips.

"Man, you need a remedial course in having a little faith in your brothers. Believe it!"

"I will never doubt you again, my friend," Abe replied solemnly and lifted Derek in a comprehensive hug that left the shorter man's feet dangling.

Disengaging himself with an effort, Derek brushed himself off and said severely, "Okay, okay, you can save all of that," waving off Abe's embrace, "for Amy. Let's get some food before the game starts."

"Absolutely." Abe grinned and turned to the others around him. "But first I must thank you all for such a splendid idea. You had me worried for a while, but this – everything," he said with a gesture that took in the spectacular seats, the immaculate field groomed for battle, and the arching roof overhead, "is more than I could have hoped for. I don't know who planned it or how it was pulled off, but I humbly thank you."

"Enough with the hugging and the speeches, already." Derek insisted on moving past what he considered unnecessary sentiment. "This is *supposed* to be a par-tay. Let's do this!"

And they did. The match-up on the soccer field ended in a draw, making it impossible for either team, or their respective supporters, to claim victory or to go home losers, but the rival fans continued to contest the event all the way back to Tinkers Well.

Though slightly less rambunctious, Amy's hen party was just as memorable. Elegance replaced athletics, and stadium fare was shelved in favor of savory canapes and fruit shish kabobs. A lively game of charades broke down any vestige of awkwardness among guests from different age groups, ethnicities, and cultures, with a final act that brought the curtain down to screams of laughter. Granny Gert, Aletha, and Amy's Aunt Ruth joined forces to enact their clue like a chorus line of aged Rockettes run amuck. They jumped up and down, kicked, and waved their arms while chanting slogans from a bygone era, causing those nearby to lunge for lamps and vases in danger of immediate annihilation by Aletha's recklessly flailing cane. The "Cheerleaders" won the round and the game for the over-fifties team. Amy was still wiping tears of laughter from her eyes when she was reminded that it was time for her bridal shower.

Knowing that Amy wasn't likely to pamper herself at unnecessary expense with a recent home purchase, coupled with the associated costs of Abe's seminary career not covered by the VA, Rose had added to the invitations for the party a comprehensive list of gift suggestions for a bridal shower. Amy's initial response to Rose's suggestion that it be included in the evening's program was one of misgiving. She was worried about potentially opening gifts of a personal nature, such as lingerie, in front of the older ladies who would be in attendance. When she found out that Abe's mom and sister would be joining them, her anxiety grew. Though assured that she had nothing to worry about, it was with some misgiving that Amy peered into the contents of the first frilly gift bag. But as each thoughtful present followed the next, hesitation was replaced with heartfelt gratitude.

Stretched out on her temporary couch bed later that night, she glanced at the pile of shower gifts in the corner and smiled. Ultimately, sleep overcame her memories of the evening, and her dreams turned to anticipation of the future.

An army of Walkers, consisting of Amy's immediate family and a host of aunts, uncles, and cousins, descended on the wedding venue Saturday morning like a swarm of locusts, transforming the old barn into a romantic, earthy fairyland. Swags of fresh greenery draped the rail of the musicians' gallery, liberally interspersed with candles mounted in clamped brackets. On the main platform, underneath the gallery, a rustic trellis of branches made by the father of the bride, was stuffed with wisps of tulle and spring flowers, and wrapped around in twinkle lights. The potted plants from Amy's hen party had taken a detour to the barn for a follow-up performance before finding their way to Rose's garden. Forsythia, shining its golden splendor from wooden buckets scattered throughout the barn, was augmented with white and pink spirea.

Rose and Amy had spent some time trying to determine the best configuration of chairs and tables and finally settled on a V-shape with rows angled off the main aisle. Dinner tables were set up behind the chairs that would be moved after the formal ceremony to accommodate dinner seating and to create space for a dance floor. Each table sparkled with its own character reflected in the novel place settings the girls had accumulated over the past five weeks, and each was centered by a pot of spring flowers. Wall art took the form of delicate quilts made by Amy's great-grandmothers and hung on rods at varying heights around the room. The heirloom pieces, treasured by later generations, displayed the artistry, thrift, and ingenuity of her matriarchal ancestors in the vibrant patterns showcased: sunbonnet, Maltese cross, grandmother's fan, and Amy's favorite – and most appropriate for the occasion – double wedding ring. And thanks to her resourceful prior planning, the hanging antique windows were covered in childhood pictures of both her *and* Abe, lovingly provided and arranged by Iffaa and Samia.

The roar of the blowers from the industrial heating system added substantially to the bustle and noise of preparation, but by 4:30 the large space had reached a comfortable temperature and peace and quiet – relatively speaking – held its sway. Soon musicians could be heard tuning their instruments in the balcony. A layer of laughter was added by the caterers, banging pots and pans in the kitchen. Male voices joined the rising din as the groomsmen, relegated to the men's room until time to move into position, offered Abe their version of critical last-minute advice, which he found more humorous than helpful.

The sound of guests arriving, the hubbub of long-distant family and friends meeting, and the energy and air of expectancy inherent in every wedding swelled and overflowed in the sonorous fluidity of Mozart when a string quartet began the prelude. J.S. Bach succeeded Mozart as Angelica was escorted by her son to a seat of honor on the front row. Husam, following suit, frowned when he met his mother at the back of the hall. Abe had guessed correctly that his brother's participation in the practices of Islam had become merely a formality to appease his father. Even so, young Husam was indignant at the sight of his mother in public without her hijab. He, irrationally, felt no guilt about his tepid adherence to the family religion, but was obviously not pleased by his mother's lapse.

Iffaa Yousef had chosen to leave her long, thick hair loose on her shoulders, draped only by a veil. But she wore the delicate lace covering with the same dignity and grace as any painted on the pious head of a Raphael Madonna. Angelica provided a smile of welcome and a well-placed compliment when Iffaa joined her on the front row. Joyce Walker took her place on the left front row next to Lucas and his wife, who waited to corral their kids if they showed any signs of unruly behavior in the performance of their duties as ring bearer and flower girl. The musicians transitioned into the lively *Hornpipe* from Handel's *Water Music,* signaling the entrance of the groom's party. Rose, not sure Abe would remember his own name, let alone his musical cue, knocked on the men's room to tell them it was time.

Derek had graciously stepped back to mere groomsman status, giving Husam honors as best man. Liam Walker and Tim completed the intentionally low-profile processional along the outside of the seating area. Once in place, all eyes turned toward the back of the room. Rose caught Tim's eye as she floated by in a chiffon gown with a gathered cross over bodice that cascaded into a flowing asymmetrical floor length skirt. The bronze-pink dress was the perfect backdrop for a bouquet of pink and white tulips mixed with maiden hair fern. Both complimented the men's dark gray suits and sage ties brilliantly. An arch smile and a wink caused Tim's heart to skip a beat as it had a thousand times before. Amy's cousin, Sarah, followed. Then it was Samia's turn.

Immediately after confirming that Samia would be one of her bridesmaids, Amy searched diligently for a similar dress in the same fabric to accommodate her new sister's desire for more modesty. Unlike Husam, Samia did not condemn her mother for her choice of head covering, but she feared breaking the dictates of Islam on her own account. Fortunately, Amy came very close to meeting those requirements in a dress with long sleeves and a level full-length skirt. The neckline was still a problem until Iffaa suggested that Samia's hijab could be adjusted to cover her chest completely. Not only was the hijab functional, but the bright floral of the fabric gave the young Muslim girl a boost of confidence as she took her place with the other women. Becky, as Matron of Honor, entered last and turned to keep a stern eye on her niece and nephew making slow but steady progress to the platform, one scrupulously placed tulip petal at a time.

Amy, being Amy, didn't want a big fanfare to announce her entrance, so the musicians made a smooth, but subdued transition to Pachelbel's

Canon in D. The cello had finished one round of the familiar ground bass when Amy and her father reached the tables set up in the back of the great hall. She saw only Abe until she gasped and came to a full stop, her eyes flying to the musician's gallery. During the second iteration of the bass line, the cello was doubled by a reedy bassoon and Emily Miller's blatty horn. Her wayward trombone slide nearly knocked over a music stand.

Amy couldn't believe it! Four of her middle school students augmented the professional string quartet that took on the intricate melody note patterns of one of the later variations while the students squeaked, honked, and blared their way through a simple underlying harmony. Some of the guests present winced at the loosely controlled cacophony, directed by a fellow music teacher, but Amy wouldn't have traded it for a finely tuned symphony. She listened to the performance with ears of pride until her father urged her on. Amy's eyes once more found Abe. He grinned and pointed to the gallery overhead, then he gave her a two-thumbs-up sign. It had all been *his* idea! She laughed out loud in her delight at his wedding surprise. As she drew nearer, Abe's grin transformed into an expression of humble adoration as he beheld his bride.

Every bride is beautiful, but on that early spring day in Kansas, Amy outshone them all. The glow of her smile seemed to radiate from the top of her shining, loose brown tresses, crowned with a wreath of glossy leaves and baby's breath, to the hem of her flowing white chiffon dress. The fluid movement of the fabric gave the illusion that she was floating on a cloud. A fitted, brocade bodice, dropping to a point between the hips, accentuated her slender, lithe figure. Long loose sleeves looped over the third finger of each hand, and a high stand-up collar plunged to a modest V in front, highlighting the long, noble line of her neck. Amy embodied all Abe thought to be unattainable. He felt a little light-headed and his legs began to tremble.

"Don't you dare pass out on me, Ahmad," Husam hissed by his side, "or I'll never forgive you! Move your legs and breathe." Abe complied without thinking. "That's it, keep breathing."

Whether due to Husam's timely intervention or the touch of Amy's hand, Abe regained control of his shaky limbs as the two moved to stand under the trellis. Pastor Lindeman performed the simple, but meaningful vows, then moved smoothly into a message requested by the bride. The strikingly tall couple had been provided temporary seating, enabling the Pastor to address the guests present as well. Mark Lindeman was one of the other people Amy had contacted when she confirmed that Abe's family would be in attendance. She apprised him of her mother-in-law's roots in Christianity and asked him to present the message of the gospel in a way that fit into the wedding setting without losing any of its import and meaning. The words were spoken primarily to the bride and groom, but everyone listened respectfully. Iffaa Yousef listened intently, hanging on every syllable.

She and Abe had talked about his new faith when he tried to share his heart with her during his visit home the previous autumn. She had listened to him then but had been afraid to accept the full meaning of his words. She too had sought to maintain the fragile peace that kept the family together for that short season. Now she heard the story of a God who loves his followers, of Jesus who looks upon his church as a groom who delights in his bride. And with the words came flashes of deeply buried memories from the faith of a child. The pastor spoke of Jesus' first miracle at a wedding feast. He drew on scriptural references from letters written to churches in Ephesus and Philippi – cities of historical significance in Iffaa's part of the world. But it was his admonition to the bride and groom that brought her up short. He read words instructing Amy to submit to her husband's position as the spiritual head of the family. Submission, honor, and respect were concepts easily understood by Iffaa. Then he told Abe that husbands are to love their wives "just as Christ loved the church and *gave himself up for her.*" That spoke of personal sacrifice!

"Abe, that's what you signed up for," Pastor Lindeman said, looking intently at the groom. "Who do you believe is required to show the more extreme expression of devotion?"

Abe squeezed Amy's hand and spoke to her. "I am. And I do so willingly."

Then the pastor, reading from Philippians 2, reminded them of their calling as members of Christ's body, *his bride,* the church.

In your relationships with one another, have the same mindset as Christ Jesus: Who, being in very nature God, did not consider equality with God something to be used to his own advantage; rather, he made himself nothing by taking the very nature of a servant, being made in human likeness. And being found in appearance as a man, he humbled himself by becoming obedient to death—even death on a cross! (NIV)

Humility, service, obedience, sacrifice. This Jesus, who was somehow equal to God, gave his life for those he loved. And in so doing, he miraculously freed his people from the penalty and guilt of their sin. Iffaa definitely understood the burden of guilt. She wanted to hear more, but the Pastor was inviting those present to participate in communion. *Communion!* She was to have taken her first communion as a child, but her family had been killed, and her life changed forever. Now she spoke the words of the service, as printed in the bulletin, and tried to understand their meaning. The bride and groom were served the elements representing the body and blood of the Savior who died in their place, then all were invited to come as they felt called to do so. Abe and Amy waited under the trellis with their heads bowed, their thoughts full of one another and the solemnity of the moment.

Iffaa looked uncertainly at Angelica, who smiled and nodded her head gently. "Come. I'll go with you." Angelica took a broken piece of matzah from the plate held out to her. After eating it, she drank from a tiny cup filled with grape juice.

Iffaa found herself hesitating, but when she glanced at the pastor, he spoke with gentle compassion. "This is the body of Christ broken for *you*, Iffaa Yousef." His words compelled her to take a piece of the unleavened bread. "This is the blood of Christ poured out *for you*." She drank the juice and followed Angelica back to their seats. Her heart swelled, but she wasn't sure what had just happened.

"Am I a Christian now?" She whispered so quietly Angelica barely caught the words.

"Takin' communion does not make you a Christian. Admitin' your sin, understandin' that it can only be forgiven through belief in the power of Jesus' sacrifice on the cross, and choosin' to follow Him as the only *true* God – that makes you a Christian. And that happens when God's Spirit speaks to your heart. But I think you know that, because you've been listenin' to his voice, and you're ready to make that choice now, aren't you?" Iffaa nodded, amazed that Angelica could discern her thoughts so clearly. Angelica put an arm around Iffaa and prayed with her new sister in Christ. Abe may have been oblivious of his mother's actions, but Samia and Husam were not. One was alarmed and the other critical, but a discussion would have to wait.

Pastor Lindeman wound up the ceremony with a prayer of blessing. Abe contributed his part by supplying an enthusiastic kiss when duly instructed, and Mr. and Mrs. Abraham and Amy Yousef were introduced to exuberant applause. A proud and impatient young husband was about to step out with his wife before the closing music began, but Amy held him back, murmuring, "Wait for it…" Just then a thundering brass intro was heard over the sound system heralding a familiar triumphal march. Abe stared at his bride, amazed at what he was hearing. Then he threw back his head and laughed in exaltation. "*My* little wedding surprise," Amy said with smug satisfaction. The happy couple led the recessional to the unforgettable strains of the theme from *Star Wars*.

As Abe had requested, the follow-on reception involved a very full meal, and cake – lots of cake. It was only after dinner and the last of the ceremonial activities that Abe finally noticed Amy's footwear as they moved through a Texas line dance. Under her ethereal chiffon skirt, she wore white western boots.

"I am a Kansan, after all – cowboy," she said with such a provocative smile that he suddenly remembered the time.

They managed to make the rounds of the room and thank everyone for joining them for their wedding gala. Abe was only sorry that he had shared so little time with his family, but he had new obligations now, and knowing that they all supported him in *this* life choice, at least, filled him with profound peace of mind. Abe kissed his mother and wondered fleetingly at the strange expression on her face, then he hugged his brother and sister. Their presence had meant everything to him.

While Amy was sharing parting words with her much larger family, Derek pulled Abe aside and demanded his cell phone. Too happy to be suspicious, Abe surrendered his phone without question. Derek handed it back to him a minute later with explicit instructions.

"Don't look at the address. Just hit 'Go' and follow the GPS instructions. Got it?"

"Derek, believe me when I tell you that there is only one place I intend to go tonight, and I could find my way there with my eyes closed."

"Yeah, but that's not where you're going." Abe was more perplexed than ever. "And don't dilly-dally. You don't want to burn the place down."

"What on *earth* are you talking about?"

"And stop asking questions! This is a gift from Tim and Rose and me. Trust us!"

The newlyweds had planned to start their life together in their own place rather than in a hotel, and until they could move into their new home after the honeymoon, that meant Amy's duplex. Though counter to their original plans, Abe wasn't about to hurt his friends by turning down the generous gift of a nice hotel room, so he simply thanked Derek. In his turn, Tim pressed a key into Abe's hand, telling him it would open either of the exterior doors, then handed him a garage door remote and assured the bewildered groom that he would need it.

Final good-byes shared, the couple set off for a celebration of their own. Amy had no more insight into the unexpected "gift" than her husband, but both were more curious than concerned. Ten minutes later they sat staring at the iron gates protecting the new Yousef estate. Both were so shocked, they looked at one another without speaking. Abe pushed the remote button and the gates, previously opened solely by manual power, swung wide, welcoming the new owners. Still stupefied, they drove through the gates and peered more closely at the house. Muted light shone through the darkness from an upstairs window, now uncovered.

"Amy, love of my life, I don't know what this means, but I am fairly certain it's good."

"Abe, is it possible that someone got into the house and…" She didn't dare finish the question. She couldn't bear the disappointment if her guess was wrong. Abe helped her to alight, and the two walked, with growing excitement, toward the front door, now clearly visible in the glow from a new porch light. Using the key provided by Tim, the door opened smoothly on freshly oiled hinges.

"I think this is going to be a *very* good night," Abe said with a grin and swept all 72 inches of his bride over their very own threshold. A single bulb was the only light in the hallway, but it was enough to illuminate a trail of flower petals leading up the stairs. "A very good night indeed," Abe muttered softly under his breath when he followed his more agile wife up the stairs after locking up. He found Amy standing in the doorway of the front bedroom and put his arm around her as they stared in disbelief at the scene that met their incredulous gaze.

White crepe panels hung on either side of the triple front window and the single end window near the fireplace. Flickering candles, scattered across the mantle and along the raised hearth, cast a warm glow into the room. The subdued lighting turned Amy's somewhat lumpy queen-sized bed into a soft, sumptuous divan fit for a sultan. Lush pillows and satiny sheets offered the weary, and not so weary, a place of implicit comfort. Rickety, mismatched nightstands, long past their prime, were draped in more filmy crepe and topped by mellow lamplight with a vase of tulips on one and an elegant tissue holder on the other. In a room beyond, fresh towels hung next to a sink.

Amy's eyes filled with tears, and Abe fought to control his voice with an effort. "It would seem that our friends have given us another wedding miracle."

Amy nodded her head in silent agreement, then spoke through her tears. "When did they find time to do this? Your mother and sister slept in that bed last night. And look," she said, pointing at suitcases in the corner, "I just finished packing mine this afternoon. Derek must have gotten yours from your car." Overwhelmed by the gesture made on their behalf, she turned to her husband. "Oh Abe, I feel so unworthy of such thoughtfulness. Everyone has been so good to us."

Abe took her hands and looked into her eyes. "Amy, we are *all* unworthy, but God is not only a God of mercy. He is also a God of grace and blessings, and I am now more convinced than ever that one of the greatest blessings we will ever know is our friends."

He pulled her gently into the room – *their* room in *their* house, then more forcefully into his arms. "Now, are we going to stand here all night feeling humble, or are we going to honor their efforts by making use of this magical place?"

Amy carefully removed his boutonniere and reached to place it on a nightstand. She needed time to collect herself before daring to look again into eyes that glowed with suppressed longing. "I think it would be foolish to neglect so generous a gift," she said, finally lifting her gaze to meet his challenge, "and neither of us is a fool."

"No, my darling wife," Abe whispered, his lips a breath away from hers. His arms tightened around her. "And I can assure you, there will be *nothing* neglected tonight."

Sighing in deep contentment, Amy nuzzled his nose playfully and whispered back, "Promise?"

If actions truly do speak louder than words, Abe's answer nearly shouted the house down while his ever-supportive helpmate cheered him on. He was guilty of only one misstatement. There was something neglected that night – the world beyond the four walls of their own makeshift paradise.

CHAPTER 11

"Mama, Rose will be here soon to take us to the airport, and you haven't packed a thing!" After a search of Fern Cottage, which took less than a minute, Patty Gunn had discovered her mother sitting on the porch swing next to Aletha. Each lady was wrapped in a colorful, warm blanket against a blustery morning breeze. Scout had been given leave to roam the front yard in search of interesting scents.

Gert adopted a somewhat belligerent air and replied without looking at her daughter, "I know I probably should have talked to you about this before we left Kentucky."

"Talked about what?" Patty asked in a tone that reflected her misgivings. She knew from experience to anticipate trouble when her strong-minded mother decided to act independently.

"Now don't get all upset. Letha and I just thought that since I came all the way out here for the wedding, it would be silly to fly back after only a week, then have to do it all over again when I come to stay for the summer in June. So, I've decided to stay put." Her chin jutted out mulishly, daring her daughter to overrule her decision.

Judging it to be the most auspicious moment to add her mite, Aletha said helpfully, "That's right, Patty. Please say Trudy can stay. You see, I

170

didn't realize how lonely I had become until she and Rose came to visit me last year. And then we had such fun over Rose and Tim's wedding, and we've also been able to share in Abe and Amy's. I just can't bear the thought of her leaving now. You *will* take pity on a poor, helpless old woman, won't you?" she added for effect. Aletha Mason was neither poor nor helpless, but it suited her purpose to play her sentimental trump card. It rarely failed, except, perhaps, when trying that tactic on her more perceptive son and grandson. Luckily for the success of her plans, neither man was present.

"Aletha, are you sure? Mama has spent so much time with you in the past year, I'm afraid you may think she's imposing."

"*Imposing?* Patty, I taught you to have more sense than that. Can't you see that I am a big help to Letha." Gert's co-conspirator nodded on cue. "And to tell you the truth," she said hesitantly, not wanting her daughter to feel unappreciated, "as grateful as I am for you taking me in and all, well, Versailles is not my home. Never has been. All my old friends are in Winchester, and with you gone at work all day, I get awful lonesome." She shot a glance at Patty's face, which bore the blank look she usually reserved for the political arena. What Gert didn't know was that the lack of emotion in her daughter's expression hid the ache Patty felt on her mother's behalf.

Patty and her sister Beth had agreed on the need for their mother to leave the farm she and her husband had owned for over 60 years when their father, Ernst Gunn, died a few years earlier. It made sense to the two sisters that their mother should move in with the eldest – a spinster who had lived her whole adult life alone – thereby providing company for one another. But they failed to take into account Patty's absence during the day, and the wider social interaction so critical to many people as they grow older. Though gruff and opinionated, Gert loved her daughters and gave them full credit for their efforts to look after her. She put on a brave front and found purpose in taking care of the house and looking forward to outings with her three granddaughters. It wasn't until she accepted an invitation from her old school chum to visit Kansas the previous summer that she faced what had become the hollow reality of her life.

During the two short months of her initial visit, however, Gert and Aletha managed to unmask a ruthless villain, survive a threatening tornado, and perfect the art of matchmaking when they contrived to bring Rose and Tim together despite the odds. The old friends joined forces again to toast the success of their ploys as unlikely cupids when their grandchildren tied the knot in October. After a long, frigid winter that had driven them both into forced isolation, Gert leapt at the invitation to attend the Yousef wedding. Amy had written a note on their individual invitations, saying that "Grannie Gert and Aletha were everyone's grandmothers, and she couldn't get married without both of them present." An idea was planted, took root, and came to fruition on that brisk spring morning while they waited for Rose to arrive.

Patty said with as much sentiment as she ever revealed, "I'm sorry, Mama. I didn't fully think through how the move from the farm to Versailles would impact you. You know Beth and I only did what we thought was best."

"Of course, I do! When I was your age, I probably would have done the same thing if Mutti had lived longer. You won't understand completely until you're my age, and by then, Rose and her sisters will have to figure out what to do with you and their parents. But just for now, mind you, I'd like to stay here until the end of the summer."

Gert and Aletha had the sense to look a little wistful and expectant as if they hadn't decided the matter between them already. Scout looked up from his yard inspection to hear the verdict.

"I don't know what Beth will say, but if Aletha really wants your company…" Patty looked at Aletha, who threw her hands in the air and declared blithely, "Absolutely!"

"Then who am I to say no?" That settled, Patty took her mother to task for not telling her earlier. "I wouldn't have booked you a return ticket. Maybe I can change it to a later date," she mumbled as she retreated into the cottage to gather her things.

Rose was ecstatic over the news. The *only* downside to marrying Tim Ludlow had been the separation from her family in Kentucky. There would always be visits back and forth, but she knew that those with her grandmother would grow fewer and farther between as Granny Gert aged. Now she would be here for another four and a half months! Rose wasn't the only one who greeted the news of Gertie Gunn's extended stay with pleasure.

For some time, Miles Hawthorne had been, humbly, happily, and helplessly in love with his ex-wife. He wanted to spend every moment not claimed by the demands of his real estate development projects with her. But he was equally committed to rebuilding his relationship with his mother. The desire, born initially out of respect tinged with guilt, grew into renewed affection that continued to grow as he learned to better appreciate the woman who had given him life. Her courage and intellect inspired and humbled him. She faced more challenges daily than he did in any given year. Yet she always had a kind word and a hopeful outlook to share, even while maintaining a shrewd understanding of human nature and a philosophical acceptance of life circumstances. It had worried Miles for some time that she lived alone, though Angelica Warner continued her practice of visiting Aletha several times a week to care for her practical needs. He also took solace in knowing Tim and Rose lived nearby.

But he couldn't help noticing his mother's lack of energy and enthusiasm for life after the excitement of the holidays had waned, and her grandson's wedding had settled into a pleasant memory. Miles also noticed her complete turnabout in attitude with the arrival of her old friend, Trudy. The other elderly woman was hardly more independent than her blind friend, having lost driving privileges due to a string of minor fender benders. But the two seemed perfectly content to do nothing more than talk for hours about old school days, the life of Community Church, and the likelihood of a shared great-grandchild in the future. While Gertie Gunn was present to keep his mother company, Miles felt free to devote more of his time and attention to wooing Marilyn Ludlow in earnest.

He was still in the dark as to her affections, but at least they were friends – good friends; probably better friends than they had been when they were married. A much younger Miles had taken for granted Marilyn's devotion and unstudied beauty, not understanding the true worth of her character. An insecure young wife had known only how to admire and love her husband. It wasn't until the night she left him that she finally stood up for her principles and attempted to help him recognize the pitfalls of the path he was following. In the present, there was no taking up where they had left off. Both recognized the futility and undesirability of such an endeavor. They were very different people than the two who had married over 30 years before.

When they came together again in an almost unbelievably unexpected way, Miles had been immediately impressed by Marilyn's strength and dignity. And though she couldn't help but notice his handsome façade and engaging manner, it wasn't until he was confronted by elements of an unknown past, that she saw glimmers of hope for Timothy Miles Hawthorne, the man. Since then, they had reconciled over what had separated them and gloried in what they shared.

Long, comfortable chats over leisurely dinners, walks through the city after a symphony concert or visit to an art gallery, and the easy communion of worshipping together on Sundays drew the two together again. They built a new relationship, but this time it was rooted in trust, common interests, and mutual respect. Marilyn seemed to be content with that. Miles had hinted at something more a few times but had always sensed an emotional battle on her part. It was almost as if she wanted to let him further into her heart, but she had drawn a line she would not allow herself to cross. If he had to guess — and he *always* had to guess — he would have sworn that it wasn't a matter of her not trusting *him*; she didn't trust herself.

Miles had witnessed the personal struggle many times: in her youthful exuberance when they danced together at Christmas before she retreated into her shell; in the perfect peace they shared under a silent snow fall on Christmas Eve until the wind extinguished their candles and the moment; in her almost marveling reaction to his offer to help some of her struggling students with tutorials; and in the wistful smile that appeared whenever she watched him and Tim interacting as father and son. She seemed to long for the reestablishment of their family but was afraid to let herself accept such a possibility.

He continued to make progress on the special gift he planned for her and drew contentment simply from being near her. Miles Hawthorne was not a patient man, but with his recently expanded insight into the depth and breadth and height of sacrificial love, he was learning patience. He would continue to apply patience in his relationship with his Mari if it took the rest of his life — though he fervently hoped it wouldn't.

"Now Letha, what's going on between that boy of yours and Marilyn Ludlow?" After receiving news that her oldest daughter had arrived safely in Kentucky, Granny Gert decided it was time to get down to business. She and Aletha were playing *Go Fish* with colored braille cards at the kitchen table. Rose, looking on, scooped out baked potatoes and mixed the contents with some chopped ham, cheese, and sautéed bell peppers and onions before refilling the skins and sliding them back into the oven for a second baking. Tim was working late at a project in a neighboring county, so she had invited herself to Fern Cottage for dinner.

Aletha, who was winning, asked for twos.

"Go fish," Gert replied absent-mindedly, barely looking at her cards. "I'd say he's nutty on her. I guessed as much when I saw them together at Rosie's wedding. Why, she was glowing like a bride herself. So, what's taking so long? We might be ancient, but they're not getting any younger either."

Aletha drew from the deck. "Quite right. But I can assure you that he *is* pursuing her in earnest. And while I agree with you that Marilyn is obviously quite happy in his company, she still maintains a certain reserve. Your turn, dear."

"Oh. Do you have any fives?" Gert's luck was out again.

"Do you have any tens?"

"Here you go, Letha." Gert's opponent placed another group of four cards on the table. "But don't you have *any* idea what her feelings may be?"

"I am so glad you asked." Rose set the timer and joined the other ladies at the table. "Tim and I have been trying to figure that out for months. We *have* noticed that they seem to be spending more time together, but as closely as I've been watching them, Marilyn doesn't give anything away. They are obviously very *comfortable* together..." Rose concluded lamely, thinking that was hardly the mark of a hopeful romance.

"I'll try once more. Do you have any twos?" Aletha added the card from Gert to her remaining hand and laid it on the table. "And I'm out again," she said smugly.

"Are you sure you're not cheating?" Gert asked suspiciously.

"Shame on you, Trudy! I am merely paying attention to the game. But if you prefer, I'm willing to put the cards away for now and turn our minds to more important things."

"Now you're talking," Gert said, consigning the deck of cards to a nearby basket. Turning to Rose, she offered a pointed reminder. "Seems to me I recall a young woman who was quite *comfortable* with her tall giant of a friend until she opened her eyes one day and realized she was head over heels in love with him."

"That's true," conceded Rose, "but I practically had to be slapped in the face with the truth before I recognized it."

Granny Gert snapped her fingers. "That's it! What we need is a cata…catalophe…catastrophe? What's the word?"

"I believe you mean catalyst, dear."

"You're right, Aletha," Rose agreed enthusiastically. "We need a catalyst – like another tornado!"

"Merciful heavens! Let's not go through that again." Aletha appreciated inspired ideas, but there were limits.

"Catalyst," Gert muttered softly. "If a tornado is a catalyst, it sounds more like an act of God. I'm not sure how to pull that off."

"I don't know if it falls under the category of catalyst or not, but there *is* some secret that Tim and Miles share. I've noticed them talking quietly together and glancing at Marilyn as if it has something to do with her."

"Well, can't you wheedle it out of that mountain of man of yours?" Granny Gert demanded.

"Believe me, I've tried! But when he wants to, Tim Ludlow can be totally unwheedle-able."

Aletha suggested gently that they leave it in the hands of Providence. "I am as anxious as anyone to see Timothy and Marilyn truly together again, but perhaps we should trust the right circumstances will happen naturally to bring that about. Such a surprise might make things more exciting for everyone concerned."

Gert thought her friend's suggestion pathetically tame, but as the timer dinged just then, signaling potato perfection, matchmaking was shelved in favor of complimenting Rose on her cooking.

"Mr. and Mrs. Rosenbaum, thank you so much for agreeing to meet with me today. I know it may seem odd – a Christian clergyman asking for your help – but I believe your input could prove invaluable toward the success of an event planned for our church during what we call Holy Week on the Christian calendar. It was actually Derek Warner's idea that I approach you. I believe you know all the Three Brothers construction guys, or at least the original ones."

Isaac Rosenbaum radiated warmth and life despite the effects of age on his bent form. His drooping mustache and thick ring of white hair surrounding a bald crown reminded Mark Lindeman of pictures of Albert Einstein. His wife was a plump, kindly woman who took almost as much pleasure in talking as she did in cooking, her hands keeping tempo with her voice beat for beat.

"Of course. Such nice young men." Mrs. Rosenbaum clasped her hands together and smiled like an indulgent grandmother.

Though the Jewish seniors had been somewhat surprised to receive a request to meet with a local Christian leader, they respected his position as a man of faith and were truly desirous of getting acquainted with more of the population calling Tinkers Well home. They knew of no other Jewish families in town, but people are people after all, they reasoned, and all created by Adonai.

"Just so, my dear. Now what can we do for you, Pastor Lindeman?" asked Isaac. "Or would you prefer we address you in some other way?"

With a boyish smile, the younger man replied, "I'd be happy if you just called me Mark."

"Mark it is then. And we are Isaac and Deborah." The restraint of strangers was lifted. "Please take a seat and try one of Deborah's rugelach. Our young friends Derek and Abraham always seem to enjoy them when they do little jobs for us." Mark Lindeman would have preferred not attempting to speak around a mouth full of food, but he didn't want to reject their hospitality. He took one bite and realized the courteous choice had also been the wise choice. The pastry was delicious.

"First of all," he said, when he could, "my wife, Lisa, needs this recipe, and secondly, I'd like to lay out my vision for our event and your part in it. This will be a first for our church in many ways. It will not only meld Jewish and Christian traditions; it will also be a sort of 'Reality TV' kind of lesson in understanding more of Jesus' Jewish history. I've introduced many of these themes in sermons and particularly in our men's Bible study, but nothing quite replaces hands-on learning. And this would incorporate the entire church, young and old."

The Rosenbaums looked at one another, no more enlightened than they had been when the pastor had called them earlier in the week. Isaac commented doubtfully. "Of course, we are happy to help in any way we can. Jewish we know, but how can that help a Christian church?"

Strictly speaking, Isaac's claim to knowledge of Jewish traditions had been quite limited for a number of years. That had all changed when, as a much younger man, he met Deborah Steinmetz at the wedding of mutual friends. As the daughter of a rabbi who followed the conservative, middle ground of Judaism, Deborah had been inculcated with all things Jewish since birth and followed the teachings and traditions of the *Torah* and the rest of the *Tanakh* as her life's grounding. She had fully intended to marry a nice Jewish man of similar orthodoxy, but her heart was captured by the handsome young man in the tailored suit who wore his *yarmulke* as if it made him feel self-conscious.

He *had* felt self-conscious. Isaac Rosenbaum had grown up in a Jewish family that paid only token attention to holidays like *Hannukah,* celebrating them more as secular cultural events rather than religiously sacred ones. His parents left Germany just before Hitler's rise to power in the mid-1930s and learned of the full horror of the Holocaust from afar. They turned their backs on the God who had apparently turned his back on his own people. Assimilating as ethnic, non-practicing Jews into the melting pot of America, they vowed to protect their children from being ostracized by antisemites. Christmas trees and stockings were as prominent as the *menorah* and *dreidels* in their home, and Isaac grew up not believing in much of anything but hard work and success. He might just as easily have fallen in love with a Christian girl and been drawn to her faith. But it was Deborah God brought into his orbit, and with her advent, a return to Judaism.

Deborah married Isaac in the face of her family's disapproval with only his promise to attend synagogue regularly and to observe Shabbat and all religious feasts as appeasement for Rabbi Steinmetz' objections. Isaac would have agreed to almost anything to marry his beloved Deborah. But in the course of honoring his pledge, he discovered a spark of innate longing for knowledge of the God who had formed and guided the nation of Israel since his covenant with their great ancestor, Abraham. Isaac connected almost effortlessly with his centuries-old heritage in the timeless prayers and rituals of worship and learned to read and speak Hebrew alongside his children. So ingrained was his observance of yearly festivals and the weekly Sabbath that he effectively forgot they had ever been foreign to him.

Isaac became thoroughly Jewish and took great pride in the ancestry he had spurned before meeting Deborah. His only stumbling block centered around the prophecies pointing to a Messiah. Having embraced Judaism as an adult, Isaac was more inclined to challenge tenets of his faith than Deborah, who, for the most part, believed implicitly without question. Though even she had occasionally expressed doubts on that score.

How could Messiah arrive as a conquering king and a suffering servant simultaneously? This question had arisen after the two studied several passages in Isaiah – passages that were curiously and consistently omitted in synagogue. They discovered no answer, so the unsettling problem remained. Other questions persisted also. Were the prophecies meant to be taken literally? Perhaps he would not come now because he was no longer needed. After all, the Jewish people had weathered many storms without him. Isaac sometimes wondered if he would even recognize Messiah if he did appear, but he kept any uncertainty to himself, only speaking of the great mystery as it might encourage his wife.

As his knowledge of Judaism grew so did his awareness of those who were less enamored with his religion and people. In an ironic twist, Isaac's unexpected zeal for his native faith had not only given him direction; it began to make him suspicious and judgmental of anyone *not* Jewish. Only in the past few years had he come to realize that much of the distrust and animosity directed at him, or expressed by him regarding people of other faiths, was due largely to dogma and ignorance. Mark Lindeman's timely proposal intrigued him, for in it, Isaac recognized a mutual desire to break down those barriers. Perhaps in this act of sharing by the two groups who ostensibly worshiped the same God, he and Deborah could learn something too.

"Before I go into that," Mark said, "I must be upfront in telling you that core Christian beliefs will be presented as they tie into Jewish history and theology. I don't expect you to buy into those concepts, but you must understand that they will be present. If that's a game changer, I won't be hurt at all if you choose to pass on this project. I'll be disappointed, but I won't be hurt."

Deborah appreciated the man's honesty. "I think you need to eat more," she said, adding another pastry to Mark's empty plate, "and we'll talk." Having mastered the art, conversation flowed as easily as her stout coffee.

The Rosenbaums had never heard of such a venture as that outlined by Mark Lindeman, but they were intrigued by the pastor's vision and his desire to create a better understanding of, and appreciation for, Judaism within the Christian community. The date was agreed upon and their contribution to the script was set. Deborah was delighted that some of her kosher recipes would be incorporated in the evening meal. It never occurred to either of them to be concerned over any ideas they might be exposed to. They were firm in their beliefs, and both agreed that the occasion would be a golden opportunity to share their rich heritage and traditions with a sympathetic crowd.

The letter came as something of a shock. Until the unwelcome arrival of that jarring missive, Brittany Murdock had all but forgotten her absent husband. The initial disquiet she had experienced while settling into the obscurity of Tinkers Well had been somewhat mitigated by her frequent trips to Kansas City in search of distraction. But, as Aunt Reenie had astutely deduced, those interests began to lose their allure as the intrigue attached to them waned. The general malaise that followed evaporated the minute she made the acquaintance of one Tim Ludlow and his adorable sidekick, Derek Warner. The fact that Tim was married gave him an edge in the desirability stakes. She loved a challenge, and she couldn't imagine any woman, particularly one from such a dreary little hamlet, capable of offering her any competition. When she met Rose Ludlow, Brittany was convinced of her superiority.

Seeing Granny Gert and Aletha safely installed at Tanya Miller's salon, Rose acted on the guilt that had been nudging her conscience ever since Brittany Murdock and her family stepped into the diner and into the life of Tinkers Well. Rose wanted to atone for her unusually critical comments, despite a similar vehemently expressed assessment by Tim. She was determined to give Brittany the benefit of the doubt. Accordingly, she knocked on the door of the little blue cottage on Third Street with her sunniest smile at the ready. She had come armed with a gift bag containing a variety of small items: tea bags, a purse-size package of tissues, a few generic stationary cards, and a container of cookies fresh from the oven. If nothing else, Mrs. Murdock's little boys might enjoy the latter.

Rose had booked 10:30 hair appointments for her grandmother and Aletha, thinking she might run her little side errand at a time when the hostess of the house might reasonably be unengaged and available. Luckily for the success of her mission, Brittany spent less time on her toilet that morning than was ordinarily her custom, because she was still preoccupied by the letter the principal had handed her the day before. Rose's knock broke into those thoughts as an unexpected, but welcome diversion.

Brittany opened the door to find a fresh-faced young woman standing on the front porch, dressed in jeans and a loose sweater, her auburn curls tossed by the wind. At sight of the bag she carried, Brittany moaned inwardly, assuming the stranger was selling something, and nearly shut the door in the girl's face. Just as she moved to close it, she heard,

"Mrs. Murdock, my name is Rose Ludlow. I won't take up much of your time, but I wanted to welcome you to Tinkers Well and introduce myself. I believe you've met my husband Tim."

Brittany's perpetual expression of sullen boredom transformed instantly into a perfunctory social mask — the one she reserved for women. Rose entered the house when the other woman stepped back and nodded her head toward the interior in a meager show of hospitality. When the door closed, however, Brittany neither moved into the room nor offered Rose a seat. She took a certain perverse pleasure in knowing that Aunt Reenie would have scolded her over her rudeness. But Aunt Reenie was out shopping. Leaning against the door, Brittany surveyed Rose from head to toe: a little too short, a decent figure, but deplorably "All-American girl."

"Tell me your name again. Reese, was it?"

Rose had never met anyone of Brittany's ilk. The naïve young woman was almost tempted to describe her hostess as a female version of her nemesis, Simon Atherton, except that Brittany made no effort to charm at all, choosing rather to insult and summarily dismiss at the outset.

Controlling an uncustomary urge to slap the smirk off the other's face, Rose collected herself and tried again.

"No, it's Rose. Rose Ludlow. I brought a little something by way of welcome. I tried to think of things you and your boys, and your aunt of course, might enjoy. And I wanted to invite – "

"I'm sure that's very nice." Brittany interrupted without ceremony. "You can just set it on the table." Once again, she nodded, this time toward the kitchen, then followed Rose and leaned on the back of an easy chair. "You know, you are one lucky girl." Rose lifted her eyebrows in surprise. "You were right about your husband. I have met him." Brittany made the simple statement sound a bit vulgar. It certainly brought the color to Rose's cheeks.

"In that case, you won't be a stranger at our Easter gathering." Her hackles now firmly raised, Rose wasn't about to let the other woman have the upper hand. "Tim and I are hosting a fellowship meal at our home after Sunday services on Easter for those who may not have other family to celebrate with. The address is in the bag," she said, pointing at her gift. "And since your aunt and Mattie and Drew have become regulars at my mother-in-law's weekly potluck brunch, we wanted you to know that you are welcome, too. I would have invited you at church, but we haven't seen you there yet." Rose's guileless expression contained a hint of steel, and her open gaze never wavered.

Touché, Brittany thought. *So, the little creature has teeth. What fun!* Aloud she said, with the shadow of a smile, "Thank you. That sounds lovely. Is there anything I can bring?"

Rose wanted to say, "Some manners!" but bit her tongue. "Oh, anything that goes with baked ham and roast lamb."

"That sounds delicious. Maybe I'll just – surprise you." Again, the implication of something not quite nice.

The entire visit couldn't have lasted more than a few minutes, but the whole time she was there, Rose felt like a mouse being toyed with by a particularly twisted feline. The invitation having been duly delivered and accepted, she made a beeline for the door and managed some civil words of farewell. Brittany, closing the door behind her guest, did bear rather a striking resemblance to a sleek Cheshire cat. With suggestively arched eyebrows and a malicious smile, Brittany began to plan her big entrance to Tinkers Well society. She wadded up the letter from Matt and tossed it into the trash.

A balding man with a pencil behind his ear flipped through page after page of designs laid out across a large drafting table. He pointed out several options incorporated into the detailed drawings and answered astute questions about possible future expansion. Thomas Maxwell had come up through the school of architecture that valued function and flexibility over frills. The plans for a unique multi-use facility incorporated those qualities brilliantly, while still allowing for artistic elements that provided welcoming aspects to the façade and common areas. Miles Hawthorne could not have been more pleased. Such structures had rarely fallen within his bailiwick in the past, so he doubly appreciated the insight and vision of the architect.

He tossed the tube of drawings into the back seat and drove to Tinkers Well with a perpetual smile that he could not banish, had he actually tried. It hardly seemed worth the effort. It was Friday afternoon on a beautiful day heralding the advance of spring. He was spending the weekend with Tim and Rose since his mother's guest room was otherwise occupied. And the young couple would be joining him and Marilyn on Saturday for an evening of Twentieth Century "folk" favorites as performed by the Kansas City Symphony – the music of Vaughan Williams, Copland, Bartok, and Stravinsky. Miles chuckled softly as he recalled Marilyn's ecstatic response to receiving tickets for the symphony, and her excitement in discovering the program for each concert.

He was a man on top of the world, and all his plans were falling into place. Never had he felt more at peace with himself and his fellow man. For a fleeting moment, he wondered if he wasn't getting a little ahead of himself, but he quickly banished such a thought. Everything *must* be smooth sailing from this point. It was only a matter of time.

CHAPTER 12

*You denied the holy and innocent one, and instead asked for the reprieve
of a murderer! Now, brothers, I know that you did not understand
the significance of what you were doing; neither did your
leaders. But this is how God fulfilled what he had announced
in advance, when he spoke through all the prophets, namely,
that his Messiah was to die.*

Acts 3: 14, 17-18 (CJB)

Abe and Amy's wedding had a trickle-down effect beyond that
experienced by the greater Yousef family. With his two best
buddies now married, Derek was left as odd man out and suddenly
bereft of housemates – except for his mother, of course. Angelica knew in
her heart it was past time for him to strike out on his own again, however
much she would miss his company. She had been mulling over possibilities
for several months in anticipation of the change in their household. Her
efforts essentially coincided with Tim Ludlow's emergence from his
extended honeymoon season.

Tim had been considering for some time the prospect of extending the
parameters of *Three Brothers Construction, Inc.* beyond renovation and
remodeling for other people. As a hedge against lulls in client project
demand, though an unlikely contingency, and as a direct investment with
clear profit, he had been looking into the prospect of house flipping. Because
he knew Derek was already experienced in dealing with the challenges of

living in a house while it was being renovated, Tim wondered if he might consider occupying the property while working on it and taking payment in the form of a profit percentage.

Derek would never admit to his loneliness, but Tim knew his buddy too well. The life of every party suddenly felt like the last living bachelor. When Tim broached the idea of being a resident flipper a month before Abe's wedding, Derek had hesitated a bit. He wasn't sure about the advisability of living completely alone, for he was a true extrovert; he drew energy from being around other people. The idea of losing not only Abe's, but his mother's companionship as well, was a little daunting until he hit on the notion of asking José Nuñez to join him. As co-workers and accountability partners in their VA counseling group, Derek was aware that José was now considerably more emotionally sound than he had been when he first signed on to the Three Brothers team. He might just be ready to leave the security of his aunt and uncle's home.

José had never quite gotten past the enlisted/officer status previously held by him and Derek, but they had forged a working friendship as civilians. José appreciated Derek's support and encouragement and looked up to him for his spiritual leadership. Being a nominal Catholic himself, José respected the optional offer of participation in a group prayer often led on workday mornings by Derek, Tim, or Abe, believing it to provide him with an excuse for not attending Mass on Sundays. He readily agreed to join Derek in the house-flip.

The house in question was a 1,500-square-foot ranch near the elementary school – an optimal location for quick resale. As an architectural carpenter, Tim had done a thorough inspection and satisfied himself that the building was structurally sound enough to invest in. Most of the needed renovation was restricted to the kitchen and two small bathrooms, all of which were hopelessly stuck in the 1960s. The day after closing, which coincided with the arrival of the Yousefs to attend Abe's wedding, Derek and José each moved in enough furniture to make life at least marginally comfortable, though that was a fairly low bar. For two army veterans, any living conditions that improved on stale water out of a canteen and a sleeping bag on the cold hard, ground, were decidedly manageable. To aid in development of ease in their relationship, Derek asked Tim to give the new roomies some intentional one-on-one working opportunities.

On the Monday following Abe's wedding, the two found themselves on the way to look at a rather simple remodeling project for a former client. They pulled into the client's driveway on the east side of town. The entrance was barely discernable amid overgrown shrubbery that continually threatened passersby on Perkins Road. But having worked for the owner the year before, Derek was able to navigate the hole in the bushes without too much difficulty. Once past the natural barricade, the drive led through a front yard densely populated with a random intermingling of pine, oak, and sycamore trees before reaching the house. The building was deceptively large and beautifully maintained, and inevitably took visitors by surprise after navigating the surrounding forest. The trees provided both privacy and a sound barrier for the retreat – a retirement home of peace after 50-plus years of working in finance in Kansas City.

"Come, come, Derek," said the homeowner in answer to Derek's knock. "You must say hello to my Deborah before we discuss our joint enterprise. I warn you – she has been baking!" Isaac's drooping mustache came to life with his effusive welcome – a welcome reserved for those he considered friends. Derek knew himself to be part of that fraternity and hoped José would be too. Deborah emerged from her perpetual hideaway – the kitchen – and wiped her hands on a bright floral apron before engaging them as an extension of her mouth.

"Derek, I made for you your favorite – fallen chocolate cake," she said, beaming with hospitality.

"With lots of whipped topping?"

Her hand gesture reflected her affronted expression. "You think I don't remember? Of course, with lots of whipped topping, but no mascarpone – like I make for *Pesach*. Without thinking, I hoped perhaps Abraham would be with you today. I know how he loves my baking – almost as much as he loves your mama's delicious island cooking." Then she leaned closer and put her hand on Derek's arm, her eyes twinkling. "But I saw in the paper that he was marrying that nice schoolteacher, so maybe she will put some meat on his bones. And ach, such beautiful babies they will make!" she added ecstatically, touching her hands to her cheeks. Derek grinned, wondering how soon he would have the pleasure of teasing his friend mercilessly by recounting the old woman's words.

"Mama, you talk too much," chided her devoted husband. "Let Derek enjoy your delicious cake in peace while we meet our other guest." He extended his hand to José, who had been quietly standing some distance away, saying, "You are very welcome to our home, young man. Any friend of Derek's is a friend of the Rosenbaums."

José, who normally competed for talking honors with whomever he met, was oddly reticent, almost to the point of appearing rude. His gold-capped teeth, usually displayed with his broad smile, remained hidden. He briefly shook Mr. Rosenbaum's hand, before shoving his own back in his pocket, then avoided eye contact with the other man. "José" was all he offered by way of introduction. Derek, confused and embarrassed by José's behavior, stuffed the rest of the cake in his mouth, then hurried to provide further explanation.

"José Nuñez," he said, briefly giving José's shoulder a warning shake, "is one of our new team members. He's pretty good with a toolbox, even if he is a shrimp." Finally, a reluctant smile emerged to break the unusually hostile set of José 's facial features. Derek took great pleasure in lording his superior height over his co-worker's (a mere two inches) because he was no longer the perpetual shortest man in the room. After a few more pleasantries, he got down to business. "Now what can we do for you, Mr. Rosenbaum?"

An hour later, measurements taken, and estimate given, Derek and José left the Rosenbaums' home armed with enough well wishes and food to keep their fridge full for a week. Derek had let slip a mention of their living situation during his introduction, and Deborah, like Angelica, was worried that the two would starve without a woman to cook for them. While the men were discussing the proposed enclosure of the back porch, she dashed about the kitchen, filling a large shopping bag to overflowing. Her three children were long since grown, and they and their families lived on opposite coasts, so the pleasure of cooking for healthy young appetites rarely came her way.

"You bring these containers back with you and I'll fill them again for you. And be sure to give Abraham *his* cake. I included both recipes – with and without yeast - but if the young Mrs. Yousef needs help to make them, you just send her to me." Derek felt no need to remind her that Abe was on his honeymoon. There would be no leftovers to pass on.

He responded with a hug that nearly lifted her out of her shoes and a kiss on her cheek that left her beaming. José was already in the truck having made no attempt to take even polite leave of their generous clients. The Rosenbaums were the last business call of the day, so Derek pointed his battered white pickup toward what had become their temporary home. He could see the couple waving goodbye in the rearview mirror.

Once clear of the house and back on Perkins Road, Derek glanced at José 's sullen profile and demanded, "What the *heck* was all that about?"

"I think maybe Tim needs to send somebody else on this job, you know," José answered evasively. "Maybe JT. He'll eat anything, but I can tell you, ese, I won't eat that sh – stuff."

"What is *wrong* with you?" Derek demanded, still perplexed by José 's attitude. "This is perfectly good food. I should know. I ate enough of it when Tim and Abe and I worked out here last September. And the Rosenbaums are two of the nicest people you'll ever meet, though I have to admit they weren't always that way."

José merely grunted.

"When the three of us first met them, they were a little more – oh I don't know – I guess I'd say standoffish, maybe defensive, or even suspicious. But after I dazzled them with my charm – " Derek was interrupted again, this time by a snort. "As I was saying, my charm dazzled them, and Tim's expertise and fair business practices (Mr. Rosenbaum is *very* big on value for money) impressed them even more. But when Abe introduced himself very formally as Abraham (you know how he sounds like a foreign diplomat) and told them we all attended church together, they finally thawed and couldn't have been easier to get along with. My mom had them over for dinner after we finished that job because she was so grateful for the way they took care of *us* when we were *supposed* to be working for them. We must have sat talking till almost midnight. I think they're kind of lonely, like maybe the quiet and solitude of the country are more than they bargained for."

"So maybe they're okay, but I don't, you know, work for their kind," José responded with finality.

"Their *kind?*" Derek couldn't believe what he was hearing.

"Yeah, you know, *Jews.* I ain't goin' to do nothing for no Jews." Seeing Derek's exasperated expression, he added defensively, "Hey, *mi madre* told me when I was little that the Jews killed Jesus, so they're bad people. And you know, you don't argue with your mother."

"Unbelievable," Derek muttered to himself. They had reached the cottage they shared and began the daily routine of securing the tools they weren't using on their house flip before entering the gutted kitchen. The stove and refrigerator were still plugged in, but all the cabinets were gone. A sheet of plywood lying across sawhorses was the only countertop they had.

A strained silence filled the small room until Derek pulled some cold drinks from the fridge after stowing the Rosenbaum's food stash. He invited José to join him in the living room where secondhand couches offered the only comfortable seating in the house.

"I should, you know, probably get the studs marked so we can hang the cabinets when they get here. And we still need to tear out the rest of this old flooring so we can even out the sub-floor." José 's lame excuses had little effect on Derek who leaned against the doorframe of what used to be a small formal dining room. The wall separating it from the neighboring kitchen had been reduced to framing studs prior to being torn out completely to make room for a larger, open living space. He watched José locate the first 2x6 with his stud-finder, but before he could move on to the next one, Derek stopped him.

"That can wait. Look, I'm not mad at you. I'm just – concerned. And as your accountability partner, I've shared enough of my hang-ups with you that you should know I don't take the role lightly. Come on," he said, nodding his head toward the living room, "I just want to run some ideas by you. What do you say?" Derek waited as José wrestled with respect for his housemate versus his innate desire to avoid controversial discussions. Respect won.

Derek and José were not close friends, not in the sense that he and Abe and Tim were. They had built a relationship of professional comradery and consideration of each other's life experiences as they related to dealing with varying degrees of PTSD. But they shared little in common other than a love of family and a solid work ethic. José's earlier comments and his reaction to the Rosenbaums worried Derek, because even though they weren't the best of buddies, he cared about José. And Derek realized, as José did not, that the misplaced anger and blame José carried hurt him more than the people it was aimed at. Derek knew he must speak with humility and honesty if his words were to have any impact.

"José, why do you say that the Jews killed Jesus?" Despite lounging comfortably on the old couches with their heavy work boots laying on the floor, Derek could see José immediately stiffen. "Like I said, I'm not mad at you, I'm just trying to understand why you believe what you believe."

Relieved at Derek's apparently nonjudgmental attitude, José said simply, "Because they did. I remember hearing it many times when I went to mass on Good Friday. Don't you know that?"

Derek chose his words carefully. "I think before you get that far into Jesus' story, you have to fully understand who Jesus is."

"Who he *is*? He is the son of God, the Savior," José said, as if he couldn't believe that someone he knew to be a regular church goer didn't understand that basic truth.

"You're absolutely right, but do you realize that Jesus was *Jewish*? He was arguably the most Jewish person who ever lived. He was a direct descendant of King David on both Joseph's side (even though Joseph was only a sort of adopted earthly father) and on Mary's side. Their family lines are recorded in the gospels of Matthew and Luke."

"*Jewish*?" José responded in disgust. "Jesus is the heavenly head of the Church. How could he be Jewish?"

"Because he *had* to be. He was the *Jewish* Messiah prophesied in the Old Testament. Have you ever gone to a Maundy Thursday service; you know, when the Last Supper is commemorated?"

"Yeah, sure, when I was a kid." José looked at Derek suspiciously, as if expecting a trap.

"The Last Supper that Jesus shared with his disciples was the feast of the Passover. Do you remember today when Mrs. Rosenbaum told us she made the cake like she did for *Pesach*?"

"Yeah, sure."

"*Pesach* is the Hebrew word for Passover. That's what Jesus was celebrating. It wasn't just a random meal in an upper room. There's a lot of symbolism involved in the Passover story, but we can get into that later. Anyway, it was the Jewish priests and officers of the temple guard that dragged him away from the Garden of Gethsemane, all right, but – "

"You see, it *was* the Jews," José interjected, feeling that he had scored a significant point.

"Yes, but they could not order his death. All the known world at the time was ruled by the Roman Empire. So only Pontius Pilate, the Roman governor, had the authority to put Jesus to death, and he found *no reason to do so*. But, for political expediency, he allowed the Jewish religious leaders and their spiritually blind followers to use him as their weapon, and he eventually ordered the *Roman soldiers* to carry out Jesus' execution."

"Jesus was killed by Romans, *not Jews?*" José shifted his position on the old plaid couch, as if he found it suddenly uncomfortable, and glanced at Derek with overt skepticism. To occupy his hands, and to provide himself an excuse for not maintaining direct eye contact with Derek, José grabbed a Rubik's Cube™ sitting on the windowsill. On his final deployment, his squad leader had taught him how to solve the puzzle using a story narrative, and even though he had solved it countless times since then, José still needed to mentally recount the story to make the correct twists and turns. He didn't want Derek to think he was buying everything he heard. But his distracted attention caused several missteps in movement of the rows and columns because he couldn't completely tune out all that Derek said.

"Yes, but don't you see, that was all part of God's plan. A plan that was in place from before the beginning of time. When the first man, Adam, sinned – "

"When he ate the apple," José said, looking up momentarily from the square in his hands. He felt a measure of confidence in being able to contribute to the discussion.

"Well, the whole apple thing is more tradition than biblical fact. What Adam and Eve actually ate was fruit from the tree of the knowledge of good and evil." Derek stopped when he saw José looking defensive again. "Okay, we'll go with apple. So, the perfect interaction between God and man was broken because God is holy and could no longer be associated with Adam and Eve who had sinned by disobeying God's instructions. Later, when God called the nation of Israel into existence and set them apart to be his chosen people – "

José broke into Derek's speech without apology. "Wait, why do you say the Jews are God's people? That's the Christians, you know, the Catholics and Protestants like you who follow Jesus. That doesn't make any sense." He was almost belligerent now, daring Derek to disprove him.

"Because God made a covenant, a special kind of promise, with Abraham." Derek continued in the level tones of a storyteller. "God promised Abraham a large chunk of choice land that would eventually be home to the nation of Israel. God also promised him boatloads of descendants and that through him and his descendants, all the world would be blessed. The greatest blessing came in the person of Jesus, the Jewish Messiah.

"In fact, just before Jesus ascended into heaven, he told the disciples to be his witnesses, or I guess you could call them missionaries, and he gave them a specific order they were to follow in spreading his story. First to Jerusalem – the Jewish capital and site of the Jewish temple. Then to Judea – what had been the southern kingdom of Israel. Next to Samaria – what had been part of the northern kingdom of Israel. It was inhabited by a sort of half-breed people called Samaritans who descended from the intermarriage of Assyrians with the Jews they conquered. And finally, after all those Jews and Jewish descendants had been introduced to the gospel, the disciples were to take it 'to the ends of the earth.'

"Even the apostle Paul, who was credited with taking the gospel message to the Gentiles – that's people like us who are not Jewish – said it was 'salvation to everyone who believes: *first* to the Jew, *then* to the Gentile.'

And believe it or not, the first church in history was established after the coming of the Holy Spirit at Pentecost – *another* Jewish feast day, called the Feast of Weeks. The church was located in Jerusalem and made up almost entirely of *Jewish* believers." At José's look of astonishment, he added, "I'm not kidding. They met in the Jewish temple court and were initially considered a sect of Judaism referred to as 'Followers of the Way' – not as Christians. But I'm getting a little ahead of myself."

José was beginning to think Derek was making the whole thing up. The commentary certainly wasn't helping with his progress on the Rubik's Cube.

"Like I was saying, you have to go way back in the Old Testament to understand the need for Jesus and his death. After Adam and Eve disobeyed God, they were separated from God by their sin, and were kicked out of the garden. Centuries later, after the flood and after God rescued the nation of Israel from slavery in Egypt, he established a system of sacrificial offerings. They were performed by the Aaronic priests, from the tribe of Levi, on behalf of the Jewish people to make atonement…" Derek saw disbelief turn to confusion on José 's face, so he tried to break it down a little more. "…to pay the penalty for all their sins so that they, the nation of Israel, could be close to God again."

Confusion now turned to a frown of mental reasoning. "Think of a convicted bank robber who is sent away to serve a sentence in prison as a penalty for breaking the law. When the sentence has been completed – when the punishment for breaking the law has been fulfilled – he can be part of society again. It's kind of the same idea when we sin against God. Does that make sense?"

"Yeah, sure. I guess so," José answered, without much conviction.

Derek was more determined than ever to help José understand, so he retraced his steps a little. "You know that we all make mistakes, right? We screw things up in a way that hurts ourselves or other people. We disobey God's instructions. We violate Jesus' teachings. We sin." At José's nod, he continued. "Well, those sins separate us from God, just like the bank robber's crime separates the prisoner from society. And before Jesus came, sacrifices had to be made over and over again because the people kept sinning over and over again. So, God made a way that would pay the penalty for sin forever – one final, perfect sacrifice, once and for all, for *all* mankind, Jew and Gentile alike. That could only happen through the death of Jesus on the cross. Are you still with me?" he asked.

"Yeah, sure," came the habitual reply, though with considerably more conviction. The puzzle in José 's hands was momentarily forgotten.

"Okay. Here's the really important part. We tend to think of Jesus as most human when he endured the physical agony of the cross. What we forget is that he was still *completely God the Son,* and he had the power to stop the crucifixion at *any time* from his arrest on, but he *chose* to be obedient to God the Father and went *willingly* to the cross as a sacrifice to pay the penalty for *our* sin. And his blood *is* on the hands of those who made it necessary for him to do so. But if you're going to hate those people, you'll have to hate me too, because *I also* nailed Jesus to that cross." Derek paused to allow his words to sink in. José stared, not wanting to accept what he heard. "And Tim nailed him to the cross, and my sweet mama, and our pastor, and every human being who has ever drawn breath because, like the apostle Paul *also* said in the book of Romans, '*All* have sinned and fall short of the glory of God.'"

As he spoke, Derek noticed that José's expression had become more intent and focused. His defensive manner was gone altogether as he considered his long-held beliefs in a new light – not a particularly favorable one. He began to speak slowly as if processing every word. "Then that means..."

"...that José Nuñez nailed Jesus to the cross? Yes, my brother. And when you look at what happened to Jesus from *that* perspective, it becomes *very* personal." Derek spoke gently. "Can you see now how futile it is to blame others for what we're just as guilty of? But Jesus doesn't want us to live in a prison of guilt. He paid that horrible price so that those who sincerely regret their sins and *choose* to follow him, can be forgiven; *not* because of any righteous acts – good things we do ourselves – but because of faith in the power of Jesus' shed blood on our behalf. No special words we recite, or ceremonies performed by religious leaders can save us from the penalty we deserve. Our salvation comes *only* by God's grace poured out on us because of our faith in Christ. When we receive Jesus' forgiveness, we can have an eternal relationship with him. It's that relationship that makes us *want* to live lives that honor him. And every time we take communion, we're *reminded* of Jesus' incredible selfless act of love."

José sat quietly for some time, no longer looking at Derek but rather into a nebulous haze of uncertainty. Finally, he looked up and asked, "But how do you know all this? Why should I believe what you're telling me?"

Derek reached for his Bible lying on the couch next to him. It was the place he read his daily devotion. "It's all in here, man," he said, handing the Bible to José, who seemed reluctant to take it. "I quoted from two different books – Acts and Romans. I suggest you read those two books – it's pretty intense." Then Derek carefully planted another idea. "If anything, we should feel sorrow and compassion for the Jewish people. We *know* who Jesus is and what he did and still does for us, but most of them missed their own Messiah when he came to earth and walked among them. Though some of them, like the Rosenbaums, obviously honor God and worship him, they still carry the burden of following a complicated set of ceremonial, dietary, and moral laws as their only hope of being free from sin. And because the whole of humanity possesses a sinful nature, I don't know how much hope they really have. But at least we can let them see Jesus in us, and in our actions on his behalf."

José's frown deepened while he considered the implications of Derek's words. Unable to take in anything more, he stood and walked down the hall to his room still holding the Bible. The abandoned Rubik's Cube fell to the floor unnoticed.

The Rosenbaums waved until Derek's truck disappeared into the forest of their front yard. Deborah folded her arms and commented, "That Derek is a real mensch, no? His smile lights up a room."

"He is a good man," Isaac agreed. "But would you be so quick to praise him if he did not enjoy your cooking so much?"

She nudged him playfully with her elbow as they stepped back into the house. While Isaac reviewed the project bid, Deborah bustled around the kitchen, gathering what she needed to begin dinner. She hummed a little tune while she went about her preparations, only pausing to ask her husband how many fish he wanted. They were tiny in her estimation, and she worried perpetually over his lack of nutrition – a total fabrication of her imagination. After calling to Isaac twice with no response, she tracked him down to the back porch where he sat looking out over the garden in a brown study.

"Isaac, you'll catch your death out here without even a sweater. You wait till those boys finish closing in this porch, then you can sit here staring at nothing."

"Ach, Deborah, you worry too much. And I'm not staring at nothing. I'm thinking."

"And this you can't do inside where it's warm?" Without waiting for an answer, she plunked herself down in a neighboring chair. "What is so important that you must think about it here?"

Isaac reached out to take his wife's hand. "This thing we have been asked to do by Mark Lindeman – I think it is a good thing."

She patted his hand comfortingly. "And what brought on such a thought, today, when we saw our old friend Derek again?"

Isaac looked at her searchingly, though it was difficult to discern much of her countenance in the fading light. "Did you not notice anything about

Derek's friend? The curious way he avoided speaking directly to us and left without saying goodbye?" The memory of their own initial hesitancy in welcoming *Three Brothers Construction, Inc.* into their lives had faded into inconsequence.

"Oh, I'm sure he is just a little shy. You know how overwhelming you can be to strangers."

"*Me? I'm* the overwhelming one? *Oy vey, meshuggeneh* woman!" There was no mistaking Deborah's charming smile despite the gathering darkness.

"Come, let's go inside and you can stuff me with whatever delicacy you have prepared for dinner." Isaac pulled his wife to her feet, and she immediately began reviewing the menu, insisting he eat at least two fish. Isaac Rosenbaum was a man of wisdom and peace. He ate the better part of three.

Derek did not see his housemate again that evening, but when an unusually solemn José appeared for breakfast, he greeted Derek with diffidence and asked if they would start on the Rosenbaum project that day, adding some of his own ideas to make the finished project more suitable for the older couple. He concentrated on peeling a piece of citrus before saying awkwardly, "Hey, man, you know that Bible stuff you told me about? I didn't really understand it all, but I read some of the things you told me to read, and dude, that Paul guy, or whatever his name was first…"

"Saul."

"Yeah, Saul. He was one bad *hombre*. First, he's *killing* all the Jesus followers, then he *becomes* one – that's messed up."

Derek tried not to laugh as he shouted a silent "Hallelujah!"

"Pretty amazing what God can do with people, right?" Derek patted his friend on the back on the way to the door, and added, "Now let's see what he can do with us. You sure you're ready for this project, short man?" He jumped nimbly aside just as a half-eaten clementine whizzed by his ear.

"Hey, ese, one of these days I'm going to get some boots with some seriously thick soles, and then we'll see who the short man is."

Assuring José that they did *not* need to pack a lunch because Mrs. Rosenbaum would have more food than they could eat, they hopped in the truck and headed to the local building supply store to pick up materials.

"We are both very grateful for the beautiful work you all did. We will think of you every time we sit in our porch room and admire the garden." Mr. Rosenbaum shook first Derek's, then José's, then Derek's hand again. Mrs. Rosenbaum was too busy speaking with her hands to shake anything.

"Don't forget we will see you tomorrow evening, Derek," she said. "And maybe José? We are so looking forward to sharing our Passover Seder with you and your friends. Thank you for suggesting your pastor contact us."

José was a little mystified by her parting words. He would ask clarification from Derek presently, but first things first. "Hey, ese, why'd you run us out of there so fast? I was still eating!" José complained as they drove toward Perkins Road after taking protracted leave of the Rosenbaums.

Thanks to Tim's timely appearance earlier in the week, when he added his special touch of craftsmanship, the back porch enclosure had far exceeded their clients' vision and had been finished for less than the bid price. Mr. Rosenbaum showed his appreciation with the unusual gesture of a padded check. Mrs. Rosenbaum expressed her gratitude in more tangible, and immediate, ways. After six days of eating their fill of her cooking, José was her newest fan.

"Because you would probably have spent the *rest* of the day eating," Derek pointed out. "I saw the gleam in Mrs. Rosenbaum's eye when you asked for seconds of her roast chicken and *kreplach*. As it is, we'll be eating it for the rest of the week anyway – not that I'm complaining. I'm just saying."

"And *I'm* just saying that those dumplings are *awesome*. Do you suppose your mom could make those?" José asked hopefully.

"My mama can cook anything," Derek replied, as if stating a proven law of nature.

"And what did Mrs. Rosenbaum mean about seeing you, and maybe me, tomorrow night?"

"She and her husband have been invited to lead our church in the Passover Seder on Maundy Thursday. Remember when I explained that it was the Passover feast Jesus shared with his disciples for his 'Last Supper?'"

"Yeah, so?"

"Instead of holding a communion service this year, we're having a Passover feast of our own, and the Rosenbaums are going to share the Jewish history and meaning of the meal. Our pastor will explain the Christian symbolism behind it. We've been studying a lot about the Jewish Jesus lately, and he thought it would be a helpful teaching tool." After a short silence, Derek added, "She was right, you know."

"Who was right?"

"Mrs. Rosenbaum – when she hinted at you being there too. You should come."

"Oh, I don't think so, man," José said with misgiving. "Me, I only go to *my* church on Easter and Midnight Mass on Christmas. Why would I go to *your* church?"

"But this isn't a service. It's a dinner, and we're meeting at the Ludlow's barn because it's the only place big enough to hold everybody. The meal is potluck, including some of Mrs. Rosenbaum's kosher recipes, so we're talking lots of good food. *Comprendevu?*"

José looked at Derek in comical dismay, then burst out laughing. "If you promise *never* to try to speak Spanish or French, or whatever that was, again, I'll think about the dinner."

"Deal."

The two pulled up to the Willow Walk barn promptly at six o'clock the following evening.

CHAPTER 13

Get rid of the old hametz, so you may be a new batch, just as you are
unleavened — for Messiah, our Passover Lamb, has been sacrificed.

1 Corinthians 5:7 (TLV)

Candles, as a rule, provide a rather paltry source of lighting. The scope of their power is limited and unstable as the wick burns its way through the dripping wax – one minute flaring brightly, the next struggling for air in a mounting sea of melting fuel. But light a single candle in the gloom of a cloudy, moonless night, or in the smothering darkness of a vaulted cave, or in the vast well of human ignorance, and it has the capacity to glow like a signal fire, to dispel weighty fears, and to illuminate the mind and heart. Multiply that single candle by 40 or more, and that frail light becomes a beacon of welcome and peace.

Such was the effect experienced by those gathered to celebrate the Passover Seder led by Isaac and Deborah Rosenbaum. As the first match leapt to life when struck by Mrs. Rosenbaum, she held it to a candle then quickly lit a second, signaling each of the designated women at more than 20 tables to follow suit. Flickering candlelight strengthened and spread throughout the huge expanse of the old barn where overhead fixtures had been dimmed to insignificance. A gasp of delight rose from the assembled crowd, followed by shivers of awe, as the old woman spoke Hebrew words of blessing born aloft on an undulating wave of heat vapor. The English words followed.

"Blessed are you, O Lord our God, ruler of the universe, who has set us apart by his Word, and in whose name we light the festival lights."

It was a mystical moment bridging time and space, inviting those present to recline at the table shared by Jesus and his disciples at that last supper. "*I have really wanted so much to celebrate this Seder with you before I die!*" Jesus told his followers, as recounted in the book of Luke. Pastor Lindeman had reminded them of the Savior's words during a brief overview of the program before introducing his special guests who would inaugurate the evening's formal events.

"Because this is meant to be an instructional evening, time constraints won't allow us to cover all details of the Jewish Passover Seder, but you should be afforded a clear enough picture of the rich history and ceremonial aspects of the celebration to stimulate your imagination. After you have experienced the significance of the Passover, you may wonder why the events of Holy Week don't always coincide with the Feasts of Passover, Unleavened Bread, and First Fruits, given the magnitude of their relevant symbolism as fulfilled in the death and resurrection of Jesus. It all has to do with phases of the moon and how they determine dates on the Gregorian calendar we follow versus the Jewish calendar and is way too complicated to go into right now. Just know that in God's flawless timing, those world-changing events coincided perfectly with specific Jewish festival days on the calendar of human history – and be amazed."

Isaac Rosenbaum, humbled by a very warm welcome, had taken his place to begin his teaching role. Speaking into the mic that carried his voice throughout the vast space, he had explained the preparation of insuring that all *hametz* is removed from the house while gesturing at the huge walls of the barn surrounding them. "This means all bread and cakes down to the last crumb, because *hametz*, or yeast, represents sin, so the gathering place must be thoroughly cleaned. Just as each person must consider themselves freed from slavery in Egypt, we must put away the sin hidden in our hearts.

"*Haggadah* – the program we are following together – means 'the telling.' Passover is a story that has been retold for thousands of years; a miraculous story of transitions; from slavery to freedom, from despair to hope, from darkness to light. Its greatness is the greatness of God; its timeliness the eternal truth of his involvement with his people. God cares for all who are his today just as he cared for the children of Israel in ancient times."[6] He had then commented on the *Seder* plate present on every table and named each element. "I will explain their individual meanings a little later, but each element allows your senses to participate in the story. Taste, smell, see, and feel the truth of God's love. Now, a mother at each table will light the candles, just as my Deborah does. She will speak the appropriate Hebrew words first, then you ladies will echo the text in English."

And so, it had begun. The candles lit by Deborah and the other women had not only brought light and warmth to the darkness; they had ignited a spark of excitement and anticipation in the room, momentarily diminished by the intrusion of practical necessity. The house lights once more grew in strength to better light the big space, and with their brightness grew a collective groan. Pastor Lindeman laughed apologetically as he moved the evening forward. "I know, I know. I'm sorry to spoil such a magical moment, but I remind you that this Seder is meant to be a learning experience, and for that we all need to see the *Haggadah* clearly. You will notice that the text is printed in different colors. The words in black are the traditional text and the words in red highlight what we, his followers, believe to be the fulfillment of Passover symbolism in the person of Jesus."

The magnitude of such a claim registered merely as a blip of passing interest on Isaac's philosophic radar. It drew a subdued gasp from his wife which was hidden by the pastor's continued introduction.

----

[6] Barry and Steffi Rubin, *The Messianic Passover Haggadah,* 2d ed. (Clarksville, MD: Messianic Jewish Publishers, 2005), 3.

"All scripture passages are from the *Complete Jewish Bible*. And with that piece of housekeeping, let's continue. Isaac…"

"I can assure you there are many exciting moments to come." Isaac beamed and adjusted his reading glasses. "At Passover, we remember Adonai's plan of redemption for the children of Israel." The room read collectively words from Exodus, chapter six:

"*…I will free you from the forced labor of the Egyptians…rescue you from their oppression…redeem you with an outstretched arm…I will take you as my people, and I will be your God…*"

"We celebrate these four promises the Lord made to *Moshe*, or Moses, by drinking from our cups four times. Each cup has special meaning." He lifted his cup and gave a blessing to God for the fruit of the vine. "*Baruch atah Adonai eloheynu melekh ha'olam borey pri hagafen.*"

Mark Lindeman added, "The 22nd chapter of Luke recounts that Jesus, or *Yeshua* – his Jewish name – began his final Passover Seder by taking what would have been the first cup and telling his disciples:

"*Take this and share it among yourselves. For I tell you that from now on, I will not drink the 'fruit of the vine' until the Kingdom of God comes.*"

Isaac continued, "Let us all drink of this, the first cup of Passover, the Cup of Sanctification."

A pitcher of grape juice had been provided at each table so that all ages could participate in the "fruit of the vine." A careful seating plan, worked out weeks in advance, ensured that every table included children, a father or grandfather, and a mother or grandmother so that speaking parts and actions performed by those respective groups could be experienced by everyone present. Despite the presence of a large crowd gathered in an enormous space, great effort had gone into infusing the evening with the feeling of an intimate family dinner in keeping with the manner of Passover celebration within the Jewish community.

"Who may go up to the mountain of Adonai? Who can stand in his holy place? Those with clean hands and pure hearts..."

After reading the passage from Psalm 24, Isaac lifted a basin of water and invited everyone to share in the hand-washing ceremony. Mark Lindeman pointed out that Jesus took the gesture a step further during the hand-washing after the meal, by washing his disciples' feet and thereby providing another example of humility and selfless service to others.

Isaac read from Exodus 2 of the suffering of Israel under the yoke of slavery then lifted from the seder plate the *Karpas* – parsley – representing life created and sustained by God. He held up his cup of salt water and instructed everyone to dip their own parsley into the salt water to remember the tears of the children of Israel living in captivity. The pastor spoke of the tears of all who live in captivity to sin.

"The crushing reality of slavery under brutal Egyptian control vividly illustrates the hidden, though no less crushing, effect of human bondage to sin. This includes both our own transgressions and the cruel practices perpetrated against mankind by the host of lost souls driven by the control of Satan in a fallen world. Man's inability to free himself from sin's tyranny, or to wash it away through centuries of religiosity and the shedding of innocent animal blood, cried out then, and continues to cry out, for a savior – a Messiah."

Deborah Rosenbaum tried to listen respectfully to the teaching, but her state of umbrage grew as Mark Lindeman seemed to have an answer for, or differing understanding of, everything Isaac said. When the elderly Jewish couple agreed to lead the Christian congregation in an evening of teaching, they did so out of a desire to impart a greater understanding of Judaism to their Christian neighbors. Neither had anticipated so many additions to the traditional ceremony, though Mark had been forthcoming about such possibilities. They never imagined how the deep meaning of each Passover moment could be so deftly altered or amplified. Nothing of the original had been taken away, but much had been added. Deborah found it unsettling and maintained an attitude of complacence with an effort.

Everyone turned a page in the Haggadah, and the children suddenly became more animated. It was time for their special contribution. The kids at some tables read in turns; others read in unison. But at the head table, where the guests of honor were seated, one young boy stood to read on behalf of his younger, less experienced tablemates. In addition to the Rosembaums, those seated around the table included Mr. Taylor, Aunt Reenie, and Mattie and Drew. Next to Drew sat his newest best buddy, KC Thatcher, KC's little sister Cookie, and their adopted parents. Mattie cleared his throat nervously and prepared to read with the others in the room. Mr. Rosenbaum nodded his head to begin, and catching Mattie's eye, winked in encouragement. The boy smiled shyly in return and began reading.

"On all other nights we eat bread or *matzah*.

On this night why do we eat only *matzah?*

On all other nights we eat all kinds of vegetables.

On this night why do we eat only bitter herbs?

On all other nights we do not dip our vegetables even once.

On this night why do we dip them twice?

On all other nights we eat our meals sitting or reclining.

On this night why do we eat only reclining?"

"It is a duty and a privilege to answer the four questions of Passover and to recite the mighty works of our faithful God," Isaac said, in tandem with each table's "father," then began an explanation of the other Seder elements.

Lifting the plate containing three *matzahs*, he told the people that some rabbis teach that the three represent the unity of the patriarchs – Abraham, Isaac, and Jacob; others the unity of worship – the priests, Levites, and people of Israel. "The *matzahs* are placed in a compartmentalized bag called an *echad*, meaning 'one' in Hebrew." He took out the middle *matzah* and broke it in half, though providing no reason for doing so, then replaced one piece in the bag and invited the leaders at each table to do the same. He was about to move on to the next step when Mark Lindeman again interjected.

"I'm sure some of you have already thought of another unity of three, the tri-unity of God – the Father, Son, and Spirit. Let's focus for a few moments on that middle piece – the Son. Look at the appearance of the *matzah*. We know that it is flat because it contains no yeast and represents the bread made in haste by the Hebrew people before their exodus from Egypt. But also notice how the *matzah* has blotches of darker spots like bruises, and see the stripes across its surface reminiscent of the torn flesh Jesus sustained during the scourging he received after his unjust trial. Let's read together from the prophet Isaiah, chapter 53, verse 5."

> *But he was wounded because of our crimes, crushed because of our sins; the disciplining that makes us whole fell on him, and by his bruises we are healed.*

"Also, take note of how the *matzah* is pierced, a necessary step in cooking the bread, and read Zechariah 12:10."

> *"I will pour out on the house of David and on those living in Yerushalayim; a spirit of grace and prayer; and they will look to me, whom they pierced. They will mourn for him as one mourns for an only son…"*

Mark smiled at the valiant attempt by a bunch of Kansans to pronounce the Hebrew version of "Jerusalem" and nodded at Isaac to take up the story. The old man hesitated, unsure of the actions he had performed for decades, but he was there to teach, and he meant to honor his promise.

"Take the second half and wrap it in linen cloth. This is called the *afikomen*. Now, if the children will cover their eyes… ach, I see some of you peeping through your fingers. Cheating is a sin, and remember, we have swept every hint of sin from our homes and our hearts tonight. I am still waiting…" Finally convinced that most of the youngsters in attendance had complied with his request, Isaac told the leaders at each table to hide the *afikomen* until time for the children to search for it after dinner.

"There are a few significant points in this ritual I want you to consider through the lens of Christ followers." The pastor had again taken over the narrative. "One half of the middle *matzah*, suggesting the Son – Jesus – is returned to the *echad*, possibly illustrating his deity as part of the Triune God. The other half, by which we recognize his humanity – broken, bruised, and pierced for us – is wrapped in linen and hidden away. This *afikomen*, meaning 'the coming one' is wrapped in white cloth just as Jesus' body was wrapped for burial and placed in a tomb.[7] And just as the sinless Messiah completed his initial mission on earth when he rose on the third day to conquer death, so the return of the *afikomen* will indicate the Passover Seder is nearing its completion." He paused as he watched lightbulbs going off everywhere in the faces of those present. "I don't know about you, but I've already got goose bumps, and the good news is – there's more to come!"

Unlike his wife, whose consternation grew more apparent, Isaac found himself caught up in the shared anticipation of those around him. He began to wonder how the story of Passover could possibly be any more modified, but rather than listening to such augmentation in growing resentment, he discovered an unlooked-for curiosity suddenly aroused by Mark Lindeman's words. Knowing Deborah would regard such interest as bordering on heresy, he dutifully took up his portion of the tale and waited for what must surely follow. He offered a blessing for the bread and proceeded to answer the rest of the four questions.

Taking another piece of *matzah*, Isaac invited everyone to scoop up and taste a little of the other elements of the Seder plate. Some grimaced while sampling the bitter herbs, called *maror* (horse radish), reminding them of how bitter life was for the children of Israel during their time of slavery in

---

[7] Marvin Wilson, *Our Father Abraham: Jewish Roots of the Christian Faith* (Grand Rapids, MI: Wm B. Eerdmans Publishing, 1989) 237.

Egypt. But most enjoyed the *kharoset*, a mixture of chopped apples, honey, nuts, and wine, representing the mortar used to build cities for Pharoah out of brick and clay. The presence of a lamb shankbone on the plate would be explained later. *Baytzah*, a hard-boiled egg eaten during the Seder meal in remembrance of the loss of the Jewish temple, completed the plate. Isaac explained that they eat the Passover Seder reclining at their ease because they have been set free from slavery, unlike the first Passover meal which was eaten in haste while standing in preparation for Israel's deliverance from bondage.

"The story of Passover is a story of miracles, a story of redemption, a story of the mighty power of God to overcome evil."[8] Isaac stepped back to allow the other readers access to the microphone. The fact that they were all teenagers was a testament to Pastor Lindeman's efforts to engage the youth of the church in more congregation-wide events so that they might find their place in the larger fellowship. One after another, each designated teen stepped up to the mic to recount a step in the Exodus story: the enslavement of the growing number of Hebrews in Egypt; the killing of infant Hebrew boys and Moses' miraculous rescue and adoption into the royal Egyptian family; his flight into Midian after killing an Egyptian who was beating a Hebrew slave; and finally, Moses' calling by God to be his messenger to the king of Egypt to "Let My people go!"

Isaac led everyone in a responsive telling of Pharoah's refusal to heed Moses' words and the infliction of the ten plagues. Everyone's cup was filled a second time and Isaac further explained, "We are filled with joy at God's mighty deliverance. But we also remember the great cost at which redemption was purchased." He instructed everyone to dip a little finger into the cup with the recounting of each plague, allowing a drop of liquid to fall. "This symbolizes the reduction of the fullness of our cup of joy this night."

---

[8] Rubin, *The Messianic Passover Haggadah*, 18.

The teens took ghoulish delight in the process as all present called out in order: "Blood! Frogs! Lice! Beasts! Cattle disease! Boils! Hail! Locusts! Darkness! Death of the firstborn!"

"Before we proceed to the heart of the Passover, consider this: the gospel accounts of Jesus' final Passover speak of the first cup and the third cup, but not of the second – the cup symbolizing judgment. Now think for a moment of Jesus' prayer in the garden of Gethsemane where he and his disciples gathered after the dinner." The crowd seated in the old barn had by now been conditioned to expect something of deep spiritual significance every time the pastor took the floor. He did not disappoint.

"'Father, if you are willing, take this cup away from me; still, let not my will but yours be done.'

Jesus knew what was coming when he prayed in anguish that night. The bitter cup of judgment loomed as a dreadful task before him. It was a cup that *only* he could partake of to purchase our freedom from guilt and slavery to sin, yet he accepted it in humility and obedience."[9]

Derek had been aware of José 's growing silence as each layer of the Passover's dual meanings was revealed. The symbolism of the second cup was new to Derek, but it was an echo of all he had shared with José the week before. Sensing his friend's eyes on him, José looked up from contemplation of the cup he held. He neither smiled nor frowned, but rather considered the other man with new respect as the credibility of everything he had spoken of regarding Jesus' sacrifice was driven home by Mark Lindeman's comments, leaving little room for doubt.

While José Nuñez confronted his own misunderstandings and lack of knowledge, Deborah Rosenbaum grew more and more agitated as she listened to the ceremony sacred to her people being co-opted by the

---

[9] Amir Tsarfati, *Jesus and the Passover Through Jewish Eyes* (video of teaching, Calvary Chapel, Chino Hills, CA) posted April 8, 2020. https://www.youtube.com/watch?v=MvfUeZyVrHc&t=3000s 1:00:00/1:07:04

Christians around her. It seemed to her that the miraculous rescue of the nation of Israel from Egypt had been overshadowed by references to a Messiah – the same Messiah foretold by the prophets, if one could possibly believe such nonsense! It was as if a clearly defined topographic map, representing her faith, had been covered by a map overlay, causing the altered landscape to draw all eyes beyond the familiar and obvious toward a previously hidden pathway. She found that she resented the change even as she felt her innate longing for *Meshiach* subtly roused.

"We have eaten the *Matzah*, reminding us of the hasty manner with which the children of Israel fled Egypt. We have tasted the bitter herbs, reminding us of the bitterness of slavery there." Isaac lifted the lamb bone. "And this roasted shankbone symbolizes the lamb whose blood marked the doorposts of the Hebrew slaves, signifying their obedience to God's command and their protection from the plague of death."

A series of readings from Exodus 12 followed, detailing instructions to the people of Israel as to the selection, slaughter, and consumption of the sacrificial lamb. Then the leader at each table read segments of Exodus 12:12 with Isaac, after which everyone else responded in unison:

"For that night, I will pass through the land of Egypt...
I, and not an angel.
"and kill all the firstborn in the land of Egypt, both men and animals;
I, and not a seraph.
"and I will execute judgment against all the gods of Egypt;
I, and not a messenger.
"I am *ADONAI.*"[10]

"Since the destruction of the second temple in AD 70, lamb is no longer eaten at Passover, but the shankbone reminds us of the sacrificial lamb,"

---

[10] Rubin, *The Messianic Passover Haggadah,* 24.

Isaac said and again pointed out the symbolism of the roasted egg as it related to the loss of the temple.

"You know I can't let this go without pointing out what is probably obvious to you by now." Mark Lindeman appeared to be pinging with about 220 volts of electricity. "It was *not* an angel *nor* a seraph *nor* a messenger who redeemed us from sin and death, but *ADONAI* himself in human form. Jesus, the Lamb of God, being completely pure and without sin, was sacrificed in our place to redeem us from the bondage of sin and the penalty of death." With each word his excitement and intensity grew. "Do I hear a 'Hallelujah?'" For a man not ordinarily given to charismatic speech, the pastor's zeal, and demand for a response, both surprised and inspired his congregation. Some clapped, some shouted "Hallelujah!" or "Amen!" and many surged to their feet.

Isaac was unprepared for such a display of emotion. While the first part of the *Hallel* – Hebrew for praise – was to be shared at the *end* of the *Haggadah* with the drinking of the second cup[11], he had rarely approached this portion of the evening in the face of such exuberance. The impromptu eruption of what one could only call unrestrained joy, threw him out of his stride. Sensing the older man's confusion, the pastor spoke over the noise. "Since most of you are already on your feet, we'll move ahead to the reading from the Psalms." He looked at Isaac, again passing the torch of leadership.

Thankful for a segue he was at a loss to contrive himself, Isaac smiled and nodded. "You are quite right, Pastor Lindeman. We would ordinarily sing the words of the Psalms, but we will read them together, then I will teach you to sing the *Dayenu*. It is the response meaning 'It would have been sufficient' and recognizes God's rich mercy and blessings – blessings that went far beyond what our ancestors expected in their liberation. Is this not a God worthy of praise?" The cheers that had momentarily subsided during Isaac's instruction, began again, compelling him to initiate the formal

---

11 Benjamin Galan, *Christ in the Passover*, (Peabody, MA: Rose Publishing, 2008), 5.

portion of the *Hallel* in the hope of maintaining order. The church pianist, along with Amy Yousef, who added a touch of Hebrew flavor with her violin, accompanied Isaac for the *Dayenu*. It took the boisterous crowd a few repetitions to master the lilting melody, but after a final, joyful rendering, everyone readily drank the second cup at Isaac's invitation. It was time to eat!

Long tables on the raised front platform, and more in the back of the great hall near the kitchen, groaned under the burden of potluck dishes and casseroles too numerous to count. A special place on each length of table had been reserved for Passover Kosher foods, prepared for the feast according to Deborah Rosenbaum's recipes by the more adventurous chefs. In addition to a flock of slow-cooked chickens with root vegetables purchased by the church, Bobby Taylor had volunteered to supplement the meat supply by contributing several slabs of beef brisket baked in his new outdoor oven.

The feast signaled not only time for food but fellowship as well. Isaac and Deborah weathered a barrage of gratitude, welcome, and invitations to various Tinkers Well community events with grace and dignity. They enjoyed getting to know their tablemates and discovered an unexpected connection with one of them. With the exception of four-year-old Cookie, who rested contentedly in her father's arms after an exciting evening that was quickly catching up with her bedtime, the kids were excused after dinner to seek out some of their other friends. Irene, as Aunt Reenie had introduced herself to the Rosenbaums, explained the absence of the boys' father, telling her table neighbors he had been called away on business.

"And what sort of business is he engaged in?" Isaac enquired politely.

Reenie replied evasively, "Oh, I don't really understand it all; something to do with finance."

"But that is my field! What a coincidence," he said, pleased to have found some common ground. "What is his name – if you don't mind my asking, Irene? Perhaps we have met."

"Oh… well, I'm sure you haven't. His name is Matt, that is…Matthew Murdock. Mattie is named for him." *Please don't say anything if you recognize the name,* Reenie pleaded in silent dread.

"Murdock, Murdock… now why does that sound familiar?" Isaac glanced up to catch a glimpse of anguish on Reenie's face and the name clicked, but he would not add to the woman's worry. "No, I don't believe I have ever had the privilege, but I *have* heard good things of him," he said with a reassuring smile.

Reenie breathed a sigh of relief just as Gertie, ever mindful of her friend's limitations, arrived with Aletha's hand clasped tightly in her own. She had cleared a path through the crowd with all the panache of a native guide wielding a machete through an overgrown jungle. Navigating across an unfamiliar room filled with tables, chairs, and children on the loose was not a feat to be left to a blind woman alone.

"I can't tell you how interesting your talk has been. I may be close to 83, but I learned something tonight, and that gets harder to say the older I get," she said in her blunt, friendly way. "I'm Gertie Gunn, and this is Aletha Mason." Aletha smiled and waved in the general direction of her friend's voice. "Besides thanking you for helping us to appreciate our Jewish neighbors a little better, we wanted to invite you to join the other town seniors for Thursday Bingo Night."

Deborah might have declined the invitation on the grounds of Jewish law prohibiting gambling, but Gert never gave her a chance.

"Now I know you can't do anything on Friday nights on account of starting your Sabbath then, but Thursdays are good for everybody unless, of course, you have something special like tonight's shindig." Deborah drew breath to respond, but she might as well have tried blowing into a whirlwind at maximum velocity. "And it's not like one of those bingo parlors where everyone looks like grim death while they throw their money away. We have a potluck dinner first, and then we play bingo — when we're paying attention enough and not yammering away at 19 to the dozen. And it doesn't cost anything — just a donation if you feel like it. *And* what's left over after prizes goes to our local *Meals on Wheels* ministry."

Thankful for the welcome change in conversational topics, and because she had already become a Thursday night regular, Reenie added her voice of encouragement. Not wanting to appear boorish, the Rosenbaums felt compelled to assure their new acquaintances that they would make every effort to join them at the community center on the following Thursday. They admitted, in a silent shared glance, that becoming involved in community activities had been a goal since their move to Tinkers Well.

"Splendid! We'll save you a place at our table," Aletha said with her gentle warmth.

Deborah might well have agreed to anything if only to see the evening end so that she could vent her chaotic emotions on Isaac. Everyone had been more than kind and friendly. The preparation for the *Seder* had been completed precisely as they had instructed. And she had been touched and gratified by the number of Kosher dishes prepared for the occasion. But the words, the symbolism, the story, the very essence of Passover had been turned upside down! It was nearly over, though — only praise and celebration of God's provision. *How can that possibly be modified?* she wondered.

Conversation was abruptly suspended when the pastor called everyone back to their tables and bid the children seek the *afikomen*. Shrieks of success echoed throughout the barn as the most enterprising searchers held aloft their find in exchange for a "ransom payment" by the table leader. The winners received a small fleece lamb as a reminder of the Lamb of God.

Following Isaac's example, leaders at each table poured a third cup of juice. But he was only granted the opportunity to explain that the third cup is the Cup of Redemption. The blessing was preempted when Pastor Lindeman stepped forward.

"This is it, the moment we've all been waiting for, when Passover meets Communion." He took a piece of *matzah* and began reading a familiar passage from Luke, chapter 22.

> *…taking a piece of matzah, he made the b'rakhah, the blessing, broke it, gave it to them and said, "This is my body, which is being given for you; do this in memory of me." He did the same with the cup after the meal, saying, "This cup is the New Covenant, ratified by my blood, which is being poured out for you."*

Mark suited actions to words just as he did every Sunday they shared Communion as the body of Christ, but this time it was different. The disciples, who had celebrated the Passover Seder every year of their lives, failed to understand the profound significance of Jesus' words spoken while holding the cup shared *after* the meal, the Cup of Redemption. The full meaning of those actions and words had likewise been hidden from his modern disciples. Finally making the powerful connection between Passover and The Last Supper, many present found their vision blurred with tears.

"Even as the blood of the lamb brought salvation in Egypt, so the Messiah's atoning death can bring salvation to all who believe," Mark said, then nodded to Isaac.

The name "Messiah" rang in Isaac's ears each time Mark spoke it with such authority. Resentment, doubt, and curiosity ran rampant through his brain, but he put all such thoughts aside to offer the Hebrew blessing. They drank the third cup together, then read again from the Psalms for the second half of the *Hallel.* Isaac instructed everyone to fill their cup for the fourth and last time. "This is the Cup of Praise and signals the end of our *Seder.*" He lifted his cup to speak the final blessing for the fruit of the vine, but Mark forestalled the moment with an apology as he raised his hand.

"Before we drink of this Cup of Praise, I want to leave you with another thought as we conclude this beautiful evening. The scriptures speak of the first cup and the third cup. We have already considered a possible meaning for the second cup in the context of Jesus' final Passover, but no mention is made of the fourth cup either. Matthew records these words:

> *'I tell you, I will not drink this "fruit of the vine" again until the day I drink new wine with you in my Father's Kingdom.' After singing the Hallel, they went out to the Mount of Olives.*

"I have committed much study to these events and read countless commentaries by brilliant Bible scholars far more knowledgeable than I, but the explanation that makes the most sense to me is that the fourth cup was not drunk at all! The final fourth cup of the Passover will be drunk at the wedding feast of the Lamb as described in Revelation 19.[12] Whether that is true or not, I encourage you all to do your own study. And remember, it is not only the New Testament that contains Jesus' story; it is clearly stamped on the full canon of scripture from Genesis to Revelation." Turning to their guests, he lifted his cup. "We will complete this evening's celebration by sharing this cup together, for we have much to offer in praise and thanksgiving now. I think we can all agree that we have been richly blessed by the leadership of Isaac and Deborah Rosenbaum who brought to life for us the deep historical meaning in the sacred observance of Passover."

Waiting for the thunderous applause to subside so that the final blessing could be heard, Isaac then lifted his cup and led the Community Church family in the traditional Passover wish, "Next Year in Jerusalem!"

During the ensuing chaos, when clean-up began and families gathered kids, coats, and casseroles, Abe managed to catch up with the Rosenbaums before they slipped away. He had watched Mrs. Rosenbaum from a nearby table and had witnessed the play of emotions across her face. Over the course of the evening, her naturally twinkling eyes had gradually assumed a

---

[12] Galen, *Christ in the Passover*, 6.

shuttered look, and her broad smile had narrowed to a polite, thin line. He recognized, as few others could, the indignation – perhaps even anger – that filled her generous heart, and he felt led to pour his compassionate balm on her wounded spirit. He and Amy caught up with the elderly couple just as their last well-wishers bid them goodnight.

"Mr. Rosenbaum, Mrs. Rosenbaum, do you remember me from my work at your house last year?" Deborah's reserve softened at Abe's humble approach.

"Of course, we do! And this lovely young woman must be your wife." The twinkle reasserted itself as Amy shyly took the other woman's hand.

"She is the light of my life," Abe confirmed simply.

"Spoken like a man who desires a happy one," Isaac said.

"A happy life?"

"A happy wife. One will ensure the other!" Isaac congratulated the newlyweds, then Amy excused herself to put her violin away after agreeing to some cooking lessons.

"You are a lucky man, young Abraham," Isaac said.

"I am a blessed man," Abe replied. "But I did not approach you just so you could meet Amy, though it gives me great pleasure to introduce her to everyone I've ever met. I hoped I might have a few minutes to speak with you before you leave. You see, I believe I understand your reaction to what you heard tonight, because I felt the same way you did at one time."

The guarded look stole over Deborah's face again, so Abe thought it best to get straight to the point.

"You know me to be a Christian now, but until a few years ago, I was a devout Muslim, a follower of Islam my whole life." They had assumed that having been born and raised in Lebanon, young Mr. Yousef was a Maronite Christian. Neither had guessed that his religious roots were in Islam.

"You left *Islam* to become a Christian?" Deborah asked in shocked surprise.

"When Derek first started sharing his faith with me, I was initially outraged by claims that Jesus was the Son of God. I knew of Jesus as a holy man, a prophet, but I was taught that Allah could have no son. That's when Derek told me about the God of Abraham, Isaac, and Jacob and explained that he is *not* the same as the Allah worshipped by Muslims. Despite explaining the five pillars of Islam to him, he insisted that there was no amount of righteousness on my part that could assure my place in heaven. 'How could the death of one man accomplish that?' I asked. 'Where did that leave me?'

"I asked about a thousand questions and found that all the answers could only be found in one man – the man who was also God. The choice to follow him cost me my family and the only identity I had ever known. The glorious exception is my mother, who called me after my honeymoon to tell me she became a Christian at my wedding! I fear for her when she tells my father, but her faith is unwavering. I can only pray for her."

He went on to recount the decision to change his first name and the reasons behind it. They were nothing short of amazed that a former Muslim would champion Isaac, the Jewish seed of Abraham, over Ishmael.

"I know much of what you heard tonight was disturbing, especially references to the Messiah, but it is the only way the words of the prophets make sense. Excuse me, I should say it is the only way they make sense to me and to other believers."

As Abe spoke, Isaac's eyes gleamed with curiosity. Deborah's reflected only doubt and trouble. Abe would have gone on to share his full testimony with the Rosenbaums, but it was not the time. They already had much to think about, and it was getting late.

"I will bid you goodnight now, but I humbly ask that I might call upon you for your insight on the writings of the prophets. I am learning every day as I study the scriptures, and I would enjoy learning more of Jewish tradition and God's interaction with his covenant people from you both. Though I would be *most* gratified if you could just teach Amy to make your rugelach, Mrs. Rosenbaum."

His parting comment inspired the glimmer of a smile, and her dimples flashed briefly when Abe kissed her cheek. He waved to them as they drove away.

Anticipation of emotional venting by his wife, damped throughout the evening and therefore intensified, had instilled in Isaac a dread of the drive to their forest hideaway. But Abe's timely intervention had given the couple a great deal to contemplate, diluting Deborah's outrage to thoughtful introspection. Silence is not the same as peace, but Isaac gladly accepted the substitute.

CHAPTER 14

Go quickly now and tell His disciples that He is risen from the dead.
Matthew 28:7 (TLV)

I t should have been a morning of unalloyed rejoicing; of total focus on the resurrection of the Lord of lords and King of kings; of getting lost in the majesty and lyrical depth of the music; of being transported to a beautiful garden filled with flowers and the fragrance of spring and hope and promise. It should have been.

But before the pastor could finish his words of welcome to a packed sanctuary and lead everyone in the perennial Easter proclamation and response; before the snare drummer and music leader could bring the crowded room to its feet; and before the bagpiper could strike in for the stirring intro to the opening hymn, *"See, What a Morning,"* a perfectly timed entrance by one individual brought everything to a screeching halt like a ten-car pile-up on the freeway. The calculated move drew all eyes in her direction and momentarily distracted those present from anticipation of a deeply moving worship experience.

"Oh, I am *so* sorry. It looks like I accidentally took two bulletins. How silly of me!"

The simple words of apology to the usher sounded more like an invitation to flirtation when spoken by a strikingly beautiful woman. She intentionally pitched her voice to carry over that of the pastor as he offered his greeting of, "Happy Resurrection Day!" Not wanting to appear ungracious to a newcomer, he paused before beginning the proclamation to allow the late arrival to find a seat. Brittany Murdock had no such qualms.

Fairly certain that her aunt would plant herself firmly in front of the preaching source, Brittany deliberately walked slowly down the outside aisle on the opposite side of the church, gazing at each pew she passed, evidently looking for someone. It wasn't until she reached the front of the church that she made much of spying her family seated midway down the other side of the sanctuary. But instead of hurrying back in the direction she had come, then up the center aisle, she sauntered across the front of the room. Smiling at Mark Lindeman and the others on the platform, she turned and performed a full-frontal assault on Community Church as she made her leisurely way to the seat she had asked Aunt Reenie to save for her.

"You and the boys go ahead. I'm not quite ready," she had told them 20 minutes earlier, still wrapped in a bathrobe. Aunt Reenie had come to accept her niece's quirks without question. That she was destined to be late for her first day of church attendance, and on Easter at that, hardly raised Reenie's eyebrows. Had she bothered to notice, she might have wondered at the delay given the fact that Brittany's face was already made up flawlessly, and every strand of her deep bronze hair had been fashioned into an elegant French twist. A few stray, wispy curls highlighted her ears and the nape of her neck.

How long does it take to don a dress? Reenie might have asked. But the boys were anxious to find their friends before finding their seats. And knowing that attempting rational thought was futile, as regarded her niece, she had gone ahead, walking the short distance to the church on a glorious morning that reduced Brittany's eccentricities to irrelevant nonsense. However, as she sat watching her niece's shameful behavior in silent dismay and embarrassment, she bemoaned her own weakness in not confirming that the younger woman was dressed decently. Though Brittany was always dressed *stylishly*, modesty had never been her guiding principle in clothes selection. This Sunday was no exception.

Brittany might have stepped off a designer runway, so perfectly did the linen suit in a pale shade of buttercup yellow fit her equally perfect figure. The color should have made her look sallow and anemic; instead, it gave her the illusion of sunshine personified. Maddeningly so, thought the envious women around her who felt positively frumpy by comparison, despite their own new Easter attire. A long-sleeved jacket, held together by a tiny bow tied under her fulsome bosom, was shed as soon as she reached the pew. The moment could not have been better stage-managed for effect. Delighted at finding herself located immediately behind the Ludlows' pew, Brittany carefully smoothed her dress before taking her seat.

Her tailored sleeveless frock featured a wide, scoop neckline cut a little too low, and a straight skirt hemmed a little too high. Everything in between was a little too tight. The gathered populace looked on like unwilling witnesses of the car crash image her presence evoked. They wanted to look away but continued to stare in stupefied horror. Accomplishing all she had intended, Brittany took her seat and nodded at Mark Lindeman as if granting him permission to go on. The fascinated congregation shifted their gaze from the center ring to the ringmaster, wondering how he would handle such an awkward interlude. With commendable sangfroid, the pastor judiciously ignored the smoldering wildfire in their midst and continued the service without missing a beat. His calm command of the situation salvaged the morning and the message and helped everyone to focus once again on the empty tomb.

"He is risen," he said, beaming.

"*He is risen, indeed!*"

Three times the call came, and each time the congregation responded with growing excitement and volume until the very walls reverberated with the sound. Under cover of the music that followed, Aletha nudged Granny Gert to ask what she had missed.

"I don't remember hearing such a deafening pall since the last time Mark spoke about sacrificial giving!"

Gert grunted derisively. "We've just been joined by Jezebel in the flesh. And I do mean flesh! What I can't figure out is how a nice woman like Irene Fields could have such a hussy for a niece! All I can say is that I hope that young woman doesn't plan on joining the more chaste members of her family at Rosie's Easter dinner."

"Now Trudy, she can't be that bad."

"Hmph!" was her friend's only reply before contributing a loud monotone to the hymn.

Granny Gert wasn't the only one disgusted by Brittany Murdock's behavior. Rose gave Tim an earful on the way home and found an appreciative audience in Derek, who had volunteered to help them with last minute set-up rather than waiting to arrive with his mom.

"I know it's not a Christian thing to say, but… ooooh! That woman really yanks my chain; to use this Sunday, of all days, to make a spectacle of herself. And you! You practically encouraged her!"

"*Me?*" said Tim, caught off guard by the unexpected attack. "What did *I* do? I tried to *ignore* her."

"That's right, Rose. Hold his feet to the fire," Derek supplied helpfully from the back seat.

"You've got no room to talk either, mister," Rose said, turning to glare at him. "You were all smiles and charm."

Well, I can't help that," Derek said, grinning. "Besides, I could see how uncomfortable my buddy was, so I tried to field a little of the lovely lady's attention. You know I've always got your back, bro."

"Right," Tim replied with heavy sarcasm. "Your sacrifice is duly noted."

"Anything to help a friend."

"You two can laugh it off, but I really believe she *enjoys* stirring up mischief." Rose sat gazing out the window at nothing, an unfamiliar frown on her face. Tim took her hand, holding it in his strong, comforting clasp.

"We are not going to let whatshername or anyone else ruin this wonderful day. Now, let me see the smile that always melts my heart."

Rose returned the pressure of his hand and said, lovingly, "Thank you for being such a patient and understanding husband."

"Ugh, just shoot me!" Derek muttered in the back seat and clapped his hands over his ears.

Rose's spirits restored, she set to work like a dynamo when they got home, completing last minute kitchen duties in preparation for the 20-odd guests expected. Decorating was already complete. It had been a gradual process, with God the Creator doing most of the heavy lifting.

Jonquils, early tulips, and hyacinths, in various stages of bloom, graced the planting beds around the house, reaching to the warmth of a strengthening sun. Tender yellowish-green leaves had begun their creeping conquest of the willow trees' branches, while the ornamental maples provided an early hint of ruby foliage. Clothed in reddish-purple blooms, the redbuds offered a regal welcome where they lined the long drive. And dogwoods, bearing the bloom of the cross with its crown of thorns and four pedals, each tipped with a drop of blood, paid homage to the resurrection in variations of pink and white. The potted bulb plants, used during the Yousef wedding, spread the last of their glory throughout the house before drying and dormancy would prepare them for a permanent fall planting.

But Rose's favorite symbol of spring stood on the dining room table, it's branches spreading to make room for the whimsical ornaments hanging between the golden yellow forsythia blossoms. The *Osterbaum* or Easter Tree, was a tradition perpetuated by Granny Gert's mother, who had continued the Lenten ritual after immigrating to America from her German homeland. Rose and her sisters had always admired the display at their grandmother's home. When Granny Gert left the farm that she had shared with her husband for 60 years, she had offered the ornaments to her granddaughters.

Lily, never one to place much value on anything not considered *au courant* as determined by the latest home decorating craze, had taken only a few ornaments in token of her childhood. Violet had been immersed in getting through her midwife courses at the time and couldn't be bothered with anything but studying and pursuing her then boyfriend, Steve. So, the bulk had come to Rose. Recognizing the former pagan fertility symbolism in the eggs and bunnies, and ladybugs and bumble bees, she had added to the collection three wooden crosses, a tiny woven wicker crown, and little felt lambs. Clipped several weeks earlier, the buds of the forsythia opened right on schedule, and Rose's Easter Tree drew accolades from both her husband and grandmother.

She had just relocated the decorative tree to the sideboard when the first guests arrived. The kids were thrilled to have their own table in the kitchen and were charmed by the diminutive *Osterbaum* placed in the center, hung with tiny birds and flowers. Ages ranged from four to twelve years. Abby – the eldest Lindeman – assured Karen Thatcher that she would help little Cookie with her food so that "Mommy" could enjoy a grown-up lunch. Other than briefly wondering what was keeping Mattie and Drew, Rose almost forgot to worry about the full Murdock entourage. She congratulated herself on dodging that bullet a little prematurely.

Phase 1 had gone as planned. Now, speeding to the home of Tim Ludlow, Brittany smiled in anticipation of Phase 2. Aunt Reenie fretted in the passenger seat.

"I don't know why you couldn't have filled the gas tank yesterday, and as to the *side dish* you promised to provide… well, all I can say is, I've never been more embarrassed. And why you had to wait until today to buy it…" Her agitation found expression in her twisting fingers. "We'll probably be the last family to arrive. They may even be waiting on us! Oh, how could you be so thoughtless?"

"Hush, Reenie. You worry like an old woman!" Brittany answered in a waspish tone. "Everything will be just fine," she added and produced her best feline smile. The boys in the back seat tuned out the squabble in favor of taking in promising sights on their way to a new destination. Anticipation grew as they turned off the bypass and through the wrought-iron gates.

Screaming down the long driveway, Brittany slammed on the brakes and skidded to an abrupt stop in a cloud of dust. Blocking the egress of several other cars without a thought, she climbed out of the low-slung vehicle and paraded to the house, leaving Aunt Reenie to unload the boys. Brittany waved indiscriminately at the crowd gathered in the kitchen, held out a bag of potato chips vaguely in Rose's direction, and made a dead set for Tim who had tried, unsuccessfully, to hide in the corner.

Turning her back to him, Brittany once again made a show of unfastening her jacket and waited expectantly for him to remove it. She smiled coquettishly over her shoulder at his face which glowed with embarrassment. Tim took her jacket as gingerly as he might have approached radioactive waste and stood there feeling like an idiot until his mother swept the contaminated garment out of his hands. Tim had no thought but that of flight. Unfortunately, his dazed brain slowed his actions and before he knew it, Brittany had wrapped her hands around his muscular arm.

"Since everyone is here now," she said, oblivious of the guest list, "will you show me to the table? I'm sure I would get lost in this big house all by myself." Her lips pouted prettily, but as she turned to preen herself before the assembled fellowship, she sustained a shock, and the pouty smile froze on her lips.

Brittany had never been a favorite with women. She had always been carefully circumspect in her behavior as she had gathered female social contacts in Kansas City who could open doors to the attention of their wealthy husbands. Once she had made conquests of those most susceptible to her charms, she cared little for the displeasure aroused in the hearts of their wives. Her present reckless, attention-seeking behavior might be attributed to the enforced seclusion of Tinkers Well and the loss, or dismissal, of those fawning admirers. Perhaps it grew from the vacuum created by her husband's absence and the slavish devotion now denied her. Matt was no longer there to kiss away any doubt concerning her superiority over the rest of the female sex. Whatever the reason, Brittany had grown daily more obsessed with the need for adoration and less discreet in her demand for it.

Aunt Reenie certainly never supplied any, and her sons only answered with an indifferent affirmative when queried as to whether Mama looked pretty. She had neither sought, nor expected admiration from other women of her acquaintance. But as she stood there in the homey kitchen filled with those who shared deep friendships of long standing, she was amazed to see frowns of disapproval on the men's faces, too. The male population in the room, rather than being drawn like a throng of moths to a bright flame, seemed more inclined to look away. And Derek, who had offered kindly attention during the service when his friend displayed defensive aloofness — even he frowned. Shaking his head almost imperceptibly, he warned her to think better of her behavior.

A small voice broke the silence when four-year-old Cookie Thatcher asked the million-dollar question, "Why does duh pwetty wady wook so funny?"

Brittany had never been made to feel gauche by an entire assembled body at a social function, and certainly not by a child. The unpleasant sensation brought her up short and stirred a sense of ill-use and anger deep within her. Looking frantically for support in the faces confronting her, she watched with relief as an unlikely rescuer approached. She had hardly expected the pastor to be the one person to appreciate her worth.

"You must be Mrs. Murdock," Mark Lindeman said in a friendly, avuncular way. Brittany was compelled to loosen her hold on Tim's arm in order to shake the hand held out to her, so he took the opportunity to bolt for the dining room doorway where Rose stood. "I missed you in all the hubbub after the service. Please forgive my tardiness in welcoming you to our community."

It was hardly the enamored greeting she had hoped for, but she had worked with less. Summoning her most alluring smile, she said, "*You* may call me Brittany," and tweaked the corners of his collar with undo familiarity.

Mark glanced at her hands, then looked steadily into her eyes. Without a word, he simply raised his eyebrows in a gentle rebuke, and waited until she released his collar. "I imagine you must be missing your husband and old friends. I hope you will find new friends and purpose here," he said, then turned away from her to greet another parishioner.

Her hands fell, numb, to her sides as she experienced another unpleasant jolt. Brittany had read not condemnation in the pastor's expression, which she could almost have understood; she had seen pity.

Pity! she thought with disgust. *This pudgy man with thinning hair, a forgettable face, wearing rumpled khakis and an inexpensive off-the-rack sports coat — this man pities me? Brittany Murdock?*

Resentment joined the anger bubbling within her. She had *never* sought pity. That would be a show of weakness, and she was not weak. She didn't want pity; she wanted power. And the unassuming, unimportant, insignificant people surrounding her had all but stripped her of that power. They had rejected and judged her, then offered her compassion. Brittany would have felt less offended by a slap in the face. The pastor's dismissal of her self-promoted irresistibility was the final rejection. Never mind that he had shown her kindness and forbearance; she felt like a social pariah, an outcast. Nobody appreciated her.

And for that, they will pay! Brittany pledged to herself.

An immediate, tacit agreement to intercept any more of Brittany Murdock's antics shot through the minds of the other women present with the force of an interstellar radar beam. Angelica and Marilyn, who rightly interpreted Brittany's response to Mark Lindeman's well-intentioned words, stepped quickly to her side and each took one of her hands in theirs. Bowing their heads, the two women maintained a strong hold on Brittany while Tim offered a prayer of thanksgiving for the feast and the occasion that had brought them together in celebration.

Thoughts of revenge, already swirling in her brain, were sidelined when Brittany found her hands clasped by the two middle-aged women who seemed to have materialized out of nowhere. Immediately following the "Amen," her captors propelled her to the dining room, where she found herself marooned amid what she considered the dregs of society – the elderly.

Aletha Mason, who Brittany labeled an old blind woman of no interest, occupied the chair to her right, and beyond her sat a short barrel of a woman with a voice as big as her beak-like nose. Granny Gert would have roared with laughter at the description by the younger woman had she given her the opportunity to voice her opinion. But she had no intention of letting Brittany poison any of that blessed fellowship with her malicious tongue. Instead, she kept up a lively flow of anecdotes and encouraged Bobby Taylor, sitting on Brittany's left, to share some of his legendary stories which were as colorful as they were harmless. Aunt Reenie was enormously entertained and held her new friends in awe for so neatly managing her niece.

Brittany sat in high dudgeon, refusing to respond to Mr. Taylor's friendly conversational gambits. Her sartorial soul simply would not allow any kind of interaction with a man dressed in a plaid jacket, checked shirt and paisley tie, and worn corduroys. She eventually lowered herself enough to ask of her other dinner companion the names of unfamiliar faces at the table.

"I believe you know Tim and Rose. Aren't they a lovely couple? And absolutely devoted to one another. Oh yes, absolutely *devoted*. Then there's Abraham and Amy Yousef who are newlyweds. He's the very tall, handsome, middle Eastern man who, no doubt, is smiling at his equally tall bride. I find the planes of his face so interesting. And I expect Amy's big brown eyes are gazing adoringly at him. They usually are."

Brittany stared more closely at Aletha, wondering if she had somehow misread her blindness.

"You understand, of course, that my descriptions are based on what others have told me and what I can discern with my hands, but I can picture them in my mind's eye as clearly as if I could actually see them. Now, as to the others; Derek you've already met. I've always imagined his smile to be as bright and charming as his personality." She went on to list Mark and Lisa Lindeman, Landry and Karen Thatcher, Angelica, and Marilyn.

"Yes, yes, I'm sure they're important to someone," Brittany said impatiently, "but who is that very attractive man who just arrived and is sitting next to Tim's mother, Mattie's dowdy schoolteacher?" Aletha grimaced at such an unflattering description, but Brittany never noticed. She was overtly ogling the stranger.

"That gentleman is my son, Timothy Miles Hawthorne, and, as you may have guessed, he is Tim's father and Marilyn's former husband. Through God's miraculous grace, they are a family again, quite inseparable, really."

If Aletha hoped her words would act as a deterrent to Brittany's predatory nature, she had underestimated her tablemate, who sat with her eyes fastened on Miles' elegant figure. It was not only the square jawline, piercing eyes, and athletic physique, however, that drew her gaze. Brittany recognized money when she saw it, and money declared itself comprehensively from the excellent cut of his suit to his silver cuff links to his exquisite manners and carriage.

Aletha may have been unaware of Brittany's absorption, but the other ladies at the table were already planning to thwart her next campaign. At an unspoken signal within that sisterhood, the meal was declared finished.

"Rosie," Granny Gert shouted from the opposite end of the table, "Why don't you have all these fellows trot on along to the family room, or conservatory, or whatever you're calling it these days, and they can work on this great performance we've all heard so much about. I know it's a Bible story, but they'll probably have us all laughing. Hmm, I wonder if that would be considered irreverent…"

"That's an excellent idea, Trudy." Aletha could always be counted on to back up whatever scheme her friend concocted. The gentlemen excused themselves with haste. Tim threw Granny Gert a broad wink by way of a thank you. "And since there are so many of us," Aletha continued, "I think we can excuse Lisa, Karen, and Brittany to prepare for the egg hunt on the front lawn. The rest of us can clean off the tables. I'll help where I can."

"Oh, but I'm much better with theatricals. I adore acting, so I'll just – "

Brittany's protests were cut short when her newly appointed guardians propelled her through the wide opening to the parlor before she could make a break for the family room. As she was pulled into the foyer, she could hear men's voices arguing.

"I, of course, will be Jesus," she heard Derek say.

"There is no 'of course' about it. I am from the Middle East, so I am certain I more closely resemble what Jesus must have looked like." The voice was unfamiliar, but she guessed it belonged to the one named Abraham. "Besides, I have black hair."

"Hey, I have black hair too, bro."

"*What?* Your head is cleanshaven. You don't have *any* hair!"

Laughter was the last sound heard drifting down the hallway before the front door closed behind the trio. A stack of pastel colored wicker baskets was thrust into Brittany's hands with instructions to fill each with shredded green paper while Karen and Lisa checked the placement of plastic Easter eggs scattered around the garden.

Waiting until she heard the front door close, Rose hurried around the table to plant a kiss on first, her grandmother's cheek, then on Aletha's.

"Ladies, I salute you. You may have just saved the day."

"Oh, there's nothing to it," Granny Gert replied nonchalantly. "The only way to handle a baggage like that is to be decisive." Then, remembering she was talking about Reenie's niece, she added, "No offense meant, Irene."

Reenie's usual hovering frown had dissipated like magic, and her weathered cheeks radiated sunshine. "Oh, none taken, I assure you. In fact, I applaud all of you. It's remarkable, really." So impressed was Reenie by such swift, resolute action, she would have followed these women on any crusade of their choosing. They had accomplished in a few minutes what she had failed to do in eight years of living with Brittany's machinations.

A spirit of lighthearted gaiety infused the prosaic acts of clearing tables, loading the dishwasher, and packaging leftovers. The scrubbing of large pots and pans and serving bowls could wait. Rose and Marilyn helped the younger children into their sweaters, and Angelica made sure the older ladies were wrapped warmly in coats and scarves. The afternoon had warmed to a pleasant 66 degrees under a sunny sky, but a slight breeze might chill Aletha and Reenie. Gert had already grabbed her own sweater.

Chores complete, the women and children made their way to the front of the house where they found Brittany standing on the wide verandah with a scowl on her face and baskets in her hands. She had only attempted an escape once, claiming that it was a little too cool outside without her jacket. Lisa had gently but firmly pushed her back onto the porch swing and retrieved the jacket for her.

"Okay, kids. This is your special event – the first Willow Walk Easter Egg Hunt!" Rose had to dampen the resulting cheers and whistles to explain important rules.

"You have to find five eggs apiece, and I've labeled every egg with each of your first initials. *Do not* pick up any that are not yours." Rose looked pointedly at ten-year-old Jonathan Lindeman, who liked to make up his own rules. He looked away, his face that of a blameless angel. "Let me spell it out for you. A is for Abigail; J and *only J* is for Jonathan; S for Stephen; and P for Miss Pris."

"My name is Prithilla!" The youngest Lindeman, like Drew Murdock, was missing a few teeth. "So it is," acknowledged Rose with a wink before moving on. "M for Mattie, D for Drew. If I use the name Andrew, your eggs might get confused with Abby's. Is that okay, Drew?"

"It's okay. Bethides, the only one who callth me Andrew ith Mama, usually when she'th mad at me." Unlike young Jonathan's face, Brittany's did *not* look angelic.

"K for KC – only one letter per kid, buddy; and finally, C for Miss Cookie." Kneeling before the little girl, Rose said, as if amazed, "Your mama told me that you know all your letters now so you can find your eggs all by yourself!"

"Of couwse," Cookie said, confirming the obvious. "I'm a big giwl now!"

"When you find all your eggs, take them over to that side of the house," said Rose, motioning around the corner to the east façade where prevailing westerly winds would cause less disturbance, "and we'll open them together. Mrs. Lindeman, Mrs. Thatcher, and Mrs. Murdock will be watching, so make sure you don't grab anyone else's eggs. These are special eggs that contain a treasure even more precious than candy." The older kids looked a little skeptical, but when she said, "Ready, set, go!" they took off like horses out of the starting gate.

During Rose's instructions, the men had come around the back of the house to join the ladies already seated in folding chairs on the east lawn. At the sight of far more interesting company, Brittany began slowly backing around the corner of the verandah toward stairs that led from the library to the side yard. When she turned to make a break for freedom, she ran smack into Granny Gert, who could move with remarkable stealth for one of her girth and stature. Brittany wanted to scream.

"Rosie left this fancy mug of hers in the kitchen, and I didn't want to interrupt her and the kiddies by coming out the front door, so I just moseyed around the side of the house. Fancy running into you!"

Brittany was beginning to feel trapped. Everywhere she moved, she ran into an impediment. There was no escape now. Gert grabbed her arm and drug her back around the verandah just as the children ran down the wide steps and into the garden.

"Look at those young'uns go!" Gert chortled with glee. "Let me just hand this mug thingy to Rosie, and you and me'll go see how they're doing. There goes that little Drew of yours. He is a pistol!"

Brittany almost wished she *had* a pistol. Mentally, she waivered as to whether she'd rather use it on the evil genius beside her who (she was convinced) had somehow orchestrated this social debacle with an invisible hand, or on herself. Her fight or flight instinct, however, was definitely leaning in the flight direction. Hope soared when Granny Gert let go of her long enough to deliver the mug and chide Rose on her forgetfulness. As she stepped away in relief, Brittany felt another arm linked in hers.

"Mrs. Murdock, I'm so glad you were able to join us today. I've wanted to tell you how much I enjoy having Mattie in class this semester. He really is quite bright, and such a gentleman. That's a compliment to you, you know."

It was a compliment to Aunt Reenie, and Brittany knew it, just as she suspected Marilyn Ludlow knew it. *How much more of this stifling niceness must I endure?* she wondered.

They strolled around the garden until all the eggs had been found. Everyone gathered in front of a big board shaped like a cross and anchored with twine and stakes against the effects of the wind. The cross was marked with numbers from 1 to 40. Each child opened their eggs carefully so that the contents would not fly away. Brittany reluctantly helped Mattie and Drew, at Marilyn's suggestion, and noticed the other parents doing the same. When Rose called a number, Abby Lindeman took each sticky note "clue," covered with two to four words printed in large font, and placed it on the board in the designated spot. Rose purposely called the numbers out of order. With the final sticky note in place, the kids began to read the message aloud.

While they concentrated on the story of the women visiting Jesus' tomb early on that first Easter, Brittany concentrated on seeking an avenue of escape. She spied an empty lawn chair next to Miles Hawthorne and looked for an inconspicuous route to his side. She took a few tentative steps just as the children reached the text about sharing the news with the disciples. Before she could make any more progress she was forestalled by Rose.

"Now that we've unveiled the secret message, maybe we can all find someone to tell this good news to. What do you think?" Raising her voice to carry over the noisy affirmative, Rose gestured at the cross behind her and added, "Since you've been so good at finding *this* treasure, you will each receive an extra treasure."

Brittany was about to make a desperate dash toward the prize when Rose held up a large shopping bag and announced, "Why don't we ask our newest guest, Mrs. Murdock, to help hand out the treasure?"

"Yay!" the kids yelled.

Noooo! Brittany shrieked silently.

She was trapped again. By the time the enormous plastic eggs, packed with goodies, had been distributed, all the men were standing off to the side, waiting to begin their drama. As the exception, Mr. Taylor gallantly stood and asked Brittany to join him in a neighboring lawn chair. She sat down, defeated. She heard nothing of the cleverly combined stories: one of Jesus walking with his spiritually blind disciples on the road to Emmaus; and the second, the tale of doubting Thomas who had to see and touch his risen Savior to believe. She neither knew the stories, nor found any amusement value in amateurish performance. She was alone in her indifference.

Granny Gert had been right about the laughter. It was hard to take seriously the sight of grown men wearing bathrobes or oversized, belted burlap bags. Each also sported long sections of cloth, either wrapped around their heads or draped across their shoulders like they had just stepped out of the shower. But the stories were timeless and reminded everyone present of the monumental events that occurred all those years ago, and of the joy and wonder felt by Jesus' earliest disciples.

Following the drama, while friends mingled and everyone congratulated Tim and Rose on a wonderful event, Brittany finally made good her escape. Without a thought for her children or her husband's elderly aunt, she ran to her car and drove off with tires squealing.

Anticipating Reenie's dismay, Angelica encouraged her and the boys to enjoy themselves as long as they liked. She and Derek would be honored to escort them home later.

Unaware of Brittany's scorn of pity and of those who offered it, Rose felt a momentary twinge of sympathy for the other woman. Then she remembered Brittany's single-minded pursuit of Tim and her total disregard for her own children. There is pity, and there is regrettable awareness of a life ill-spent. Rose's tender heart was no less sympathetic or kind or caring than it had ever been, but after closer association with Brittany Murdock, it was certainly more wise.

CHAPTER 15

And not only this, but we also celebrate in our tribulations, knowing that tribulation brings about perseverance; and perseverance, proven character; and proven character, hope...
Romans 5:3-4 (NASB)

A sense of well-being rested on the old house much like the contentment inherent in reading the predictable ending of a favorite romance novel. The chaotic energy of a large gathering had mellowed to quiet and calm as the nucleus of the Ludlow family sat in companionable ease in the parlor of Willow Walk. Rose and Marilyn, seated together on the long plush couch, spoke in an undertone to one another, sharing a wager over whether Granny Gert would wake herself from her nap. Seated in a neighboring chair, the subject of the bet snorted from time to time while her head gradually fell forward, but her nap remained otherwise uninterrupted. Scout followed her example with the controlled silence and posture of a gentleman. Rose doubted the eventuality, having watched her grandmother fall asleep in the middle of a lively crowd, but Marilyn, ever the pragmatist, was inclined to choose the more likely probability. They had agreed to leave the dregs of kitchen clean-up until after the big surprise Miles had promised ever since his late arrival for lunch.

As it happened, neither won the bet. Despite Miles' obvious impatience, his equally determined son insisted they stow all the extra lawn chairs and the cross in the garage before taking a break. It was their entrance on the scene that caused Granny Gert to jerk up her head and demand to know if it was time yet. Aletha sat bright and alert in the wingback chair reserved for her comfort, while Rose moved to join Tim on their favorite love seat. The stage was set, and Miles took the floor, directing everyone's attention to the mysteriously draped easel standing in the corner. An imposing sign with bold lettering cautioned, "DO NOT TOUCH."

"I know that we all agreed today's focus would be about celebration of the resurrection with our church friends, and rightly so, but I'm afraid I simply could not wait any longer to present you, Mari," Miles said, turning to his love who was totally unprepared for his announcement, "with your birthday gift."

"But Timothy," she protested, "my birthday isn't till next month, and I don't expect or need anything special – "

"I'm afraid we will never agree on that," Miles said, silencing any more objections. Rose waited impatiently for the reveal. She had no idea what lay behind the shroud, despite pestering her husband for a clue after catching the two men completing set-up following the departure of their last guests. Tim had warned her of dire consequences if she peeked.

"Everyone here is well aware that a miracle took place in my life nine months ago, and I have been on a journey of discovery ever since. My concepts of worth, morality, and love – so long twisted by my own distorted understanding and total lack of wisdom – collapsed into meaningless rubble when I was confronted with the futility of my existence. That which I thought I most desired had been there for the taking all along, but I had allowed everything I most *needed* to slip away." Miles stopped for a minute to clear his throat before plowing on.

"I am happy to report that the challenges and revelations of the past nine months have not been in vain. You have each aided in my education in your own way. Mother, you taught me to trust in the power of prayer. Tim, you modeled integrity and honor. Rose, you welcomed me without reserve and provided gentle encouragement." Finally, he turned to Marilyn who waited a little breathlessly for whatever tribute he had to offer. "And Mari, a woman in a million, you gave me a kick in the pants." She stared at him, stunned into silence.

"Mari, you have changed – not in essence, for you will always be a tender, nurturing woman of faith – but in character. You have developed great strength and independence and a fierce devotion to the welfare of children. Ironically, the latter quality probably surfaced when you discovered that you needed to protect our child – from me. That disclosure, in the aftermath of an emotional and physical tornado, more than anything else, was the wake-up call I needed. And it showed me what an extraordinary woman had walked out of my life."

The room was deathly quiet. Everyone focused on Miles and Marilyn. Even Granny Gert managed to ignore her inner demon and kept her mouth shut.

"But Timothy…" Marilyn tried to say something – *anything* – to mitigate such harsh self-censure. For she, more than all the others, had witnessed the greatest change in Miles.

"No, Mari, let me finish. It was your courage that allowed Tim to become the man he is today, and a son that any father, deserving or not, would be proud of. It was your independence that drove you to resume your calling as a teacher. And it continues to be your devotion to children that fires your concern for their minds, their hearts, and their futures. I've witnessed that passion firsthand, and it inspired me with a vision – a vision that has given me the direction I lacked.

"I no longer want to make money for the sake of money itself. I don't want to waste my life pursuing empty goals simply because I can. You gave me purpose, Mari – clear, challenging, fulfilling purpose. And for that I will always be grateful. Now I want to give you something in return, something with meaning." He moved over to the easel and whisked away the covering to reveal an architect's rendering of a low, broad building with a playground on one end and a taller structure protruding off the rear. Taking a seat next to Marilyn, Miles handed her a portfolio. She opened it slowly as if afraid of its contents.

"It's a school, Mari," Miles explained in the face of her total shock and bewilderment. "The first Christian school in Harrington County." Disbelief continued to render her speechless. "Here, let me show you. This is the front elevation," Miles explained, then pulled another sheet from the folder. "And here you can see the gymnasium off the back, which will have to double as a lunchroom for now. These covered areas outside," he said, pointing to another drawing, "will allow students access to fresh air during inclement weather." Now well away on his subject, he indicated the library and music room, then showed her the mock-up of the school's letterhead. "You can name the school anything you like, but I thought of *Word of Truth Academy*. I got the idea from this verse that's printed under the school's name."

Reeling from the impact of Miles' actions, Marilyn could barely take in the words she read.

So Jesus said to those who believed in him, "If you obey my teaching, you are really my disciples; you will know the truth, and the truth will set you free." John 8:31-32 (GNT)

Her silence and total lack of reaction left Miles feeling suddenly unsure of himself. As she became more uncommunicative, he spoke with increased eagerness, fearing he hadn't made himself clear. "I thought it would be inspiring to have the final phrase emblazoned on the wall opposite the entry doors. 'The truth will set you free.'" he said, gesturing with his hands. Still no response. He stood and walked back to the large drawing, fumbling for words. "Or you could simply call the school 'Tinkers Well Christian School' or…"

"Or 'Options Academy'," Tim suggested weakly.

The folder, with its colorful drawings, fell to the floor in a jumbled heap when Marilyn rose abruptly. She looked in dismay from father to son before running blindly from the room. Tim and Rose looked at each other but didn't dare say a word.

"I…I don't understand," Miles said with a blank expression. The wind had been completely knocked out him. The consummate businessman had failed to impress his most important client. "I was sure she'd be thrilled by the idea. Why, she as much as told me she wanted a school option for families in the area that would protect young minds and hearts from all the nonsense being forced on children today." He looked helplessly at Tim, who had previously congratulated his father on such an inspired idea.

Aletha, who had, heretofore, been merely an interested yet silent witness to the interchange, asked her son, with some impatience, "Well, do you mean to just stand there like a ninny? Don't you know why she left?"

"I have no idea. That is… surely you don't think…?"

Uncertainty still held the upper hand.

"Oh, for heavens' sake, Timothy. You let her walk away once before. Don't make that mistake again," Aletha said, wondering how an otherwise perfectly healthy man could be even more blind than she was.

"You're not *serious*?" Miles asked in wavering disbelief. Aletha merely rolled her eyes and threw up her hands. He turned to his son for inspiration. Tim was as genuinely surprised by his mother's reaction as Miles was.

"Don't look at me. I haven't even been married six months yet. What do I know?" But as a man who had almost given up on a future with Rose had it not been for the encouragement – and plotting – of his friends, he shrugged and added with a supportive smile, "You'll never know until you try." Miles squared his shoulders and walked toward the kitchen.

Not sparing any concern for the turmoil she had left behind, Marilyn hurried into the kitchen in search of a refuge from Miles and the unexpected rush of conflicting emotions that left her shaking after the revelation of his gift. She looked around frantically for something to do that would blot out her thoughts and calm her jangled nerves. Eyeing the pile of large pots and pans that waited for attention in the sink, she donned a cheery red checked apron and mechanically began scrubbing. Her breathing had barely slowed when she sensed someone walk up behind her. Without turning, she knew it was Miles. Marilyn could hide no longer.

She didn't trust herself to speak, so she continued her task, bracing for the challenge that must come. Without saying a word, Miles rolled up his shirt sleeves, grabbed a dishtowel, and began drying the items already stacked in the dish drainer. She may have been surprised by his actions, but Marilyn was also relieved and grateful for the respite, allowing postponement of the inevitable confrontation. The minutes passed and the pile of pans dwindled while silence reigned.

The whims of a woman's deepest desires being somewhat arbitrary, the verbal lull gradually became oppressive. Marilyn turned impulsively to her assistant, resenting his apparent unwillingness to help her unburden her heart and mind, and thought irrationally, *Why doesn't he say something? He must know I need to talk!* She saw in his expression politeness, impassivity, and – *surely not* – a hint of humor. If he refused to make the gallant gesture and speak first, she would.

"Timothy Miles Hawthorne, how *could* you? Men are supposed to offer sensible gifts like jewelry, or…or perfume, or a…a piece of…oh, I don't know… porcelain. *No one* gives a woman *a school.* Why it's… *preposterous!*" When he refused to respond like any civil man would, she added resentfully, "What were you *thinking?*"

Miles was as calm as Marilyn was agitated – irritatingly so, she thought. He replied in a level tone, "But you never mentioned requiring jewelry or perfume. And I don't know the name of your particular scent, but as it is extremely alluring, I would hardly suggest you wear anything else. And as to porcelain, I can't imagine you would enjoy anything I could offer you half so much as one of your flea market finds."

While he spoke, he offered her a dishtowel to dry her hands and would then have taken them in his, but she was not about to let herself be so easily distracted. She spied a broom leaning in the corner and put it to use by sweeping the same few crumbs all over the kitchen floor. Miles followed leisurely in her wake.

"And I suppose I *asked* for a school," she demanded, intent on her task.

"Why, yes. That is precisely what you did. And a very fine idea I thought it at the time."

Momentarily brought to a standstill, Marilyn gasped in outrage. "I *never* said any such thing!"

"But you did, darling, the first time we dined at Louis' Bistro." She either missed, or willfully ignored, the endearment.

"Now that is unfair! You know I was only conjuring up a…a fanciful dream in response to your absurd question. You couldn't possibly have taken me seriously," she cried, torn between a deep sense of gratification at his regard for her unguarded outpourings and a feeling of acute embarrassment that her wishful thinking had led him to such extremes.

Miles gently pulled the broom from her slackened grasp and replaced it in the corner. But before he could make better use of her hands, Marilyn moved quickly to the kitchen island and emptied the fruit basket to rearrange its contents over and over. Amused and encouraged by her agitation, Miles leaned negligently against the counter on the other end of the island.

"As I recall, my love, your words were anything *but* fanciful. I was so fired by your passion that I decided on the spot to do everything in my power to help you realize that dream."

Marilyn stared in wonder at his sincerity. Though Miles looked relaxed and at ease, his voice had taken on an undercurrent of something she was hesitant to name. When he started toward her, his hand held out, she frantically looked around the now spotless kitchen for a diversion. Walking purposely to the old farm table in the corner, she stepped behind it and set to work "straightening" the perfectly aligned pictures on the wall, leaving them all lamentably askew. The corner of Miles' mouth twitched into a crooked smile. He was ready when she turned after reaching the last picture. Her back was to the wall, where a row of cock-eyed frames bore witness to her misguided efforts.

"My dearest Mari," he said gently, finally capturing her hands between his. "Will you *please* accept my gift? If not for yourself, then for the children of Tinkers Well."

"Oh, Timothy, that is so unfair!" Marilyn exclaimed for the second time, keenly aware of her own erratic pulse and legs that seemed suddenly unstable. She avoided his eyes as she added, "You know I could *never* turn down such a…a welcome offering. But why couldn't you have simply donated the school to the town instead of tying it to me?" she asked, a little reproachfully.

"Two reasons," he answered calmly. "One, if I gift it to the town, I will receive a hefty tax benefit and I don't want to make any gesture simply for my own gain ever again. I have set up a non-profit organization called 'Joshua's Way,' in honor of my noble ancestor. After an administrator has been appointed, he or she, can purchase the school from me for one dollar."

"Oh," was all she said, keeping her eyes downcast. After a few minutes, she dared to ask as nonchalantly as possible, "And the second reason?" Miles had slipped one hand around her waist and softly stroked her cheek with the other, willing her eyes to look into his.

"Because as much as I was moved by your passionate speech about the educational needs and moral dilemma of your students, I wanted to give you something that would genuinely please you and bring you relief from your worries." He added gently, "If it would make you more comfortable, I will say nothing about the school in connection with you and me. It's enough for me that you know." Marilyn looked up at that, moved by his words, though nearly unable to think at all – let alone rationally – due to his closeness and the electric jolt of his touch. But she had to know all before she could begin to trust again.

"How did you do it, Timothy? You promised me you wouldn't ask Aletha – "

"And I kept that promise. I raised the start-up capital myself through honest – and I do stress the term *honest* – aboveboard business transactions. You can ask Tim if you don't believe me."

"*Tim?*" Marilyn said, incredulous. "Tim *knew* about all this?"

"I asked him not to say anything, but yes, he knows everything. I will happily supply you with all the boring details, but I would much rather use this precious time we have together to better purpose."

"Now Tim, I know you don't approve of – " Aletha began.

"– surreptitiously gathering information?" Tim finished on a wry note. "Ordinarily I would agree with you because I would be nosing into to someone else's business."

Aletha turned away as if she had never been guilty of doing any such thing. Rose watched the entertaining exchange between grandmother and grandson, wondering who would emerge triumphant. She was surprised when Tim walked toward the hallway, saying, "But one could argue that the outcome of events in the kitchen *is* my business, so if you ladies will excuse me…"

"I knew he was a right one!" Granny Gert said.

He returned a few minutes later, frowning, to report, "They're cleaning the kitchen, and mom is… well it sounded like she was almost… *yelling* at Miles."

"*What?*" The three women cried out in unison.

"I don't remember her *ever* yelling at Dad," Tim continued, puzzled. "She hardly ever raised her voice to *me,* and I certainly gave her provocation enough when I was a kid."

"Perhaps a few more details would be helpful," said Aletha, gently prodding.

"I don't know what more to tell you. They were washing some pans at the sink, and then Mom started sweeping like her life depended on it. After practically taking the finish off the floor, she rearranged the oranges and bananas in the fruit bowl."

"Yes, but how did they *look,* dear boy?" Aletha persisted.

Tim responded thoughtfully, "Well, Miles looked perfectly calm again, you know how he usually appears so sure of himself."

"And Marilyn?"

"That's the really odd part. She must have rearranged that fruit bowl three or four times. When I left, she was 'un-straightening' all the pictures on the wall behind the table. If I didn't know better, I'd say she was… nervous or keyed up maybe. After the way she ran out of here, I was worried she'd be sitting in there crying. Instead, it looks like she's preparing for a visit from royalty!"

"Now I find that very interesting," Aletha said, nodding speculatively.

Tim just shook his head. "I find it baffling. I guess I will *never* understand women."

Rose gave Aletha's hand a meaningful squeeze. The older woman said to Tim, as if explaining the obvious to a simpleton, "We prefer it that way, dear."

"Mari, you asked me why I couldn't have just given you a simple gift. I'll tell you why. Because it would have cost me nothing." Miles hesitated before going on. His self-assurance deserted him, and there was a note of uncertainty and longing in his voice. "Mari, I'm getting too old to slay dragons or perform amazing feats of daring and courage to earn your favor, but I don't deserve *anything* from you unless I'm willing to lose something of myself in return." She let her guard down for an instant and reached up to smooth his furrowed brow as she had done so many years ago. When she saw his expression soften, she realized the enormity of her gesture and would have stepped away but for the power of his arm holding her tightly.

"That is so unfair," she accused him, for the third time. "You know exactly how to… to push my buttons." The nerve at the corner of his mouth twitched again. "I obviously can't be trusted to keep my wits when I'm near you. But I'll have you know," she said severely, "that I am not an impressionable, soft-hearted girl anymore. I'm a…a level-headed, middle-aged woman." Her decisive delivery was somewhat diminished when she dropped her eyes and straightened his collar.

"You may be level-headed, my love," he said. His relentless string of endearments was having its inevitable effect. "But you will always be a beautiful, tender-hearted girl to me." Miles kissed each of her hands and pulled them behind his neck. Both arms now circled her waist to draw her closer.

"That is so unfair!" Marilyn said yet again and tried to draw back, but she was held in place by his unyielding embrace. She looked up into his face just inches away.

Miles no longer made any effort to hide his smile. "You mentioned that before." Marilyn attempted to debate him in a composed manner, but the words came out in a breathy, uncertain voice against the sheer magnetic pull of his presence. She grasped the well-defined muscle in his arms, barely concealed by his dress shirt, to lend weight to her argument.

"If you'd had a shred of… of common decency, you'd have shown up with flabby arms and a pot belly, at the very least, instead of striding back into my life looking like a…a mature, well-dressed Adonis!" His eyes gleamed. She knew her last defenses to be weakening under his intense gaze when, suddenly, every vestige of humor was gone.

"Mari, it was my selfishness that drove you from me, and ironically, it was my selfishness that brought you back. God turned my greatest failing into my redemption and my only hope." He stopped, searching for the words that were so critical to their future. "I know that no man has the right to be blessed twice in one lifetime by the same woman, and I know it is so *unfair* of me to ask," he said and caught the shadow of a responsive smile on her lips, "but my dearest Mari, dare I believe in a life with you again?" He held his breath while he watched her wrestle with conflicting emotions.

With eyes downcast, Marilyn responded. "I have tried *so* hard to maintain my reserve when we are together, but every time, I have felt betrayed by my desire for something that is past, something that can never be again." She spoke with genuine regret.

"But my darling," Miles said, gently lifting her chin to drown once again in the depths of her eyes now misted with tears, "I thought we agreed that we were done with the past. I don't *ever* want to be that man again, and you are infinitely more beautiful and wise and dear to me than the girl you once were. Can't we begin anew? *Please* say yes," he pleaded.

For the first time since seeing Miles on that fateful day when a tornado and unexpected revelations rocked them both to the core, Marilyn felt at peace. Meeting his gaze, she responded shyly, though with a newfound certainty, "Yes, Timothy, I believe we can."

Chapter 16

It was Thursday night, a week after Maundy Thursday, when deeply symbolic revelations had inspired the many and confounded the few. Swelling the ranks of the regulars streaming into the Tinkers Well Community Center for their weekly bingo battle, Gertie Gunn and Aletha Mason greeted their many acquaintances and claimed their table for the evening. The room was abuzz with the news of Miles and Marilyn's engagement, and Aletha happily confirmed the stories. At her friend's repeated request, Gert produced her cell phone to show a short video of the engagement ring. Rose had instructed her months earlier on taking pictures and recording videos so that Gert could keep her daughters updated with more than mere phone calls. Now she favored those interested with a short recording of dazzling blue and green fire revealed in an opal stone as Marilyn shifted it in the light.

"He told her he chose that particular stone because – I'm quoting now, you understand, 'it reflects the depth and ever-changing facets of your character.' Isn't that just lovely?" Aletha sighed.

Gert secretly thought all that sentimental drivel was a bit maudlin, but she would have cut out her tongue before saying anything that might spoil Aletha's happiness.

Bingo night had been a favorite of the town seniors since its inception ten years earlier, but the addition of Gertie Gunn brought an extra measure of fun to the mix. Her many new friends were quite pleased to welcome her return after the long winter absence. She was not the only newcomer, however, to have found a sense of belonging within the diverse group vying for optimal seating either near the food or the bingo caller, depending on individual preference. Irene Fields, though inherently shy, had discovered an inner strength and confidence through association with members of her Sunday School class and those who gathered regularly for church social functions. But Reenie had also found a place in the larger senior community of the town. Ironically, for the first time since joining the Murdock family, she had more steady social engagements than her nephew's flighty wife!

Reenie's innate qualities of self-doubt and insecurity had touched the generous hearts of Gertie and Aletha, who had made a place for her at their table, providing her the much-needed assurance of being truly wanted and appreciated. She, in turn, looked for opportunities to do the same for others. But because few strangers penetrated beyond the portals of the once-a-week bingo hall, there was little hope of rendering that service – little hope, that is, until meeting the Rosenbaums.

Unlike the others surrounding her, who had longstanding ties to the community or one of its residents, Reenie understood the reluctance of exposing oneself to isolation within a tight-knit group. She had sensed the same reluctance from Isaac and Deborah Rosenbaum, and though it may have been rooted in something more profound than mere personal diffidence, she saw two people who longed for friends and their place in a new social circle, just as she had. Gert put little faith in their promise to attend the event, but Reenie kept her eyes on the door and was rewarded for her vigilance when the two appeared, looking uncertain and on the verge of retreat.

Isaac tentatively removed a dated felt fedora, exposing the gleaming crown of his head, while his wife looked warily around the room, clutching her purse and a covered dish like defensive weapons aimed at the unfamiliar natives. Reenie moved quickly to intercept them, guiding Deborah to the perfect spot for her platter of roast chicken and *kreplach,* and ushered them to her table where two empty places awaited them. Gert and Aletha added their welcome, and Bobby Taylor gripped Isaac's hand saying it was high time another man populated the heavily female assembly. The presence of another reminder from the problematic Seder the week before might have been a stumbling block, but the two men had established a friendly relationship that evening based on mutual respect despite, or perhaps because of, their religious differences. Bobby admired Isaac's adherence and dedication to the faith that had given birth to his own. Isaac envied Bobby's enthusiasm and acceptance of new teachings – that and his thick thatch of gray hair. Deborah had mentioned it several times.

Being greeted by Reenie like an old, established friend had given the Rosenbaums the courage to embark on a new social adventure in the face of lingering misgivings. As a diversionary tactic against the resentment Deborah eventually gave vent to regarding the shocking Passover takeover, and because Isaac knew she could be trusted with such a secret, he had shared with his wife the story behind the absence of Irene's nephew from Tinkers Well. With that knowledge fresh in her mind, Deborah's kind heart ached over the anguish the other woman must live with daily. Reenie exhibited boldness beyond her comfort zone to ensure Deborah's ease, and the two were drawn together out of a mutual compassion that neither fully understood.

Little by little, Isaac and Deborah relaxed enough to compliment Reenie on the delicious bean dish and fruit salad she had prepared according to Kosher instructions (just in case the Jewish couple joined them), and to admit to enjoyment in an evening spent with relative strangers. They agreed wholeheartedly with Gertie Gunn's droll but blistering comments on contemporary life and culture and were greatly impressed by Aletha's ability to feel her way effortlessly around her braille bingo cards. They even discovered a competitive streak that pitted them against one another and their neighbors in good-humored rivalry.

Taking advantage of a lull between games, when the others at the table were revisiting the dessert bar or chatting with acquaintances scattered throughout the large hall, Reenie dared broach the unspoken subject to the only other person she believed to know the truth about her nephew.

"Isaac, I can't thank you enough for not speaking last Thursday of my nephew's incarceration," she said, and noticed a barely perceptible glance between husband and wife. "Oh, it's quite all right if you told Deborah. In fact, it's a great relief for me to be able to talk to you both about the whole terrible business. You see, I am so worried." Her voice broke on the last words.

All social, cultural, and religious differences were abruptly forgotten. Isaac and Deborah saw a soul in need and responded accordingly to Reenie's cry for help. Deborah reached out to pat the other woman's twitching, restless hands.

"We do know about your nephew's improbable arrest and sentencing, which are enough to upset anyone, but that's a settled thing to be endured and mourned. And those two little boys, Mattie and Drew, they will survive, especially since you were wise enough to tell them their papa is away on business. Surely, your nephew has assured you he is all right."

"That's just it – I haven't had a call or note from him since he went to prison! I've known him his whole life, and a more thoughtful, kind young man I've yet to meet. Whatever can have happened to him?" she asked, her desperation mounting with every word.

"Now, now," Deborah replied calmly, "There is no need to work yourself into a fever." She looked around the crowded room. "This is not the place to speak of such things. Sabbath begins tomorrow evening, so I have a few chores I'll need to get done during the day, but I'm sure Isaac and I can find time to pay you a short visit." She was surprised when Reenie's agitation increased.

"Oh, no! You can't come to my home. Matthew's wife, Brittany, will be there." She dropped her voice to a near whisper. "I don't trust her. And I can't possibly drive the only vehicle we have – her monster of a sportscar." Reenie was almost frantic.

Isaac saw people getting settled for the next round of bingo and stepped in to provide a simple solution that stilled Reenie's fears and helped her regain an even, emotional keel.

"Nothing could be easier. I will come collect you here, at the hall. You mentioned you live only a short walk away, yes?" Reenie nodded, hope shining in her eyes. "You will come to our house. Deborah can teach you to make *challah,* and you will tell us how we can help you. So," he said, placing his hands on the table in the manner of a judge mediating a minor dispute, "it is settled."

His beaming smile reassured Reenie in the same way the miraculous appearance of a lifebuoy might restore courage and strength to someone floundering in dark waters that threatened to overwhelm them. Reenie had, in fact, been slowly drowning in a sea of troubles she felt powerless to rise above. But now she had help. She was powerless no more.

Driving away from the Community Center, after dropping off their grandmothers, Tim reminded his wife that he had no intention of going anywhere near Brittany Murdock. Rose would have to call for the boys at their home while he waited in the truck. She readily agreed, guessing that her presence at the door, in lieu of her husband's, would infuriate their mother. It did – momentarily. But Brittany refused to be drawn off course. She had already written Tim off as a loss and was reassessing her goals.

When she finally cooled down enough to take stock of her situation after the disastrous Easter outing, Brittany had to admit that, through no fault of her own, the reactions of yokels living in a backwater town had failed to live up to her expectations. They, meaning members of the male populace, were clearly not sophisticated enough to appreciate her unique attributes. But she knew what she wanted, and she would not rest until it was hers.

Rational, thinking people usually recognize the signs of failure, criticism, or personal missteps. They either make an effort to change their course to something more productive or force themselves to look inward, to examine their errors, and to learn from them. Such a lifelong pursuit generally results in maturity and wisdom. Not so with Brittany Murdock. She was incapable of critical self-examination because she was incapable of recognizing any fault in her actions or attitudes. Any setbacks in her single-minded pursuits were clearly evidence of others' shortcomings, not her own.

Money, adoration, and power were her gods. She had never had all that she desired of any one of them, but the need to command all three drove her to recalculate her strategy. In her estimation, there was only one man in her restricted world who could offer what she craved. He obviously had money, evidenced by his impeccable attire and his superior intelligence. He alone had allowed a gleam of interest to show on the only occasion their eyes had met during the interminable Easter dinner. And he alone exuded the kind of power she craved. A conquest of Miles Hawthorne would provide her ultimate power – power over him, power over her miserable existence, and power over those who had dared judge her.

Though not willing to own any error on her part, Brittany had the sense to realize she must shift her strategy to attain a goal she estimated to require no more than two weeks. She dismissed the stuffy inhabitants of Tinkers Well as a means of gaining access to Miles' inner circle and adjusted her tactics accordingly.

"He'll soon forget his middle-aged schoolteacher," she purred, while admiring her reflection in a full-length mirror. Michaelangelo, Bernini, and Rodin might well have contended for the honor of capturing her face and form, with its generous curves and white, almost translucent skin, in the cold immortality of marble. Brittany would certainly have reveled in modeling for the undertaking. But, for the present, she was focused on contending for, and capturing, Miles Hawthorne.

"What a lovely home!" It was a generous comment by someone who had visited the grand halls of Willow Walk and the more modest, but stylish rooms of Marilyn Ludlow's house with its imaginative, eclectic décor. The Rosenbaum home reflected a shared lifetime and a shared faith. Gleaming furniture from a decades long marriage anchored each room where old lace and fine needlework ornamented highly polished tables or hung in gilded frames. Reenie was particularly fascinated by the symbols of the Jewish faith. Deborah named each one as she guided her guest through the house: the *mezuzah* fastened on the front door post; the *menorah* candelabra stored in the dining room; and the Star of David, fractured yet brilliantly whole in an artistic stained-glass setting displayed in the front window. Reenie's innocent praise pleased her hostess. Like any woman, Deborah took understandable pride in her home.

"The *mezuzah*, I believe you called it, is that what holds... now what's that term we learned in Sunday School last month?" Reenie hesitated, trying to recall a recent nugget added to her well of knowledge where 70 years of Bible study facts and observations jostled for prominence. The memory surfaced, and though eager to share even this simple understanding of Jewish traditions, Reenie spoke shyly, not wanting to offend. "It contains the *Shema*, is that right?"

"And what is the *Shema*?" Isaac asked, gently teasing. He had joined the ladies in the dining room after hanging coats.

Reenie was determined to please. "Now, I *think* it's from Deuteronomy and begins, '*Hear, O Israel: The* LORD *our God, the* LORD *is one! You shall love the* LORD *your God with all your heart, with all your soul, and with all your strength.*' I can always remember that last bit because Jesus said that it was the most important commandment," she added naively.

"I see that we have something in common," he replied kindly and proceeded to recite the remainder of the passage from Deuteronomy 6. "There is more from later in Deuteronomy, but that's the main idea."

"Well, I think it's a wonderful idea." Reenie caught a glimpse of the backyard and asked timidly if she might be allowed to see it.

"But of course. Come, my dear. You are the expert horticulturist. I just plant things where you tell me." Isaac had noticed his wife stiffen at the mention of Jesus in connection with another sacred text, and hoped she might be diverted by talking about her garden. He knew her so well. They stepped into the covered porch room still enclosed with glass until rising temperatures would signal the change to screens. Deborah pointed out hydrangeas emerging from slumber and a sturdy arbor framing a suspended bench swing.

"That will be covered in clematis vines by early summer and the weigela bushes, which now only look like scruffy, shapeless shrubs in the wood line, will burst with colorful blooms like the tulip magnolia you see over there." Deborah pointed toward the laden ornamental tree with tulips scattered at its feet.

"Why, it will look just like paradise – your own little Garden of Eden!" Deborah looked sharply at Reenie, who continued to gaze in rapture at a garden still in partial dormancy. Isaac and Deborah had, for some time, been debating the wisdom of having left their Jewish community in Kansas City to move to this gentile community where they were isolated by their own faith practices. What had drawn them in the beginning – the privacy, the wooded retreat, the garden – had lately caused them to question the decision. Their friends from Kansas City had not made the frequent visits promised, and the burden of making new friends, at their age, among those they appeared to have little in common with, had proven more difficult than expected. Now they stood with a new acquaintance, poles apart in many ways, yet appreciating the qualities of their home that they had first recognized themselves.

"The drive through the front yard recalled childhood stories of forest animals and gnomes." Reenie blushed as she turned away from the promising view. "I'm sorry. You must think me terribly foolish and romantic."

"We find you refreshing and welcome. Now, we must turn our attention to the kitchen," Deborah said and ushered Reenie into her inner sanctum where breadmaking paraphernalia was already scattered across the surface of the center island. Over mixing, kneading, and braiding the dough for the *challah* loaf, Reenie unburdened her weighted soul. Isaac, sipping coffee at the table, interjected adroit questions, and gained more insight into the inner workings of the Murdock family than Reenie realized. Her unguarded words also ignited speculation in his mind as to the exact nature of the crime laid at her nephew's door.

Three hours later, noting that Brittany's car was not parked by the little blue cottage as they neared it, Reenie agreed to let Isaac drop her there so that she needn't walk from their earlier meeting place carrying a loaf of warm bread. He waved goodbye after assuring her that he would begin inquiries over certain points discussed. He had also promised Reenie that he and Deborah would escort her to Lansdowne Correctional Facility before another week was out.

Locating the Emerson office building with the aid of GPS, Brittany squeezed her sports car between two SUVs parked on the street, stuck a worn "Out of Order" sign on the meter, and headed for the elevator. Astute enough to realize that her plans would hardly prosper if she knocked on Miles' office door only to find him out of the office or in a meeting, Brittany had called to schedule an appointment using some improbable pretext. Upon meeting Miles' secretary, Mrs. Castle, Brittany felt she already knew the woman, so closely did her appearance live up to her voice. Iron gray hair, swept severely into a clip at the back of her head, pulled her features into sharp, unflattering relief. A modicum of makeup hardly softened her edges, nor did her shapeless polyester gray suit. The whole was a sort of bland efficiency devoid of personality. But when Mrs. Castle bent her shrewd gaze on the newcomer, Brittany lost some of her assurance under such unyielding scrutiny. She found the effect of being dissected with the accuracy of an electron microscope somewhat intimidating.

"I suppose you're Mrs. Murdock, young lady," Mrs. Castle demanded, barely concealing her contempt. She felt she had accurately taken Brittany's measure when making the office appointment the day before. Her suspicions were borne out by her employer's reaction following a review of his daily schedule three hours earlier.

"Now, what can that minx be up to?" he had murmured, a speculative look in his eye. They both soon found out.

At Mrs. Castle's summons, Miles stepped into her office to greet his suspect guest. She almost ran to him in her desire to rid herself of Mrs. Castle's penetrating stare. He ushered Brittany into his office and asked, politely, how he could be of service to her. It took much of his supreme emotional control to keep from laughing out loud as he watched his guest change from subdued child to sultry siren in the blink of an eye. She saw in his smile an indication of interest and the appreciation of a connoisseur and knew herself to be well on her way to success.

Brittany had erred on the side of modesty in her choice of clothing — at least from her perspective — not wanting to appear too obvious. To her mind, the simple knit dress with long sleeves, a high turtleneck, and a hemline that at least flirted with her knees, was the perfect blend of discretion and style. A tailored coat was soon discarded to fully reveal her sober attire. From Miles' vantage point, the stretch fabric clung to her every curve and hollow with the tenacity of plastic wrap. The smooth swath of black was alleviated only by a single diamond pendant dangling from her neck, drawing all eyes precisely where she wanted them. She looked as sleek as a panther and twice as dangerous. Miles proceeded with caution.

"I'm not sure that I can help you in any way, Mrs. Murdock, unless, of course, you are somehow able to hide a considerable amount of investment capital somewhere on your person. Though, I think that hardly likely."

A laugh of effortless delight greeted his polite banter. "First of all, you can call me Brittany. And secondly," she said, standing and turning a very slow 360 degrees to reveal a bare back held together by spaghetti strings tied in a bow, "what you see is all I have to offer."

A few years earlier, or even one year ago, Miles might have accepted the implied proposition. Using her only until she bored him or until her claims on his financial resources outran her petty services, he would have cast her aside, as he had others before her. But Miles Hawthorne was Timothy once again: loved by his mother and the only woman he had ever known who brought him true happiness and contentment. He looked at Brittany's vibrant young face and thought of Mari's, whose fine lines and thinning lips smiled only for him, and whose eyes still took his breath away. Through God's miracle, he had reclaimed the treasure he had lost and had gained the wisdom to know it. He saw in Brittany's obvious advances evidence of the empty soul that had once been his, and shuddered.

She saw nothing amiss. Having taken advantage of the timely opportunity to parade her wares, she sat down, made a spectacle of crossing her legs, and explained her visit.

"Everything was so hectic and chaotic last Sunday that I didn't get a chance to meet and talk with everyone. And I could tell you wanted to meet me, too," she said, with relentless intent, "so, I decided I would just have to get together with people individually if I wanted to… get to know them. I think you understand," she added, with a slow wink.

"Well, I'm sure that's very resourceful of you, but I am rather a busy man. Perhaps you would consider joining my fiancée and I for dinner at her house after church this Sunday. You know Marilyn Ludlow, young Mattie's teacher. I'm sure she would enjoy knowing you better, as well."

Brittany had no intention of ever meeting with the piety patrol of Tinkers Well again. For an obviously interested party, Miles was certainly acting strangely obtuse. She pouted coyly and tried another tack.

"I'm not very good with crowds. I do much better with one-on-one interactions. And I know someone as important as you must be busy, so, I've come to take you to lunch. Even important men have to eat." As she spoke, she walked around the desk, took Miles' hand, and resolutely pulled him to his feet, all the while maintaining a flirtatious air.

He looked at her, an enigmatic smile hovering on his lips. Brittany read calculated desire. She admired his hesitation, reveling in the challenge of breaking down his reserve. Miles saw as devious and manipulative a little schemer as any that had ever crossed his path. He knew precisely what she was thinking, and it suited his purpose to encourage her in that belief. For in that moment, he resolved to do what no one else of his Tinkers Well acquaintance could accomplish – rid the community of a cunning, mischief-making she-devil. He would take great care that her innocent children and aunt were not hurt in the process, if at all possible. They had been hurt enough.

Mrs. Castle switched off the intercom as Miles and his guest emerged from his office. She had grown quite fond of her employer and his fiancée and, therefore, felt it her responsibility to keep an eye on their best interests. Since she worked under the maxim that men in general are summarily clueless when it comes to knowing what is good for them, especially where women are concerned, she spent her lunch hour devising a plan to protect Miles from someone she labeled "no better than she should be."

Matt Murdock nearly fell off his bunk when a guard brought him the message that he had a visitor. *Brittany!* was his first and only thought. He walked on air all the way to the large room set with tables and chairs to allow prisoners visitation from the outside world. Reaching the doorway, his hungry eyes sought the vision he had dreamt of for over three long months. He overlooked his aunt on that first scan, but her sweetly smiling face and her absurd straw hat, crowned with blue silk daisies, eventually caught his attention. Her heart sank when she saw the disappointment in his eyes, but he quickly recovered and joined her at a table in the corner where he gripped her outstretched hands like they were his last hope.

"Aunt Reenie! Oh, thank God you're here, finally! But why didn't you return any of my letters? What happened to the phone? Every time I've tried to call you or Brittany, I get an out-of-service recording. Where on earth is she? I don't understand. I just don't understand."

The torment in his voice caused her tears to flow in earnest. Reenie's eyes had teared up the minute he walked through the door. She wanted more than anything to give him the answers he sought, but she had nothing but her own questions to offer.

"Matthew, let me look at you. You look so tired and worn. Have you been getting enough rest and exer – "

"Aunt Reenie, forget about how I look," he said impatiently. "*What is going on?*" His forceful insistence and obvious anguish caused her to become flustered and increasingly inarticulate.

"Oh, Matthew, I don't know what to… where to begin. I wrote so many letters… she said they were mailed… and the boys colored pictures… my phone is gone… but it never rang, even though I waited for the postman – "

"Wait, wait. Aunt Reenie… Aunt Reenie, stop!" He clasped her agitated hands and told her to catch her breath and to answer his questions one at a time, slowly. "Are you telling me that you never received any of my letters?" She shook her head mournfully while dabbing at her eyes. "And what's this about losing a phone that never rang?"

She began an explanation that left him baffled, angry, confused, and badly frightened. "Brittany got rid of our cell phones. She told me that she was protecting us – her and I and the boys – from annoying calls from people who knew about your… about you going to jail. She replaced it with a regular phone for the house, but *it never rings*. How is that possible? My friends from church have called me, and they say there is only an option to leave a message for a different number, not our answering machine. Brittany told me it was somehow malfunctioning and that she would get it fixed, but she never has."

"*What?* But surely, she must have received calls from the boys' school, or a utility company, or *something*." Even as he spoke the words, he was afraid of the answer.

"Oh, she gets calls, all right. She tells me that the phone often rings while I'm out, but I'm hardly out of the house during the day – only to do my walking errands and to attend a women's Bible study on Tuesday mornings. And Bingo is on Thursday evenings, and then church on Sundays, of course. Still, I don't see how it could *never* ring while I'm at home. Do you?"

Matt's face had grown increasingly grim with every detail, but all he said was, "No, I don't." He continued in a cold, deliberate tone. "Tell me about the letters."

Hating herself for adding more pain to this man who had suffered so much already, she tried to be as matter of fact and unemotional as possible. "I have written you a letter twice a week since we moved to Tinkers Well. I always place them in the letter box just outside the front door first thing in the morning. It's a small town, you see, so the postman still delivers and picks up the mail on foot. Isn't that quaint?" Matt failed to appreciate the novelty of the old-world practice. "As I was saying, I put them in the post box myself, though Brittany often offers to drop them at the post office with her own letters. I check the box every afternoon, but we never receive anything but circulars and advertisements. Not a single letter. Never."

"But at least you saw the letter I sent through the prison chaplain to the principal at the boys' school. He responded to Chaplain Reardon to say he had handed it to Brittany personally. She must have shared it with you. I specifically asked her to."

Reenie looked at him blankly. "This is the first I've heard of it."

Matt groaned, rocking back and forth with his fingers clutching his hair. "No, no, no," he muttered. He was frantic to disregard everything he had heard, but it had the ring of truth about it. Aunt Reenie was too ingenuous to make all of it up. What did it mean? His heart cried out for Brittany, needing her reassurance and plausible answers. But it wasn't his beloved wife who had come to see him, even though he had begged her to. It was his aunt. His Aunt Reenie. Finally emerging from his fog of dismay, he focused on his visitor.

"*You're* here. You're *here*. Why, in God's name, did you not come sooner, Aunt Reenie?" His accusation hurt her, but she knew he wasn't thinking clearly.

"I would have come every day, if I could, but Brittany insisted on keeping her sports car for transportation, which as you know, I simply cannot drive. I'm here today because of the kindness of some new friends. I met them just two weeks ago."

Matt, still struggling to put everything together, fastened on his aunt's last illuminating disclosure. "Wait a minute. Are you telling me that you've been *walking* everywhere – the grocery, the bank, your church? Surely, Brittany offers to drive you…"

"Oh well, she takes the boys to and from school every day, and the walking is good for us. I have groceries delivered, and the Community Center, where I meet with other seniors for Bingo, is near the house. As to church, I find that walking to church helps rid the boys of some of their excess energy, so they pay attention better."

He was so bewildered by unwelcome truth after unwelcome truth that he completely missed the comment about the boys attending church. He fastened instead on his aunt's ability to reach him at last.

"You spoke of some friends. They're here with you?"

Reenie nodded. "The Rosenbaums. Isaac has been looking into what happened to you, and I think – I hope – he may be able to help you. Will you speak with him now?" She rose to vacate her place for Isaac, who was waiting with Deborah in the Visitors Lobby. Matt took her hand and kissed it.

"Please forgive me for the way I've treated you today, Aunt Reenie. I haven't even thanked you for making the effort to see me or for taking care of Mattie and Drew. You are a miracle, and I love you."

She smiled fondly, patted his hand, and left. A few minutes later, Matt was approached by an elderly man with a shining dome and a diffident manner.

"You are Matthew Murdock, yes?" Matt nodded. "My name is Isaac Rosenbaum, and I am here, as a friend, to discuss this terrible business with you. I know you have been confronted by much that has upset you today. I can do nothing about that, except to assure you that your sons are well. My wife and I had the pleasure of sharing an evening with them and your aunt a few weeks ago. They are fine boys, and I am happy to know them. Now that that is settled, we may look at your problem."

Nothing had been settled from Matt's standpoint, but he was intrigued by the attitude of this stranger who spoke in a measured, respectful tone. He not only knew Matt's family, he also, apparently, knew of Matt's arrest and the mystery behind it. Little urging was needed before Matt was rehashing every detail of the sordid affair. He went through the evidence, barely aware that Isaac scribbled occasionally in a little notebook. He talked about the adjusted commission charges, the limited access to accounts, and the impossibility of anyone getting his passwords – he had never written them down. And then there was the fake charity and bank account, established in his name, about which he knew nothing.

"It is easy enough these days, for anyone to set up an account in someone else's name, provided they have that person's social security number. But tell me about these passwords. They seem to be the sticking point to the whole thing. If you did not record them anywhere – "

"Not in a computer file, not on paper, nowhere. There is simply no way they could have been stolen."

Isaac sat in silent contemplation of the young man before him. He knew of him through newspapers and inuendo within the finance world, but those he quickly discounted. Irene Fields was an honorable woman, and if she said her nephew was an honest man, Isaac believed her.

"I don't suppose you will be using those passwords again, so would you mind sharing a little of the creation of such varied, yet memorable codes? You see, I quite understand that you must have created some system that could be altered for each client yet required no documentation. So, only you knew of it. Yes?"

Matt frowned, fearful of trusting anyone again, but his aunt trusted this man. *What do I have to lose?* he thought. Aloud, he began to lay out the ingenious yet relatively simple system. "I changed the passwords on the first business day of every month. Each password began with the client's first and last initials, in lower case, followed by five numbers. If the month was an odd-numbered one, the digits began with the odd-number one, followed by two, three, four, and five. If the month was even-numbered, the digits began with the even-number six, followed by seven, eight, nine, and zero. Next came the keyboard symbol associated with each month's numerical designation. For January, the first month, I used the exclamation mark; for February, the second month, the 'at' symbol; March, third month, hashtag, and so on. For November and December, I used the upper-case symbols for the two keys next to zero. And finally, I added my wife's first initial, an upper-case 'B.' That's it."

"Do you know, that is quite inventive, Mr. Murdock. And how did you come to develop this system, if you don't mind my asking?"

"I hardly have anything left to hide," Matt said with resignation. "Now, let me think. I've been using it for several years now…" He frowned, trying to remember details. "It was about the time my wife started volunteering in my office." Remembering her selfless involvement in his work helped him to block out the horrors hinted at by his aunt. He would face those later. He chose, instead, to reflect on a more positive past.

"I think she may have come up with the idea, or something like it. Yes, I remember her suggesting the pattern because she insisted that her initial be capitalized rather than the client's, to remind me that she was more important to me." A tragically crooked smile marred his expression. "She wouldn't let me use 'BM' for obvious reasons, just 'B' for Brittany. And then she came up with several other ideas like starting the odd and even numbers backwards; zero, nine, eight, seven, six or using the symbols from the opposite ends of the keyboard; plus for one, dash for two, exclamation mark for twelve." Recalling her ridiculous, adorable nonsense, Matt laughed softly. "The more complicated the ideas she came up with, the more confused I got until I finally just went with the first one and stuck with it. I remember her asking me not to tell her what I ultimately decided on so that she wouldn't be burdened with the responsibility of knowing something that could get me into trouble. She was so supportive."

Based on comments made by Reenie, Isaac had reason to believe that Brittany's behavior was quite the opposite. "You are a clear-headed, organized man. Usually, such persons choose the most straightforward, uncomplicated course of action in any given situation. It is an admirable character trait, and one I'm sure your wife admired." Matt frowned at Isaac's observation. "Good. Now, I ask you, could you access the accounts from any computer — say, a personal laptop — or did you do so only from your desktop at work?"

"Oh, I only used my office computer. Brittany never wanted me to bring work home."

"And you say she helped you often at your office? Very commendable. But I am wondering, were you always there together, or did you perhaps leave for appointments or meetings while she remained in the office?"

"What difference could that possibly make?" Matt's features hardened, and his pulse began to race.

"Calm down, young man. I am merely attempting to gain a clearer picture of who might have had access to your accounts. Your wife volunteered in your office, yet you must have had an administrative assistant of some kind."

"Alisha. Yes, but she had to support four different advisors, so as Brittany took over more and more tasks, Alisha was free to step back and focus on the other three guys. Brittany was a godsend. She scheduled my meetings, kept my client data current, took care of any correspondence. She was my right arm, but she had no need to come near my computer. She had her own laptop. Besides my desktop is password protected, and she – "

Brittany knew his desktop password. She had always known it. On their honeymoon she had insisted they keep no secrets from one another, convincing him that a marriage could not survive without mutual trust. His password was their wedding date and their first initials. Matt used it on all his devices – computers, phone, tablet. She had access to everything. His mind flashed to random memories of regret at missing out on time spent with her at the office because she had scheduled a client meeting in a different location. She had encouraged him to attend financial seminars away from work, pouting before kissing him goodbye. She had routinely set up business lunches, then bowed out graciously, supposedly to catch up on paperwork while he was out. She knew the day and hour of every Hibbard and Associates gathering – official meetings she did not attend.

The inconsistencies in Brittany's actions and words, hinted at earlier by his aunt, forged back to slap Matt in the face as a second wave of indictments, exposed by Isaac, washed over him. Every remnant of rose-colored memories faded to be replaced by hideous implications that smacked, inescapably, of truth. He wanted desperately to denounce every monstrous allegation, but honesty compelled him to examine them in light of the facts. And they fit – with appalling accuracy.

Matt never heard Isaac Rosenbaum assure him that he would help Irene get to the bottom of the phone and mail puzzles, or that he vowed to engage the help of a jurist friend to look closer into the trial transcripts. He never heard the older man's parting words of optimistic comfort. All he heard were the deafening screams building to a crescendo in his fevered brain until they seized control of his voice, and he became merely a mouthpiece of profanity and denial. Without conscious thought, he knocked over tables and chairs in the throes of a violent rage that stripped him of his very humanity.

Restrained by two guards, Matt was dragged back to his cell and left lying on the floor, sobbing. Eventually, overcome by the nightmare he had finally been forced to recognize as Brittany, he fell into a blessed coma of mental oblivion.

CHAPTER 17

The wicked make evil plans against good people. They grind their teeth at them in anger. But the Lord laughs at the wicked. He sees that their day is coming.

Psalm 37:12-13 (ICB)

Hmph," grunted Granny Gert.

"Precisely," replied Aletha.

The two were swinging in a desultory fashion on the front porch of Fern Cottage on a fine spring morning that, at any other time, would have inspired them with peace and contentment. But their coincidental dark blue and gray clothing seemed to dull both the sun's rays and their attitudes.

"Rosie and Tim are happier than two squirrels living in a nut factory, and the Yousefs are still walking with their heads in the clouds," Gert commented in a curiously critical tone.

"Isn't it wonderful." Aletha's response was tepid at best. "Timothy and Marilyn have finally sorted everything out, too." After a short pause, she added a little wistfully, "It appears that our efforts have met with universal success. Still, I *am* pleased…" Silence fell between them.

"That's it!" Gert said suddenly, jerking herself upright.

"What's it?"

The swing began to move faster. "We're sitting here feeling like we're stuck in a bog. What we need is someone else to help! What good is having all the wisdom and brains and experience in the world without spreading it around a little? Letha, it's time we started noticing."

Aletha's sightless eyes began to shine as she, too, became more animated. "I knew you'd think of something Trudy. What should we notice?"

"Anything. Anyone. Keep our eyes peeled. Well, you know what I mean," she added gruffly.

It was only a few days before the next recipient of their beneficence revealed herself through the counter process of almost hiding. On the Sunday following Reenie's visit to LCF, Aletha noticed the other lady's unusual silence during brunch, despite having become a lively occupant of the seniors' table. Gert noticed her woebegone expression. When questioned closely – some might have described it as an interrogation – Irene Fields poured out all her pent-up worries over her nephew and the part that Isaac and Deborah Rosenbaum had played in helping her to see him. Not content with merely consoling their new friend, Aletha responded to a pointed nudge from Gert and invited Reenie to tea on Tuesday, saying she would invite the Rosenbaums also. They were not about to pass up the opportunity to delve more deeply into the hint of intrigue surrounding the suspicious activities described by Reenie.

Angelica, pleased to hear that the Rosenbaums had agreed to another outing among the locals, offered to guide Aletha and Gert through the preparation of curried egg salad sandwiches and cucumber sandwiches. They added simple chocolate chip muffins as a sweet, and brewed both tea and coffee, not knowing the Rosenbaums' preferences. Gert spread the coffee table in the living room with a small, antique lace tablecloth. Aletha had dug it out of a buffet drawer and presented it for use, oblivious to its stained and yellowed state. Angelica carefully covered the worst spots with the sandwich trays and the basket of muffins, though it was doubtful that the elderly guests noticed the tablecloth's condition at all.

The Rosenbaums, who appreciated the value of well-built and well-preserved furniture, approved heartily of Fern Cottage and its décor. They were also pleased to find another familiar face in Angelica. Reenie, always disposed to enjoy an invitation to anyone's home, found Aletha's charming, and the company welcome. They ate their fill while learning the history of the cottage and how Aletha had come to live there. Gertie provided a much-embellished account of their friendship as young co-eds, and the adoption of nicknames for one another. She also proudly explained how their providential reconnection after so many years had made the marriage of their grandchildren possible.

Waiting until everyone sat comfortably sipping their tea or coffee, Angelica slipped quietly away, judging accurately that Gert and Aletha would get down to whatever plan they had hatched between them if she was not there to inhibit their schemes. She had seen the glint in Gert's eyes when Aletha suggested the tea party. So, she left the seniors to their fun. *After all,* she thought, *how much trouble can they get into?*

It took less than 10 minutes for the conspirators to strategize and form their plan of attack. All agreed that Isaac would be best suited to pursue the legal side of Matthew Murdock's predicament. Deborah volunteered to drive the ladies on their various errands beginning on the morrow, and the party soon broke up.

At one o'clock the following day, the Post Mistress of Tinkers Well received a visit. Mary Ellison, whose harsh features were matched by her acidic tongue, found herself confronted by four elderly women, all talking at once, demanding an explanation for Reenie's lost mail.

"Pipe down and let Reenie have her say," Gert shouted over the noise. No one dared point out that she had been making most of it. "Go ahead, Reenie."

After explaining her predicament, Mary looked up the address and solved the mystery. "The reason you're not getting any mail at the house is because it's all being forwarded to a post office box here. Don't you have a key?" she demanded, glaring at Reenie.

"Oh dear. I don't know anything about a post office box. My nephew's wife, Brittany Murdock, must have set it up. I'm afraid I don't have a key."

"Then I'm afraid I can't help you, ma'am. Only the person whose name is on the registration can authorize access to the box's contents. Perhaps you can ask her about it. Now if you'll excuse me." Mary, turning to intimidate another customer, felt a gently restraining hand on her arm.

"Now Mary – I do hope it's alright to call you Mary – my name is Aletha Mason. I hope you remember me. I know *I* can't forget how helpful you were to my husband and I when we first moved here, and we had forwarded mail from Chicago going to the big house, then had to forward it again to Fern Cottage. You kindly made sure we received everything."

Mary thawed a little under the influence of Aletha's gentle words. "That's my job ma'am," she said in a voice roughly akin to soured milk. "This lady a friend of yours?"

"She is indeed. I think you'll find that she has a government issued ID." Reenie eagerly produced her card. "And surely if she can prove who she is, it must be lawful to hand her any letters with her name on them. Couldn't you just take a quick peek in the Murdock box to see if there is anything for Miss Fields?"

"Well, it's a not strictly legal…"

Mary disappeared and returned a few minutes later with a letter from Matt. Reenie almost wept with relief.

"That explains why I haven't received any letters," she said, "but why hasn't my nephew received any of mine. I either put them in the box at the house or hand them to my niece to mail."

"Seems to me you need to have a little talk with your niece," Mary replied evasively.

Deborah, helping Aletha to the car, applauded the other's strategy. "That was cleverly managed, my friend. Are you sure you're not Jewish?"

Aletha patted the arm guiding her, and said with a smile, "I'd like to think we're all part of the same family if we look back far enough."

The ladies encountered much the same tale when a gentlemen called at Reenie's home to check the phone line. They had just finished a cup of tea, and a discussion of the unexpected information gleaned at the post office, when he arrived to assure them that both the line and the phone were in perfect working order.

"But you don't understand, young man. This phone *never rings*, and my friends tell me that when they call, they get a message directing them to leave a message for an entirely different number. Oh, I don't understand any of this," she fretted.

The man from the telephone company took pity on her obvious distress and suggested an experiment. "Let me just call this number from my cell phone and see what happens." He put the phone on speaker, and they all waited impatiently for an answer. The phone on the table was silent, but the voicemail message was stated clearly on his cell phone. "I'd say your phone has been call-forwarded. Just give me a minute…"

Whipping out a small electronic tablet, he tapped the screen a few times and put his hand on his hip, nodding his head. "That explains everything." It explained nothing to the four women staring at him, waiting for enlightenment. "*This* phone," he continued quickly, afraid the sweet, little old ladies surrounding him might attack if he failed to provide immediate clarification, "has been forwarded to a cell phone. It looks like the cell belongs to the same person who had this land line hooked up. A Brittany Murdock. Does that mean anything to you?" he asked. Four faces, showing varying degrees of dismay and disgust, indicated that the information did indeed explain everything.

Isaac drew up to the house about the same time Deborah returned from taking Gertie and Aletha back to Fern Cottage. It was nearly time for Brittany to bring the boys home from school, and Reenie worried that the presence of strangers might anger her. The more she learned about the treachery of her nephew's wife, the less safe she felt in her home. The Rosenbaums stayed only long enough to reassure her and to tell her not to confront her niece until Isaac had more details about the incident from the files of the State Securities Regulator. Reenie forced a brave smile as she waved goodbye, but it disappeared when she spied Brittany's lethal looking sportscar roaring down the street. She nearly caught her foot in the front door during her hasty retreat into the house. Reenie may have been growing increasingly frightened, but she would not desert those two little boys or spurn the faith placed in her by their father.

There was apparently, however, no immediate need for personal concern over Brittany's volatile temper or incalculable actions. She showed only supreme contentment in all that life had to offer in the present. Reenie encouraged the young woman's regular absence each day, enjoying the only peace afforded her in a situation fraught with uncertainty. Brittany experienced no such concern. Her path was unfolding before her just as she had planned it – almost.

Miles Hawthorne had proven to be every bit the man she believed him to be – charming, urbane, generous. He showed every sign of welcoming her overtures. They dined out for lunch almost daily. He treated her to the finest cuisine Kansas City had to offer and was clearly proud of being seen at each venue with such a ravishing creature. They strolled through parks or along shopping districts where he purchased small, but expensive trinkets for her. She was ready to offer him everything. Still, he held back.

At first, she found his hesitancy intriguing, making him even more desirable. But after a series of her calculated advances had been deftly deflected, Brittany began to feel a twinge of irritation toward her elegant cavalier. If she attempted to link her fingers with his while walking, he pulled her hand into the crook of his arm. When he solicitously held her chair at a restaurant, she slid slowly to her seat being careful to draw close to him with her low décolletage displayed to best advantage. He merely smiled in a perfunctory manner, drew back, and moved quickly to the other side of the table. She made a thinly veiled suggestion about the comfort of guest rooms in the building above one particularly cozy venue while attempting to slide her bare foot along his leg. Without blinking or missing a word in the conversation, Miles shifted his position and crossed his legs just out of range of her touch.

A week after Reenie had discovered Brittany's carefully planned and executed control over communication with Matt, her niece returned from her daily amorous excursion earlier than usual. She had declined the offer of another stroll through the park after lunch. She had had enough of parks and public places. Instead, she had invited Miles to accompany her on a drive. She decided it was time she took control. As he held the door for her, she turned in a flash, grabbed his tie and pulled him toward her for a kiss that must surely break down his defenses. But a surprised Brittany found her wrist gripped so tightly, she released his tie, crying out in pain. Miles loosened his clasp to take her hand gently in his.

"I'm so sorry, my dear. Did I hurt you? I do apologize. You see, this tie was a birthday gift from my daughter-in-law. Now let me see if I can help you forget any lingering pain," he said, and kissed her hand with great tenderness while directing the full force of his piercing eyes at her. She gasped at the touch of his lips on her skin and felt her heart beating faster. His next words sent it into overdrive. "Can you be at my office by 11:00 tomorrow, my sweet? My secretary will be out then, and there's something of a very… personal nature I wish to discuss with you."

Brittany had speculated on the meaning of his words all the way back to Tinkers Well. She believed she was on the verge of success, but during their short affair, if one could call it that, she had never been quite sure of his desire. He was either a master of control or deliberately building the tension between them. She wasn't sure which explanation she preferred. Miles had gone from being an enticing conquest to an inexplicable enigma, and her growing impatience was reaching a boiling point. Tomorrow she would demand his capitulation and leave him wanting more. She smiled smugly to herself, hardly aware of the raucous sounds made by her sons on their way home from school. She was mentally selecting her wardrobe for the promised liaison as if her future depended on it.

"Mrs. Castle, you know what to do?" That austere lady would have walked across hot coals to assist her employer in his agenda. He had finally taken her into his confidence when she all but ordered him to explain his actions following his first few excursions with Brittany. He rose about ten points in her esteem that day.

"Good. You had better be on your way, then, lest our little temptress arrives early."

She hurried down to the lobby where she stood in a corner ostensibly reading a newspaper. The entire staff of *The Kansas City Star* might have been waiting with her, and Brittany would have overlooked them all. When she entered an elevator, Mrs. Castle began her lookout for the other guest due minutes later. The two conspirators waited just long enough to allow Brittany her solo entrance to Miles' office, then followed her, careful not to attract attention.

Brittany managed to make her knock on Miles' open office door sound sexy. His eyes glowed at her entrance, but he remained seated. She slowly removed her tailored coat to reveal a mini-length dress beneath. It was hardly appropriate for day wear, but then most civilized people would have found it inappropriate for evening wear as well. The dark green dress, which set off her deep red hair to perfection, seemed to reveal more than it covered up. An off-center slit almost to her hip formed an enticing front flap. She swept it to one side, while maneuvering herself like a writhing snake onto his desktop, and slowly crossed her legs clad in nothing but silky-smooth skin. Miles steeled himself, recognizing the need for haste. He stood and walked to the door, closing it softly. Brittany was forced to slew herself around to maintain eye contact and the obvious hold she believed to have over him.

"Now what was the little personal matter you wanted to discuss with me?" She made the simple question sound like the advertising slogan for a five-star brothel.

"What do you think it is?" Miles replied evasively, with a crooked smile she found both promising and provocative.

Sliding off the desk, Brittany slithered toward him. "You're finally willing to admit that *you want me*, and I am here to tell you *I am all yours*," she said, reaching for a clasp behind her neck.

"Enough!" Miles shouted. The single word succeeded in startling Brittany so thoroughly that she halted with her hands in mid-air. Her smiling, flirtatious lover had disappeared. Instead, Brittany confronted a man of stone who spoke in glacial tones. "Carefully lower your arms, Mrs. Murdock. I wouldn't want you to expose yourself any further. It would be an act as futile as it is unnecessary."

Slowly lowering her arms, Brittany spoke in the voice of an angry, confused child, "Mrs. Murdock? But I'm *Brittany!* I know you desire me. *All* men do. They can't help it. You *must* want me." His cold stare said otherwise. "You can't possibly make me believe that you would refuse *me* in favor of that… that… schoolteacher. She's old enough to be my mother!"

"Young lady – and I use the term loosely – that schoolteacher, as you call her, has more class, intelligence, and allure in her little finger than you have in your entire pathetic being. And having had the privilege of being married to her once before, I know that if she were any more of a woman, I would not be man enough to satisfy her. I only share such personal confidences with you so that you may fully understand my next statement." Miles leaned forward and spoke with icy clarity. "I wouldn't worship at your tawdry altar if you were the last woman on earth!"

"*Tawdry?*" Brittany gasped, enraged.

"If you prefer, I might suggest cheap, common, course, vulgar…"

Miles waited for her reply, but astonishment bound her in silence. He took the opportunity to retrieve her coat, lying negligently across the back of a chair, and handed it to her as if his skin was sullied by contact with it. She received the coat with unseeing eyes.

"I will admit that my methods have been somewhat unorthodox, but you refused to behave with decorum around the men of your acquaintance in Tinkers Well, always attempting to stir up mischief. And because your outrageous behavior makes *everyone* acutely uncomfortable, I resolved to beat you at your own game. I am hopeful that I have finally penetrated the cloud of narcissism that shrouds your oversized ego and underdeveloped brain. You are unprincipled, unintelligent – and to the man with even a modicum of decency or taste – unappealing."

"*Unappealing? Me?*" Touched on the raw, Brittany found her voice once more.

"Oh yes, and annoying," Miles added politely.

"Why you… you…"

"Quite." His voice was now almost amiable. Watching her struggle in silent fury to don her coat, Miles graciously offered his assistance while keeping her at arms' length. She stopped flailing her arms abruptly as a cunning look stole over her bitter countenance. A feline smile, signaling base designs born of her worst instincts, lifted the corners of her bronze-red lips. She spun around, almost purring.

"Even if you're stupid enough to choose your schoolteacher over me, I'm sure you can imagine how displeased she would be to learn of our little trysts. I can be very persuasive with details. I don't care whether they're true or not, but I'll bet she will." Brittany watched Miles' face harden again and pushed home her point. "Who do you think she'll believe: little Mattie's tearful mother who didn't know how to fend off your advances, or her worldly tycoon boyfriend?" His piercing blue eyes glinted. "Care to change your mind about who shares your favor now?" Brittany finished on a challenge.

Miles walked to the door and turned the handle.

"You have no hold over me, you little witch. I think you will find that your son had a substitute teacher today. My fiancée and my secretary have been listening to this entire conversation on the intercom." Brittany's jaw dropped. "I have kept nothing from Mari. She didn't necessarily approve of my methods but agreed that something had to be done about you, if for no other reason than to assure the comfort of our son and daughter-in-law."

He swung the door wide so that she could see Marilyn Ludlow and Mrs. Castle. The latter switched off the intercom and sat with folded arms, gloating triumphantly.

"Should you have any misguided idea of spreading vicious, unfounded rumors around Tinkers Well, think again. If you take such an unwise step, I will be forced to report the jewelry I gave you as stolen. Who do you think the police will believe: a respected businessman or the wife of an embezzler?" Brittany's eyes flew open, and she looked warily at Miles. "Oh, yes, I know all about your husband's unfortunate arrest, and I can't help wondering if his devoted wife wasn't somehow involved. I have no proof, of course, only a thorough knowledge of your techniques and motives." Her overly made-up complexion turned ashen, leaving blotchy patches of artificial color. "Now go home and try to behave like a decent wife and mother. I bid you good day," Miles said, and bowed slightly.

Color rushed back into Brittany's face as her entire being was suffused with rage. She bared her teeth like a cornered animal and let out a high, unholy, primal shriek before running past the other women and through the outer door.

Miles held out his hand to Marilyn, still glowing from the tribute he had paid her. Mrs. Castle turned away until the door shut behind them, then addressed her favorite captive audience – the empty room.

"That was certainly worth the price of admission!" she said and resumed her duties with commendable excellence.

"Yes, she's packing. She came home in a towering rage, screaming about how men can't be trusted and vowing to take revenge on the entire male sex. It looks to me like she's planning to leave just as we're starting to get some answers. And what about Mattie and Drew? I can't let her take them. Though, knowing her, she probably doesn't even remember she has two sons. Oh, what should I do?… You'll come?… *Thank you*, Deborah. I'll feel so much better… oh, Gertie and Aletha just arrived. I called them, too… what's that?… Yes, we'll put our heads together and decide what is best to be done."

Reenie hung up the phone to head off Gert and Aletha before they could ring the doorbell. Rose dropped off the two friends on her way out of town to visit a bridal shop promising to advertise *Willow Walk Weddings*. As Granny Gert helped Aletha out of the car, Rose adjured her elders to stay out of trouble and received a tart reprimand for being so impertinent.

"Don't be a such a goose," her grandmother said. "Letha and I *never* get into trouble." Far more skeptical of such a dubious claim than Angelica, Rose drove off with her fingers crossed.

The unusual absence of Scout was explained to Reenie by his mistress. "Angelica has taken him to the vet for his three-year booster shots. I agreed that it was the perfect opportunity since I'll be with so many friends who can help me, if need be. Though I can't imagine the possibility of any problems."

The Rosenbaums arrived ten minutes later to find the other three ladies still on the front porch. Reenie was afraid that Brittany might otherwise hear their discussion.

"Oy vey! What is all this worry? Come, Irene, tell it from the beginning." Isaac's calm approach helped Reenie focus on the facts.

"Well, Brittany came home about 30 minutes ago, fit to be tied. All I can gather is that some man – and from all I've learned about her recently, I'm not surprised that she's been seeing other men; I've always suspected it. Oh dear, now where was I? Oh, yes, some man rejected her – and I say bully for him! She's been packing suitcases ever since. I don't know why, but I can't help thinking she's running away from more than a mere broken love affair. And if she gets away, we may never find out why she cut us off from contact with Matthew."

Isaac stilled Reenie's habitually twisting fingers. "I agree. In fact, after talking to your nephew, I believe her to be directly complicit in this business. I have people looking into it now. The important thing is to stop her from leaving. If she has no transportation, she cannot get away. So, we steal her car. Simple."

Deborah gasped; Gert slapped him on the back and congratulated him on an excellent plan; Aletha clapped her hands together gleefully; and Reenie began twisting her fingers again.

"Isaac! Have you been drinking?" his wife demanded, her eyes narrowed in suspicion.

"Hush, woman! We won't take it far – just far enough that it will take her some time to find it. By then, she may have simmered down. And if she's up to no good, as I suspect, she won't call the police. That could be very telling. Meanwhile, *we* will call them and enlist their aid." Deborah and Reenie agreed reluctantly. "Good. So. Reenie, can you get the keys without asking for them?"

"I think so. Brittany usually throws them on the kitchen table or coffee table. But Isaac, it has a manual transmission. That's why I can't drive myself anywhere," she said in defeat.

"But that is wonderful! I haven't driven a stick shift in years. What fun!"

Deborah snorted. "We'll probably end up in a ditch, you old fool!"

Disregarding his wife's comments, Isaac laid out his master plan. Grasping the keys retrieved by Reenie, he ushered Gert and Aletha into the back seat of Brittany's car, with some effort, while Deborah drove their car around the corner and out of sight. She hurried back and climbed into the passenger seat next to Isaac. Reenie remained at home to distract Brittany and hopefully stall her. She waved her friends off, watching the car lurch with a few false starts, and turned reluctantly to enter the cottage. Opening the door, she saw Brittany walking toward her with a business-like pistol in her hand.

"Isaac, where are you going? Back that way is the church," Deborah cried. Her husband was heading north out of town toward the bypass.

"Hush, Deborah. I know what I'm doing," he said, grinding into third gear. "Do you want she should find the car so soon? Besides, I'm starting to get the hang of this clutch."

"What an inspired idea, Isaac," Aletha said from the back seat. "Perhaps we can keep that despicable woman guessing until the police arrive."

"But Letha, nobody's called the police yet. We all piled into this buggy and started tooling around town and forgot all about them."

"Ach, you are right, Gertie. I confess I was having such a good time with this beautiful machine that the police flew out of my brain." Isaac was now headed west on the bypass. "Deborah, can you reach the phone in my pocket? My hands are a little busy."

"And what's wrong with *my* phone?"

"Okay, okay. We use your phone. Now, call 911."

Their plan hit a speed bump when the operator explained that they had no real emergency. When connected with the police station, Isaac was informed that there was no evidence to detain Mrs. Murdock or to request a warrant. It was a setback, but they all trusted in God to take a hand in the affair and headed back to the church to thwart Brittany's getaway.

"I mean it, Reenie. You know I'm not an inherently violent person. But with my back against the wall, I find that I have a very strong sense of self-preservation. Now, where did your friends take my car?" Brittany spoke through clenched teeth, her upper lip curled in a sneer.

There was no standing up to a much younger woman in the grip of desperation. "Brittany, don't do anything rash. If you hurt me, everyone will know who did it, and think about the boys. They would be horrified to know their mother had assaulted me."

"Don't try to con a con, honey. You know as well as I do that you're the only real mother they've ever had, which suited me just fine. It gave me the freedom to run my long game. But Matt got arrested, and I had to recalculate my exit strategy. I thought I could stick it out in this little hovel until it was safe to move on, but I've had more than enough of this town and its stupid, narrow-minded inhabitants."

Reenie understood nothing about long games or exit strategies. She fastened, instead, on the last part of Brittany's speech, and experienced an unrepentant delight in goading her niece.

"You must be talking about whatever man had the sense to turn down your… offerings."

The courageous observation landed on Brittany's last nerve. Without thinking, she slapped the other woman hard across the cheek, then grabbed Reenie's arm before she could fall.

"I'm only going to ask you one more time. *Where have your new BFFs taken my car?*"

Reenie had done all she could and was wise enough to recognize defeat. "I expect you'll find it parked behind the church. I believed it to be the last place you would look for it."

Brittany gave a harsh shout of laughter. "Not bad," she said. "But isn't this pitiful attempt at theft a violation of your precious Bible – something about 'Thou shalt not steal?'"

"Judging by your disgusting behavior of late, you're hardly in a position to quote the Ten Commandments," Reenie retorted with heat.

"Shut up, you old hag." Dragging Reenie to the table, Brittany shoved the older woman into a chair. Her gift of improvisation inspired her to grab a bungie cord dangling over the back of another chair. Mattie used it to secure his ball of choice onto the back of his bicycle when meeting friends to play soccer or football. His more enterprising mother wrapped it around Reenie's hands and pulled it taut, hooking the ends to the chair back spindles. "That should hold you for a while. At least long enough for me to find my car and get out of here." She slipped the pistol back into her purse and grabbed her mink coat. She wasn't about to leave it behind, despite its patent incongruity in the mild April weather.

"I would ask you to leave me the phone, but I know it won't ring." At Brittany's arrested expression, Reenie hurried on. "Oh yes, I know all about the phone and the mail, and my friends are looking into suspicious points surrounding Matthew's arrest and how you may be involved." Reenie's hands were growing numb from the pressure around her wrists, but she fought for any stall tactic. "You wicked, wicked woman! You won't get away with this. They'll find you!"

"Oh, I don't think so. I'm too clever for that. I was too clever for Matt, and too clever for the state investigators, so I'm certainly too clever for the local boys in blue. Give them my best when they knock down your door." She stood in the doorway and looked back at a pile of luggage. "I don't think I'll be back for my things after all. I have enough money stashed away to buy anything I want." Brittany slammed the door, locked it behind her, and threw the key into a nearby clump of weeds before striding away in the direction of the park.

Minutes later, she rounded the far corner of the Community Church building just as her car turned into the parking lot. It came to a standstill pointed away from her, which allowed her to creep up behind it undetected. Brittany jerked open the left door and pointed a gun at the startled driver.

"Get out of my car, old man, or I'll use this on you."

"Please, please, young lady, give me a minute. This is not for me so easy." Isaac took his time climbing out of the driver's seat, hoping that someone might notice them. But the parking lot was almost empty on a Friday afternoon and the car undetectable from the building due to its position under the portico.

"I don't have a minute. I've got a plane to catch, and you're in my way." Brittany grabbed his wrist and hauled him out of the car. Then, in a vicious act that surprised even herself, she struck the man on his temple with the pistol and watched him crumble onto the pavement. Far from being repulsed by her action, she felt a strange surge of empowerment.

Deborah screamed and watched in mute horror as her husband fell. After frantically exiting the vehicle, she ran to his inanimate form and fell on her knees next to him. "Isaac! Isaac, speak to me!" She turned her furious gaze on Brittany, who calmly slid behind the wheel. "You *Hexe*! What have you done?"

"I'm just claiming what's mine, dearie," Brittany said, and tossed her mink coat and bag into the now empty passenger's seat before negligently dropping the pistol into a cup holder. Waving her fingers at the distraught woman, Brittany moved her sunglasses into place and screeched off.

CHAPTER 18

Bring us back to you! Give us a fresh start.

Lamentations 5:21 (CEV)

*H*urry, *hurry hurry!* Brittany Murdock fought the frenzied, inner voices urging her to undo haste as she navigated the turns around Settlers Park. Having let off a little steam, she immediately became more circumspect in her progress. She almost sensed a warning in the cautioning shadow cast by the imposing façade of the Harrington County Court House on State Street. But when she turned right onto Commerce Street her breath came a little faster. She shifted into a higher gear and sailed past the elementary school without a thought to spare for two little boys who would soon be waiting for a ride home. Reaching the bypass, Brittany slowly released her breath. The last of Tinkers Well was in her rearview mirror. Assuming a steely calm, she approached the limited access highway that would take her to Kansas City, the airport, and freedom.

Freedom! Still stinging from her recent humiliation at the hands of Miles Hawthorne, Brittany set about convincing herself that this untimely departure was entirely her doing. She simply had to get away from the tedium of life in a small town and the cloying demands of a family who, for some time, had been little more than a necessary smokescreen. Once on the highway leading into the city, Brittany unleashed the powerful engine and focused her attention on maneuvering through the slower-moving vehicles.

A surge of exultant triumph engulfed her, and she gave herself over to full possession by her inner Daytona 500 driver.

She missed a big tractor trailer rig by inches when she swerved in front of it from the right shoulder. Cutting across the outside lane to the opposite shoulder, she passed a utility truck traveling at a mere 80 miles an hour. Brittany shouted with wild laughter in answer to the other driver's angry horn and set her sights on Kansas City. She was cruising along at 90, weaving through traffic with a recklessness bordering on mania, when, out of the blue, an unexpected, stifled scream from the backseat nearly caused her to lose control of her mechanical monster. Slamming on the brakes, she fought to bring the beast out of a skid and back to a safe position among the terrified drivers around her. Only then did she dare lift her eyes from the road to glance over her shoulder.

Aletha crouched on the floor behind the passenger seat, praying silently for the gift of invisibility. Granny Gert, whose eyes were the size of saucers, stared at Brittany in the rearview mirror.

"What the *hell* are you two old crones doing here?"

"I think the better question, you lunatic," Gert pointed out furiously, "is why are you so determined to *kill us all?*"

When Gert and Aletha realized they had no hope of escaping their four-wheeled prison after watching Brittany's assault on Isaac, their only thought was to hide. With any luck, she wouldn't notice them before she had to abandon her vehicle at the airport. Neither passenger had any desire to share Isaac's fate. But it didn't take them long to conclude that there are worse endings than being cold-cocked or shot. Gert had dared to peep out of the side window while Brittany careened haphazardly through traffic and found herself envying Aletha her blindness. One particularly close call drew an uncontrolled shout of terror from Gert's lips, precipitating the near disaster.

"Damn!" Brittany swore furiously. "I should have known you'd try to get in my way, but I've got news for you, you nosy, interfering old biddies.

No one will stop me now. So, just sit back and enjoy the ride." Her lips formed a sadistic smirk as she accelerated, pushing the speedometer to near 100. Laughing at her two passengers cringing in the back seat, she reckoned without their sense of dignity, self-worth, and sheer determination not to let Brittany defeat them. Granny Gert was the first to recover.

"Oh, we know you're in a hurry. You can't wait to get out of Kansas. I wonder if it wasn't that man we heard about who spurned your pitiful advances?" It took all of Gert's stubborn self-control to maintain a calm front.

"Shut up!" Brittany yelled and laid on the horn until the car in front of her changed lanes.

"You may be right, Trudy." Aletha found courage in her friend's attack. "But she is probably anxious to leave before more details are unearthed about her illegal actions regarding her husband's client accounts."

"You don't know anything, you decrepit, old blind woman!"

"I think we know more than you realize." While she spoke, Aletha reached out to give Gert's arm a warning squeeze. "Now aren't you sorry you don't have a cell phone, Trudy, despite Rose insisting you carry one? I believe I'll just give the police a little call on mine."

Without taking her eyes from the road, Brittany lifted the pistol from the cup holder and pointed it directly at Aletha, who didn't need eyes to know the hammer had been cocked. "Toss your phone into the front seat, or I'll shoot you where you sit. I don't much care whether you arrive at the airport dead or alive."

Not willing to test the other woman's resolve, Aletha obeyed without demur, her bravado temporarily squelched. Granny Gert fingered the cell phone she perpetually kept in her sweater pocket and mentally blessed Rose for teaching her how to use it. She silenced the ringer and held it up behind the driver's seat.

"Now, there's no need to get so huffy. You've got us properly trussed up, and that's the truth. I don't know what we'd have told the police anyway. You can't possibly be smart enough to plan some elaborate embezzlement scheme. It was probably your husband all along." Gert's prod hit the mark.

"Well, you're wrong there. It was me. It was *all* me. Poor, naïve Matt never had a clue. Though, to be fair, he had a real instinct for investing; he just didn't have enough to invest." Far too conceited to realize she was being cleverly manipulated, Brittany took great pleasure in finally being able to boast of her successful campaign, even if her audience appeared unimpressed.

"There was never enough money, you see, so the first thing I had to do was drum up some wealthy clients for Matt. I enjoyed that – very much," she said, purring like a lioness on the prowl. "Dear Matt thought I was sacrificing my time for his career. And I let him think so.

"Initially, I was forced to endure a lot of boring meetings with wealthy women who chaired social clubs and charity boards. I dressed and acted as conservatively as they did until I got my first invitation to a party where husbands were included. Oh, I still kept up the dutiful little woman routine for the benefit of the wives, but I made it clear that I was open to more… adventurous interactions with their husbands. Unwittingly, those snooty women not only helped me to reach the top rung of the social ladder, their pious gossip and sugar-coated comments about their best friends' shaky marriages and questionable business practices pointed me toward my most likely conquests. And I know just how to judge when a man is willing to dance. I wasn't blessed with this perfect body for nothing." Brittany's lips twisted into a devilish smile.

"It didn't take long before I had regular rendezvous with a select number of rich men vying for my favor. With some, I took long drives in the rear cabin of limousines, hidden from chauffeurs' prying eyes. Others preferred assignations at discreet inns. My personal favorite was to meet a client in his office where the threat of discovery made the liaison more dangerous – and more fun. And because I was especially… generous on such occasions, the investor allocated more funds accordingly." Brittany glanced in the rearview mirror and caught a different kind of horror on Gert's face.

"Why, you… you're nothing more than a dressed-up, painted trollop! *For shame!*"

Brittany's brittle laugh mocked such strait-laced convention.

"Oh, but I have no shame. I thought you knew that." She, in turn, began to manipulate.

"Ooh! Hussy, tramp, harlot, *jade!*" Gert spat the words, working herself into a state of righteous indignation. Aletha grabbed her friend's hand and gave it a little shake, hoping to dampen Gert's wrath. They couldn't afford to lose what limited control they had over their destiny.

"I quite see, if you'll excuse the irony, that you are a woman without conscience and that you revel in such wanton behavior. But that doesn't explain how you managed to hide all that money. It simply can't be done." Aletha's diversion calmed Gert and stimulated Brittany's eagerness to brag.

"Wrong again. Of course, Matt, as expected, played right into my hands. I demanded the boys attend a prestigious school on the opposite side of town, supposedly for their educational benefit. But I knew it would open more doors of opportunity for me. And it gave me the excuse of waiting to drive them home to explain my absence from the house all day. Within two years, I had amplified Matt's client list enough, keeping those new clients… well-invested, you might say, that I deemed it time to shift my focus to skimming my little nest egg. I convinced Matt that he needed to beef up his account security and offered enough password variations to thoroughly confuse him. The simple fool stuck with the first, most uncomplicated one, as I knew he would. It was easy from there on out.

"I offered him my administrative services, which was enough for him to nominate me 'Wife of the Year.' Then I gradually began managing his schedule to ensure he was out of the office when I needed to adjust the accounts. His standard commission payment went to our joint bank account, but as I began to ratchet up the commission percentage, I set up an online account in the name of a fake charity, organized in Matt's name, naturally, and funneled the overages to that. He denied it all at his trial, of course, and was furious that I was even questioned about it. I put on one of my better performances for his benefit. I don't know whether it was my passionate tears that convinced the judge or Matt's insistence on my innocence, but it was Matt alone who took the fall. All I had to do was wait until the heat died down to disappear. I just hadn't counted on it being so soon. But I suppose it's all for the best. When I had extracted what I wanted from them, my friends in Kansas City began to bore me. And since the blind, prudish men in Tinkers Well were foolish enough to reject me, this seemed the opportune time to leave."

"Why, I've never heard of anyone so depraved in all my born days!" Gert declared in disgust.

The explanation of her cleverness had momentarily taken Brittany's focus off the road and onto herself. But at Gert's words, she laughed and pressed her foot harder on the accelerator.

"Oh, I understand how you were clever enough to embezzle all that money, but you can't possibly hope to get away with it." If Aletha's words were meant to distract the driver and slow the speed at which they all hurtled through traffic, they failed. But they did succeed in drawing out more information.

"With the help of one of my conquests, I opened a crypto currency account. I'd hardly expect you to know anything about that. It's the newest craze in money management since the gold standard, though I must admit, I don't completely understand it myself. But when a gentleman chose it as an unexpected topic for pillow talk one afternoon, I knew I had to have it. I found the idea of investing in essentially make-believe money too delicious. And since I convinced him that 'poor wittle me' couldn't possibly handle anything so complicated, he set up the account for me, including a crypto wallet where I could hide all that lovely money, and no one could trace it to me. And the best part is that I can access it from anywhere. So, I'll just hop on the first plane to a country with no extradition treaty — I keep a list in my phone — and I'll start over somewhere else. I have enough money to purchase a new identity and more than enough to catch the attention of any number of wealthy men on the prowl for a new wife or a new mistress — preferably the latter."

Making their way to the north side of the city, the unlikely trio miraculously arrived at the airport unscathed. Brittany parked in a towaway zone, too impatient to hide her distinct sports car in a parking lot, and turned to her reluctant passengers. She waved her gun between them and lifted the corners of her mouth in a mirthless smile.

"Don't move a muscle, ladies. I was serious about my willingness to use this, though I'd rather not, so I expect you both to be good girls and give me plenty of time to get away." She was too thoughtless to recognize the near impossibility of two elderly women escaping the backseat without assistance. "And just in case you get any crazy ideas, I plan to lock you in," she said, and gathered her mink and her purse. Stepping out of the car, she fulfilled her threat. Gert watched helplessly as Brittany threw her keys and gun in a trash can then disappeared into the terminal.

"Oh, my gosh! What on earth…" Mark Lindeman, returning to his car after retrieving some notes he had left in his office, opened the door of the education building, and stared in horror at the sight of Deborah Rosenbaum bending over her inert husband. Dropping his backpack, he rushed to their aid.

Deborah looked up, beside herself with worry. She was so relieved to see the cavalry arrive, she forgot any lingering anger toward the man she believed to have, unwittingly, misinterpreted her Passover.

"Pastor, you see what that horrible woman has done to my Isaac," she said, with tears coursing down her cheeks. "She hit him with her gun and left him lying here. Is he still alive?" she whispered fearfully. She had been keeping watch over her husband's body for what seemed like hours but had, in fact, only been about ten minutes.

Mark felt Isaac's wrist and was relieved to report a strong pulse. "But he needs more help than I can give him." Between them, he and Deborah staunched the bleeding until an ambulance arrived. In the interim, he heard the story of Brittany's attack and subsequent departure. He worried for the safety of Irene Fields, who must have encountered the desperate young woman when disclosing the location of her niece's car. After calling for an ambulance, Mark reported possible danger at the blue cottage to the police and advised them of Brittany's plan to flee the area by plane. Airport security officials were alerted. It wasn't until all these wheels had been set into motion that Deborah remembered her other friends trapped in the car.

"Oy!" she exclaimed, clasping her hands to her head. "Gertie and Aletha! What must have happened to them?"

At that very moment, those two intrepid adventurers were attempting to explain to airport security that they were unable to move the car or to get out of their seats, for that matter. The conversation was hindered by attempting to communicate through closed windows. Eventually, Gert remembered a notebook buried in the bottom of her oversized handbag. Scribbling quickly, she held up the note to the side window and all became clear. One of the security agents dug the keys and gun out of the trash can, and presently the ladies were assisted out of the car, only to assault their rescuers with incoherent phrases.

"What are you standing there for? Get after her!" Gert demanded.

"Look for extradition treaties. I believe that's what she said," Aletha added helpfully.

"You can't miss her. She's looks like Jezebel in a mink coat."

"I can't help but feel she might find that coat somewhat cumbersome, Trudy," Aletha pointed out. Speaking in the direction of the bewildered agents, she said, "Perhaps you should just look for a startlingly beautiful young woman with deep red hair. That's only what I've been told, of course. I'm blind, you see." She beamed, happy to have been of assistance.

With some difficulty, the patient security agents extracted the gist of the ladies' story and contacted their team leader. After escorting their elderly charges to a comfortable airport lounge, where the two regaled everyone within hearing range with colorful commentary on their heroic exploits, the agents joined their comrades in pursuit of the young woman described. By then, the airport had been contacted by Tinkers Well police, and ground forces were closing in. Brittany, secure in the misplaced belief of her own infallibility, checked the departure schedule and sauntered to the airline desk for the next international flight. The airline official looked at her passport curiously and took it to confer with an associate. She returned, smiling, and asked pleasantly that Ms. Murdock step aside while she assisted another customer.

Something was wrong. Brittany snatched her passport and hurried to another airline counter where the procedure was repeated. Suddenly losing interest in the clean architectural lines of the terminal, she walked purposely toward the entrance but stopped short when she saw a security guard standing next to her car. Quickly reassessing the situation, she refused to let panic take hold. After evaluating her limited options, she turned away from the security checkpoint, knowing she couldn't possibly get past the agents without a boarding pass. A sign for luggage claim caught her eye, and she skated down an escalator, blind to the flow of its colorful terra cotta waterfall.

As Aletha had predicted, Brittany discarded her mink coat in favor of more freedom of movement, though she still clasped her purse. Glancing around with a hint of desperation now in her eyes, she spied a baggage carousel surrounded by passengers eager to claim their suitcases. While the passengers concentrated on the conveyor belt, Brittany moved to the exit end where items would disappear before beginning another loop on their journey. Confident that everyone's eyes were focused elsewhere, she made her move.

Hopping on the belt, Brittany held the plastic strips aside and passed through to the delivery area. Her luck held. All the handlers were busy unloading baggage carts, so she ran around to the other side of the towing tractor and jumped into the passenger seat, crouching down to avoid detection. It gave her all the time she needed to form her next plan. Easing herself into the driver's seat, Brittany waited until the last suitcase was offloaded, shifted the tractor into gear, and pointed it toward the large opening to the tarmac. It took just enough time for the weary handlers to figure out that none of them were driving the vehicle for her to make her getaway. She turned a deaf ear to the growing sound of shouting behind her and continued her desperate flight. What she needed was another means of escape, something other than a plane seat.

Brittany began to feel like a caged animal. A caged animal! That was the answer; she knew what to look for. "I need a plane transporting an animal!" she shouted out loud as if calling out to her gods of power and fortune.

If an animal could survive in the cargo hold, so could she. Exhilaration replaced fear, and she drove as quickly as the electric vehicle would allow. *There must be a plane for me. There must be!* Brittany told herself. The roar of jet engines deafened any other sound. She scuttled under one airplane that had just parked at a gate and spotted the prize. A huge St. Bernard in a kennel was being loaded onto a neighboring plane. She drove toward the jet like it was the gateway to heaven. Brittany threw her head back and laughed with wild abandon bordering on hysteria. She had outwitted them all. So blinded was she by her egotistical tunnel vision that she was taken completely by surprise when a security agent jumped into her moving tractor and slammed on the brakes.

"*How dare you?*" she screamed at him. They were the last words she uttered before being forced roughly to the ground. Brittany felt a heavy boot in her back. Her wrists were jerked behind her and handcuffed. She felt the manacles locking her ankles together. Uncompromising hands lifted her and slapped a piece of duct tape over her mouth while she stared into 10 rifle barrels aimed at her with deliberate intent.

The game was over, but Brittany refused to surrender. She fought wildly against her restraints and screamed rage through her distended nostrils as her captors drug her away. Nevertheless, the overweening egotism that ruled her life had finally been defeated by harsh reality.

The sensational arrest made national news. It was all anyone talked about in Tinkers Well for two weeks. Gert, Aletha, and Reenie were the toast of Bingo night, but not before Rose drove them to visit the Rosenbaums who stayed at home to allow Isaac to recover from his injury. The five shared all the little details lamentably left out of local and national news coverage. They marveled at their own cunning and congratulated one another on solving the Case of the Wayward Wife. Only Reenie seemed a little subdued.

She had insisted on having her meager wounds treated at home by the first responders who untied her, then hid the bruises on her wrists and face with a long-sleeved blouse and a little makeup. She wanted to be there to greet Mattie and Drew, who were brought home from school by an obliging police officer. Aunt Reenie once again told them that a parent had been called away on business, but this time the subterfuge failed.

News of Brittany Murdock's arrest was common knowledge. The boys began to experience the malice that only children can direct at their peers. Their classmates snickered and whispered and pointed at Mattie and Drew until Marilyn finally suggested Reenie take them out of school for a few days while she and other teachers managed damage control. When the boys ventured to school the following week, they were met with guilty kindness and shamefaced mercy.

But there were still questions left unanswered. If their aunt had lied about their mother being away on business, where was their father? They never asked because they couldn't face a similar truth. They weren't able to truly mourn their mother because they found that her absence was much like a millstone being lifted from their necks. They could now speak freely without censure and get their clothes dirty without criticism. But her absence seemed to intensify the ache they carried for their absent father. Tim noticed it when he picked them up for the Pinewood Derby workshop. He, and Derek and Abe, took them out for lunch one Saturday to try to cheer them up. The men made a point of playing soccer with them on Sunday after brunch. Mattie and Drew politely showed their gratitude, but their spirits were heavy.

While the Murdock family adjusted to changes, Isaac, fully recovered and bent on seeing his part of the money mystery through, made several trips to Lansdowne Correctional Facility to encourage Matt. After conferring with the prison chaplain, he decided to share with Matt the portion of Brittany's confession that dealt strictly with her embezzlement scheme. The entire story, cleverly recorded by Gert on her cell phone during that reckless drive to the airport, had been given to the police. But she also shared it with Isaac who carefully edited the content to exclude any discussion of Brittany's adulterous behavior. He and Chaplain Reardon agreed that Matt must face the truth of her duplicity as regarded his business irregularities and subsequent arrest. But exposure to her truly evil, wanton nature was something that would remain hidden, if possible.

A month had passed since Brittany's incarceration. Though ultimately subdued by her inescapable circumstances, she roused herself enough to gloat over the knowledge that her spoils would remain hidden until she could claim them and a new life for herself. When she was confronted with the unwelcome information that her crypto wallet had been traced and confiscated by employing the same password system she had suggested to Matt, all that was left of her self-centered world collapsed. That final blow drove Brittany into an almost catatonic state, leaving her unable to speak other than to babble unintelligible phrases like a baby. Her condition warranted confinement in a federal institution for psychiatric care until she could be moved to a regular prison. The indictments against her from the Office of Homeland Security, alone, were enough to put her away for decades. Embezzlement, aggravated assault, reckless endangerment, and perjury charges were the nails in her coffin.

Mattie and Drew never again asked about her or their father. They went through their daily routine like wounded beasts, waiting for the inevitability of some further disaster.

The Pinewood Derby was held in the gym of the elementary school on a Sunday afternoon when rain threatened, and the boys' spirits were as low as they had ever been. Despite wearing their sharp Cub Scout uniforms, of which they were quite proud, they each smiled wanly at Tim who gave them a pep talk before the race. Derek tempted Drew with his best knock-knock jokes, and Abe wore shorts, hoping his prosthesis might distract them. The well-meaning attempts to boost morale were only marginally successful.

An unprecedented crowd had turned out for the event. Unnoticed by the young Murdocks, the better part of Community Church was present to cheer them on. The Rosenbaums also swelled the number of spectators.

Other boys and their fathers made last minute adjustments to their cars and found their lane assignments. Tim was about to do the same when he saw Pastor Lindeman approaching them from the hallway door. The pastor ruffled the heads of the two brothers and asked if he could borrow "these scallywags" for a few minutes.

He ushered them down the hall to Mattie's classroom where Miles, Marilyn, and Angelica stood near the doorway to give the boys an encouraging smile. A little confused, and worried that they might miss the race, they looked into the room to see a man standing there with his back to them. His brown hair was liberally streaked with gray, and his shoulders slumped a little. He turned when he heard the door close. The reaction was all that Mark Lindeman had hoped for.

Drew was the first to challenge the disbelief that wrapped them all in silence. "*Daddy?*" He was afraid to trust his own eyes. When Matt smiled tentatively and held out his hand, the little boy ran into his father's welcoming arms and clung to him, weeping uncontrollably. Mattie's face dissolved into tears, but he couldn't move. He just stood there, shaking. Still holding Drew tightly, Matt knelt before his oldest son and pulled him close. The three seemed to breathe as one. Together again, they savored the miraculous reunion and embraced the palpable waves of hope and love that washed over them, drowning despair and emptiness. The pastor left the room quietly, wiping away his own tears.

Until that moment, Matt Murdock had still been living in a prison, a prison of remorse. He had officially been granted a conditional pardon based on new evidence and was released from Lansdowne Correctional Facility that morning. But he had stayed long enough to worship with his fellow inmates who understood only that a miracle had taken place as they celebrated their brother's good fortune. It was the only church family Matt had known for a very long time, and he needed their emotional support to face a future even bleaker than the one that had greeted him on his arrival at LCF.

Matt may have been acquitted of any premeditated crime, but his negligence in allowing his wife access to his accounts – whether intentionally or not – ended his career with Hibbard and Associates, and he knew himself to be a complete failure. He had failed his sons beyond forgiveness. He had failed in his choice of a mother for them. He had failed because he lacked the courage to see the glaring faults in her character. And he had utterly failed them when his willful blindness ultimately left them under the influence of such a depraved woman. The only comfort he allowed himself was the knowledge that Aunt Reenie had also been with them, and her guiding hand had always protected them. Still, it was with great trepidation that he waited in Mattie's classroom after being driven to the school by Isaac Rosenbaum. Like Chaplain Reardon, the older man had become a friend, someone he respected and trusted.

When Matt saw Pastor Lindeman through the door, he had turned away abruptly. He needed more time to prepare himself for the disappointment, anger, and resentment he must face, knowing he deserved every ounce of it. But when he steeled himself to face his two young accusers, he was greeted instead by blessed, undeserved clemency – the same forgiveness and unconditional love that had been lavished on him by his Heavenly Father and righteous judge. It was a lesson he would spend the rest of his life reliving with his children.

While father and sons were rejoicing in their reunion, the situation was explained to the race officials who happily waited for the Murdock men to join the rest of the competitors. At their approach, Tim handed Matt two wooden cars and stepped aside. He joined Rose and Derek at the end of the course where they held up brightly colored signs rooting for Mattie and Drew. The Yousefs stood with the Rosenbaums to cheer from the sidelines while Aunt Reenie, glowing with happiness, sat with Gertie and Aletha to patiently await race results.

The Murdocks didn't win that day, but no father or sons were more content with the outcome of the race. Tim and his friends were temporarily forgotten, supplanted in Mattie and Drew's esteem by their father, as was right and proper. The three young men applauded the turn of events that set a topsy-turvy world to rights for two little boys who had bravely born the weight of loss for so long. Pain, fear, doubt, and longing melted away as a family began the process of healing.

Though Matt had prayed daily for vindication, he was totally unprepared to receive it at the point of a double-edged sword. The future held nothing but questions and uncertainty. He still had much grieving to do over a treacherous wife who had stood by and watched him go innocently to prison, and a marriage that had been a lie. But holding his sons, and watching their joy restored, bolstered his hope that, someday, he too would find peace and happiness again.

Everything had come full circle. All the pieces had fallen neatly into place. Contentment and peace covered Tinkers Well inhabitants like a soft blanket.

After 30 years of separation, Tim Ludlow's parents were together again and looking forward to their engagement party. The young Ludlows still enjoyed the twilight season of their honeymoon while Abe and Amy Yousef continued to celebrate every day of their marriage as if it was their first. *Three Brothers Construction, Inc.* juggled more contracts than they could keep up with, not the least of which was a bathroom addition to Fern Cottage, with a bump out space to be added beyond the kitchen for use as a family room. Being sensible as well as sentimental, Aletha anticipated the day she must leave her home, when age and physical limitations would make living alone there impractical. It pleased her to think a young family might occupy it in the future and prepared it accordingly.

And *Willow Walk Weddings* was the success Rose knew it would be.

She contemplated with wonder the calendar on her computer screen. At least two weddings were scheduled each month through early fall with every Saturday booked for the entire month of July. Two large gatherings for churches in the city and a corporate employee family day completed the event line-up so far. (One of the original investors in the venture believed the best way to gage its success was to see it in action.)

Business prospered, relationships prospered, and the halls and walls of Willow Walk grew more inviting and charming with the completion of each inspired decorating project. Rose was happy. Her love for her husband grew daily, and she delighted in the secondary joy radiating from her friends and family. Granny Gert was certainly in high fettle after her adventures with Aletha and their new friends. She continued to recount the story to any willing audience, though she had just about exhausted that pool in Tinkers Well. All was well. Everyone was healthy. Rose Thompson Ludlow was living the dream!

Then what is wrong *with me?* she thought. *I* am *happy. I am* very *happy. So, why do I feel so close to tears all the time? Am I going crazy?*

Knowing Granny Gert would soon put to flight such disquieting thoughts, Rose turned off the computer and walked the short distance to Fern Cottage. Though her grandmother's matter-of-fact, commonsense approach to any apparent crisis often irritated Rose, she suddenly felt the need for calm, rational advice. The older woman's straight forward yet kindly words had reassured her in the past when Rose had sought comfort and counsel. She sought that same reassurance now.

Granny Gert will make it right. She always does.

On that hopeful thought, Rose let herself into Fern Cottage. She discovered her grandmother and Aletha in the gazebo, where they were finishing their lunch and enjoying the warm June weather. At the sight of their welcoming smiles, Rose suddenly felt overwhelmed by an inexplicable surge of emotion. She fell to the floor between them and poured out her heart through coursing tears, while Granny Gert stroked her tumbled curls.

Rose didn't quite know what to make of the suggestion that followed.

Excerpt from Intersecting Destinies

Prologue

Thus saith the Lord God: In that day projects shall enter into thy heart, and thou shalt conceive a mischievous design.
                                                    Ezekiel 38:10 (DRA)

Nine months earlier:

Thousands of milling locals and tourists filled the *Nepomuk Terrasse* and the Philosopher's Walk, then overflowed to line the banks of the Neckar where the *Alte Brücke* spanned the river in the heart of Old Town. Thunder from a passing summer storm could be heard still rumbling in the distance, and the occasional flash of heat lightning illuminated a dusky sky, quickly succumbing to velvety darkness. Pale stars began to appear here and there, but their luster soon faded into insignificance when a collective expression of awe rose to greet the slow spread of eerie light from a well-stocked arsenal of flares. The wavering, red glow flooded the massive ruins of Heidelberg Castle, transforming the ancient stone into molten lava.

Held to commemorate the burning of the castle at the hands of Louis XIV in the late 17th century, the impressive spectacle was repeated each summer and never failed to grab the viewer's imagination, bringing history into stark relief in a way that dry textbooks never could. The visual senses eventually returned to something approaching normal as the glow died to an ember at the base of the brooding edifice. But those same senses, and their auditory partners, were assaulted once again, this time by millions of shimmering lights exploding in the night sky. As each dimmed and fell toward earth, they were followed by another round of fireworks bursting with brilliant color and light. Each barrage eclipsed the one before until wonder filled the hearts of all present, inviting them to step back effortlessly into childhood. All, save one.

An old man, stooped and infirm, made slow progress behind the mesmerized crowds, finally entering a *Wirtshaus* on the *Nepomuk*. Exposed half-timbered exterior construction was echoed inside where decorative plates and medals lined the interior walls. The colorful hardware provided evidence of years of *Volksmarsch* participation by the proprietor and the regulars of the *Stammtisch* crowd. Beer *Steine* from local breweries and those farther afield topped an oversized bar. But the cozy ambience hardly registered with the old man who seized on an empty table in a lonely corner. He sought a place of refuge in the small bar-restaurant, anticipating the clamorous mobs who would surely demand sustenance following the sound and light show currently still in full force outside. A shock of white hair framed a face whose formerly smooth black surface was pock-marked and lined with age. Tinted lenses hinted at a sensitivity to light – even in the dim recess of the corner.

"*Guten Abend, mein Herr. Was möchten Sie trinken?*" inquired a roving waiter.

"*Hauswein, bitte.*" The answer came in a rich voice quite at odds with the overall weary essence of the speaker. Even at a soft level, it hinted of strength and power.

"*Rot oder weiss?*"

"*Rot, bitte. Danke sehr.*"

When presented with his order, the man threw a bill on the table and muttered *"Stimmt so,"* the ring of his voice, even at a lowered level, still striking an incongruent note when compared to his outward appearance.

He sat sipping the deep red liquid, enjoying the leisure of old age and the peace of languor. Occasionally, he lifted his head to study those who came rushing into the building as the last sounds of explosions faded away. Young couples, boisterous groups of university students, retired couples on long-anticipated holidays all flocked in until the room was filled almost to overflowing. Presently a nondescript middle-aged gentleman in slacks and a casual sport coat approached the table occupied by the elderly man.

"Ist hier noch frei?" At the old man's affirmative nod, the newcomer claimed the only empty seat remaining in the bar. The practice of sharing a table with a perfect stranger was a common practice in Germany. Neither showed any signs of unease. The obliging waiter appeared once more and provided the gentleman with his requested *Bock Bier,* but in the act of collecting payment, he was jostled by a passing *Fräulein* on her way to greet friends. Metal serving tray and coins fell to the floor with a crash. Cursing under his breath while simultaneously apologizing for his clumsiness, the harassed young man squatted to recover the fallen objects. He bowed stiffly to the two men at the table and turned to be swallowed up by one of the large university groups nearby.

The men sat in silence until the din in the room grew to such proportions there was little chance of anyone listening to their conversation. It seemed unlikely they would be able to hear each other! But when the older man eventually lifted his gaze from the dregs in his wine glass to look aimlessly around the room, he spoke in clarion tones, giving full scope to the subdued resonance that had only been implied earlier. The voice could be heard distinctly by his table mate. So remarkable was its rich vocal timbre that it had been described over the years – mostly by women – as deeper than the throbbing depths of the ocean, and smoother than waves washing up on a pristine beach. The utterance of such accolades never occurred to the younger man. He merely showed himself alert and ready to converse, albeit ostensibly as strangers.

"*Guten Abend, Herr Richter.*"

"*Nein, nein! Auf Englisch, bitte.*" The gentleman in the sport coat spoke with agitation and a pronounced German accent. "Despite being in the center of what is apparently the destination for every international tourist in Europe at the moment, I feel safer steering clear of *Deutsch*. I am convinced that, even here, native speakers outnumber those of other tongues, and discretion is essential for the success of our plans. I am in agreement with you that the exchange of information in person, while rather a dated technique, is perhaps the safer option now when computers can be hacked by school children and cell phones cloned at will." In a quarrelsome manner, he added, "Such intrusions make our jobs damnably difficult."

"As you say." The man of the white hair pulled a wry smile and bowed his head again, but he continued to speak in deep, lyrical tones that would have brought glory to any Wagnerian opera. "My contact has informed me that a convention will be held in Kansas City in the United States some time next summer. Those attending will be introduced to the latest in industrial security technology."

"Kansas City? I do not believe I am familiar with this city."

"Precisely. The generally prevailing belief amongst practitioners in the field is that, while able to boast of the amenities of a cosmopolitan metropolis, Kansas City can only do so on a small scale. Its relative obscurity is its greatest asset."

"I see." Taking a final swig of his beer, the other man wiped his mouth and sighed. "It's a pity, but so it must be, I suppose. I would have enjoyed an excuse to visit Las Vegas, or New York, or Miami." Putting his disappointment aside, he asked, "But the jewels – they will be there. Yes? You are sure of this?"

"Jewels, Euros, gold. Oh yes, my friend. How better to sell a failsafe system than to test it with something of value at stake."

"And you are sure of your contact?" There was an edginess to the question.

"He is beyond reproach. I have been in this business long enough, I should know who I can trust," the other replied rather sharply, then sat brooding for a few moments. "Despite enjoying a lifetime of risks and subsequent lavish rewards, I find that I grow weary of this game. This will be my final score, Richter, after which I shall retire to the islands – Caribbean, Polynesian, Greek – who knows, but I *will* live in style. This I have promised myself."

"But you haven't yet told me where specifically I am to meet you in this nondescript city of no importance. I will not be double-crossed, not at this juncture. I have plans of my own."

The clearing of the deep voice caused the table to vibrate. "Do not push me, *Herr* Richter. If you have no faith in 'honor among thieves,' we will never succeed." An address was passed between the two men on a crumpled piece of torn paper. "The hotel is scheduled for a grand opening in July. I will be present at the soft opening in June. I mean to thoroughly acquaint myself with the facility before the conference. I suggest you do the same, but we must have no contact until the appointed time. Now, much as I have enjoyed this delightful interlude" he said, lowering his voice to a quiet rumble, "I think it best that we part company. You will, of course, leave first. An old man cannot move quickly."

He bowed his head lower until his chin rested on his chest. When he heard the other chair scrape back accompanied by a soft-spoken *"Tschüss,"* he waited five minutes and appeared to wake himself with a snort. Making a show of rising with an effort, he made his way to the door.

A busboy in jeans and t-shirt seemed to materialize out of nowhere. If he bore a marked resemblance to the waiter, no one seated nearby bothered to notice. Wearing latex gloves, he picked up the wine glass and beer *Stein* at their bases and lowered each carefully into a greasy canvas bag slung across his upper body. Intentionally dropping a spoon on the floor, he bent down to pick it up with one hand, while reaching under the table with the other to remove a small device attached there. It followed the other objects into the bag, and, leaving a basin of dirty dishes on the table, the youth disappeared into the night.

About the Author

Linda Edmister is a self-proclaimed lifelong vagabond. She has lived on four continents and made a home for her army husband and their two children in 13 different residences over 40 years of globe-trotting. She is a former US Army Major, State Department Community Liaison Officer, and Church Music Director. Linda holds a Bachelor of Arts degree and a Master of Music. Her favorite authors and literary influences are Agatha Christie, Georgette Heyer, and Elizabeth Cadell. When not teaching piano lessons or volunteering in her church library, she enjoys gardening, travel, and Bible study.

Find links for book purchases and study discussion questions on her website.

www.misteredbooks.com